ENEMY
IN THE WIRE

ANDY SYMONDS

WITH NAVY SEAL CHRIS McKINLEY

When you're wounded and left on Afghanistan's plains,
And the women come out to cut up what remains,
Jest roll to your rifle and blow out your brains
An' go to your Gawd like a soldier.

--Rudyard Kipling

www.mascotbooks.com

For more information, please contact:
Mascot Books
620 Herndon Parkway #320
Herndon, VA 20170
info@mascotbooks.com

Library of Congress Control Number: 2017913737

CPSIA Code: PBANG1117A
ISBN-13: 978-1-68401-648-8

Printed in the United States

WASHINGTON, DC

I am not a hero. Despite what Mom must tell her friends, I'm just not. I've fought next to a lot of guys over there who are, but each time I've come home. That, in my humble opinion, precludes me from the title. For now.

I slide the shades back, just a touch. Enough so that early-morning sunlight meanders through the cracked window. Five floors below and 750 meters ahead, the ordered chaos that is Dupont Circle during rush hour plays out before me. I watch it all with a cold focus. Fresh beams bouncing off clean, sharp buildings. Long, architecturally perfect rows funneling into Massachusetts Avenue. Right angles, shiny glass. Capitalism and Democracy. In all its unwitting glory.

I take a moment to enjoy the brightness, the crispness enhanced by reflecting light. It's pure, new, an impartial witness to the mayhem it is about to watch unfold.

The commuters dance in and out of the MRAD scope attached to my SR-25 sniper rifle, naively making their way to and fro, framed for what could be eternity. I watch them scurry about their day, reflect on their obliviousness. The complete unawareness that so many of their lives are about to be over. Gone, forever. Just like that. What would they think if they knew? What would they change?

No, I am not a hero. Not yet.

RURAL NORTH CAROLINA

Finally. Senior Chief (SEAL) Dan Westhead spotted the first sliver of morning light, a friendly slit of sun taking its time to rise over wooded hills. Just that first peek of daybreak began to warm his bones. Before long, brilliant flashes crisscrossed the openings afforded by thousands of trees: pine, oak, and fir as far as the eye could see. Before long, an oppressive humidity would kick in, but for now the sun's arrival was welcome.

The brightening sky took him back to cold deer stands and early mornings with his father in West Texas. Often just the two of them: silent, patient, watching their breath march forward into the dawn. The dulled scent of coffee and sweat and gun cleaner, staring across a scraggly landscape pocked with canyons and mesquite.

Or of his first SpecOps missions, playing army in the neighborhood with his brothers. The youngest of three rough-and-tumble boys, Westhead often was the one captured and executed as a Soviet spy. Like most good memories, the later reflection brought more gratification than the act. That, he realized, was part of the attachment.

In another time, another setting, he would have appreciated the scenery before him as beautiful. The smell of fresh dew, the start of a new day. But as he'd been lying prone in this sniper hide for the past fifteen hours, his only focus was completing the mission and extracting quickly. Stretching, a bathroom break, and eating actual food would rank high on the priority list after that.

He allowed his mouth the slightest of movements to draw a sip of water from his Camelbak. Blinked twice, slow and exaggerated, exercising his eyes, flexing his jaw. Quad-coned night vision goggles (NVGs) had been painstakingly removed a half hour ago, and it was becoming a struggle to maintain eyeball discipline in the haze of first light. A dilapidated cabin, 1,000 meters away, was starting to blur through the .300 Win-Mag's scope. Westhead's left elbow screamed, long numb from remaining stationary since the previous evening. He was considering taking a leak, which would mean doing it where he lay. All in all, not a comfortable situation, but one that he had trained for extensively as a Navy SEAL and had experienced countless times in real-world ops all over the planet.

Quit your whining, he told himself before starting another math problem. *Ten million, nine hundred four thousand, four hundred and seventy.* Challenging himself with complicated puzzles was a trick he had come up with back in BUD/S to keep his mind sharp and energy present. A way to disassociate from the pain. He began to create the next riddle: the number of days since he had lost his virginity divided by the number of women he had slept with. This one might take a while.

While pondering the tallies, Westhead kept a careful, unmoving eye on the cabin, where, per the warning order, his target may or may not appear sometime in a forty-eight-hour span. His task order was to recon the area, photograph it, and take out any confirmed high-value targets (HVTs) who appeared. That order had been delivered by Commander Hagen, his Tier 1 Special Operation unit's assistant officer in charge (AOIC) two-and-a-half-days ago. And twenty minutes after he had to cut his date short with Jan, the pretty little blond cashier from the Portsmouth NEX.

Westhead had just rounded thirty, and while he hadn't yet fully settled down, he had slowed somewhat from his hell-raising days as a young invincible Naval Special Warfare Operator. He even saw long-term potential in this one. They had been eating pizza and playing games on the boardwalk—him sipping water since he was on a twenty-four-hour recall, Jan working her second beer—when his phone had emitted a God-awful foghorn sound. That alert meant only one thing, and after ordering his confused date an Uber, he raced to his Jeep and double-timed it back to base. Now, here he was, two days later, in the middle of nowhere, trying to complete this mission and get back to civilization. He corrected himself. *Not trying. Trying is failing.*

Westhead's mouth actually watered thinking about that uneaten pizza. Of all the sacrifices, all the hardships men in his profession were subject to, that was becoming, for him, the most difficult to accept. It wasn't the lack of sleep which most gnawed at Westhead. The truth was, nowadays he barely slept even when given the opportunity, and when he did, it was a restless, unproductive slumber, usually ending in a nightmare or flashback of some sort. Episodes which he, of course, kept to himself.

Nor was it the training or the travel. Not the danger, not the physical pain, the mental anguish, the impossibility of normal relationships or even the loss of brothers.

No, it was the shitty MRE's, the dearth of regularly scheduled and consumed meals. The lack of hot food tasted and enjoyed with utensils. The inability to make a reservation at a steak house that he was confident he could keep. A leisurely brunch with bottomless mimosas. In his younger years, the discomfort and abstention had been a source of pride. Now, the train was a-comin' 'round that corner, and while it wasn't in the station yet, he could hear the whistle blowin'. And that whistle was telling him that before long, he wanted the pleasure of three solids a day at a set table with the option to finish that bottle of red if he were so inclined. And a second date wouldn't be bad.

He wondered if Jan would take his calls when he got back. He doubted it. That was the way it usually happened. He was not unaware of the irony—the secretive nature of his job and untraditional schedule had been the easiest way to remain unencumbered in his younger days, but was now the biggest hindrance to sharing a life with someone. *Maybe when I get out,* he thought, for that deficit too. In his line of work, thirty was more like sixty. It wouldn't be long until his operational career was over, and it was getting to the point where he was actually happy about that. But he and his team had a few loose ends to tie up before that happened.

The day continued to brighten as he watched, waited, and thought. The shadows' persistent movement meant he needed to sink his body even further into the small indentation he had carefully selected yesterday as his home for this op. *Think invisible, be invisible.*

After the quick briefing, he had rushed onto a stealth Blackhawk flown by pilots from the elite 160th Special Operations Aviation Regiment (SOAR), fast-roped into these mountains under the cover of darkness after several false inserts, then stalked through miles of enemy-infested terrain while being hunted with thermal imagers and night vision devices. It had taken six hours to low-crawl the final half mile, face scraping mud, overtaking the ground inch by inch while maintaining strict noise discipline, alertly focused on every twig and leaf while evading counter snipers and spotters. After donning a ghillie suit created with the leaves and shrubs of the landscape, Westhead had completely camouflaged himself and the sniper hide, blending into the elements so expertly that the enemy would trip over him before they would spot his position. He had scarcely moved a muscle in—his eyes flicked toward the Suunto watch on his left wrist—sixteen hours. He was confident that even if a spotter was staring right at him, they'd never know he was there. One of the many skills he had mastered in the California desert at SEAL Sniper School. A course he had later taught.

The sun's progress meant many things when conducting reconnaissance, not least of which was the warmth it provided. But more importantly, if Westhead had left one piece of metal unscuffed, one shape on his kit too rigid, there was a good chance one of those spotters would see him and take him out—which meant, obviously, mission failure. Unacceptable. The good news was, since Westhead was facing east, his target would be silhouetted nicely as the sun continued its ascent. The bad news: It could potentially blind him. Didn't matter—either way he had no choice but to make the shot. This was a no-fail mission.

Thoughts that were never far continued to run laps in his head while he waited. Westhead did his best to not think of Cheyenne or her father. Or of Bull, Spencer, Guzzo, the men of Operation Atlas, thirty of his brothers he watched get shot out of the Iraqi sky six years earlier. And too many more over too many years of war to even think about not thinking about.

Naturally, this wasn't the easiest exercise for a man alone with nothing other than his thoughts. Often those most unwanted feelings arrived on just these occasions. He started another math problem in an attempt to drag his focus back to the cabin. Sweat now oozed from his armpits, his lower back, his brow. Wiping his face was, of course, not an option.

And then, just when he was under the impression that birdcalls and rustling leaves were the only noises left on earth, he thought he heard something new. A moment later, he was sure. His pucker factor spiked. With no man-made sounds reaching his ears for almost two days, there was no mistaking the slow crunch of approaching vehicles from what sounded like the rear of the cabin.

Still unflinching, Westhead lowered his thumb slightly, moving the safety on his sniper rifle to the Off position. His focus and senses were back where they needed to be.

Dust kicked up behind the cabin as two black SUVs appeared. They parked adjacent to it, one on either side. No one got out. Westhead rested his sights on the rear passenger door of the south-side vehicle. It had been second in the convoy, and he figured his target would be riding shotgun in that vehicle.

Westhead's eyes moved to his right wrist, checking a three-inch monitor strapped to it. Grainy footage from the MQ-9 Reaper drone circling invisibly ten thousand feet overhead showed no activity other than the two parked SUVs. He waited.

WASHINGTON, DC

I think I have my first target. It's the lunchtime crowd now, leaving their midtown offices. Headed to McCormick & Schmick's, Capital Grille. Unknowing and uncaring, each stuck in their own world, unaware of what people sacrifice all over the world so they can enjoy Cobb salads while billing another hour. Lawyers, lobbyists, the policymakers, and if ever there was a poster child for what is wrong with this country, for the rampant indifference that makes boys fatherless and fearless men dead, it's this guy: mid-forties, dapperly tailored navy-blue suit, slicked-back hair and iPhone to his ear. He's responsible for Operation Atlas, he just never realized it. Or stopped to care.

My breath slows, a conscious effort to regulate my mind, my heart rate, my thoughts. I feel the oxygen flow into my nostrils, send it out evenly through pursed lips. My earlier migraine mercifully forgotten. A thought crosses my mind: *Maybe I shouldn't do this.* I push it out: *They have to pay.*

I have the high ground, which makes this a relative chip shot, but instinctively my brain goes through its calculations just the same. As always, it automatically considers wind speed and direction, distance, drop rate, even the rotation of the earth, along with dozens of other subconscious permutations that are by now second nature. I put a few clicks on the top turret to adjust for my elevation. Dope is set. The man's cherry-red tie swishes in my crosshairs, dead center mass. I lead him, but just slightly. Sound, peripheral vision, even this room, disappear, just for this fraction of time. My chest swells, pauses. Then:

The hiss from the suppressed sniper system sounds like someone whispering a secret—a secret that no one else will hear, delivered by a heat-shielded, 220-grain, 7.62 polymer round. Through the scope, I watch the man's chest explode. Direct hit. Tango kilo. He crumples, shock across his face. Other pedestrians sidestep him, unaware that one of their own has just been shot. For another sluggish second they go about their lives. It's not until they notice the blood that the screams begin. Then panic. Pandemonium. Through my scope at this distance, they seem to be screaming underwater.

I calmly move the rifle left to right, lining up another target.

FSSST.

Another, then another. I don't notice sex or age. Just targets, just moving targets. They fall, one after another. I smile, but it seems forced. *This is what I want. Right?*

RURAL NORTH CAROLINA

It took almost an hour for one of the SUVs' doors to open. When it finally did, it was the north car and the driver who cautiously stepped out. Large, muscular, wearing a plain baseball cap and sunglasses, he stood behind the protective cover of the open door, automatic rifle slung out front. A knowing, confident stare penetrated the woods, eyes scanning behind dark lenses angled in Westhead's direction. The driver knew that if there was a sniper out there trying to take out his principal, that's most likely where he would be.

He thinks like the enemy. *How would I set up if this were my mission? About half a mile back, just past the tree line, with a clear path to the extract point.* Once the target was eliminated, there would no longer be a need for stealth, so he would expect a nearby HLZ. Shoot and scoot. He knew from his maps that there was a clearing a klick west of the cabin.

The guard rubbed his mustache in thought. *Yep, that's exactly where I would set up. Close enough to take the shot and immediately call for a quick extract.*

He continued to stare into those woods, that tree line. This was when it got interesting. Even though they were half a mile from each other, even though there was no way the guard could see Westhead, still there was a connection. Something between two combatants who have been in this position so many times. A telekinetic association. A sense not easily definable.

Westhead watched through his mil-dot scope as the man slowly walked around the SUV, eyes never leaving the tree line, weapon on line. His Kevlar vest bunched under a too-tight polo shirt, designed more to show off his biceps than for tactical efficiency. He called to someone in the other vehicle, too far away for the sound to reach Westhead. The man didn't divert his gaze when the other driver exited, cautious, the same automatic HK416 at the ready. Then, stillness.

Imperceptibly, Westhead keyed his handset and whispered, "Geronimo to God, activity at the X. Over."

After a beat, his earpiece crackled. "Roger that, Geronimo. Sat shows only the two vehicles, tangos unknown."

Alert but patient, he prepared for the shot.

WASHINGTON, DC

The weapon continues to spit, over and over, until the thirty-round magazine (loaded with twenty-eight rounds to avoid jamming) is empty. Sound is nonexistent; it always is. People blur in front of me, red messes intertwined with flashes of light. I never stop to think how many individual bodies lie prone as a result of my actions. This is a job, just another job, and they taught us a long time ago to not add humanity to jobs.

My eye stays locked on the scope while reloading, the clatter when the empty mag hits the tile floor especially jarring. I don't need to look down at my work. It's muscle memory, an activity I have done thousands of times. A more refined snap echoes in the nearly furniture-less office when I slam the new magazine home. Both sounds overpower the softer screams just beginning to reach me from below. Everything speeds up again while I scan for additional targets. As expected, 18th Street, normally a scene of manic activity as the country's power base hustles to keep the machine running, is now empty save for the bodies. Always, the bodies.

I come off the rifle, careful to control my breathing. To keep the adrenaline in check, to steady my heart rate. A long career in SpecOps means those precautions are second nature.

The hysteria five floors below tells me the first part of my mission is complete. I disassemble the rifle, zip up the case, make one last sweep of the room to make sure no brass is left behind (not that it will matter) and set the digital initiator before easing into the hallway and down the stairs.

RURAL NORTH CAROLINA

Westhead continued to observe the security detail closely. A professional respect. He would have approached this the same way: namely, with an abundance of caution. In that sense, protection work was similar to a sniper mission. In both cases, every sense must be alert, hyper-aware. That old lady on the sidewalk may be a suicide bomber; a bush could be hiding a counter sniper. It was about patience and attention to detail. Always about attention to detail. That mantra had been drilled into him since the first day of BUD/S well over a decade ago.

His trigger finger glided over the guard, moving just enough to keep the balance that would allow the tiniest of motions to send a 220-grain, MK 248 MOD 1 .300 Winchester Magnum match-grade round 869 meters per second across this clearing and into the center mass of his target. *If* his target appeared.

He felt his heart rate pick up when the south car's passenger door opened. This was where Westhead expected his target to come from. A smaller man slid out and turned toward the cabin, his back to Westhead.

"Possible tango sighting, over," Westhead whispered, his finger now gently resting over the trigger. Pucker factor to nine.

The new man was squinting into the overhead sun, an arm raised above his eyes to shield them. He was the right height, the right build, but Westhead wasn't yet able to get a positive identification.

"We don't deal in 'possibles,' Geronimo. Over."

Westhead thought, but didn't reply, *No shit.* Instead: "Good copy."

Then, a slight movement to his right caught Westhead's attention. He shifted his weapon just as someone bolted from the other SUV, Westhead's shot path blocked by the first driver as he sprinted with the subject toward the cabin. Westhead smoothly swiveled his rifle in front of the targets. He'd have to make two moving shots, cold bore, before they got to the cabin's front door. *Aim small, miss small.* There was no time to adjust his sights. He'd have to use Kentucky windage to hit his mark.

Inhale, exhale, squeeze. The driver fell. Inhale, exhale, squeeze. Now it was the target's turn to stumble. He crashed into the side of the cabin, falling to one knee. His head rotated wildly, searching for the source of fire but knowing deep down that it was too late. It was over. Westhead squeezed off one more shot that hit the target directly in the forehead, and he crumpled to the ground, still.

Whoops, was his first reaction, knowing he would pay for that later. But for the time being, he didn't move, didn't breathe. He tried to make himself as small as possible, to be one with the earth. *Think invisible.*

Half a mile away, he watched the security detail fan out and form a perimeter, weapons drawn. They would be headed toward his position any second. He needed to extract, and quick. No one tended to the downed tango. They knew the job had changed from protection to pursuit. Two had thermal binoculars out, scanning his tree line. Unpanicked orders were called out. One man was on a sat phone, no doubt calling in reinforcements.

Now came the scooting part. If he was captured or killed, that would be considered mission failure.

"Geronimo to God, two tangos down. Request immediate evac. Over."

"Roger that Geronimo, HLZ Alpha in five mikes. Out."

Westhead began a cautious pullback until reaching the cover of a large cluster of shrubs. Keeping his eyes downrange, he tucked the sniper platform into its drag bag and began a hunched sprint toward his extract point.

WASHINGTON, DC

I pick up the pace when I hit the stairwell. It's muscle memory now, the exfil the same as it was in Ramadi, Kabul, Colombia, Sinaloa, Tingo Maria, Yemen, or the dozens of other shitholes I've operated in throughout the world over dozens of combat deployments. Get me and my gear out.

From floors above, I can hear furious footsteps, panicked voices. I hit the bottom stair, hard. My ankle rolls, and I almost fall, almost drop the rifle kit. The adrenaline keeps me moving, keeps me from acknowledging any pain.

My Suunto watch beeps once, and then I am outside, into the brilliant midday sun. Oakleys tint the world, keeping it protected and clean. The summer heat overpowers, pushing down on me. Sounds are now crystal clear, slow and amplified, like they are meant for my ears only: the wind, the birds, the sirens. And the screams, the screams cut through it all. Soon, my watch beeps again. Walking past the confusion, my gait doesn't slow, and I don't turn back when the first explosion engulfs all those sounds. The air rushes past me, debris clouding my shoulders, my light-colored wig. I maintain my pace, head down, ears now ringing so loudly no other sensations get through.

RURAL NORTH CAROLINA

The forest was remarkably quiet. Despite the picturesque vision of nature, there didn't seem to be any birds, any bullfrogs or crickets calling to their friends. No gurgling brooks or scurrying squirrels. A blanket of stillness, of silence, lay leaden over the backdrop. Westhead's Salomon Quest 4D boots floated over the undergrowth, leaping fallen logs and side-skirting angry branches. He knew his pursuers wouldn't be far behind.

When he reached the cutout in the forest briefed as HLZ Alpha, Westhead dropped to a knee, setting his pack in front of him. His hands skimmed over the canvas quickly, knowing by touch exactly where everything was located. From a side pocket, he pulled out a roll of green 550 paracord and cut off four arm-lengths, about twelve feet. He ran the cord through an infrared chem light, cracked the stick. Behind him, he heard distant shouts, an ATV. The reactionary force had already deployed. It would be close.

He stood and began to wave the cord above his head in a wide arc.

The arc got wider and wider as he whipped it faster and faster. Through his earpiece, a pilot spoke over the troop channel.

"Geronimo, I have you on IR. Touchdown in one mike."

Westhead lowered the buzz saw and glanced at the screen on his wrist. Drone footage showed ten to twelve tangos converging on his position with what looked to be small arms and shoulder-fired weapons. Closing swiftly. He took a knee into a shooter's stance, removing a frag grenade from his webbing and placing it at his feet. There was no time for air support. He was on his own. If his pursuers made it to him before the chopper arrived, he'd take out as many as he could before pulling the pin. When they reached him, he'd drop the handle, taking out whoever was within the kill range. It was something he and his teammates talked about often; he just couldn't believe he actually might have to do it. *Fuck it,* he thought. *Kill 'em all, and let God sort 'em out.*

Suddenly, the air stirred, then grew violent with the thumping of a helo's rotors. *Right on time.* He replaced the grenade in his vest. A wry grin couldn't be helped.

The stealth Hawk, nearly silent, hovered just feet off the ground, bending branches and furrowing the long grass. Still in a crouch, Westhead squinted into the rotor wash and began to sprint. He leapt through the open door while the door gunner rotated his M134 minigun left to right. The pilot turned in his seat, getting a thumbs-up from his new passenger. He returned it, and the skids jerked off the ground. The helo leapt forward, rising urgently, soon clearing the tree line.

Below, at least a dozen armed men had reached the clearing and were looking skyward at a shrinking target. Westhead leaned out, offering his middle finger. The door gunner laughed, handed him an orange Gatorade.

"Good to go?" he shouted.

"Check," he replied. "Good to go." Within minutes, he was dozing.

LITTLE CREEK, VA

It's not until I'm on 95, passing Quantico with the windows down, that my nerves begin to settle and the impact of what I've done hits me. Not remorse, not by a long shot. But appreciation for its enormity.

I reach down, loosen my boot. The ankle is swelling.

The radio announcer's voice is harried, panicked. Distracted, I spin the dial. Information comes quickly; then there is none. Estimated casualty amounts, then retractions. Guesses as to responsibility followed by conflicting claims. I skim each channel, none giving me any information I don't already know.

When I place the battery back in my phone, I have an encrypted text telling me to muster at base for a sensitive compartmented information briefing. *Shit.* We're required to acknowledge any communications within one hour, and report within two. It's been fifty-five minutes, and I'm still eighty miles away. I accelerate and hope my Joint Special Operations Command (JSOC) badge is enough to get me out of any speeding tickets. The last thing I need is a record of me being this far north at the same time as the attack.

I try not to panic, wondering if the recall has anything to do with what just happened in DC. It occurs to me that there's a real possibility that I'm already caught, that the feds have tied me to what I've done and I'll never complete the full mission. That consideration almost fells me, makes me seriously consider driving the pickup off an overpass. The anxiety quickly subsides: If they do know it's me, there's nothing I can do about it now.

I take out a tin of wintergreen Copenhagen Long Cut and pack a lip. It's been my post-mission ritual since that first Iraq tour in 2003. The tobacco's bite, its minty smell, remind me of death, yes, but also of life. *My* life: I am still alive, and the enemy is not.

I love the smell of wintergreen.

When I get back to Virginia Beach, I head straight to HQ. My mind races, hoping I'm not walking into an ambush. It's a fear of failure, that my mission has been compromised and I won't be able to fulfill my ultimate goal: to kill the president of the United States and the rest of the bureaucrats responsible for Operation Atlas.

The graying skies calm me, the gloom a fitting setting to my mood. A familiar one, at least for the last six years, when thirty of my brothers were set up and killed by their government. I flick on the pickup's wipers, slowly and methodically picking my way toward the remote corner of base where my SpecOps unit is headquartered.

I flash my badge to the uniformed desk jockey at the duty station and make my way to the team room to see who's already here. My head feels a whole lot more secure on my shoulders when I find out that the whole team hasn't been recalled. I get a quick SITREP, pleasantly surprised at the new mission we've been given. Hearing the target's name makes me grind my teeth. After taping my ankle, I head to the gym for a quick workout, hoping it will soften the digging in my brain.

Westhead didn't wake until the chopper wheels bumped the tarmac at Little Creek. A quick summer storm had passed and the concrete was still wet. He swung his legs out the open door and jumped off, stomping his feet to get the circulation going before reaching back in for his kit and rifle. He had gone slick on this mission, choosing lightness over protection due to the strenuous infil. Even without the trauma plates, his tac vest and pack still weighed a combined sixty-five pounds.

"Commander."

The athletic older man Westhead greeted as he hauled himself into the passenger seat of a black Suburban gave him a tight smile. The greeting was neither friendly nor cold—merely one of authority. But held somewhere in the look was a nostalgic fondness. His deeply set eyes, the position of his head, spoke of competence. It was clear by his mannerisms, by the way he held himself, that this was a capable man.

CDR Hagen may not have technically been in the Teams any longer, but his rank and reputation were still fully intact. And within the covert organization, where he was second in command, rank didn't matter nearly as much as reputation. Which, as required by his station, was unassailable.

"Pig," he replied in his wispy, almost hoarse voice, using Westhead's SEAL Team moniker when he had served under Hagen as a Team 2 new guy. "Good op?"

"Hooyah, sir. Good op." His Texas roots shone through his response.

Hagen nodded at his team leader. They never had bad missions. Almost never.

Westhead adjusted his seat and wondered when his former SEAL platoon leader's temples had taken on their current salt-and-pepper landscape. He seemed tired — dare he say, old? The deep creases in his forehead, around his temples, intimated battle scars rather than wrinkles. Worn leather, maybe, weathered with use. Hagen still kept his hair tight and face clean, unlike most of the other members of their SpecOps group, and could have passed for a fit congressman or CEO. He was one of the few without any tattoos, although there was a standing offer that if he did get one, each operator in the unit would get Hagen's likeness tattooed on his ass cheek.

Westhead sighed, closed his eyes. "You're looking old, sir," he told him. "May be time to think about Botox."

"Well, you look, and smell, like shit."

Even if Westhead's eyebrows raised slightly at the obscenity, he barely stirred, just chuckled slightly. While CDR Hagen was, in general, a serious man, he occasionally flashed a unique brand of humor that wasn't always advertised. Cursing did not come natural to him, meaning his insults, an important component to leading SpecOps fighters, were notoriously bad. Probably his only shortcoming as a leader. His wife of twenty years—that length of marriage a rarity in the Naval Special Warfare community—said he only smiled when kneeling in God's house, a prayer for his men whispered across his lips. He admitted it was the only time he was truly at peace.

"Glad you're not offended," the commander said. "We'll debrief in the ready room in twenty. Bravo Team should be landing momentarily. In the meantime, wash up, hydrate. We have some chicken and beer waiting for you guys." The words were offered gently. CDR Hagen's Great Plains sensibilities had not waned even in the harsh landscape of the elite military groups he had served in over the years. He was still a kind and true gentleman, ascending the vulgarity of Special Operations the same way a show dog will still happily roll in mud if given the opportunity. Arguably more impressive was the fact that he had a track record of doing so without offending his men.

"He pissed?" Westhead asked.

"Whitey?"

"Yeah, Whitey." Whitey was (SEAL) Master Chief Adam White, Westhead's opponent on the sniper-counter-sniper training exercise, and the teammate he had just double tapped with a nonlethal but plenty painful simunition round.

"I suppose as mad as is possible for Whitey," Hagen opined of their notoriously pleasant and humble teammate. "He's not happy, which as you know is a rarity for that man. I think he even called you a bad name."

"A bad name, huh? Which one?"

"Not one that I will repeat. But one I wasn't aware was in his vocabulary."

Adam was oddly similar to CDR Hagen, both from a religious and etiquette standpoint. He even looked like a younger version of their AOIC. Regular attempts to get either of them to curse, as a rule, failed, if only because they knew maintaining a wholesome, Christian vocabulary was a surefire path to infuriating their coworkers. The rest of their brethren happily preserved the "swear like a sailor" stereotype. For them, cursing was a tool. Not a tool of expression, but one of disconnection. A manner to add the same shadow of obscenity to each scenario, the depth of vulgarity maxed whether it be to describe a fucking cocksucking, shitty-tasting MRE or a rat-bastard, goat-fucking, piece-of-shit muj just shot your best friend in the face. A way to express, *hey, this shit fucking sucks*, no matter what *this* is. Suck it the fuck up, and embrace the fucking suck. Even more shocking, Adam's piousness extended to his personal life, where he didn't touch alcohol and regularly attended mass. At least Hagen enjoyed a cold beer.

"Deep down, are any of us, really? Happy, I mean. Even him."

"Don't spout that philosophical mumbo jumbo. Sim rounds hurt."

"You don't think I know how bad sim rounds hurt?"

"You got him in the forehead. That's gonna leave a mark."

"I can't help it I was honor man in sniper school. Guess he should have been faster through that door."

"Maybe you don't want to tell him that. Next training evolution you might be the bad guy. Although, who knows with Adam. He may congratulate you for the head shot." Then, changing subjects: "How's Cheyenne?"

Westhead's headshake was answer enough. The ride continued in silence while CDR Hagen gazed out the window, absentmindedly fingering a worn piece of cloth. The faded red-and-white NYFD patch had been given to him in May 2011 by the mother of a 20-year-old fireman lost on that day nearly ten years earlier—by all accounts, a fine, exuberant young man who had reported for duty at Rescue 1 the Tuesday morning after graduating from the Fire Academy. Shortly after beginning his first shift, at 8:46 am, he found himself in the back of his Chief's Suburban, lights and sirens screaming, weaving south through rush hour traffic toward Lower Manhattan. He never had a second day on the job, and his mother, having met then–LCDR Hagen at a private event for 9/11 families after the killing of Bin Laden, presented the warrior with the patch as a thank-you. It had gone with Hagen on every mission since.

When the SUV exited the airfield, it sloshed its way through the main part of base, eventually turning down an unmarked street. No signs or identifying markers were visible along the single-lane, isolated road. When they stopped, it was in front of a nondescript cluster of gray buildings, angry Keep Out notices dotting the double chain link fence ringing it.

"Thanks for the lift, sir," Westhead said, hopping out and showing his identification to the guard at the compound entrance. Together, he and his AOIC walked into the unofficial headquarters of the Joint Operational Element - Combat Application Group. Unofficial, because with JOE-CAG, nothing was on the books.

The multibranch group had been formed by the president when it was deemed that the high-profile SpecOps forces like SEAL Team 6 (DEVGRU) and 1st Special Forces Operational Detachment-Delta (Delta Force) were just that. The operators picked for JOE-CAG were hand-selected from across US Special Operations Forces—the SEAL teams, DEVGRU, Ranger Regiment, Delta Force, Special Forces, Rangers, STS, PJs, MARSOC, Force Recon, and other secretive three-letter agencies. It was invite-only for the most experienced and decorated warriors the country had to offer. They were the absolute best of the best, battle-hardened fighters scouted throughout all groups under the Special Operations Command (SOCOM) by the JOE-CAG commanders. Once selected, candidates attended an intense six-month training and selection course known as The Dump in several secret locations throughout the country. The Dump was said to be a different but equally strenuous combination of BUD/S, Q-Course, RASP and Ranger School, OTC, Superman School, Green Team, or any of the other nearly impossible selection and training courses these men had already successfully navigated over their careers. The test of wills, marks-

manship, toughness, intelligence, strength, stamina, and fighting abilities took place once a year and was said to make most other military
training seem like Boy Scout camp. All the men invited to The Dump
had already proven themselves in elite units on the battlefield time and
time again, but still only half made it onto JOE-CAG. Hagen had been
one of the founding officers and had quickly plucked Westhead and
Whitey from SEAL Team 6. Now JOE-CAG was the president's personal Tier 1 Special Operations element, and per his orders, unadver-
tised and out of the public eye. Just where they preferred to operate.

The two men were greeted in the entryway by a harsh-looking man
whose thick, dark beard and stringy hair made him appear more biker
than head of a top-secret SpecOps group. His PT shorts barely covered hairy, tree-trunk legs. A barrel chest completed the intimidating
image evoking any immovable object, maybe an ancient statue beaten
down and discolored by the elements and years.

"You dingleberries hear about DC?" the gnarled man bellowed in
their direction. Long sleeves were rolled above thick, painted forearms,
black boots blazing in the fluorescent lighting.

Westhead, tactical vest in one hand and sniper rifle in the other,
examined the Officer in Charge (OIC) of JOE-CAG, Lieutenant Colonel Ben Stevens. While LTC Stevens, or Blade, was nearly fifty years
old, his appearance had an ambiguous air to it. He could be mistak-
en for either thirty or sixty, the degree of error dependent upon the
observer's tolerance for aggressive eye contact. Stevens had a discon-
certing way of examining his subjects through a dark mask that could
be fairly compared to a sudden thunderstorm. He didn't look *at* you
or even *through* you. Stevens seemed to look *around* you with a supernatural 360-degree awareness. The former Ranger, Green Beret, and
Delta Force officer had more than twenty combat deployments, from
Somalia to Bosnia to Iraq and Afghanistan, plus other locales American forces had never officially operated in. Blade earned his nickname
after a mishap with his KA-BAR back at RIP (Ranger Indoctrination
Program) when he was working toward his tab in the early 90s. As the

story goes, he was lubricating the knife with Vaseline before a land nav test during Mountain Phase when it supposedly slipped from his hand. Thirty-six hours later, after passing the test, dried blood covering him from the neck up, he finally headed to sick call for seven staples and twenty-four stitches in his head. No scar remained present day, but that just added to the mystique. Physical evidence was unnecessary — everyone knew the story. An instructor that day had even commented that he looked like an actor in a horror film, to the envy of his fellow candidates. Now, the grizzled, obtuse officer was the head of the president's 911 black ops group and had the leader of the free world on speed dial.

Stevens crossed the small foyer gingerly, spitting dip into a water bottle. One got the impression that the scowl he wore was part of a calculated and purposeful uniform. For a man of his size, he generally moved like a ballerina, although this evening certain movements couldn't hide that he too was aging. Even so, he seemed to swallow land rather than cover it. Hagen and Westhead met him in front of the duty-station desk. The uniformed guard at the desk straightened up, acknowledging the three assaulters as they walked past.

Westhead shook his head. "Not much news in the middle of the woods, sir. What happened?"

Steven's eyes were all pupil. Coal. His face, blank. By design, you never knew where you stood with the colonel.

"Terrorist attack in DC," he boomed. His words always seemed like they were shouted, volume notwithstanding. "Dan, wash up and get out of here. I'm getting briefed by Admiral Bradley shortly, and there will be an emergency muster in the morning. Tomorrow's going to be a long day. You'll need the rest."

Westhead realized his face was still covered in green paint and grime, and he was well past forty-eight hours without sleep. There was no doubt he was in dire need of a hot meal and shower, but his interest had been piqued. He knew he'd be pushing Stevens's patience by asking further questions, but curiosity trumped caution. "Because of the terrorist attack in DC? You think JSOC is going to task us with something domestic?"

Stevens sounded annoyed, but then again, he usually did. "Not sure yet. I can tell you that shortly after the attack, ADM Bradley put us on Alert 60 and advised me to stand by for further instruction. For what, I don't yet know. CDR Hagen and I need to sync now, but there will be a full team briefing tomorrow at 0630. You and the other team leaders come in at 0600 and I'll give you the heads-up. Make sure everyone's wills and powers of attorney are up to date, personal effects in order. I have a feeling we'll be spun up by the end of the day."

"Roger that, sir. I'll be in the head if you need me."

Westhead turned in to the gym at the end of the hallway, his bosses' footsteps echoing into the distance. He found two of his fellow operators working out in silkies and no shirts.

"Y'all want to put some clothes on? The glare is blinding me," Westhead called out over blasting Mötley Crüe.

They turned toward him, surprised to see their teammate in full kit. Westhead hadn't enjoyed the luxury of a mirror in several days, but had a pretty good idea of the effect his appearance would produce. Even for combat veterans intimately familiar with the hygienic challenges that run parallel to a three-day sniper exercise, he found respect and jealousy in their eyes.

"Shit, Dan, you look like the ol' lion done ate you and shat you out. Smell like it too."

That was Jud, a mountain of a man from deep Alabama, fond of sayings his teammates could rarely decipher. He stood over a squat rack, an ungodly amount of sweat pouring down his sizeable body, pooling at his feet. Jud was soft spoken, the way only huge men can be. He was a family man with six kids under the age of twelve, who would have to be described as a gentle giant for no other reason than it fit him perfectly. He had been a Delta sniper under Stevens before the JOE-CAG cadre had invited him to attend The Dump. Now, the operator known for needing custom-sized helmets and spouting indecipherable maxims was one of the elite group's most respected fighters.

Amongst Jud's litany of medals was a Congressional Medal of Honor that, to his chagrin, had recently become public knowledge, making him a temporary celebrity. A Fox News reporter had been imbedded with his Delta squadron in Afghanistan when they got a mission to rescue an American doctor kidnapped by the Taliban. Jud had been second through the door that night. Upon entry he immediately killed three of the doctor's captors, then jumped on top of her as gunfire erupted all around the team. While shielding her with his body, he had engaged in hand-to-hand combat with a Taliban fighter, eventually killing him with his knife. First through the door had been their breacher, a popular operator named Nick Check. During the exfil, Jud and his team had done all they could to resuscitate Nick, who had been shot in the neck, but he had died en route to Bagram. The cryptic inscription Jud now wore on his right forearm was a dedication to his fallen brother. Jud had also been one of the first American faces to greet Saddam Hussein as he crawled out of his hole in Tikrit in 2003.

"Just got back from a three-day R&S training exercise," explained Westhead. "These old bones probably feel even worse than I look." He took the time to stretch, hearing several ligaments pop for his troubles. The training and deployment cycle over the past dozen years had taken its toll on both body and mind.

"You hear what happened in DC?" Jud's workout partner asked.

Westhead nodded, trying to take Dale and his nearly shoulder-length blond hair seriously. Dale was as short as Jud was tall, and had the Napoleon complex to go along with it. As such, he drank too much, gave the new guys the most shit, and was unable to leave a bar without coming at least close to a fight. But he was also the first to pop his hand for the hard jobs, to stack first on a hot door or coolly call in danger close air support if they were at risk of being overrun. The former SEAL was young but fearless and made up for his lack of height by resembling chiseled stone.

The rule about not giving yourself a nickname had been lost on Dale. Not happy with "Smurfette," the name bequeathed by his instructors at BUD/S, Dale had instead pegged himself "Thor" after being assigned to Team 5. His teammates were convinced that once he had made JOE-CAG he had grown his hair out even longer in the hope the name would stick. In reality, his moniker varied depending on the speaker and their mood. At the moment, he was purposefully flexing his pecs while eyeing Westhead.

"Ben said something about a terrorist attack, but that's it, Smurfette."

Thor ignored the slight. "Major attack, bro. Sniper took down at least twenty-five people at around a thousand yards. His cutout was an office building near Dupont Circle that he blew on a time charge. Could be as many as 100 casualties." He paused here, his face contorting into disgust. "And guess whose offices were in the building?" The answer, which landed like a baseball bat to the gut, came before Westhead could venture a guess. "The Basting Institute."

"Really? The Basting Institute?" Westhead practically spat the name of the liberal think tank. Its founder and namesake, Dick Basting, was the president's foreign policy advisor. Westhead and his fellow SpecOps brothers were convinced that he was responsible for the change in the Rules of Engagement (ROEs) that had gotten their men killed in Operation Atlas six years earlier. The Basting Institute had led a committee that recommended hundreds of changes in how American forces engaged the enemy in both Iraq and Afghanistan. Shortly thereafter, the Chinook helicopter carrying a joint task force mostly made up of SEAL Team 6 and Delta Force operators had been shot down in a small village just outside Fallujah, killing all on board. It had been flying in daylight without an Apache escort, which the committee had deemed responsible for too much collateral damage. JOE-CAG had been born from the disaster that was Operation Atlas and was supposed to have its own ROEs far from the reach of Defense Department lawyers. Westhead certainly wasn't happy about the loss of life on American soil, but he didn't shed any tears for that organization.

"Could be ISIS," Jud offered. "If it is, I wouldn't be surprised if we got the call on something like this."

Westhead's face displayed disbelief. "Us? On something domestic? I don't know. Although Blade did just tell me we were going on alert. But I wouldn't think the president would task us on this, unless ..."

"... unless he thinks additional attacks are planned," finished Thor. "Exactly. This was too professional to just be some nut. And with The Basting Institute as the target, that's not coincidence. It has to be connected to us somehow."

"Anyone claim it yet?"

"The usual jihadi assholes. But the CIA and FBI already are saying that it could be homegrown. Maybe a lone wolf with sympathies to ISIS. Someone who fought with them in Syria and came home," surmised Thor.

"Sounds too professional to just be some muj," Jud said, scratching his beard. "I bet it's a pro. An old SpecOps guy with an ax to grind with Basting."

Westhead raised his hands above his head and let out a sarcastic howl. "I was on a training op, I promise," he said.

"I bet you were," joked Thor. "Sounds like the perfect alibi. Out alone in the woods, sneak down to DC, complete your mission and jet back to base. Did I just solve this thing?"

Westhead offered his wrists for the handcuffs. "You got me." Then, suddenly serious: "Wait, was Dick Basting killed?"

"Of course not. Most of the dead were support staff. The worker bees, innocent people just trying to make a living. That lucky son of bitch was at lunch, three blocks away. Him and the whole executive team, not a scratch on them."

"Am I an asshole if I say too bad?"

"You're definitely an asshole, but not for saying that." The hollow voice came from the gym's doorway. "You cheesedicks about done with the grab ass?"

The three wheeled toward Stevens. He glared at them, murky eyes seeming even deeper set than usual.

"Dan, don't you have an early briefing tomorrow? I thought I told you to wash up and head home. 0600 tomorrow, and be prepared for anything. Consider this country under attack, and that should piss you off."

If the mood wasn't already amplified, their OIC's warning ensured it now was. The three operators nodded at their boss and made their exit into a stifling summer evening. Jud and Westhead warily declined Thor's suggestion of happy hour. They'd be back in less than 12 hours.

LITTLE CREEK

It's still pitch black outside when I pull into the JOE-CAG compound the next morning. The beeping of my key card echoes loudly, cutting through the humidity and quiet. Another piercing headache and residual adrenaline from my mission at the Basting Institute had made sleep a challenge, but there are things I have to get done before the whole team arrives.

I'm surprised to find a light already on in Hagen's office. I show my ID to the sleepy guard, ease my way down the hallway, muffled voices just audible.

"... doesn't mean it had to come from here," I hear Hagen say.

"Only four groups officially have access to those explosives," is the static reply. Authoritative. Intense. Frustrated. I don't recognize the voice.

"*Something, something,* investigation," responds Hagen, surprisingly curt. While the words aren't clear, his lack of patience with their recipient is.

I pause in the dark hallway, knowing that the guard can see me eavesdropping from his desk, but desperate to know if they are talking about my operation in DC. I move forward, allowing the footsteps to announce my arrival. The voices stop before I turn into the tiny room.

"Morning, gentlemen," I say.

Both heads spin to the doorway.

"You're in bright and early," Hagen tells me. He's sipping from a coffee cup emblazoned with a gold Trident and the words "*There are two ways to do things: Right, and again.*" His feet are on his desk. A shiny red apple sits on a paper towel next to them. The commander is dressed casually, athletic shorts and a t-shirt, appearing unworried about whoever seems to be interrogating him.

"Not as early as you. And this is ..."

The other man rises from his chair, but slowly, and only after a beat has passed, like he is deciding whether or not I am worth the effort. A limp hand moves lackadaisically toward me. I take it, looking over his suit, the gold watch, the rotund, pockmarked face compensated for by thick gelled hair. He's even wearing a gold bracelet. It makes me think he'll be working a toothpick the next time we meet.

"FBI Special Agent Seth Kopen, Norfolk field office. I'm investigating yesterday's attack in our nation's capital." He hands me his card, which I don't bother reviewing.

A surge of adrenaline rushes through me. I push it down, examine the FBI agent. He has light eyes. Thin, tight lips. His white shirt is buttoned tight against his neck, a flawless half-Windsor knot leaving no space for air. He wants me to think he's smarter than I am, which initially leads me to believe he isn't.

I arch my eyebrows, not impressed. "And your investigation has led you to our little part of base? Well, nice to meet ya, Agent Kopen.? I'm—"

He drops my hand, holding his up to interrupt my introduction. "I know who you are. I'm working on getting to know who everyone is in this unit."

I'm slightly taken aback by his aggressive stance, and react the only way I know how. Call it a personal defect, call it a coping mechanism, but much like a cornered animal, for better or worse, I only know to fight back when challenged. I instinctively flex, raising my chin while trying to quell the anger about to boil over. Hagen notices, and tries to calm me with his eyes.

The FBI agent continues, seemingly unintimidated, which doesn't lower my ire but does earn him a sliver of my respect. "I'll tell you this— as friendly and accommodating as CDR Hagen has been, I know more about this unit than he thinks I do. And I'll continue to learn more. But I do know that there is no love lost for the Basting Group with the men in this building. I also know that your group has almost exclusive access to the explosives that were used in the bombing. So I can tell you with sincerity that if anyone in this unit had anything to do with that attack yesterday, I will find out."

I shrug as nonchalantly as I can while turning toward the door. "Congratulations, then, Agent Kopen. Sounds like you already have this thing wrapped up. Guess you don't need me for anything."

A loud crunch pulls our attention. Kopen turns back to me.

"Not so fast. What I need is a list of everyone who has access to RDX."

I laugh. "RDX? Half the damn military uses RDX, in everything from torpedoes to blasting caps. Not to mention terrorists the world over. It's the main ingredient in C-4, after all. If you're here looking for RDX, you'll find more than you could use in a hundred wars."

This time, he ignores the crunch coming from Hagen. "Did I say RDX? Sorry, I meant RDX-*X*." After emphasizing the second "X," his mouth clamps shut, letting the insinuation hang in the air. It's deathly silent for a moment. Hagen's apple munching breaks the impasse, almost comically.

Kopen continues. "As you know, only Tier 1 Special Operation groups have access to RDX-X. As well as the digital initiator the bomber used." He looks to a notepad, quoting: "Experimental RDX is more malleable and has two-and-a-half times the destructive power of traditional military-grade cyclotrimethylenetrinitramine and twenty times the power of TNT. Set off by a seventy-two-hour programmable digital initiator that is in trial stages within select United States military development groups." He looks up, setting the notepad on the desk. "Development groups like this one. Surely you both are familiar with RDX-X. Hasn't this group been experimenting with it for almost a year now?"

Hagen lifts his head up, mouth full of apple. "That's not in your notes?"

Kopen ignores him, for some reason addressing me directly. "Those explosives and that initiator are only available to Tier 1 groups under JSOC. That's four or five elements, and you're one of them. Believe me, I don't want to be investigating the men who keep this country safe any more than you want me here. But you understand,"—a sloppy grin is the agent's weak attempt to disarm, to let us know he's on our side—"I got a job to do, just like you gentlemen do. And right now, it's to eliminate the possibility that this unit had something to do with that bombing."

My heart skips a beat; my stomach simultaneously sinks. While this is not unexpected, I am surprised they've already traced the explosives and are here so soon. I quickly recover. Instinctively, the SERE training I've received on surviving harsh interrogations takes over. He could waterboard me and attach jumper cables to my balls; this fifty-something in pinstripes is no threat to me. I decide to go on the offensive.

"I would check with the guys across the street. You know, DEV Group? SEAL Team 6 has some bad dudes over there. Didn't you see that special on the Bin Laden raid? Read No Easy Day?"

"I assure you, SEAL Team 6, Delta Force, and other JSOC elements all have agents at their headquarters as we speak. You're lucky—you got me."

"I feel lucky, I really do. But this is an ordnance disposal unit. Who even says we fall under JSOC and use this experimental RDX?"

He smirks again, now to indicate anything but amusement. "I would appreciate you not pissing on my head and telling me it's raining. ADM Bradley, the commander of JSOC, was ordered by the president to provide a list of the units currently using RDX-X. We know who has it."

"In that case, I'm sure you'll be heading down to Bragg. Fort Campbell too. I think even Pendleton and Lejeune. 'Cause the way I hear it, 75th Ranger Regiment, SOAR, and MARSOC all get deployed in JSOC task forces. They probably have cases of the stuff just sitting around. JSOC isn't known for inventory control."

He furrows his brow, unsure whether or not to believe me. I motion toward the notepad in front of him.

"Far be it for me to tell you how to conduct your investigation, Agent Kopen, but feel free to jot this stuff down. Free of charge. Because I'm pretty sure SF and even some OGA direct action elements use those explosives. But hey, you're the professional investigator. I'm sure you knew all that."

His glare makes me smirk, makes Hagen smirk. I almost feel bad for him. To his credit, Agent Kopen quickly regains his color and composure.

"As I said, we have agents speaking with the other elements that the manufacturer provided those explosives to. But I'm here, and I'm speaking with this group."

"So you come in here as we prepare for war and accuse us of committing an act of terrorism against our own country?" I turn to Hagen. "Commander, what's the punishment for beating the shit out of a federal agent?"

His shoulders rise, just slightly. Casual. He throws the apple core across the room. It hits the side of the trashcan with a hard thud.

"Dang it," Hagen says, picking up the refuse. "Hate it when I miss."

Kopen ignores my threat. "Any guys limping?" he asks.

"Excuse me?"

"Limping. Walking funny. Eyewitnesses saw a person of interest limping away from the explosion. We think he may have injured himself in the commission of the attack."

"Agent Kopen, everyone in this building limps. We put our bodies through a meat grinder, every single day," Hagen told him.

"As that may be, I'd like a list of everyone you notice with a new limp, who also has access to RDX-X and those digital initiators." The agent spins toward me. "The list can start with you." His pale eyes cut into me, trying to read my reaction.

"Me?"

"Yes, sir. You have access to those munitions and seemed to be favoring that left leg when you came in. Am I wrong?"

"You couldn't be more wrong, *sir*," I spit. "And you better have some bigger balls than those Brooks Brother slacks can hold if you think we're giving you the names of the members of this unit. The last time that happened, thirty better men than you died."

I feel Hagen stiffen next to me, his hand brush my shoulder. "Easy," he murmurs.

Kopen continues, a little less antagonistic now. "I'm familiar with Operation Atlas, and I'm sorry for that loss, sir. But if I have to subpoena you to get that list, I will. Am I clear?"

"You can be as clear as glass, *sir*, but the people in this building are protected by an Executive Order. I'm sure CDR Hagen has already explained that to you." The commander nods more emphatically than needed.

"He has."

"Perfect. Then you understand you will never get names of the people who operate within these walls. Am *I* clear?"

"If one of them is a suspected terrorist I will. Look at it this way: Once I have that list, we can clear it and let you get back to ... what is it you said you do here? Ordnance disposal?"

"Something like that."

"Fantastic. Ordnance disposal." The agent takes a step toward the door. I cut in front of him and exit first.

"I wish you the best of luck," I tell him before pointing back into the office at Hagen. "You're talking to the second in command. But you already knew that. See if he can remember anyone's name." I walk out, ultra-conscious of my ankle. A stabbing pain shoots up my leg each time I put extra weight on it, but I can feel the FBI agent's eyes on me, so I make sure there is no limp.

At least now I know my adversary.

Once I'm alone in the hallway I pause, take a deep breath, and push open the outside door to the back of the building. I take a seat on the picnic table, letting the morning breeze cool clammy skin. The cigarette I light is an occasional habit hidden from the rest of the team. Smoking is frowned upon; no one wants a teammate huffing and puffing while humping a mountain or racing from a hot HLZ. I laugh to myself, thinking of some of the old dogs I came up with. Vietnam era guys. The more they drank and smoked, the better they were in the morning.

I pull deeply on my cigarette, thinking. Now is not the time to panic. I knew the investigation would get close. I'm somewhat surprised they've already tied the explosives to JSOC, but that type of RDX is more common across US Special Operations Forces than Kopen realizes. Something else gnaws at me, though, and it takes a minute to place it. I realize that it's Agent Kopen himself. The sinking feeling that there may be more to him than meets the eye. I hope I don't have to take out an FBI agent, but if it's between him and operation success, it will be an easy decision.

Four fighter jets scream past, heading out to sea on maneuvers. I blow smoke in their direction. After the planes are gone, I bury the butt, then head toward the small armory in the basement. There are a few items I need to grab before the rest of the team arrives for the full briefing. The goofy fed poking around isn't going to stop me from completing my personal mission. I missed Dick Basting in DC yesterday. I won't let it happen again.

Westhead sat with the rest of the team, most sipping their first coffee while waiting for Stevens and Hagen. He had already been read in with the other team leaders earlier that morning and knew about the FBI agent and potential tie from the DC attack to their unit. He was on edge, and even with the exhaustion from his sniper exercise, hadn't slept well. Unfortunately, that was now par for the course.

Stevens and Hagen marched to the front of the room. Stevens began the briefing.

"We just got a warning order from JSOC, and it's even bigger than the attack in DC. You won't be home to tuck the kiddies in tonight, boys."

Gunnery Sergeant Pete Hellesley, the ranking enlisted man in JOE-CAG and one of its team leaders, winced, the reaction just enough to catch the colonel's eye.

"That a problem, Hell?"

The former Force Recon Marine sent an embarrassed but emphatic shake of the head toward his OIC. His ruddy face, naturally swollen and just this side of ugly, darkened. An MMA fanatic with scarred and swollen cauliflower ears, Hell was an old, grumpy, savage brute who lived for PT, often irritating his teammates with his special sour flavor of gung ho.

"Not at all, sir. It's just—it's Mikey's birthday tomorrow. We were having cake, a clown, all that shit."

"And I wasn't invited?" Stevens asked.

"Thought I mentioned the clown ..."

The entire JOE-CAG team, sixteen operators and their two commanders, chuckled because they were supposed to. Even Brady, their Belgian Malinois, lifted her head, barked once sharply. But the laughter was an afterthought. Automatic. There was no mistake, a switch had been flicked, and the men were officially in battle mode. It was a welcome, familiar place for these commandos. Each of them had, in various capacities, been in constant war for years. It was where they excelled, where they felt most comfortable. Now they just waited to find out where the next fight was and what their role would be.

Stevens continued. "This is the big mish, gents, the one we've been waiting for. Operation Atlas Revenge. The CIA has found Ibrahim al-Baghdadi. I think a few of us have been waiting to bump into him again for oh, I don't know, about the past six years or so. And guess who ADM Bradley and the president called to send him their best wishes?"

It took just the smallest fraction of a second for the news to sink in before they erupted into a chorus of deafening cheers. High fives and backslaps echoed across the cramped room amid shouts of bravado and glee pocketed with violent curses, threats, and oaths of vengeance directed at the terrorist.

Westhead assumed the steely face expected of him, shaking Adam's hand with two of his own. This was it, this was why they trained so hard. A couple of them had been on the Bin Laden mission in 2011, and that was the only op that could compare to this one.

Ibrahim al-Baghdadi had been a young, rising officer in Saddam Hussein's Republican Guard before the US invasion. After Marines captured him in Ramadi in 2006, he had spent several years in an American prison camp in Iraq. When the president unceremoniously closed the camp and released its prisoners in 2009, al-Baghdadi began a tireless campaign to organize the many disparate terrorist cells working in the region. Since then, he had grown his organization into a regional terrorist power, replacing the remnants of Al-Qaeda in Iraq with the Islamic State, or ISIS. That alone made him the western world's number one target, but maybe even more importantly to JOE-CAG, the Iraqi terrorist had been the target of Operation Atlas. When the chopper and its thirty passengers were shot down during that mission, he had escaped into the wild west of central Iraq. A ghost ever since, al-Baghdadi had been credited with dozens of attacks and few confirmed sightings. It was fitting that it would be JOE-CAG who would go after him once again.

"One more thing, boys, and this relates to the attack on our nation's capital yesterday." A shadow seemed to cross Stevens's face, turning it even darker than normal. "There is certain evidence suggesting that the attacker or attackers had access to experimental explosives and initiators. The type only available to Tier 1 SpecOps groups."

He paused, letting that sink in. Wrinkled brows and whispered shock confirmed the men's disbelief that any elite warrior under JSOC would use their skills against their own country.

"I know, sounds like bullshit to me, too. "But if you are approached by a"—Stevens looked down at the business card he had been folding and unfolding—"an Agent Kopen with the FBI, you are not to speak with him. I don't need to remind you we are a black ops group, and we all have plausible deniability."

"You kidding me, Blade?" scoffed an incredulous Nailer, the former EOD tech and SEAL who had been raised in the wilds of Alaska. "The FBI is actually investigating us? How do they even know about our existence? That can't be good for our overall mission."

"That's why we're stiff-arming this joker. You don't admit our existence, let alone our mission. We're an ordnance disposal unit as far as Special Agent Kopen is concerned. He seems like a putz, but you never know how deep a motivated fed can dig. Check?"

Stevens met each operator's gaze, content with the vigorous response confirming their understanding.

"Good. Then kit up, and forget about this FBI bullshit. We have a flight leaving for Baghdad in sixty minutes where the op of our life is waiting." Hagen started to pass out the equipment checklists as the men filed into the hallway, the chatter excited but serious.

Conversation seemed to bounce back and forth between the terrorist attack and the mission many of them had been waiting six years for. Calls and texts home blaming a sudden training exercise for their pending absence were dispensed unapologetically. As a group, they headed to the high bays where their extensive tools of the trade were stored.

Each operator had his own cage the size of a large walk-in closet for gear, explosives, and weapons on the first floor of the JOE-CAG headquarters. While the United States military at large was notoriously cheap, budgetary restraints did not reach JOE-CAG. They were given the best of the best and had everything from portable handheld drones to Sealskinz socks and munitions and armaments most soldiers had never even heard of. State-of-the-art throat mics. Viper handheld-target-identifying devices that could send a ten-digit grid coordinate to a circling F-18 who would launch a smart bomb to within five meters of a target. JOE-CAG even had their own dedicated satellite for comms.

Testing experimental weapons was another vaunted perk of the unit. They were currently trying out the XM35 Counter Defilade Target

Engagement (CDTE) System, an airburst grenade launcher that detonated rounds midair. They had access to the latest medical advances, including hemostatic agents and clotting materials not yet available in civilian hospitals. Ultralight level-4 body armor. Each operator had multiple load-out bags packed for quick exits to anywhere in the world. By the time Westhead reached his cage, most of his teammates were already loading their gear.

"H-h-heard you shot Whitey in the face with a sim round."

The fast, almost nervous statement was directed at him. Westhead turned to face Derrick McDonald, a smallish, relatively timid former Ranger and paramilitary CIA operative who had arrived at JOE-CAG just a month earlier. That was still wholly considered a new guy, and even though he had already differentiated himself in war with other elite US military units and graduated The Dump, he still wasn't yet considered a full-fledged JOE. That distinction would take time and could only be earned on the battlefield with this group. Until then he was an FNG through and through.

"Guess he should have been faster through the door," Westhead told him.

McDonald suppressed a smile before quickly sticking his head back into his cage like he forgot something. He wasn't fooling anyone. It was his dimples, and the self-consciousness that went with them. They would be great for the ladies if he had the confidence to use them, but they, along with a slight stutter, were a never-ending source of grief from his new teammates. Red-faced, he came out with a sledgehammer and pair of bolt cutters, placing them in a custom-cut pelican case. Westhead asked if he was the main breacher for this op. That would be rare, but not unheard of, for a new guy.

McDonald, smooth-skinned with a cleft chin and those dimples, shrugged. "Not sure, but either way, you know who has to carry the sledge."

"And the M249, New Guy!" Thor reminded him from across the room. "Even with those dreamy craters, you're still humping the SAW."

His face went a shade of pink. "Right. And the SAW." You could almost see his back bow under the thought of the extra weight, but he said nothing, continued loading his gear. They all knew that no matter what, Mac would hump whatever they needed him to without complaint.

A yell pulled everyone's attention to the other side of the room. It was Nailer, flatfooted, extending a dripping wool sock from his body. He had a wide, flat face, partially hidden by an unkempt beard under a buzzed head. He was ugly, there was just no getting around it. And he didn't care in the least. His resting face normally appeared a snarl, but currently it was contorted into a mash of disgust and acrimony so extreme it had to have been exaggerated for effect.

A strange guy, Nailer was known for his eccentricity. His sense of humor, peculiar. The somewhat absurd brand of satire often amused only him, and even then only because it had to amuse someone. Nailer had grown up a survivalist and was legitimately confused by anyone who wasn't. To him, the label said it all. It wasn't a matter of *if* the apocalypse happened, it was matter of *when*. Aliens (especially aliens), foreign invaders, a plague, zombies—he didn't assume to know what it would be, only that it would happen. And that he would be prepared. As a bomb and gun nut, his house had a cache of weapons hidden throughout it—under couch cushions, inside toilet tanks, medicine cabinets. Westhead had once raised a recliner at a Super Bowl party to reveal a frag grenade taped to the leg extension.

"Son of a bitch! Who did this!" He was holding the inflammatory cloth at arm's length, offensively pinched between thumb and index finger.

"Maybe it was ET," suggested Jud, but all eyes were scanning the room for Matt Horrigan, the most devastating prankster on the team. Not finding him, they turned to Thor, the next terrestrial suspect.

"My official policy is to neither confirm nor deny pranks," Thor said, turning to face his teammates, most of whom wore intrigued grins. "But I'll say this: A sock with ... what?" He strolled toward Nailer and his cage, sniffing the air around him. "A rotten egg inside? Maybe. What else? Smells like a sea-based animal. Anchovies, maybe? Canned tuna? Probably also includes a dairy product, a nice ripe limburger or other semisoft cheese. Does that sound like the type of unimaginative caper I would undertake? A little too coarse for my sensibilities, I must say. I ask you this, Señor Nailer, et al. Would I stoop so low as to commit such a basic, uncreative prank? Do I resort to the lowest common denominator? Judgement is yours." Elocution over, he walked off, arms raised, finished.

The speech sparked off heated debates, including a theory gaining momentum that Nailer had pranked himself, an action not unheard of for bored operators. Adding fuel to that theory was Nailer's excessive animation and anger. Westhead, ever curious, walked closer to his cage, inhaling at the edges of the dangling sock.

"That's been ripening for a while, Nailer. How is it that you just noticed it now? Are we to believe that your gear smells so bad it masked the odor?"

"Don't question me, Chief. I'm the victim here!"

Westhead did a double take into the cage in question, suddenly serious.

"You planning on taking overwatches again? Thought you liked being point man."

"Huh?"

Westhead pointed to the three cases of 7.62 ammo in his locker.

"You're not going to use a sniper system on this op, are you?"

Nailer snatched a case of 5.56 ammo and stuck it in Westhead's face. "I'm bringing both. Why you all in my shit, Dan? Go harass someone else. Haven't I been through enough? We're trying to find a vile offender here."

Westhead chuckled and headed back over to his cage, fully convinced Nailer had concocted the offending sock and stuck it in his own locker.

He grabbed the load-out bag holding his desert cammies and gear. Since operations had slowed in Iraq and Afghanistan over the past couple of years, desert areas of operation were becoming more rare for them. Special Forces and SEAL teams were still stationed in that region and handled most of the missions that came with fighting ISIS and Al-Qaeda in Syria and Iraq. Most of which were supposed to be training the local armies and calling in air strikes on enemy camps and caravans. It was good to hear that the president was moving more SpecOps forces over there for direct action assaults. Even more so that it was JOE-CAG getting the call.

"Back to the sandbox," Westhead mumbled, mostly to himself. "Can't say I miss it."

"Shit, that's my home away from home. I haven't been to Iraq in almost three years. I wonder if she's missed me." The fond reminisces came from somewhere under Jud's beard. "All's I know is, I've missed her."

"You miss the sewage and death stench? Feral dogs? Kids begging for candy? 'Mista, Mista!'" Westhead mimicked, shaking his head. "Hell, I miss her like I miss the clap." He took down his modified HK416 and placed it in its case along with extra magazines, an IR illuminator, and two different optic devices. "I miss Iraq like you miss bathing."

"Roll Tide," he answered. It was a common retort from him, the meaning malleable and generic.

"You know what your problem is, Dan? You don't appreciate the finer things in life," Nailer called over to him. "You've gotta let the earth soak in your skin, taste the grit. That's the only way you can be one with your environment."

"Amen to that!" Jud agreed. "Westhead wants a mint on his pillow every night. Me? Give me blood!"

Amused and not fully denying their charges, Westhead turned back to his cage and re-checked his trunks one more time. Everything had been packed efficiently and quickly, from strobe lights to flex cuffs, glint tape, a second blowout kit, body armor and plates, batteries, knife sharpener, new Camelbak, Crye Precision cammies with integrated knee and elbow pads, a Princeton-Tec tactical headlamp, SureFire light, various explosives and charges, even an IO device in case he had to give someone blood directly into their bone marrow. While he had never been a corpsman, everyone on the team was trained extensively in battlefield medicine. Unfortunately, all had used it.

"Fuckahs, fuckahs, fuckahs," squeaked a loud voice from behind Stevens. "A hundo says I'm the one to double tap al-Baghdadi, that goat fuckah."

Matt Horrigan was trying to squeeze past their officer in charge, his usual wide smile plastered across a ruddy, child-like face. It didn't matter to Horrigan if his lips were purple while lying in the surf zone or picking moondust from his teeth in the Sunni Triangle—he was always, some would say psychotically so, happy. The Boston product was known as Mr. Positive, or simply Pos.

He had both hands on Stevens's shoulders, trying to shove him through the doorway. The rest of the guys looked up from their prep, unable to not crack up at the entrance of Pos. He possessed the lovable affectations of a worn boxer still content to get in the ring for a meager payday.

There wasn't anyone more universally liked on the team than the pudgy jokester. Even within this dysfunctional family of man-children, no one struck fear into their teammates quite like Horrigan did. His practical jokes were legendary, while generally obliterating any normal lines of decency. If Pos was around, you were constantly checking your six, making sure salt shakers had tight lids and no bodily fluids had found their way into your helmet or gloves. God help you if your cell phone was left out. Didn't matter if you had a passcode—Pos could hack into anything, and you'd soon find the language changed to Hebrew and gay porn as your wallpaper.

He had been in Westhead's sister platoon when they were both newly pinned SEALs a dozen or so years earlier, and even as a new guy had been fearless when pranking more experienced teammates. Fresh out of SQT and determined to make a name for himself, he went so far as to prank Naval Special Warfare Group 2's commanding officer. When then-CAPT Bradley went into his office after PT one morning, the bucket of water Pos had placed on the top of the door fell as designed, soaking him. The smile never left Pos's face for the eight hours he was tied to a tree and continuously smeared with condiments by his new task unit. His reputation had been forged that day, and he worked hard to live up to it.

Pos's head—the same width as his neck—possessed properties similar to that of a bowling ball: namely, hairless and perfectly round. His face: cherubic, often flushed and sweaty with exertion or laughter. Its size necessitated powerful shoulders, which seemed to rise from the stocky frame like dough. A ratty Red Sox hat was usually pushed low over wispy eyebrows, which rose higher as he addressed Stevens.

"Excuse me, suh, if I kin jus' get on ovah to my cage ovah theh," he warbled in a thick Boston accent, still pushing on Stevens's back. The colonel wasn't fooled. He spun around, shoving Horrigan into the room before reaching over his shoulder. As suspected, he removed a piece of paper that had been taped to his back.

"'Kick Me'? That's the best you could come up with, you Irish inbred?" Stevens held the paper high for everyone to read. A jagged grin through disheveled whiskers bespoke his pride in not being duped. "I was born at night, but not last night. Jerkoff."

He started to ball the paper up, but suddenly went flying through the doorway, skidding face-first across the floor.

Thor stood in his place, wearing the most innocent of expressions. When the room erupted in laughs again, Stevens stared up in shock. On his back was a second KICK ME sign.

"Sorry, Colonel, but the sign said to kick you. Just following orders."

"Two is one, one is none, right?" Horrigan was performing for the room now, his thousand-watt smile infectious. "You wouldn't single-prime a charge, would you?"

Stevens rolled to his back, both middle fingers extended to the room, while the men laughed and continued their preparation for war.

We all laugh. Mine is forced, but I know I have to do it. The sad clown, or some shit. For the guys. People notice stuff like that, if you aren't screwing around. If you act like you care too much. If it seems like what we do affects you. It's a fine line, being squared away while staying fun and loose. If you aren't, the guys'll start to wonder about you, and if that happens, it's over. You'll be deemed nonoperational and serve the rest of your contract creating PowerPoints before being turned over to the VA for shitty care as a newly minted, fucked-up civilian with sore joints and an inability to sleep.

It's an asset in our line of work to know when to be serious and when to screw around. That's why the mood is light as we prep, even though we fully understand the seriousness of the mission we are about to undertake.

"What's up, Dan?" I say as friendly as I'm capable, clasping Westhead on the shoulder. The small flag I'm holding—red, white, and blue—drapes across him. "You meet the FBI agent?" I can't help but realize it sounds forced.

He looks toward me, scowling at the flag on his arm with enough venom that I wonder if he somehow knows. If *anyone* worries me, if anyone is capable of catching me, it's Westhead. He's never been in a room where he wasn't the smartest guy. It's a testament to his humility that he doesn't let everyone know it. That, or he just doesn't want to give away a tactical advantage. We both hold the look for what feels like a long time. My heart races. Westhead is a team leader, one of our most experienced operators. He's the type of guy who makes people doubt themselves even when they're right. Fuck Agent Kopen, it's visions of Chief Westhead's suspicious looks that keep me up at night.

"Get that nasty-ass flag off me," he spits, flicking at it.

"That's some way to talk. Should hang you for treason." I pull it away, folding it and placing it in the bottom of my foot locker. I haven't yet been on a deployment without it.

"I mean, you know I'd give my life for that flag, but I'd rather it not be from cholera. Has that thing ever been washed?"

"Negative. I've worn it under my plates on every mission I've ever been on. A gift from my priest back home before my first overseas deployment. My good luck charm. Guess it works. I'm still here."

"Get a rabbit's foot. Thing smells like shit." He closes his cage. I walk away, wiping sweat from my neck, my chest. It's sweltering out, and the government air conditioning can't handle this many of us rushing around in tight quarters. Most of the team already has their gear squared away, and the bullshitting comes to a close. It's a bustle of activity, organized, but with a sense of heightened alertness. While we've all done this countless times, that experience does not mute the anticipation or dull the adrenaline. The day it does is the day an assaulter needs to hang up his guns.

I can't help but feel extra eyes on me, imagined or not, while everyone continues to discuss what happened in DC and whether or not we'll be the ones to go after the "terrorists." I'm still jacked up from that operation and our new mission is adding to my overstimulation, causing my right eye to twitch so badly I have to place my hand on my knee to stop it from shaking, and I'm holding out hope I'll be able to sleep on the flight but have a feeling my swirling head will not let me, when I answer someone's question before settling an argument about which Chuck Norris movie is most realistic and then it's time to move out.

LITTLE CREEK

Westhead, like everyone else, conducted a final sweep of his cage. People shouted to each other, borrowing extra batteries, asking about different optics, radio frequencies. They broke Pos's balls for the amount of candy and Pop-Tarts he packed. Thor wondered out loud whether if Pos's wife would even wait until they were wheels-up before inviting her boyfriend over. Pos asked him if Oompa-Loompas really do make the best chocolate. Adam offered McDonald a Bible. He declined, politely. Rucks were sealed, kits outfitted, gun cases locked. Stevens stuck his face back into the team room, yelling that the buses had arrived. The men turned toward the speaker to find their boss loaded out in a mix of desert cammies and civilian clothes, a plate carrier in one hand and EXFIL ballistic helmet in the other. His sleeves rolled up to reveal colorful artwork on powerful arms. At his feet lay his full kit and rifle case. Each operator thought the same thing: It had been a while since their OIC had gone operational—proof the al-Baghdadi mission was personal.

"Nice man-bun, Blade," Thor laughed. "Yeah, you're operator as fuck. A real pipe hitter. You look like one of those lumbersexuals who can't change a tire. Or worse, one of Mutt's surfer bros with the skinny jeans who forgot leg day."

Mutt, peaceably seated in front of his locker, turned casually, giving the room an aloof, simple once-over. In his hand steamed a freshly brewed coffee from the French-press kept in his cage. His preferred brand, named "Death Wish," was a highly caffeinated concoction which after half a cup Thor had once said it made him want to exit his skin, and that Pos described as "magic shitting beans." The caffeine content did nothing to raise his sense of urgency or limit his chill. The California product was characteristically unoffended by the joke. Mellow.

"Hey, man, leave the hipsters out of this. Give peace a chance," he slurred affably, exaggerating for effect. The casual peace sign which followed did nothing to negate the dichotomous fact that he was a highly trained killer. Mutt's bright white teeth seemed especially brilliant against such a tan face, half-covered by flopping blond hair. He was long and lean, his sharp face all angles.

Stevens snorted, addressed Thor. "Smurfette, I was wasting bad guys when you were still gumming your mama's teat. You even pop your cherry yet? Unless that was you in DC yesterday ..."

Thor chucked a chem light at Stevens, who caught it and rifled it back, hitting him in the midsection. The room erupted in laughter. JOE-CAG was the tip of the spear, but at this level the line between officers and enlisted was blurred, to say the least. Everyone was, for the most part, on equal footing, the only differentiator being your battle record and reputation. You were only as good as your last mission.

There was a clamor of boots, grunts, and curses as heavy gear was lifted. The room emptied, suddenly silent.

Outside, the men stood with their gear in front of idling buses, anxious and excited. The morning was muggy, gray, and otherwise still. When the bus doors hissed open, the operator in front of Westhead winced while pulling himself up the stairs by the safety railings.

"What's wrong with you?" Westhead asked McDonald. There was obvious pain in his face.

"Nothing," he answered too quickly. "J-jus, just my knee." He said it like he'd been caught doing something wrong. "Wrenched it a little on that VBSS training exercise last week, and it's still a little sore. I'm g-good to go."

Westhead's stare was one of suspicion—like all the men, McDonald would be loath to admit an injury, especially as a new guy. Wary but understanding, he replied, "Gotcha," and they continued boarding.

The driver, a navy seaman, just a kid really, tiptoed into the driver's seat. He took an intimidated survey of his passengers and gulped before attempting a friendly welcome.

"Don't worry, kid, we won't bite," Hell said, chomping the air in front of him while taking his seat. "Hard." The nervous sailor grinned, awestruck.

"Don't mind him." Pos winked at the kid. "He was raised by wolves." The kid smiled gratefully and started the bus.

Westhead fidgeted in his seat, repositioned his side arm. "Here we go again." His mumble was to no one.

Hagen, who had sat down next to him, glanced over. The commander closed the file he was studying and gave him a sideways look as if to say, "You all right?" Westhead blew a kiss at him and popped in earphones, hitting Play on his iPhone. Soon his eyes were closed, munching on a protein bar, lost in The Grateful Dead's "Uncle John's Band."

The ride to the airfield was short and relatively quiet. The most elite of American warriors sat impassively, some making small talk, some trying to hydrate, all mentally preparing for war. A steamy drizzle dampened them as they filed off the bus into the dawn, automatic weapons clutched tightly.

After unloading their gear from a second bus, the group trudged straight onto a waiting C-130J Super Hercules. They watched their support crew drive four desert patrol vehicles (DPVs) up the aft loading ramp of the cargo plane. The modified dune buggies were equipped with .50-cal machine guns and either TOW missiles or 40-millimeter MK 19 grenade launchers. The presence of the vehicles meant that they would be operating behind enemy lines, deep in the desert. And that they expected contact, lots of it. That was to be anticipated; JOE-CAG wasn't sent to peaceful locales.

The giant gray plane sat alone on the otherwise inactive runway, ready to take them to war.

I walk onto the plane with the rest of my team, slowly surveying the vast windowless cabin. Its dark, ambient red lighting the only thing keeping us from bumping into each other as we rush to find open pockets to stretch out in. We're old hat at this—before we even push off, guys have set up hammocks and sleeping bags, making the wide-bodied plane resemble something like a homeless shelter. For the most part, the jump seats we are supposed to be sitting in are ignored. We dare the flight crew to admonish us.

I find my own open area and stretch out on my ground pad, assault pack doubling as a pillow. Across from me, Westhead makes his space his own. He shakes a bottle of pills toward me, which I decline, before throwing several into his own mouth.

"Those stopped working on me a long time ago," I tell him gloomily.

"They just take the edge off for me," he says. "Help me relax, hopefully get a little sleep."

"Still having troubles at night?"

He looks around quickly, ensuring we haven't been overheard. "Between you and me, I haven't slept for more than a couple of hours in a row in months. Hard to stay awake during the day, impossible to sleep at night. These are the only thing keeping me going."

"To each his own," I say, settling in. We all have our own issues.

A shaky announcement from the cockpit: "Valued flyers, this is your captain speaking. Thank you for choosing Paradise Airlines, where your comfort is our top priority. Jasmine and Charity will be catering to your every need, whether it be a second serving of caviar or a champagne refill. You have your choice of in-flight entertainment and there is a top-shelf, complimentary bar available. Let us know how we can make your flight more comfortable, and feel free to press your call button now if you'd like a flight attendant to come fluff your pillow."

"I'll give you something to fluff!" someone yells at the pilots but is rewarded with only a few obligatory jeers. Like me, most guys are trying to get comfortable, earphones in and books out, some card games started. Soon there's only the whir of the giant aircraft's engines. The plane starts its shaky journey down the runway, finally jerking itself skyward, leaving me with an ominous sense of *déjà vu* as we head east.

SOMEWHERE OVER THE ATLANTIC OCEAN

"All right boys, gather 'round," Stevens called out, his gruff shout fighting for attention over the roar of quad-turboprop engines. The men stirred, working to get the blood flowing and sleep cleared from their eyes. Faces lifted from letters home, iPads. The stress ball Darby chucked at Mutt hit him squarely in the chest without causing so much as a flinch. His body, prone, face lifted, bare torso raised and chin up, remained in its stationary pose, eyelids sealed.

"Hey, Downward Dog," Stevens yelled at him. "Wanna join us?"

When Mutt finally opened his eyes, it was with a renewed concord upon his face. A bandana, bright and red, covered his forehead, sweaty wisps of light hair over the edges. He exhaled contentedly and acknowledged the address with a satisfied, "Namaste," palms together in a soothing steeple.

Stevens thanked him with appropriate sarcasm and everyone huddled closer in order to hear their leader.

"First off, I want to make sure we all have our heads in the game. The FBI investigation, cheating wives" (they all looked to Pos; he jerked off an imaginary dick) "snot-nosed kids, all that shit—we gotta leave that behind. Check?" After a robust if not edgy round of "check" responses: "OK then. We'll be landing in Germany tonight, and then"— he paused here in an attempt to draw out the drama—"we'll stage in Iraq before crossing into Syria to conduct a kill/capture mission on high-value target Ibrahim al-Baghdadi."

The shared looks were congratulatory and victorious, a palpable collection of anticipation hovering throughout the cabin.

"This will be a Joint Task Force with DEVGRU. We're going to link up with a Team 6 squadron already forward-deployed in Iraq," he continued before being quickly drowned out. It was Jud and his nineteen combat deployments with SF and Delta leading the chorus of boos. With the atmosphere re-intensified since the confirmation of their target, this time the jokes had plenty of energy and force. Jud was promptly joined by the other non-Naval operators in anti-SEAL epithets.

"Fuck those seamen!" Hell yelled out, prodding his fellow soldiers and Marines to turn on their NSW brethren with insults and headlocks. "Aren't they too busy writing their memoirs to kick any doors?"

"Settle down, dogfaces, settle down," Stevens said, arms outstretched. "I don't like working with those prima donnas any more than you do, but that's what came down from ADM Bradley and the JSOC brass. We'll do what we always do—complete the mission and then let them take the credit. I'm sure there'll be a movie deal in it for them."

Now it was the Team guys' turn to boo. Hagen shot his counterpart a glare, and after allowing for an appropriate length of spirited debate, he too raised his hands in a calming manner.

"All right, all right, enough. We're on the same team here. Don't get mad at us because you snake-eaters can't swim." He pulled out an iPad, holding up a PowerPoint presentation. "Here's the preliminary plan we developed with the team leaders yesterday. To the PowerPoint!", which the team echoed with their own resounding, "To the PowerPoint!"

He showed them a screen with a map of Syria on it. Hagen zoomed in on aerial shots of a modest town with a walled compound along the outskirts. Although the initial groundwork for the op had already been planned by the team leaders, the details would be ironed out by the full team. For the next half hour they had an animated discussion about their infil.

"And how about extraction? When shit pops off, there's gonna be

ISIS assholes all over the place," Nailer pointed out once they had reviewed inserting with the DPVs. The plan was to drive them as close as stealth would allow before patrolling the last few klicks in.

Hagen agreed. "You're right about that. Al-Baghdadi's compound doubles as a Daesh training camp. Satellite footage shows close to 100 fighters on site at any given time."

"Fucking A." Pos's excitement made his face glow. "More warm bodies to stop our bullets. We're definitely gonna get some on this mish."

"Out of curiosity, why don't we just stick a JDAM up their ass and be done with it?" Thor asked.

Nailer didn't look up from his fingernails when answering. "You know why, Thor. Collateral damage. Haji women and kids are still women and kids. Even if they're training on light machine guns and learning to plant IEDs. We're the expendable ones." He meant neither insult nor complaint. "And because our bosses' bosses' boss wants that DNA proof that only men with a particular skill set can provide. And who don't mind—neigh, enjoy—getting their balls shot off."

He had a way of phrasing things that in a traditional setting might draw the ire of his audience. If you read his comments in a bubble rather than received them directly, offense would be unavoidable. It was his complete lack of concern in what you thought about him that made it not so. Getting angry or offended would be a wasted emotion. In any event, coming from someone else, it might have sounded like an objection or protest. But with Nailer, there was no hidden agenda. No mincing words. Nailer was incapable of sarcasm, of irony, because he truly meant every word he said. He enjoyed getting his balls shot off.

Thor, who did not have those same limitations, looked skyward and started counting on his fingers.

"My bosses' bosses' boss ... Who's that, the janitor?"

"Then what would that make you, asshole?" GQ asked. Tall and lean with manicured facial hair, including an inexhaustible battle against unibrow, GQ was the only one unaware that his nickname was in jest. The anxious, easily upset New Yorker was their resident know-it-all. Most of the guys spoke more than one language, but GQ was fluent in Spanish, Italian, Farsi, and Arabic. His caustic heritage of first-generation Italian and Iranian parents gave him his dark complexion, quick temper and accent-less tongues. His claim of being a member of Mensa had never been confirmed, but was wholly believable, assuming they accepted smartasses. He allegedly had appeared on *Jeopardy*, placing second, but no one could produce the tape. Unless the team was operational, GQ was one of the few team members who actually groomed himself regularly and dressed like the international spy/model he fashioned himself after. He had three divorces under his belt, all by the age of thirty-four.

"The janitor's bitch, I suppose."

"Sounds about right."

"This is kind of like frying bacon with no shirt on, no?" said Jud, yawning, a wide stretch revealing elongating pit stains. "I mean, I wanna get this sumbitch as much as the next guy, but the intel weenies don't seem to know their asses from their elbows. They can't even say for sure he's there."

"Gentlemen, please," Hagen urged, again raising his hands to calm the troops. "Our commander in chief, who, I don't need to remind you, is responsible for this unit's formation AND giving us this mission, wants that undeniable proof of death that can only be given by a Tier 1 United States Special Operations team. I assume we're okay with that?"

Hagen's words were met with the roar he knew they would be. He and Stevens traded another look; their men were ready.

"Blade!"

"Huh?"

"Worst place you've ever shat?"

Stevens looked up from his book, worked out one of his earplugs. He was stretched out comfortably on a hammock hung between two pallets.

"Huh?"

Pos repeated the question, louder. Stevens looked back to his book.

"That's easy," he replied. "Your mom's house."

"Funny. If I wanted a dickhead answer, I would have asked Hell."

"I got this one!" Hell shouted over the plane's hard working engines. "My goddamn BDUs! Twelve-hour firefight in Falluja—AK rounds were my alarm clock that morning, interrupted my morning kale shake and protein bar. I'm quite regular, but AQI didn't want to hear it. By hour three, it was bombs away."

"If you've never taken a crap in your BDUs, do you even operate?" asked Adam. Philosophically?

"What are we talking here? Just a little shart? Some streaks in the draws? Or a full-fledged dump in your trousers?" asked McDonald.

Pos clarified. "Full-on dump."

"Shit, yeah!" exclaimed Jud. "Of course. If you don't get occasionally get a little mudbutt on a lengthy infil, you're just a liar. And what about a two-day sniper mission? Poop where you lay. Better remember jumbo-sized Ziploc bags and unscented baby-wipes. If not, your buddy is going to charge you out the ass for one."

Everyone nodded. Oh yeah, they'd all been there.

FORWARD OPERATING BASE (FOB) MONSOOR, IRAQ

It's the next day by the time we land in Baghdad. We don't plan to stay in the city long. Our next ride is already waiting as we gather our gear and disembark. I can't say I'm thrilled to be back here, especially when my mission at home is just underway, but can't deny that the FBI agent showing up at headquarters has me spooked, as is my failure to kill Dick Basting. This opportunity to get al-Baghdadi is a nice distraction; I can't complain about the chance to kill one of the men responsible for Atlas. But there are more on American soil who will go unpunished if not for me.

The air here is thick and dusty. It has a tangible quality to it, like you could reach out and put it in your pocket. Nearly visible. It's still hot, even this late in the evening. I only use that word, hot, because there isn't another that truly does it justice. Oppressive, maybe. It's actually beyond hot here. Hotter than the 116 degrees an overworked-looking thermometer hanging from a tent reads. The running joke is that Iraq is Hell-adjacent, so often told by the boots deployed here mostly because they know it to be true, though they're not only referring to the heat.

I work my mouth, trying to find saliva, squinting into the lower-ing sun. Around me, my teammates do the same. Everyone is stretch-ing, groggy from Ambien-induced sleep. I didn't bother.

"I never get used to these flights," another operator mumbles while inventorying his equipment, speaking, I guess, to me. He's rubbing his eyes, and I can smell his breath. He's one of the arrogant ones, one of the guys under the impression he's Superman. God's gift to the mil-itary. A gym rat with a head shaped like an anvil and filled with con-crete. I've never had a use for those types of operators off the battle-field, and I don't particularly care for him in social settings. But while I may abhor speaking to him in everyday life, I love having his trigger by my side in battle. He's saved my life more times than I could list.

The best I can offer in response is a slight head bob and a "me nei-ther" without really looking over.

I can feel his stare, longer than it should be, before finally break-ing away and hoisting his pack and rifle. I can't help but think: *Could he suspect?*

Blindly, blankly, we hoof it single file to a waiting CH-47 Chinook helicopter. I'm almost thankful for the throb in my ankle—it's either that or the impending chance for violence that's dulled the stabbing in my brain. Barely a word is spoken as we board for the hour-long ride from Baghdad to FOB Monsoor. The small, shabbily defended firebase in the Iraqi desert is named for Michael Monsoor, a SEAL on Team 3 who had been posthumously awarded the Medal of Honor after he jumped on a grenade to save two of his fellow SEALs on a Ramadi rooftop in 2006. The outpost had officially closed in 2012. Officially.

A too-friendly Ranger captain greets us enthusiastically on the airfield at Monsoor. This guy is gung-ho, probably pisses CIBs and dreams about PFTs. He barks at us about the quality of soldier in his command while leading us through the dusk to a series of plywood huts. We don't give a shit about his Rangers and already know where the hooches are. The Special Operations barracks sit off to the side of the tarmac, separate from the rest of the base. SpecOps forces are different creatures, and we prefer our own domain. I'm all too familiar with the housing here. Shared MREs and talcum powder in it. Given IVs and shed tears in it.

It's not easy to curb the flood of emotions that hit me in a single dream-like sequence as we reach the crude lodgings. Uncut, fast-forwarded experiences of those no longer with us. Scenes of their last hours that can't be unforgotten, right there, on the other side of that concertina wire, right where a new HESCO barrier now stands: Bull grimacing when the pilot called out "yippie-kai-yay, motherfucker" over comms. Guzzo double-checking our radio frequencies, applying eye black to my clammy cheeks. Offering Spencer a stick of gum as we stood shoulder to chest waiting to board the helos, him on one chalk, me on the other, both peering through wraparound sunglasses wondering why the hell we were operating in daylight with no Apache escort. Hagen calling out the secondary and tertiary HLZs for the umpteenth time. I can see all of them here, and it takes my breath.

"You all right, brother?" I wince under the pressure of Westhead's hand on my shoulder.

"Yeah, I'm good," I tell him, hoisting my rifle. "Let's get some z's."

"Check," he says, and I follow his back toward the series of hooches where thirty of our brothers spent their last night on earth.

"Dan, *suka blyat!*"

Westhead grimaced, turned toward the Russian curse spoken with an Ozark twang. Adam was studying the language, convinced that would be the next major theatre of war. His qualms about cursing did not include his Russian vocabulary.

Westhead had been expecting the confrontation ever since they had completed the training exercise in North Carolina. It had been merely days, but felt like a month. The mayhem in DC and the last-minute mission had delayed the run-in, but here it was.

He half-smiled at his closest friend and teammate, recognizing the same wear and tear returned harshly in his own mirror each morning.

At first glance, Adam wasn't the most physically intimidating man. But he was someone people noticed, even if they didn't know why. He had a kind face, which went against what he did for a living. He managed to come across as the sort of person truly interested in your day, and maybe even the one after that. You felt that he actually cared what kind of sandwich you had for lunch, how much of a rip-off your mechanic was. You *wanted* to tell him about how your kid got suspended from school. Maybe it was the ease with which he carried himself, the comfortability in his own skin. A genuine, unassuming smile. His countenance disarming, at least by all measurable aspects. It wasn't until proximity highlighted wide shoulders and a thick back that you could tell there was something different about him. Special. The way he didn't speak even when possessing the perfect retort. The way he moved. A confident, athletic gait. Almost a glide. An alert but subdued focus that covertly read into you, his expression seeming to know what you were thinking even before you did. And more so, that you still wanted to tell him. Adam wasn't easily forgotten, even if you weren't sure what made you think back to what should have been just one of the dozens of innocent encounters we all experience every day. A casual nod on the beach or introduction at a bar, him holding a bottle of Pellegrino or twirling a volleyball. A purchase at a convenience store. But something made you remember that icy stare and trusting grip. You wouldn't be able to put your finger on it, you would just understand he was someone you wanted to know better. Because of his job, that could rarely happen with outsiders.

"Hey, Whitey, you decide to become a Hindu? I thought you were Mr. Christianity," Westhead laughed. He was referring to the large red welt sitting dead center on Adam's forehead.

"*Ede nahou!* Hilarious, you jerk. Any idea how bad sniper-grade sim rounds hurt? You could have taken out an eye." The yo-yo Adam was working in the dark rattled in his hand. Undiagnosed ADD meant Adam rarely remained still, even when sleeping. He was a regular sleepwalker, often eating full meals without waking. It was easy to imagine what he'd been like as a well-meaning but hyperactive child giving fits to his parents and teachers alike.

"'Forgive us our trespasses, as we forgive those who trespass against us,' or something like that, right?"

The two former SEAL Team 6 Gold Squadron teammates stopped in front of one of the huts. It looked like all the others. Basic, sturdy, stained plywood and metal brackets joining four corners. Scarred knots in the wood, scuff marks on the door from dusty combat boots, calloused hands and weary knuckles. Although they couldn't see them in the dark, they both knew verbatim the scripture verses and warrior's mantras scribbled in felt pen along each wall. The messages that they, and dozens of other operators in over a decade of war in this God-forsaken country, had scrawled in blue and red and black marker, sometimes frantically, always with love: love for their country, for their families, for their mission, but mostly for their fellow warriors, because maybe they needed to leave something tangible, evidence that they were *there*, since there was no way of passing through FOB Monsoor without leaving part of yourself, although the dichotomy was that they were more full after the experience, like whatever piece that had stayed had made room for more to enter: For more love, but for more pain too. That was the challenge. The aftermath, as unavoidable as death.

"I prefer an eye for an eye," Adam responded matter-of-factly, in his unassuming, country fashion. "Although I gotta tell ya, it *was* a heck of a shot, brother. When the first one got me center mass, I already knew I was done for. That forehead tap sure left no doubt!" He had thinning hair and a narrow, pointed face. Intelligent, attentive eyes constantly darted to and fro, so afraid of missing something that they never did. He paused at the hut's entrance, pocketed the yo-yo, and pushed in the door with a creak.

"Obliged. But it's convenient how you can pick and choose which verses apply when."

"And it's a good thing you've gotten yourself accustomed to these hot climates," Adam drawled while reaching for his headlamp. "You know this place is referred to as Hell adjacent."

"You don't mean that. You'd never let me go to hell, would ya, brother?"

"I'll do all I can for you, dude. I'll pray, I always do. 'And they said, Believe in the Lord Jesus Christ, and thou shalt be saved, and thy house.'"

Westhead's cheeks rose, sincerely grateful. "'Preciate that, Whitey." Then: "You ready for this?"

Adam sighed into the blackness. "Home sweet home."

Together, they stepped gingerly into the hooch they had shared during so many deployments during their time in Team 6. They had been a part of Task Force 88 back in '07, a capture/kill team that went after dozens of high-value targets in Iraq, and had often staged at the FOB. Their team had been responsible for the eradication of a large network of IED-makers and suicide bomber recruiters, resulting in countless American lives saved—and a few lost. Now, their paces through the space were measured, slow and respectful, as if entering a temple. Their boots thumped and echoed against the plywood. The red light from Adam's Princeton TAC headlamp bobbed gently, selecting spots to illuminate, revealing pockets of the crude space they would call home, at least for the night.

"Life is not a journey to the grave with the intention of arriving safely in a pretty and well preserved body, but rather to skid in broadside, thoroughly used up, totally worn out, and loudly proclaiming -- WOW-- What a Ride!"

Of all the etchings and doodles on the walls, that was the one, centered just above the far rack, that always grabbed Westhead's attention. He knew who had written it, and for the author, it had certainly come true. He threw his pack on the cot below.

Adam flicked a switch and the room fully lit up. He paced, examining each nook and cranny, more for the activity than out of actual inquisitiveness. For a moment they didn't talk, just took in the space. Not fighting the memories but embracing them. Westhead finally sat on his bunk, sticking a hand into his bag.

"Whatchu looking for?"

"Don't worry about it."

"Gotta chill with those things, bro."

"My knees are swollen, my L1 vertebra is fused to my L2, I got screws in my right ankle, bone spurs in the left, a shoulder that won't stay in socket, and I can't feel this hand." He held up the right one, frustrated, crooked fingers angled in directions they weren't meant to go. "I appreciate your medical diagnosis, but this is the only way I'm gonna get any sleep after that flight."

"We all got injuries, Dan. I just want to make sure you have those things under control."

"What are you, my sponsor now?"

"Just a concerned coworker."

"We can't all go through life without something to kill the pain, unfortunately. Don't look down on us mere mortals." Westhead lay on the rack, staring through the ceiling. The air stagnated. A helicopter thumped in the distance. It was Adam who finally spoke next.

"Feels kind of crowded in here, huh?"

Westhead sighed, knowing what he meant. "At least they have some company tonight. I'd like to think they're happy we're here, finishing their work."

"You actually believe that?"

He shrugged.

"Dunno. Does it matter? What I believe or don't believe doesn't change anything. Just call me 'open to the possibility.' I haven't seen anything concrete in either direction. Or, more accurately, I've seen arguments for both sides, firsthand."

"Haven't we all. It's a start, though. I'll pray for you, brother."

"I'd rather you pray for Cheyenne. And Phil. And the guys. They need it, and deserve it, a hell of a lot more than I do."

Adam reached to his neck, touched the silver medallion of St. Michael that always hung there. He even taped it down during ops. "I'll pray for all of you. I always do."

Westhead sat up to remove his boots. He'd sleep in his cammies, rifle locked and loaded next to a go-bag, but he couldn't sleep in his boots. Most of the guys did, in case they had to be on the move in a hurry, but he had never been able to.

"I'd like that. Certainly can't hurt."

I wake up later than most of my teammates. That's not to be confused with getting a good night's sleep. I haven't had one of those in years.

I had lain in my rack in full gear, listening to the wind and whipping sand outside the hooch, the screams and explosions in my head. At some point, palms over ears, I had drifted into the only type of sleep I knew—a defensive, resigned half-slumber, too inside of my racing thoughts to truly rest. The reprieve hadn't lasted long, as a half-assed mortar attack jolted me upright at the same time the crack under my door began to show a faint glow. A few tired yells of "Incoming!" and "Tuck tail!" preceded the jointed spit of a Ma Deuce .50-cal, reactive return fire sent by weary Marines who didn't even bother to shout out "Get some," all too used to the sporadic bombing of their outpost. The incoming rockets didn't sound effective, and besides, worrying about getting hit by a mortar was like worrying about a lightning strike or shark attack. If your number was up, it was up.

If I fell back asleep after the shelling, the normal rhythms of the base kept my mind active shortly thereafter.

But I was lucky. I didn't have nightmares, not the way some guys did. I didn't replay the firefights or sniper shots or chopper crashes or IED blasts or suicides that had taken too many of my brothers in the decades of war. When I did sleep, mercifully, it was dreamless. I had made that clear to the headshrinker who the head shed had forced us all to talk with after Atlas. She had given me a clean bill of health. I didn't correct her, and I didn't go again. It was well known that you could lose your C-1 operational status if you went around claiming PTSD. We were all fucked up. It was a testament to my self-awareness that I realized I was just a little more fucked up than the rest of the guys. Or maybe that they weren't fucked up enough.

By the time I eat chow and meander over to the fire pit with a cup of hot but too-weak coffee, a bunch of guys are already sitting around, bullshitting. The sun is setting, I guess picturesquely or some shit, in the distance. We're on vampire hours over here, and that means the work-day starts when our targets go to bed. I'm on edge and my cup keeps going to my mouth in tiny, automatic sips. Thankfully, the caffeine starts to do its work. Soon, I feel more alert, even capable of conversation.

I stare into the horizon. Heat waves still shimmer above the sand, distorting distance. The sun makes its final retreat, the top of the sphere falling unceremoniously into the desert. Still, I am dutifully awestruck when I catch the last glimmer. Then, it's gone. Who's to say it will be back? Feeling properly philosophical, I turn to the group.

"Morning, sleeping beauty," one of them says to me with no ex-pectation of response.

I ask if he's got a dip. The can he tosses is Copenhagen. Not win-tergreen. That will come later.

I can't help but notice the conversation has stopped abruptly, right about the time I walked up. It makes me wonder what it was they had been talking about. My heart picks up speed. Could it be me? My oper-ation in DC? Does the team suspect me? A few of the glares appear par-ticularly pointed. The whole scene seems a little murky, filtered behind ballistic Oakley sunglasses. Someone starts singing Taylor Swift loudly. A few others join in, an off-beat, screeching rendition that both unites the performers and elicits head shakes from their audience. I take a seat on a crudely made bench next to the fire, rubbing my temples and staring into the cooling sand. I wonder what the guys would say if they knew the attack had been me. I would like to think they would un-derstand. After a minute and a fat lip, I throw the Copenhagen back.

"*Haters gonna hate …*" they continue belting out, song scattering across the desert setting.

Eventually, Westhead addresses me. "Operation Atlas Revenge is a go," he tells me. "That's what we were just talking about. The intelligence guys confirmed al-Baghdadi is in the compound. We're hitting it tonight."

Immediately, my head feels better, clearer. The sensation of potentially spinning off the earth's surface dissipates with the news. I'm able to take my first good breath since I woke.

"Roger that," I say, spitting into the fire. "Just another mission, right?"

"Why do we need a fire when it's still pushing 100 degrees?" Nailer asked no one, throwing another log in.

"Why does a stopped escalator still look like it's moving? Why don't my punches ever connect in my dreams? Why does Radio Shack need your phone number when you buy batteries?" Jud blinked hard, several times, looking intently at Nailer. "I don't know ..." he wailed.

"What are you talking about, dude? Radio Shack's closed."

"Seinfeld, dipshit."

"Speaking of dip, who's got one?"

A tin got tossed across the fire, then back. Thor, in only tiny shorts and sneakers, made a scene about intercepting it, tucking it under his arm like a football. When he saw McDonald in his path, he ran him over. Together, they tumbled to the sand.

"Touchdown!" Thor yelled, standing over McDonald, the sun setting on his shoulder, arms raised in victory. When he tried to stand, Thor pushed McDonald back down. McDonald rose to a knee but was thrown down again. He grabbed a boot and twisted, pulling Thor to the sand. The two men wrestled viciously, ripped arms and legs intertwined. It was hard to tell where one man began and the other ended as they clawed violently. Thor ended up on top of McDonald, more spirited than he should have been.

"Say, 'I want to bang Hillary!'" he hollered, his forearm pinning McDonald's neck. Mac's head thrashed back and forth in the sand, face red and angry.

"Fuck! You! And your whore! Of a mother!" he spat back, still losing, although not for lack of effort. They continued to struggle, kicking up sand and dust, while their teammates observed, amused.

"I swear this unit is made up strictly of deviants and psychopaths." Stevens's voice reverberated from the shadows of the fire. The men spun to him, previously unaware of their leader's presence. His ability to materialize without announcement was uncanny. He watched dispassionately for another moment, occasionally spraying the ground with tobacco juice. "Where did we find you degenerates?" Then, finally raising his voice to break up the wrestling match: "If you two have that much energy, I'll be happy to send you to Hell and have him PT you to death!"

Hellesley looked up with interest from one of his organic juices, excited that he might get to torture someone. The team leader's nickname was often used as a threat rather than an identifier. As in: "You're going to Hell," if someone screwed something up on a training op and as punishment had to run or swim with the crotchety Marine. It could also be a proper noun, as in location: "Ah, shit, we're going to be in Hell today," when he was the one to lead PT. The Gunnery Sergeant had completed eleven Iron Man triathlons and in between deployments competed regularly in ultra-marathons and open-water swims. It was said no one had ever seen him sleep. Or, for that matter, smile. Hell was known as a prick, but an alpha male amongst alpha men.

With Stevens's threat, the combatants stopped, now simply two grown men embracing in the sand. They untangled and stood, spitting grit and knocking moondust from their hair. McDonald looked angry, Hell disappointed. Thor did a back flip.

Stevens again addressed the group, quieter this time, like he was in deep thought. "Maybe it *was* one of you psychopaths who blew up the Basting Institute. Hope everyone here has an alibi. Don't be surprised if Agent Kopen gets every one of us in an interview room when we get back."

The men froze, looks of puzzlement on concerned faces.

"Can they do that?" Thor asked. "I mean, I mean, we're black ops. As secret as it gets. Isn't that why the president formed JOE-CAG?. Don't we have some protection against that?"

Stevens watched the levels of concern rise throughout the group. He studied each of them before responding.

"They're the FBI. They can investigate who they want. And I did some digging on that Agent Kopen. He's the real deal. A former Ranger, one of the first American boots on the ground during Iraqi Freedom. The head shed'll protect you the best we can, but if he gets a subpoena, not much we can do."

The men stood around, clumsy and quiet. Nailer kicked at a log on the edge of the fire. Thor perched himself on the top of a picnic table and threw in a lip. A few late-sleepers sauntered towards the casual assembly, rubbing bloodshot eyes and pouring hot water into MRE packets or putting in headphones. Adam updated them on Stevens's warning about Agent Kopen, eliciting unbelieving stares and whispered complaints.

Soon the whole team was assembled, standing stiffly around the staging area, staring into the fire or re-reading their warning order or lounging on benches or writing emails or cleaning weapons or eating Power Bars or taking Ripped Fuel or bumming chews or comparing pistol grips or stretching or working out or simply bullshitting until it was time to kit up. Hagen strolled to the edge of the group, face dark and deep.

"Gather round, gents," he told them at just above a whisper, his gravelly voice suggesting at least the possibility that he had spent time chewing glass. "As you hoped, Operation Atlas Revenge is officially a go. We stage tonight—wheels up at 2300."

The announcement led to satisfied grunts, muted affirmations. You could see each man shift into another gear, ready to do their part to ensure mission success.

They reverted to their previous activities as soon as Stevens and Hagen finished the briefing, but now in a more serious fashion. No one mentioned the Basting Institute or Special Agent Kopen further. The jokes and insults continued, but now the banter was more forced, reflexive. They still had time to kill, and didn't want to put their game faces on too early.

Jud and Thor arm-wrestled on a picnic table. Thor grimaced at the sweat pouring onto their grip, red-faced but still managing to make fun of his always-perspiring opponent. Pos refereed and talked trash. McDonald watched. GQ and Hagen played horseshoes. Nailer sat alone, drawing. Aliens and spaceships, probably. A surf magazine was laid out between Mutt and Darby, the hulking Hawaiian maybe as mellow as his California-bred compatriot. The sofa they were perched on looked out of place. Domestic. As if it had been dropped from the sky. Or at least a Crate and Barrel catalogue. Somewhere, in Seattle or Nebraska or the Jersey Shore, Betty Sue Homemaker was wondering just how her prized love seat had landed in the middle of a war zone, surrounded by jihadists and crass service members, green bulldozers and sandbags. Punk rock from Mutt's phone played louder than some of the guys would have liked, not as loud as others preferred.

"That shit sounds like a baby spider monkey getting tortured," Pos yelled over to them. His smooth head glistened in the fire, profile extending into the cooling desert. "Makes me wanna shoot somebody."

"Good thing we got one tonight then," said Mutt. "You can thank NOFX later."

Darby grinned a sloppy grin and started head banging. When he stopped, Westhead took a seat between them, spitting into a water bottle.

"You honkeys and your tobacco," Darby joked, making a face at him.

"Guess we all have our habits."

"Longboarding and hula girls, those are my habits."

While not very pipe hitter-ish of him, it would be inaccurate to describe Mutt's reaction as anything other than a giggle. He offered his knuckles to Darby. They pounded fists in agreement.

"Yeah, bro. Waves and babes."

"Red Man and shooting squirrels, that's what an Arkansas boy goes to bed dreaming about every night." Adam had walked over, scratching an unkempt beard. Even though it was mostly dark, he kept his sunglasses on, making it impossible to tell where he was looking.

"And finding a wife with all her teeth, I would imagine," offered Darby.

Adam's voice rose an octave, the hillbilly accent especially pro-
nounced. A sweaty Arkansas Razorbacks cap shielded the top half of
his face, the beard the bottom. His chuckle purposely gummy. "My
Mary Anne sure do have most all her teeth, 'cept dem two front ones!
Why do you think she's divorcing me?"

Mutt's laughter was absentminded but polite. His voice, slow.
Chilled out. West Coast.

"Bro, *that's* not why she's divorcing you."

"How is Mary Anne? I miss her. It's been a while since we've gone
out," Westhead said. "Let's all grab drinks when we're back in civilization. I mean, *we'll* grab drinks—*you* can have a Shirley Temple."

The visible parts of Adam's face contorted into a sneer. For a face
where anything other than delight did not come naturally, it was doing a
fine job indicating displeasure. He twisted the wedding ring on his finger.

"Are you serious? Don't hold your breath. When you sleep with her
sister and then tell her you're rotating to Antarctica, your invites to
Sunday dinner are probably going to be few and far between."

"You did what, Dan?" asked Darby.

Westhead feigned shock. "Ah, come on, it wasn't like that. Debbie
was a nice girl; we had fun. And I didn't tell her I was 'rotating to Antarctica.' I said 'roasting tuna tartar.' It was a dinner offer, and one she
never accepted. I guess she didn't like me very much." His expression:
mock rueful. Demeanor: Who me? "And here I thought we'd hit it off."

"Sara. Her name is still Sara."

"Sara? You sure? Swore it was Debbie, bro."

Adam palmed his yo-yo, removing the sunglasses to ensure his
glare would land. "Yeah, Dan, pretty sure I know my sister-in-law's
name. And now you're on Mary Anne's list. Which, somehow, means
my name landed there as well. Which isn't a big help when I'm this
close"—he held his index finger just above his thumb, barely a crack
in between—"to getting back in the house. And that bi—" Here he
stopped, pursed his lips, started jamming 5.56 ammo into an empty mag.

Darby looked up in shock. "Did you really almost just say what I think you were about to say, Whitey? If only Bull could hear you cursing your wife's name. Guarantee he'd choke you out."

It got quiet, the popping fire counting seconds. Each man entered a hole containing memories of another lost comrade, another doomed mission. A reflection as involuntary as it was unwanted, yet always lurking under the surface, biding its time before making a forceful appearance.

"Let the record reflect, I didn't actually curse her," Adam finally said, mostly as a way to break the silence. "Close—but as we know better than anyone, close only counts in horseshoes and hand grenades." As if on cue, a metallic CLANG rang out from the horseshoe game behind them, a modest celebratory song from GQ followed by an accusation of cheating from Hagen.   "Well, she'll get over it. She always does, every time you screw up. Or I do," Adam said. "So far, at least."

"She still mad at me about Jack getting into my Red Man?"

Darby shook his head and stood up. "I don't even want to know what that means. Someone write my blood type on my sleeve, would you? And try not to get tobacco juice on it."

Adam took the marker, writing a big O- NKA in block letters on Darby's desert cammie top, just above a dusty patch reading 6-28-05. NEVER FORGET. His head wagged back and forth in exasperation. "Your own godson, three years old, and you leave your pouch where he can get into it. God help us when you have kids one day."

The implication hung heavy in the air, unintended as it was.

"Sorry, brother. You're a wonderful godfather to Jack. We're praying for Cheyenne, and as soon as we're back stateside, the whole team is going to get tested. Someone will be a match."

"We better find a match soon, or I'm going to start picking motherfuckers off and donating their marrow myself. That girl isn't going to die before I do, I'll tell you that."

"I don't doubt that," Darby said while adjusting his rifle sling. "We're about to walk into an ISIS training compound to kill or capture the biggest terrorist on the planet. If you somehow survive that, there's a good chance Adam's wife will kill you when we get back stateside." The bench rose like a see-saw when he got up. "And if she does, don't worry; we'll make sure Cheyenne gets that marrow transplant."

Two hours later it's shadowy and cool at the bonfire, the desert having shed its warmth as fast as the sun could pull away. Wispy clouds dart in and out of sight whimsically. My breath mingles with the smoke as I stare into the fire.

Our team sits on one side of the flames, the Team 6 troop on the other. They're shadows, hard features occasionally highlighted by the blaze. I know most of them. Like us, they are fully kitted, dressed in a mix of woodland and desert camo accessorized with dark civilian clothes. I wear desert below the waist: Crye Precision pants with kneepads and Danner 7" Mountain Assault GTX military boots. I don't want my figure to stick out on the night horizon, so I'm wearing a black long-sleeve Under Armour compression shirt beneath my Kevlar. Meticulously placed in the vest's webbing are extra magazines, comms, two tourniquets, rigger's belt, chem lights, Rip Shears, cash for bribes, and grenade pouches. My ballistic helmet, fit for quad-coned night vision goggles, also is black, as is most of the paint covering my face and neck. Like the rest of my teammates, only the whites of my eyes are visible, a ghostly appearance evoking an image of floating golf balls.

Each operator's weapon differs depending on job, personal preference, and sanctioned after-market modifications. For this op, which we assume will include close quarters battle, I'm carrying an H&K MP7A2 outfitted by our armorers with all the bells and whistles, including front grip, Picatinny handguard, retractable stock, Elcan reflex sight, and suppressor. The Team 6 guys seem to be carrying more 416s, aside from the snipers, who have Win Mags and M-79 grenade launchers, or "pirate guns." I decide to wear my armor plates tonight, even with the strenuous hike to our target. I've invested too much in my op at home to get killed before seeing it through. And of course, I have my flag tucked tightly under my body armor, snug against my chest.

"Hey, look, it's the guys from across the street," someone calls over to the Team 6 assaulters. "The Hollywood Frogmen."

"What's that, G.I. Joe?"

"You heard me, pretty boy. Shouldn't you guys be doing interviews or posing for calendars?"

"If your little Cub Scout troop could handle this op, they wouldn't have had to bring in the professionals."

"Chewbacca, how's the jock itch?" I ask one of the Team 6 assaulters cutting an especially large silhouette across the bonfire. We had been on the same task unit during a previous deployment and had spent a ton of time training together over the years.

"Still owe you for that one," he says thoughtfully. I can tell he's smoothing his red beard in the dark, and I smile, thinking back to the simple prank that took place on this very FOB. It was well known Chewie never wore skivvies, and at some point we became fed up with his balls in our face all the time. Before PT one day, I had been able to convince him to try a pair of Calvin Kleins. "Supportive and comfortable," I'd told him. "Just try them once. You don't like them, throw 'em away." I bought a few pairs in his size, opened them, covered them in itching powder, then resealed the package. "Here, it's a gift. Brand new," I told him, innocently handing over the parcel.

When most of the task unit headed out for a run an hour later, I positioned myself right behind him. Most of the guys knew what I'd done, and everyone was watching Chewie with anticipation as we started along the FOB's perimeter. The symptoms started slowly, with just a few rubs and swipes of his crotch. By the time he really starting grabbing at himself, we all had given up trying to hold our laughter. Soon he was yelping—a sad, guttural sound—and had both hands down the front of his shorts, jumping up and down.

"What in the hell is going on!" he'd screamed, quickly yanking shorts and new skivvies to his ankles, clawing at his nether regions. When he turned to us for help, he found everyone hands on thighs, unsuccessfully trying to catch our breath through genuine red-faced laughter. He cursed each of us, saving most of his venom for me, before finally diving into the sand. On his knees, naked from the waist down, Chewie had scrubbed himself with a verve usually reserved for teenage boys.

Two weeks later, our Joint Special Operations Task Force had forward-deployed to Fallujah. The following week had been the disaster that was Operation Atlas. Luckily, we had both been on the same chalk. The one that had made it.

"All right, guys, listen up." A short, balding man in civilian clothes stood before us, the dim moonlight and flames playing tricks across his face. "I'm Sully, and I'll be briefing you tonight." He had an air of importance and didn't seem the least bit intimidated by the two dozen fully kitted assaulters glaring at him. My guess was Intelligence Support Activity, also known as The Activity, or one of the dozens of codenames that changed every couple of years for that group. The secretive organization also fell under JSOC, providing intelligence and operations support to Tier 1 Special Operations Groups. There was some tension between that arm of JSOC and the direct action operators, with some high-profile dustups in the past. We tended to distrust the intelligence they provided, especially after they told us that we had a clear HLZ for Atlas. They, in turn, thought we were arrogant, self-entitled meatheads. Like with most conflicts, there was more than a kernel of truth to both sides.

"I know COL Stevens and CDR Hagen briefed you on Operation Atlas Revenge on the way over, but I wanted to pass along additional intel and answer questions," Sully said. "You know your target, you've seen aerial photos of the compound. Both HUMINT and IMINT put al-Baghdadi in the compound, just outside the town of al-Shaddadi in northeastern Syria. There will be three chalks, all HALOing from Chinooks with desert patrol vehicles. JOE-CAG assaulters will be in Alpha and Bravo chalks, DEVGRU in Charlie. Once on the ground you'll drive the DPVs to the outskirts of al-Shaddadi and dismount. You'll patrol around the edges of the city, bypassing it entirely, until you reach the camp. All three chalks will converge on the compound in an L-shaped maneuver, the two JOE-CAG squads from the south, DEV from the east. Count on close to a hundred tangos in and around the camp, with spotters in the village. If you wake anyone in that village before reaching the camp, expect a firefight, and expect al-Baghdadi's men to be alerted. If that happens, you will not have air support, as we can't risk civilian deaths over the village. I recommend not waking the locals and not engaging before you reach the compound. We would consider that mission failure.

"Once you do reach the compound, expect any MAMs to be viable targets and engage. Al-Baghdadi sleeps outdoors during the summer, surrounded by at least a dozen men. I don't have to tell you, we need to recover his body, and we need any and all intel in the compound. The president has made that clear. Understood?"

Response is unnecessary. He continues the brief.

"Once you have the target secured, a Ranger QRF will secure the HLZ one klick outside the village, where your ride home will be waiting. An IRF made up of a task group from SEAL Team 2 will be loitering on station fifteen minutes away should you need the extra guns. Questions?"

"Will there be air support over the compound?" asks Darby.

Sully bobs his head. "Over the village, no. Over the compound, yes. Two Apaches will be on station. Each squad's JTAC will be in constant contact with the pilots. It will be his call if CAS is needed."

I'm happy to hear that—a big failing of Atlas was the lack of air support. Even though it's not available in the village, death from above could be an important equalizer at the camp.

We know that the briefing is over when Chewie asks the spook if we're going to get any of that good CIA chow. You know, ice cream and doughnuts. He smiles politely, tells us he eats the same shitty MREs out in the sandbox that we do, and wishes us luck.

"Ain't that always the way it is," one of the SEALs says while we jock up. "Let the doorkickers and triggerpullers get our balls blown off by Ali Baba while the intelligence weenies chill in the Green Zone with the Red Cross girls and hot showers."

After a few more prerequisite complaints, both groups are ready to move out. We clasp the arms of the Team 6 guys and wish them luck. I sling my weapon, follow my chalk onto our helo. SOAR pilots welcome us onboard, letting us know our flight time will be just under an hour. The crew chief explains that we'll be flying blacked out and close to the ground to avoid Syrian radar. It wouldn't do for a US chopper to get shot down in a country where we aren't supposed to have boots on the ground. That's why we don't wear traditional uniforms, dog tags, or any markings identifying us as Americans. If we get captured, we're to say we're Canadian soldiers searching for a downed drone. We get a good chuckle out of that, with a few practice *eh*'s and *aboot*'s." Nailer is consulted with verve, as his Alaskan dialect is about as close as it gets to our northern friends'.

Soon, the three stealth CH-47G Chinooks, each loaded with two DPVs and eight assaulters, are skimming just above the desert landscape. Not for the first time, I realize why they call these birds "flying school buses." Stealth or not, they are big, slow targets that insurgents have had success knocking out of the sky with well-placed RPGs. It was the same type of helo shot down during Atlas.

Initially, the other choppers fly close enough that with a good stretch it seems that I could almost touch near-silent rotors. I lean back to look up at the sky. The stars are specked brilliantly across the skyscape, brighter than I've ever seen them. If I focus on one, the brightest one, it doesn't feel like we're moving. I keep staring, a stupid grin across my face, enjoying the enormity of the scene.

"You losing it, or what?" Westhead yells in my ear, pulling me back in the door. My eyes go down, and I squint, not quite sure if that's the ground rushing by below.

"It's down there," I tell him, pointing emphatically toward the desert. "It's all down there."

His frown is one of concern, the shaking head confusion.

"Now is not the time to be having an episode, man."

I smile, squeeze his leg, leaving just enough doubt.

There's a hiss in my earpiece, and a garbled message comes through comms: "Charlie to Alpha. Stop looking at my balls. Over." I drop my NVGs to get a better look at the SEALs' helo. Someone is hanging out the open door, pants lowered. It's Chewbacca, of course, zipping through the desert at 165 knots with his testicles out for the world to see.

I laugh and marvel at the world racing by.

AL-SHADDADI, SYRIA

When Westhead's earpiece squawked with the pilot's "We're in Syrian airspace" call, he clapped his hands twice to get the team's attention. Wide eyes probed the team leader, who passed along the predetermined hand signal letting them know they'd crossed the border. The men responded with excited but grave smiles, subtle movements. Most of them, sitting in jump seats, stretched and stomped feet to get the blood flowing. Their dog handler harnessed Brady to him, tightening the dog's goggles. Those who didn't have their night vision lowered did so, the quad-coned devices offering their wearers an eerie green and black panoramic view.

After another twenty minutes of smooth airtime, the crew chief held up five fingers and the activity in the chopper picked up further. Westhead felt the aircraft quickly gain altitude to 15,000 feet, then heard the hydraulic whine of the rear ramp lowering. Each man lined up behind their assigned DPV, simultaneously watching the jumpmaster and string of red lights lining the interior of the helo. One minute. Finally, as if he were starting the Indy 500, the crew chief, staggering slightly in the open doorway, dropped his arms and jumped onto a side railing. The interior lights blinked green, especially bright against the black night, and Westhead's squad began pushing their DPV out the back of the Chinook. It rolled easily down the ramp, then flew into the night with a weightless reply. The double G-12 parachutes took some time to play out after deploying from the static-lines, but soon opened majestically. Westhead was first in his squad and leaned out the open door, looking down. He watched the dune buggy fall toward earth, its dark chute billowing over the top. After ensuring there were no tangles in the vehicle's parachutes, Westhead checked the strap on his free-fall rig one last time, and leapt into the black, face-first, shouting a personal "Geronimo" as he tumbled. His body shuddered against the force of the wind, a rush flowing through his body that he never tired of. He kept the falling vehicle to his left, careful not to get caught in its air drag. He free fell for a moment, slicing through the night sky while angling himself toward the landing zone twenty-five meters from his DPV. After a glance at the altimeter on his wrist, Westhead pulled the cord, consciously relaxing his taut body as he was jerked upward. The rest of his squad would be right behind, followed by the other DPV and its crew. As always, he took the time to enjoy the wind and gravity pulling his face in all directions, never taking for granted the perks of his job.

I don't turn my head at the flutter of my teammates' chutes brushing the sand around me. They touch down one, after another, and form a security perimeter. I identify my area of responsibility, my field of vision rotating from 12 o'clock to 3 o'clock, rifle down range. I know that on either side of me, the others are doing the same in their sectors. It's deathly silent, like being in a vacuum-sealed chamber. Every sense stimulated, hyper-alert. After twenty minutes or so of no movement, no communication, the call to move is quietly passed down. Half of us begin to bury our chutes and rigs in the sand. The other half continue to pull security until their turn, everyone watching for movement into the never-ending landscape. There are no signs of other life in the isolation of the Syrian wasteland.

Finished, we load into the rugged DPVs without further ceremony. These dune buggies on steroids have beefed up rear-mounted engines encased in a Kevlar shield. Modified frames are nearly indestructible, while shock absorbers and a trailing arm suspension mean they are almost impossible to flip. I hop into the passenger's seat of my assigned cart, a laminated map on my lap, rifle between my knees, gloved hand gripping the steel cage. As soon as the vehicle purrs to life, we shoot into the night, underinflated tires effortlessly skimming over sand and rock. The wind feels wonderful on my face. I raise my night vision and inspect the horizon, more to bask in the immensity of the desert than anything else. *The stars, oh the stars*, I think, staring into the sky in an almost transcendental state. *How far they are, yet how close.*

After an uneventful forty-five-minute ride, the DPVs come to a stop. Again, no one moves as we focus on our fields of fire. Still and silent. We disembark, cover the vehicles with cargo nets, and mark them with ten-digit grid coordinates. If we can't get back to them, we'll call in fast-movers to blow them up. After ensuring we haven't been discovered, my squad starts to stealthily hump the last leg of our trek. Automatically, we space out in a single, anonymous line, trudging forward in the dark, making our outlines as indistinct as possible. I recognize each of my teammates just by their posture, how they hold their weapon. One has a slight hunch, another pigeon-toed. It's like touching my own face.

The town of Al-Shaddadi lies just under four kilometers ahead. The other JOE-CAG squad is patrolling parallel to us, while Team 6 landed three klicks east of al-Baghdadi's compound.

Thor stopped suddenly and raised a fist. Behind him, the rest of the squad halted, raising their weapons and scanning for targets. Westhead came forward and took a knee next to their point man.

"What do you got, bro?" he whispered.

Thor rotated his head slowly, then pointed into the distance. "Lights at 10 o'clock." He consulted the GPS monitor. "Al-Shaddadi. One klick.

Baghdadi's compound should just be on the other side."

Westhead nodded, then keyed his mic. "Alpha team is Checkpoint Boxer." Immediately, he got responses from the other two elements: "Bravo is Labrador," then "Charlie is Hound." Everyone was in place. Slowly, they moved out, approaching the edge of the village. They were ahead of schedule and feeling good when a long shriek overtook them. The ensuing explosion sucked the air from their lungs, scattering men and sand.

"Take cover!" Westhead yelled. He didn't need to; the men had already fanned out and were searching for the source of mortar fire. His headset came alive.

"Alpha, SITREP, over."

Westhead's reply was composed even amid the outburst of increasing detonations all around him. "We're taking indirect mortar fire, as well as RPGs and small-arms. Can you tell where it's coming from, over."

His men had begun to return fire at the clay wall ringing the village. Muzzle flashes dotted its top, and that was where they concentrated their sights. Through night vision, their IR lasers swung back in forth in a lethal dance. Jud got comms up with the Apache circling overhead.

"Stealth 1, I have tangos illuminated to the north of our pos. Can you kindly blow them the fuck up?" he calmly asked the crew chief.

"Negative, Alpha," was the unemotional response. "ROEs will not allow air support over a civilian village." A resigned curse before Jud updated Westhead.

"Guess we'll have to do this ourselves," Westhead replied. A rocket screamed past, causing him to duck and take cover. He screwed his face tight, spitting grit after the ensuing dusting of sand rained over him. To his left, a modest hole smoked dangerously. "Fuck, that was kinda close."

He called Nailer forward with the XM35. The grenade launcher had a preprogrammed high-explosive air-burst capacity, allowing the operator to set the distance he wanted his grenade to detonate at. "Can you pop a round over that patch of wall where we're taking fire from?" he yelled out over the cyclical burst of belt-fed machine gun fire from his 3 o'clock.

"I gotcha," Nailer replied, taking aim through the weapon's laser range finder. When he fired, the 25-millimeter grenade exited with a whoosh and a thump, and the men watched, awestruck, as it exploded in mid-air just above the village wall. After four more grenades and a refocused concentration of fire at that section of the wall, the enemy fire ceased.

"Fuck yeah, Nailer! Get some!" exclaimed Pos, lowering his smoking MK 46 MOD 1 light machine gun. He grinned at his teammates as the village fell silent. The scene before them was now encased in a gray haze, motionless, the outer wall of the village smoking and crumbled. The calm after the storm.

"Anyone hit?" Westhead asked his squad. The negative responses were subdued, a little surprised even.

"So much for the element of surprise," said Jud. "*Di di mau* time."

"Copy that," Westhead told him, waving his men forward. "Alpha on the move," he reported into his mic.

"Affirmative, Alpha. Bravo is breaking off and will rendezvous at Shepard. Be advised, target compound is hot."

Westhead clicked off and turned to his men. "Double-time, gents." Those that needed to reload did so, and they moved out.

The rendezvouses with the other JOE-CAG squad occurs at the edge of al-Baghdadi's training camp. I take in the three main buildings, the high outer wall, scrutinizing them for any surprises. The complex sits alone in the desert, just past the now-smoldering village. It's still; even so, it seems alive, breathing, like it's waiting for something. Us? They may not know where we are, but they know we're here. The need for stealth has passed. Now it's about speed and violence of action.

"You have approximately fifty MAMs inside the target compound," the Air Force stick pilot back in Langley reports. I smile to myself, loving those odds. The drone he's flying from 6,000 miles away circles unseen above the battlefield, equipped with night vision and thermal capabilities. Next to me, Darby appraises the compound with FLIR thermal binos.

"I got sentries on top of each corner of the security wall, plus two guys on the roof of each building," he reports. "They look fortified, but I can't tell what type of weapon. There's a roving detail on two dirt bikes circling the compound, one clockwise, the other counter. I can see Charlie team in position."

I go to the SEALs' frequency for a SITREP. Chewbacca colorfully agrees they're in position and ready to go. The immediate reaction force from Team 2 will be on station in two minutes. *Good*, I think. The more fighters the better. We've been burned too many times by poor intelligence to not have contingency plans for our contingency plan.

The team leaders check in one last time before we move out toward the compound for the main assault. A thin cloud cover has overtaken the sky's natural nightlights. It's dark here—*dark* dark, so much so that with my night vision off, I can't tell when I'm blinking. I'm fascinated by this development and periodically close my eyes for seconds at a time just to see if I can tell the difference. I'm barely aware of the man in front of and behind me, and as we patrol I'm able to imagine I'm on a different planet. The trance is broken by a single crack. Our point man stops, and suddenly the air around us is again alive with gunfire and tracers.

We spring into action without instruction. Alpha squad peels left, Bravo to the right, in two separate and distinct fire teams. Spreading out allows us to increase our fields of fire while limiting the chance of being taken out by an RPG or machine gun.

"Alpha, moving!" someone calls out. Bravo immediately starts to lay down a heavy wall of suppressive fire, allowing Alpha to leapfrog closer to the compound. After two minutes, we switch, and Bravo closes the gap. Soon, the whole team has backs against the compound's splintered outer wall, chests heaving, each one of us taking personal and combat inventory.

"Need someone to take out those sentries!" I order down the line.

"I got this!" Darby's voice ascends over the sounds of battle, surpassing the blasts, the booms, the pings, the rocking thuds. He pops into a crouch, Omen Match 2.0 .300 Win Mag MSR in his right hand,

and sprints to get a better angle at the inner buildings. While he gets into position, we engage targets as they present themselves. Several scarf-wrapped heads peek over the wall, laying the muzzles of their AKs to the side while spraying and praying down at us. Ineffective fire. Focused more on their screams of "*Allahu Akbar*" than aiming. They actually believe their god will guide their bullets for them. Good for us. They may have the high ground, but by spreading out and staying low, we maintain a monopoly on firing lines and angles.

I watch a fighter slowly lift himself. He peeks over the top, no more than twenty yards from me. Five or six rounds splinter in my direction. Dirt sprays upward behind me. He ducks back down. A second later he does it again. Same spot. This time, I watch his face crumple into itself when I send a 31-grain projectile into it at 720 meters per second. I continue to scan, searching for my next target. I find one. Then another.

"Sentries are down!" Darby is back, big grin on his face. Now his shouts struggle to carry over the noises of the gunfight. "They'll have a hard time identifying them for the funeral!"

"Good!" I tell him, turning to the rest of the men, knocking against my helmet. "Breacher up!"

The volley of incoming from the compound has slowed, but still we lay down a steady blanket of suppressive fire while the breacher runs forward. He sets charges in two different places against the wall and makes sure we're clear of the backblast area. Then:

"3 ... 2 ... 1 ... execute, execute, EXECUTE," comes through my headset, a muffled explosion shaking the ground on the third "execute." The vibrations and sudden light and shockwave of the blasts make it feel as if the entire compound has left the earth for a brief moment. As rubble and smoke rain down, the brilliance subsides, and we swiftly stack and flow through the new "doors" in two trains. We know the ISIS fighters inside will be blinded, ears ringing, disoriented, and confused. That's the idea.

Once inside, the compound becomes a frenetic kill zone. To my right, I make out the DEV guys breaching their side, perpendicular to us, knocking down stunned fighters preparing to fire on our squad. Kill teams ebb and flow in and out of the two secondary buildings, clearing them as they go. Everyone in the compound is considered a viable target, and we take out scores of insurgents. Just as I'm really beginning to enjoy myself, I hear a whir behind me. Looking up, I find a Black Hawk hovering on the other side of the wall, SEALs from the IRF fast-roping in. *Cool*, I think, engaging another target.

Westhead felt the wind from the chopper before he saw it, knowing what the sound meant and grateful for it. His fire team set security for the hovering Black Hawk until the ten SEALs from the IRF were on the ground and it had safely taken off. A hawk-nosed lieutenant hustled up to him, calm even after being dropped into the middle of battle. Westhead greeted him by bugling "Ride of the Valkyries" through inflated cheeks, the intones barely carrying over the sounds of the gunfight.

"Wagner! I love *Apocalypse Now!*" the SEAL officer shouted, crouching in front of Westhead. "You guys don't worry about a thing, the cavalry's here!" His grin was wide and bright, and he seemed genuinely thrilled to be where he was.

Westhead couldn't help but laugh. "Does that mean I can take a water break now, sir?"

"Roger that. Your whole team can catch some z's if you'd like." Then, serious: "Where do you need us?"

Westhead wiped sweat and grime from his forehead. "We've cleared the two outer buildings, we just need a main assault group to hit the big house. That's where we think al-Baghdadi is holed up. I could use more guns for the breach. The rest of your men can provide overwatch and keep an eye out for squirters." He jabbed an arm toward the two smaller structures. "Your snipers can set up on the roofs of the cleared buildings." A sudden volley of shots sent the men lower without slowing the conversation.

"You got it," the SEAL officer responded. He turned to his men, already fanned out and in the fight. "Butler, Dobbs, you're with JOE-CAG!"

He gripped Westhead's shoulder in gratitude before taking off toward one of the buildings. Two of his SEALs ran over, hunched at the waist.

Westhead raised his NVGs as they approached, eyes narrowing, then whole face widening with surprise. "HO-oh-ly SHE-it," he drawled. The words came out deep and strong, with emotion. "No one told me I was going to be babysitting out here!" A familiar affection seeped through his words.

The two SEALs took a knee before Westhead. One smallish, curly-haired, with a nervous expression under thick, bushy eyebrows. He continually skimmed the area over Westhead's shoulder, changing his rifle position from high ready to low ready, careful not to muzzle-sweep anyone while fidgeting continuously. His baby-faced partner would have had a hard time buying beer, but even with his youth there was a quiet confidence, just this side of cockiness. That square-cut face you'd expect from a SEAL. His brash smirk expanded, undoubtedly due to the audience.

"Petty Officer Butler, reporting for duty," he told Westhead smartly. It was all he could do to not snap off a sarcastic salute.

"Good to see you, son." Westhead's reply was genuine. "What took you so long?"

"Traffic was a bitch." They shook hands, but another barrage of AK rounds sent them to cover behind what appeared to be a brand new Toyota pickup truck, black ISIS flag hanging limply from its bed. Westhead stood and sent return fire toward the incoming assault while the newly arrived SEALs took firing positions. There was a second, nearly imperceptible, where Butler froze in the face of the fire. He quickly recovered, diving to safety with the other men, a serious, determined mask upon his face as he lined up his first real shots at another human being. The years of training, the countless rounds, push-ups, blood, and pain all amounted to this, to this moment. Protected behind the vehicle, his eyes just a little wider, rifle gripped a little tighter, he took a deep breath. Turned to Westhead. Waited for further instruction. The one called Dobbs adjusted the keffiyeh wrapped tightly around his neck. As they peered into the darkness for the source of fire, Darby and Mutt ran up.

"Welcome, boys," Westhead told them. "Our target is the main house. We'll breach in two fire teams." A hand motion to Darby and Dobbs directed them to peel right. He then tapped Butler, indicating they would go left. Mutt took a prone position under the pickup's bed, sniper rifle trained on the front of the building. When Westhead nodded to the other fire team, they simultaneously left their concealed position to begin a mad dash toward the house. Rounds cracked overhead, encouraging an urgent swiftness. Mutt's suppressed long gun began to spit faster into each window and onto the roof until both fire teams met at the front of the house.

"Ready to do this?" The voice came from behind Westhead, and he turned to find McDonald and Pos on his six, ready to stack. Pos wore his infamous goofball grin in the dark, McDonald with a slider charge in hand. He peeled the backing off the double-sided tape, sticking four small blocks of C4 along the door's hinges.

While they waited: "Psst. Psst. Chief."

Westhead turned, facing Pos, eyebrows arched, not happy.

"What?"

"Knock, knock!"

"You serious, Pos? Fucking now? Really?"

"Knock, knock," he repeated.

"Who's there?"

"Theodore."

Westhead sighed. "Theodore who?"

"Shooter on the roof!" Darby shouted suddenly. He had already spun toward the threat, getting off three quick shots. A shemagh-wearing fighter fell at their feet, the top of his head missing. On the roof, two more men took his place. Westhead and his men returned fire, hugging the side of the house.

"Get that SAW up!" he directed. McDonald moved quickly, hefting the M249 to his shoulder. Despite the increasing gunfire raining down on them, he sprinted into an unprotected area and let loose with a ball-and-tracer burst that ate up a corner of the roof. The enemy fell silent, allowing them to restack, ready to breach. Pos tapped West-head's shoulder:

"The-o door's locked!" he hissed, cracking himself up.

McDonald shook his head at his teammate, a sideways smirk before cooking off the slider charge. "Fire in the hole!" he called out firmly, but the train had already retreated to a clear zone. He ignited, and the house rattled with the small explosion.

Through black smoke, the assault team filed through the open-ing. Quickly and smoothly, they cleared each room of the house. Soon, calls of "clear" and "coming out" echoed across the first floor, then the second. The house was empty; of both people and furniture it seemed, save for the roof.

"Thor, give me a SITREP on that roof," Westhead said into his radio from the top floor. The last thing they wanted was to walk into an ambush.

"Sat shows three heat sigs. They look fortified."

Another voice came through the troop wire. It was the SEAL lieu-tenant. "Chief, we have eyes on that roof. Three tangos. Our snipers are getting into position and will immediately engage. Will advise when they are tango kilo. Over."

"Copy." Westhead turned to his men. "The SEALs are going to sniper check the rooftop tangos. Prepare to move once that's con-firmed."

It didn't take long for the SEAL lieutenant to get back on the radio. "Highboard security achieved. Move at will."

Westhead removed his helmet, wiped sweat. The young SEAL from the IRF, Butler, stood close, wide-eyed and breathing heavy. His eyes didn't stop scanning the room, checking the windows, doorways, rifle still shouldered.

"Easy, Nate."

He looked to the chief, and as if slapped across the face, came out of his trance. He forced a smile, nonchalance. Westhead squeezed his shoulder, and they excited the building.

Once back outside Westhead found Stevens. The big commander was standing stationary under a palm tree, helmet under his arm, squinting into the night. The fog had passed, and the last of the moon was just visible, casting a shadow under the tree. The compound was eerily quiet.

"Blade? You okay?"

The colonel turned gingerly, his gaze stopping before it reached Westhead. His orders came softly, the voice almost too calm. "Collect any intel you can, then move your squad to HLZ Final. We need to scoot before it gets light."

"Sir, what about al-Baghdadi? Have we confirmed he's KIA?"

"Bad intel. He ain't here," Stevens said and turned into the night. "Never was." His head and face, save for the whites of his eyes, were covered with a jet-black balaclava. To Westhead, he looked like an apparition as he coasted away.

"Yes, sir," he said to his back. Butler still stood close.

"Chief, who's the intelligence officer? I grabbed a laptop out of the main house," he said, holding out the computer. "That was all I saw in there. Pretty much empty."

Westhead was impressed. He looked over the young man before finally taking the computer.

"Grab a couple of your guys and take anything you can find from the other two build—" Before he was able to finish the sentence a long burst of AK fire rang out. They dove for cover behind a small stone retaining wall, pieces of rock and cement sprinkling their faces. Westhead blinked back grit and lowered his NVGs, searching for the shooter through fields of green and black.

"Anyone see the source of fire?" he whispered into his radio. Reports of "no joy" came back quickly, followed by another, longer spray of fire. He heard the distinct sounds of Butler's SCAR-H respond.

"Butler, you have eyes?" he asked.

"Negative," came the call from the other side of the wall.

They waited, the night air shiftless, dust and smoke-filled. The smells of battle wafted over them. Death and cordite, raw sewage and garbage. War. Until they knew where that enemy was, they would hold tight and let him make the mistake. Westhead reached to his carrier plate and pulled out a thermal handheld periscope. Raising the lens just over the top stone, he appraised the 180 degrees in front of him. That's where the shots had come from. He switched the polarity from white-hot to black-hot but found nothing of interest in the buildings or on the ground. The only human outlines were unmoving, fading slowly into the background as they lost their heat, or blinked with the IR strobe designating a friendly.

"Moving to your six." The whisper in his earpiece was Darby, low-crawling to their position. Westhead sat up, back against the wall, his head just below the top. On the other end, Butler was in a prone position, scanning the buildings for any sign of the sniper. He watched as Darby approached, his hulking mass sliding slowly and smoothly toward cover. As he got closer, the dirt in front of him suddenly came alive, spitting up in a straight line five feet in front to five feet behind him. Darby's body bucked, then lay flat. He remained still.

"No!" Westhead shouted, leaping to his feet. He immediately left cover and bolted toward his comrade. Butler reacted, jumping to a shooter's stance with his weapon already raised. He let loose on full auto, spraying the area ahead of them while Westhead struggled to get Darby's big body to safety.

He pulled for all he was worth, grunting, "Take it easy big boy, I got you." Westhead's body covered Darby's, hands gripping his vest. Darby's face was covered with shock, like he couldn't believe what was happening. He licked his lips, opening and closing his mouth like a starving fish. There was a tiny gasp as he sucked at air.

Suddenly, movement came from behind a mound of dirt. It appeared an innocent enough knoll even with night vision, just past the palm tree Stevens had been leaning on. The ground shifted, and slowly, an ISIS fighter's head and AK rose over the top, barely visible. His eyes were cold, hate-filled. They were focused on Westhead, his slow-moving, hunched body a perfect, and unaware, target. Methodically, purposefully, he aimed his weapon at Westhead. He and Darby were in the open, still ten meters from the safety of the wall. Butler spun toward the fighter, getting a burst off just as the AK's muzzle flashed. The dirt kicked up in front of the shooter, sending him back behind the concealing mound. His weapon discharged into the air, then fell quiet. Butler loaded a round into his modified M-79 Spudthumper, violently snapping the weapon shut. He thumbed the safety up and sent a high explosive 40 mike-mike directly into the rise. The crater smoked and remained still. Satisfied the threat was neutralized, he turned his attention to Darby, who was stretched out in front of Westhead, his uniform stained red.

FOB MONSOOR

Darby's eyes have gone gray. That's how I know he's not going to make it. The PJs move furiously over him, yelling instructions to each other, cutting the uniform away, inserting an IV, giving blood and freeze-dried plasma, but I can tell it's too late. I double-check that my weapon is on safe, barrel pointed down, away from the rotors. The steel wall of the chopper is hard and cold as I lean against it, wiping sweat from under my helmet. The bird banks dramatically, gaining altitude, and then we're clear of enemy fire, heading into the horizon. I'm still out of breath, can feel my heart beating erratically, hands shaking. Not for the first time, I wonder if I've lost grip on reality, have drifted off into the ether. I take solace in the realization that if I had, I wouldn't be questioning it.

Even under the stimulation of combat, my thoughts begin to drift to the FBI agent and his investigation, waiting upon our return. Atlas Revenge is now over, in what only can be described as a complete disaster, and I have to refocus on my work back home. I have no way of knowing how close Agent Kopen is, if I will be caught before completing the ultimate mission. It occurs to me that his image has become somewhat of an obsession since he appeared at HQ, his imprint seemingly burned into my retinas. When we get back, I realize, something drastic may have to be done.

"Hey, kid, first casualty?" I address a young SEAL from the IRF on the bench seat across from me. He nods slowly, as if embarrassed.

"What's your name?"

He answers, but wary, like he's surprised I care. "Nate. Butler. Petty Officer Butler."

"You feel bad for him?" I have to yell over the even thump of the CASEVAC's rotors. They whir rhythmically, offering a trance-like environment. The helo cuts hard again, sliding us both toward the cockpit. The kid squints through the wind rushing in through the open door. It blows his hair, his camo blouse. The Mylar blanket the PJs are fighting to keep over Darby. He examines Darby, a blank stare freezing shockingly young features. When he realizes I'm still talking to him, he looks up, his face coming back to life. I motion toward Darby's body. He doesn't know how to answer.

"Don't," I continue. "Feel bad for him, I mean. Him, you, me. We're already dead. Problem with you is that you just don't know it. Not yet. You will. Darby accepted his death a long time ago. So should you. It'll make all this a lot easier."

"You've accepted your death?" he finally asks. It's a shout that sounds like a whisper.

I grin, a deranged, toothy one. "We're all just breathing corpses, brother. Just hope you go out while making a difference. That's all that matters."

A nervous smile because he doesn't know what to make of me, then his gaze returns to the body. To the gore pooled on the litter. The tattered uniform, a lifeless hand stretched toward him. Wind blows Darby's black hair across his still face, dulled with dirt and blood. A single black string tied across his wrist. I don't know what significance it holds. I can't help but think he looks like a life-sized doll.

"The name of the game is to take out as many of them as you can before you go. Remember this feeling. Taste it. Hold it tightly. Never let it go. That's what we're here for, to get those bastards for every teammate who has ever been KIA. For every American life taken by the hand of these savages. The next one will be for him, and the one after that, and the one after that. Until it's your turn."

He doesn't know if he should respond.

After a few more minutes of flight time, I catch his eye again. His puzzled expression tells me he's still trying to gauge whether or not I'm crazy. I contemplate his baby face and smooth skin. Almost all the other SpecOps forces in country wear beards —he does not. I suspect that he can't, that it would grow in thin and patchy and make him a target for nicknames like "Mexican Mustache" or simply "Pubes." Either way, he stands out because of it. Hell, he's probably just out of BUD/S and SQT. But I saw him in that firefight, and he's good to go. They can train a man into the ground, but until the first round is fired at him in anger, you never really know what kind of operator he'll be. I know with this kid.

"Roger that. I guarantee I'll get my payback," he finally tells me. His face is resolute, again staring into Darby's body, but now the glare has purpose, collecting the scene to be used later.

I lean forward, put my hand on his knee. Locking my eyes to his once again, I yell over the sounds of the helicopter, "Good. That's real good, sailor."

The chopper starts to circle then descend quickly. Out the open door, FOB Monsoor comes into focus in the ashen morning light. The totality of the outpost is standing on the HLZ, respectfully awaiting our arrival. They already know. I reach under my plates, clutch my lucky flag. The red-white-and-blue cloth may be dull and frayed, but it worked again, the lucky charm delivering me from battle. Again, I reflect on what awaits me stateside: the investigation, Agent Kopen, my mission. I will do whatever it takes to complete it. A wintergreen Copenhagen goes into my mouth. I'm vaguely aware of the temporary peace in my temples.

The chalk with the other half of JOE-CAG touched down just

minutes after the one carrying Darby. Westhead could tell by the lack of activity on the ground that Darby hadn't made it. Seconds later, it was confirmed through his earpiece.

"Bagram, we do have one KIA. Request transport." The comment was too vanilla for Westhead's taste, too stunted. They weren't ordering coffee; this was his brother who had given his life in the unforgiving Syrian desert.

"Get off that open channel!" he hissed at the Air Force controller trying to organize the chaos. "The whole assault team can hear you!" The tech sergeant's eyes went wide with embarrassment before he mumbled an apology and stepped back into the Tactical Operations Center.

Westhead approached the PJs standing over Darby. They looked confused, unsure of their roles now that their charge was no longer alive. He put his hand on the taller one's shoulder.

"Thanks, Staff Sergeant. Nothing more you could do. We'll take him from here."

Adam joined him. Together, they stood a silent watch over Darby. He seemed smaller than he had been. Waxen. It was hard to picture him alive, as a person, like it was hard to imagine winter in August. Adam took a knee at Darby's head, holding a fist over his heart. The St. Michael medallion dangled from his fist. He reached under his Kevlar with his other arm. A gloved hand clutched a worn American flag. His boots crunched in the sand as he leaned forward, lowering his head, resting the flag and medallion on Darby's chest.

"Lord, your son is coming home to you. Grant him a peaceful journey and a seat at your table. Give his family strength in their time of pain and the wisdom to find peace in your name."

When he unclenched his eyes, Thor and Jud were towering overhead. Dusty faces streaked with anger. Furrowed brows, scrunched noses. The transition was taking place, that transition they thrived on. It affected all of them, every time. It was a painful fuel, but it drove them to seek perfection. Without perfection, they died.

"Military intelligence. Still the biggest oxymoron in the language," snapped Thor. "Al-Baghdadi wasn't anywhere near that compound. One big setup, yet again. I'm going to kill that sonofabitch Sully."

Mutt approached the body. The others moved to the side, opening a lane for him. He stood over his best friend, his brother, and he wept. For just a moment, he wept. Then, after a deep breath, he turned to his teammates. "Everyone responsible for this must die. Every. Single. One." With one last look at Darby, he walked away.

Westhead's concentration shifted after the moment of reflection. Suddenly the events around him sped back up. There was a ton to do, and as a team leader, he needed to deliver the after-action report. He scanned the area, finding Butler standing off to the side by himself, maybe a little shell-shocked. There was no time for that. Westhead wondered when exactly the young man had grown into just that. He figured it was like watching the tide go out; it was only when you looked away that you noticed wet sand.

"Nate!" he called out, walking toward the young SEAL. "You took out the insurgent who got Darby, right?"

It took a moment before Butler realized the question was directed at him. He spun toward Westhead, a mentor since childhood. But he found no guiding support, no soothing words in his deathly serious gaze. He quickly snapped out of it.

"Affirm," he said with a clenched jaw. "I killed him twice."

"Good. I'll need you for the after-action report with your Senior Chief and COL Stevens. Meet me in the ready room in ten."

Nate nodded, albeit somewhat hesitantly. "Roger that," he stammered, wiping dirt from his forehead with a shaky arm. His dusty face made wide eyes pop that much more distinctly.

Westhead watched Nate walk away. The young petty officer had the same easy lumbering way about him as his father had. When he turned wearily to hoist his plate carrier from the sand, the profile cut a familiar line against the early-morning sky. Westhead wagged his head, unconsciously touched his left forearm. Under the sleeve was inked an image of a Native American jumping out of the back of a military transport plane, the words "Geronimo" stenciled underneath. It was a tribute to Nate's father, Westhead's mentor, who had been killed in Afghanistan when was Nate was thirteen. "Mo," Westhead's former Senior Chief at Team 2, was someone he thought about often. Just not as often as Nate did.

The initial bedlam after returning to the FOB dissipates quickly, leaving us in an unwelcome place: alone with our thoughts. Different guys always have different reactions to the losses. We begin to exercise them as soon as our gear is squared away.

Some guys yell and curse. There are tears. Thor punches a hole in the door of his hut: ironically, it's not the only place where knuckles have dented that particular structure. A few guys hit the FOB's crude gym, blasting heavy metal and trying to sweat out their pain. Most would be deep in a bottle if available—that will come later for sure. Now, to a man, we know we have to swallow the pain, shove it deep inside, to be opened and examined at a later date. We have a job to do, and sorrow cannot cloud the mission. There are threats directed toward al-Baghdadi and fantasies of what guys will do when we do find him. There is shock that he has accounted for another American death and steadfast resolve to do whatever it takes to bring him to justice.

Me, I just sit off to the side of the small base, baking under the desert sun by myself, morosely unsurprised and unaffected. I've experienced this so many times now, there's only one thing for me to do: plan my revenge on everyone responsible for these deaths. That list just grew.

LITTLE CREEK

The bus moved too slowly through quiet, dark streets. The only signs of life were the buzzing streetlights, each one momentarily illuminating a sullen face as they passed. No one spoke, no one slept. Each man sat silently, obsessing over the failure of Operation Atlas Revenge and the loss of their teammate. What they could have done differently, what they shouldn't have done. A vicious mental game that would be played out for the remainder of their days.

So it seemed forced and strained when Stevens hung up his phone and stood at the front of the bus. He asked for their attention just as they pulled onto base.

"Gentlemen, I know it's been a difficult forty-eight hours, but we do have one stop to make before you're secured."

The men were too drained to groan or complain. Despite their exhaustion and the late-night hour, after what they had been through, any additional discomfort wouldn't even register on their pain threshold.

"A special guest wanted to welcome us home and thank us for conducting Operation Atlas Revenge, despite the result. Leave all firearms and knives on the bus and line up single file to go through security when we stop." He sat back down, not allowing an opportunity for questions.

"What did you say, Blade? No weapons?" Jud stuck his big face, incredulous, into the aisle. "I don't go talk to a man about a dog without a weapon." He twisted in his seat anxiously, wiping his brow.

"Dammit, I just want to hug my kid and eat something that actually grew from the ground," Hell mumbled.

Westhead took in his fellow operators. Hollow eyes and sagging shoulders abounded. Behind him, Nailer slumped in his seat, staring out the window. Greasy hair touched his ears. Across from him, Adam read *The Idiot* in Russian by what little light there was. His right foot tapped incessantly, fingers spinning his silver wedding band round and round. Something about the lines on his forehead, the tint to his eye sockets, made him seem older than before the deployment. McDonald's head bounced repeatedly against the window, a creased black-and-white ultrasound nearly touching his nose. They had not showered or changed since the failed mission in Syria, and it showed on each face. The C-5, refueled in flight, had shuttled them directly back to the States with Darby's body in a flag-draped casket under their feet.

Westhead looked down at his cargo pants, trying not to focus on the dark stains of Darby's blood. Most of the team hadn't even washed the paint off their hands and faces. The group appeared to be in a state of disbelief. When he held his own hand out, he quickly lowered it, fearful someone would notice its unsteadiness. He wasn't positive who this mystery guest was, but the team didn't seem to be in shape to get debriefed by someone important.

"Guys," Westhead started, standing up. "Listen, none of us want to do anything other than crawl into a hot shower and sack out for twelve hours. I get it. But we don't punch a clock here. You want banker's hours and hot meals with the family every night, submit an application to Walmart. *This* is part of the job. We may not like it, but what we do has a direct impact on lots of important people—many of whom are our bosses. So while we may not like it—in fact, we don't have to like a lot of the shit we do—we do have to do it, and we have to do it well. So quit yer bitching, slick back your hair, and put on a happy face. Besides, if this guest is who we think it is, then he has a lot of say as to whether or not we go back in and get payback for Darby. Check?"

The immediate and vigorous concurrence sent him back to his seat, satisfied. From behind, Pos gave Westhead an appreciative squeeze on the shoulder. Other guys offered their own expressions of affirmation.

"I would like to report to the world, and the American people..." Thor crooned in his best presidential imitation. Everyone laughed.

The team was squared away before the bus wheels stopped rolling. They parked adjacent to a well-lit hanger, a cluster of blacked-out SUVs and two presidential limos greeting the exhausted, and now intrigued, men.

I'm not surprised by Westhead's speech or even resistant to its intentions. Quite the opposite: I'm thrilled with it. He's a team leader, responsible for keeping the squad on task. I appreciate him leading from the front, and it's clear his address does the trick. The boys seem buoyed, ready to get this last task completed, despite its unpleasantness. Clearing the way for more important work.

So I give him a light pat on the back and appreciative nod, my way of letting him know I'm good to go. In truth, the sight of the president's limo has sent my heart racing into overdrive, knowing I'm about to be face to face with my mission's final target: the man ultimately responsible for the disaster of Operation Atlas, and now, Atlas Revenge.

I could end it here. My mind flicks through the possibilities. Maybe I can smuggle in my karambit knife or even a pistol. I quickly discard those notions, having no idea what kind of security we'll be subjected to. I could certainly kill him with my bare hands in a matter of seconds, but I can't be sure how close the Secret Service will be.

An idea starts to take shape. Carefully, I reach to the bag at my feet, head still up, grasping blindly for the right pocket. My eyes stay forward, examining my teammates for anyone who notices what I'm doing. When my fingers find their target, I casually, in a manner I hope doesn't draw attention, wind a piece of paracord around my wrist. Two feet or so, just enough to wrap around the president's neck and snap it before the Secret Service can react. I don't imagine he'll have a large detail, not on a military base in the middle of the night. The irony of using my government funded hand-to-hand combat training seems pleasurably ironic. Laughable, even. I know exactly where to position the cord around his neck and the jerking motion that will snap it like a twig. The president will be dead in less than five seconds.

We file off the bus through waiting metal detectors and his Secret Service detail. I feel light as I walk. There is no nervousness, no adrenaline. Just focus, the same as it always is. Mission failure is not an option. This is *my* big mish.

"I can't believe I'm walking out of here unarmed," someone says while we wait to be individually searched by the Secret Service.

"Seriously. If the shit hits the fan, who would the cake-eater rather have protecting him, us or these gym class dropouts? If someone attacks this hanger right now, I'm cold-clocking an agent and taking his sidearm. Let the men handle this." He doesn't try to lower his voice, and in fact purposely makes eye contact with an agent as he says it. The agent, square-chinned and smart-looking in his pressed shirt and shiny belt, is the first to turn away.

We laugh softly, knowing he is right, but also knowing that politics are not our strong suit. If the president wants face time with his Tier 1 SpecOps group, then he gets it.

Our footsteps bounce off the hanger's iron walls, gaining volume until we are all inside, standing shoulder to shoulder at attention. The heavy doors slam shut behind us, an aggressive sound that draws several guys' ire.

"And now youse can't leave," someone quotes, earning a few uneasy chuckles.

We're told to take seats on two rows of folding chairs lined up at the front of the cavernous room. Brady the dog takes up position next to me in the front. Even she seems annoyed by the meeting, and lies on the cold cement with her eyes closed. When I put my hand on her, she raises her head, bored. My sleeve pulls up and I look down, a jolt of electricity singeing me. The olive paracord, wrapped around my wrist, is visible. My eyes widen, and I can't help but turn in my seat, checking to see if anyone noticed, if anyone is watching me. The Secret Service agent who we insulted makes eye contact, even lowering his chin into his collarbone. Is he radioing someone? My mind flushes through alternatives, making secondary mission plans. If I need to disarm the agent and use his weapon to achieve mission success, I will.

After an insulting amount of time, a side door opens, and our commander in chief struts through it, flanked by four Secret Service agents. A second silver-haired man dressed in khakis and a short-sleeved golf shirt follows, but discreetly peels off to the side, considering us like groceries from the back. My excitement grows, and my mission changes again. The second man must go as well.

"He worried we're gonna attack?" someone whispers.

I alternate stares between my two ultimate targets, the men I hold responsible for Atlas, for Darby, for the deaths of so many good men. Only fifteen feet of worn concrete stands between me and the president, with the closest agent six feet away. I know I can cover that ground and have the rope around his neck before anyone flinches. But what about the second man? Can I let him escape punishment?

I sit on one cheek, face hot, scalp tingling. What will history say about me? The rogue warrior, the man trained to protect our country, the first presidential assassin since Lee Harvey Oswald. Not a man favorably looked upon by history, I realize. I see more parallels between myself and John Wilkes Booth: both soldiers taking out their commander in chief because he sided with the enemy. I may not agree with Booth's issues with his president, but I admire his dedication to his principles and ability to take advantage of opportunity. I wonder if I will end up the same, shot and killed. I'd like to survive the op, if only to let the world know why I did it.

"Gentlemen, keep your seats," the president says after we rise with a clatter and finish our salute. "Please, I know you've had a long couple of days. Sit. This won't take long. After I've said a few words, I'll leave you with COL Stevens and CDR Hagen and a nice spread compliments of the American people." At this, he motions behind us, where most are happy to see a folding table being set up with pizzas, fried chicken, Gatorade. But I only see the man who came in with him, the man now standing anonymously in the back of the room. If he stays there, there's no way I'll be able to kill them both before being neutralized.

"When I send our armed forces into harm's way, it is always one of the most difficult decisions I have to make," he begins. Despite it being just after four in the morning, he's dressed in full suit and tie, but overlaid with an Air Force One windbreaker. I wonder if that's his attempt at appearing a man of the people, someone us sled dogs can relate to.

He continues in that slow, smooth, every-man drawl he's perfected: "And when we lose one of those men, I assure you, I take that loss personally. I may not have known Chief Darby, but I've been told what an outstanding operator and man he was. Just the fact that he was a JOE tells me all I need to know. And I want to assure each and every one of you that I, along with your commanding officers, the JSOC and SOCOM leaders including ADM Bradley and Defense Secretary Bowser, will continue to revise your ROEs and the very nature of your missions to minimize our losses on the battlefield while still taking it to the enemy."

My ears burn at that comment, and there is noticeable fidgeting from the men. If he senses the irony of his words or our discomfort, there's no indication of it. I consider leaping forward now, ending this, but patience takes hold. My two top targets are in this room. If the other man gets close to the president, I can take them both out and end this tonight. I wait.

"I take my responsibility to you and your families seriously, and it's with a heavy heart that I address you tonight. When I was running the CIA ... "

It's about this point that I zone out, focusing only on the logistics for my attack. It was only a matter of time before the career politician mentioned his two years as director of the CIA, a presidential appointment by the last administration. A political favor, quid pro quo. He never had any business running the world's most powerful intelligence agency, just like he has no business now as commander in chief. Although each of us would tell you we happily serve the office and not the man, there's no love lost for him in this hanger. He tries to relate with us, to seem like he knows what it's like in the field. He has about as much business on a field of battle as a nun does in a whorehouse.

"This country has gone through a lot this week, and while our citizens may not know who you are or what you do, I assure you they sleep better at night knowing there are men like you protecting them. Now, we are still waiting on the Battle Damage Assessment from Atlas Revenge. I understand that DNA has been secured and is being tested by the FBI as we speak. We're still holding out hope that one of the terrorists your team killed was al-Baghdadi, and will be able to confirm that soon."

Several guys share looks, knowing that al-Baghdadi was never in that compound. The president is either naïve or lying.

"Now, I can assure you that through my strong relationship with Langley, if he did survive, we will work around the clock to make sure it won't be another six years before we find him again." He pauses, waiting I guess, for applause, as if he were delivering a speech on the campaign trail. There is none. "And when we do, it will be your team to get him. You have earned that much. I know that many of you were on the initial Joint Task Force that was previously unsuccessful in that objective during Operation Atlas—you have earned the right to finish the mission.

"Now, I also understand that the FBI had to stop by your headquarters last week, after the attacks in DC, as part of their investigation. I want you to know that no one in my administration is accusing you, or any other military unit, of being a part of that tragedy, and it is my hope you will not take insult from those routine inquiries. The truth is, we cannot leave any stone unturned in our effort to keep the homeland safe—something I don't have to tell you men."

His words continue to flow through and around me as a dull buzz.

The headache is back in full force, and it's all I can do not to scream. Scream at the pain, the insanity, the hypocrisy. It's time. I feel my legs extending, and suddenly I'm standing, moving toward the president, and everything looks like I'm watching it through foggy glass, but through it all, his face, the president's face, stays in focus before me, and the paracord slides from my wrist and the agents are moving toward me, a shrill sound from next to me grabbing my attention, and then everyone is standing, and the president smiles, is whisked away by his security detail, hand raised in a wave, and we're left in the hanger, Brady barking at our commander in chief as he strolls into a presidential limo, and the rest of the guys are already attacking the spread in the back.

I swallow a sickening feeling and watch the convoy's taillights fade into the night, knowing I just missed the best chance I'll get to eliminate my two most important targets. Because unlike most of my teammates, I know who the second gray-haired man was: Dick Basting.

CHESAPEAKE, VA

The white Ford Fusion pulls out of the FBI's Norfolk Field office just after 5:00 pm. Quitting time, apparently. I guess some jobs have a more regular rhythm that includes actual downtime. Must be nice.

I ease out of the 7-Eleven parking lot across the street and into rush hour traffic, careful to keep plenty of distance between myself and my target. Evasive driving and tactical pursuit had been taught at several stops in my career, including at The Dump. While an FBI agent ought to be more alert for tails than your average terrorist, I shouldn't have any trouble following him without being spotted.

Traffic is heavy, which works to my advantage. I keep at least three or four cars in between us, and stay in the opposite lane down Battlefield Boulevard until we turn onto a sleepy residential street.

His neighborhood is older, made up mostly of smallish, two-story townhomes crafted in that decaying early-80s style, fittingly enough on Townhouse Lane. I had discovered that Kopen was recently separated and had just moved from a rather nice single-family home with his wife and three kids near to the beach to this rented 2 bed, 2 bath. From what I know of Agent Kopen, I can't imagine he's thrilled with the new lodgings.

When he turns into the lot across from his building, I continue past, pulling into an adjacent cul-de-sac. I park the truck out of view but in a spot where I can still see his front door. Agent Kopen exits his car, trudging up the front steps to number 3147, head down, briefcase swinging. Without so much as a glance at his surroundings, he pulls out his keys and lets himself in. The front door remains open, with only a glass storm door for security. So much for operational awareness. I feel for the Sig Sauer P226 under my seat, fingers just grazing the handle of my daily carry. Its presence offers a tiny semblance of peace in a head admittedly awash in turbulence. This detour, or mission sprawl, is an unexpected interruption, an unneeded complication to a complex mission. I have yet to decide how I'm going to deal with it, but I know I need more information on my pursuer.

The neighborhood is calm with the serenity of an ending weekday, the time when families sit down to dinner and children arrive home from practice. Shadows descend on faded, self-effacing homes. Porch lights flick on. The smell of kerosene. A pack of teenagers riding bikes, singing a rap song in unison. Lamps brighten, vague figures cross plate-glass windows, televisions on, figures huddling over homework. I can't help but feel a tug somewhere deep in my psyche. The scene reminds me of childhood. Of my childhood? Indistinctive while still unique, secure, the patchwork of American society. On the surface, mine would have appeared to be your average suburban upbringing, I suppose, a neighborhood much like this one. And yeah, we grilled out, even played catch in the backyard with my stepfather and little brother. Two cars and tax returns. If you drove by Redwood Road at a time like this, it would probably have looked the same. It wasn't. Although who knows, maybe it was.

My dad had been a truck driver, crisscrossing the country in his eighteen-wheeler. He rarely was home, which made the times he was that much more exciting. I was just old enough to remember when he died. His truck jackknifed on a desert road somewhere in the Nevada night, flipping several times before coming to rest upside down.

There are only snippets of the funeral in my mind, still photographs of my grandparents, in town from Houston, standoffish, seated with cups of tea in our kitchen. I hadn't cried at the time, had barely spoken about the accident. While Mom had been too catatonic to soothe me, my youth had not prevented me from grasping the hypocrisy of her reaction—when he *was* home, they spent most of their time together drinking and screaming at each other. A few days later he would inevitably take off, the house feeling like a balloon whose air had just been let out, mother and sons exhausted, spent, but the pressure and tension relieved. Usually Mom would make us a big breakfast the mornings after he left. Sometimes, she even smiled, offered a kind word.

Not long after, she had met Stanley. Another truck driver, but unfortunately for me, he was local. His distributor was based right in town, rarely keeping him on the road overnight. The beatings started not long after they began dating, the first one after I got lost on a school trip to DC. I remember my mother watching silently, not daring to interfere, hoping behind sad eyes that the belt would remove my rebellious streak. It hadn't. With a pregnant girlfriend and gut-burning desire to never see my hometown again, it was the recruiter's office for me the day after high school graduation. I've been fighting back ever since.

After a couple hours of surveillance, during which I enjoy a mild cigar, Kopen's storm door swings into the dusk. I watch through the side mirror as he trots down concrete steps. He's still dressed in full suit, tie still knotted tightly at his throat. He moves quickly and agilely, even with what I would guess is a relatively new beer belly. While the wrath of time has initiated its scarring, it is recent progress. Whatever physical prowess has declined, the FBI agent is probably the last to know about it. Kopen seems to share the traits of a recently retired football player still harboring the outlook of the elite athlete he once was. Doing his best to maintain a hardened level of fitness, but probably finding motivation harder to come by without the carrot of combat and the stick of death. FBI physical fitness differed drastically from Army Ranger standards, where he had been before entering the bureau.

Chomping on the stub of my cigar while hiding its ember, I slump lower in my seat, instinctively reaching under it for the pistol. I could do it here, now, and be done with at least this part of the investigation. I would rather not have to kill an American agent, especially a combat veteran, but if it's required for mission success I will not hesitate. I place the gun in my lap, covering it with my shirt, staring into the evening as my target hits the sidewalk.

To my surprise, he doesn't get into the Ford. He walks past it, moving through the lot with purpose. He's walking toward me, head up, shoulders back, a man on a mission. I suppress a jolt of adrenaline, sit up a little straighter. The Sig goes into my left hand, index resting across the trigger guard, low against the driver's side door. I thumb the hammer down. Single action mode. Agent Kopen nears. There's no doubt he's heading straight for my truck. I crack the window, blowing smoke into the dusk.

"You my pizza delivery?" he asks.

I force a smile that's anything but friendly, pistol at the ready. I glance around the lot: Quiet and empty of any other movement. "Large, Brooklyn style with extra penis and a side of cock?"

"Oh, you're hilarious. Want to tell me just what the fuck you're doing following an FBI agent and staking out his house?"

Agent Kopen does not appear to be wearing his sidearm, which is a mistake. My trigger finger pulses, twitches slightly. I lift it, hold it momentarily in the air, ready to lower it onto the trigger, flash my arm upward about three feet and send a round into Agent Kopen's eye, already smelling the warm blood, brain fluid, and gunpowder. A decision has to be made. I'm still not sure what to make of the man. I relax my arm. I decide I need more time to find out what he is all about.

"Found myself in the neighborhood."

After squinty-eyed contemplation, he leans farther into my window. "You like scotch?"

I hunch forward, ensuring my weapon is covered. "I'm not much of a drinker.

"Oh, something tells me that's not true. A big, bad commando like you? I bet you brush your teeth with Tanqueray."

"You might be surprised, Agent Kopen."

"There's always that possibility. But I doubt it. And call me Seth." After a lengthy dick-measuring contest that no one wins: "Follow me. I know a place."

The bar is close to his home, slightly off the beaten path in a rundown strip mall. I had no idea this place existed, but he seems plenty familiar.

The bartender greets him by name, simply, not particularly friendly or caustic but casually familiar. A few other regulars nod to him as we slide into a scarred booth.

"As I'm sure you know, I'm going through a rough divorce," he explains. There is no shame in his words. Then, turning toward the bar, "Gus, two Glenmorangies. Rocks."

I place my elbows on the table, lean forward. "How would I know about your divorce?"

He feigns insult. "Please. If you're interested enough to follow me out of an FBI field office the day after getting back from Syria to sit on my home, I'm quite confident you've pulled public records. And more." He takes a large gulp of scotch, smacks his lips. The ice rattles. "Ah. Hits the spot after a hard day."

The fact that he knows we were in Syria alarms me. It's clear he has highly classified intel available to him, and I need to find out how. Is someone from our command funneling information? No FBI agent has the same clearances we do. I push my drink around in small circles, running a finger through the ring of condensation it leaves behind. It makes me realize that we all leave a trail, evidence of our lives, of our actions. They may not always be visible to the naked eye, and like these wet rings may not last long, but they're there. As long as someone knows where to look for them.

My face lifts. "If you find yourself in a fair fight, you didn't plan your mission properly," I tell him.

He smiles. "David Hackworth."

"I figured you were familiar with the colonel. Polarizing figure."

"Nothing polarizing about eight Purple Hearts and ten Silver Stars."

"As someone who earned their Ranger Tab, it doesn't piss you off he got one?"

"So you did do your homework. I'd say COL Hackworth earned his Tab. But you didn't follow me to wax enthusiastic about military history. I'm the one investigating your unit, not the other way around. Why shouldn't your actions increase my suspicions, not just of your unit, but specifically of you?"

I nod, knowing it's a good point. And judging by the way he's looking at me, I can't say for certain Agent Kopen doesn't already suspect I'm the one responsible. One more check in the column for eliminating him. The snub-nosed .357 Smith & Wesson 340 PD Scandium in my ankle holster seems to heat up. It's a long walk through a dark parking lot to our cars.

"Maybe they should. But that's not my concern. You're already poking your nose in our affairs, and I don't want to see it get bit off."

"That an offer for help? Or a threat?"

I send what I hope is an evil smirk his way. "Not to sound dramatic here, Seth, but I don't threaten people. And while you may be getting some information from the higher-ups, no operator is going to talk to you."

He finishes his drink, throws a twenty on the table, and stands. "Who says I'm getting information from your higher-ups?" His mouth puckers as he thinks before speaking again. "But you should know, I don't scare. So if that's your intent, you're wasting your time. But I do get pissed. And you following me home has achieved that." He reaches forward, his hand closing around my perspiring but thus far untouched glass. "You mind?" I don't answer, so he shrugs, bringing the glass to his mouth. He knocks it off with one tilt. "No sense in wasting good scotch. I'll be in touch."

VIRGINIA BEACH, VA

It was rare that Westhead was woken by his alarm clock. So when it went off two mornings after the team's return stateside, he was upset with himself before his feet had even touched the floor.

The fact that he hadn't slept in a bed or for more than four hours in a row in over a week was no consolation or excuse. His perceived laziness angered him, and as he made a smoothie in his small cottage overlooking the Virginia Beach boardwalk, he vowed an extra three miles and 250 additional push-ups as penance.

"Are we losing a step, Tex?" he asked the chocolate lab sitting patiently at his feet, waiting for affection and food. Tex licked himself in response.

"Nah, of course not, still hard as nails and mean as sin," he answered, giving Tex a light cuff across the head. "Ready for a little PT?" The dog barked once before turning his head and scampering to the porch door.

Seconds later it whipped open, revealing Adam's intense figure entering the small kitchen. He was shirtless, attired in tiny UDT shorts and black combat boots. A desert camo backpack was strapped tightly to his bare back, already filled with sand.

"How much does it weigh?" Westhead spat, his way of a greeting.

"Don't worry about it. More than yours will," he said, backing out the door in an attempt to hide his load. "Ready, Tex? Ready to see your daddy get embarrassed this morning?"

The dog jumped on him, and they tumbled into the morning. Westhead grabbed an empty ruck on their way down the porch steps, and the three of them walked onto the otherwise vacant, freshly groomed beach. An early rising gull stood defiantly in their path, taking off just as Tex goofily shot toward it.

"I hope you filled yours, Whitey. I'm feeling strong this morning," Westhead taunted. Adam stretched peacefully, purposefully not watching his teammate kneel in the sand and fill his pack. He didn't respond, well aware that shit-talking was not his strong suit. Still, he was anecdotally aware of his teammate filling the bag until it could hold no more sand. More penance.

They started a determined pace along the water's edge, heading south toward Rudee Inlet. On their left, the first hints of sun were peeking over the horizon, painting the waves as they loped toward land. Tex ran ahead and behind chasing gulls, the birds and regular rolling white-caps the only other signs of life on the coast.

For the first mile, the two warriors plodded along silently, each brooding on the disaster that was Atlas Revenge. Westhead felt leaden, each step in the soft sand that much more difficult, his thighs burning incrementally with each stride. Sweat soon ran down his chest, causing the ruck's straps to slide and burn. He relished the pain, clenched his shoulders to feel the friction, the ache in his lower back. He pushed harder, gaining a step on Adam. Adam pushed back. Soon they were going all out, heads up, sand spraying in their wake. They could hear each other's jagged breathing, tormented grunts. The inlet was within sight. For both, reaching it second was inexcusable. They each gave all they had, pushing themselves harder than most men alive would.

"I won!" Adam yelled, leaning forward, his shout interrupting West-head's call of "First!"

They faced each other, one with hands on hips, the other's fingers interlocked around his neck. Sweat streamed down both. They did what they could to hide their gasping, but the exhaustion was clear. They were wiped.

"Bullshit, I had you!"

"Don't even, bro. I leaned across and had you by almost a full step."

"You've always been a cheating son of a bitch, you know that!"

"You never beat me on a beach run in BUD/S, and you still can't today, Goon Squad!"

Between pants they continued to trade insults, until Adam stood upright, wiping a final stream of sweat from his face. He adjusted his pack, then took off in the other direction.

"Only one way to decide!" he hollered without so much as a glance back. By the time Westhead realized what had happened and started after him, Adam had a ten-yard head start.

This was a more frantic contest. Arms, legs, sand, and invectives swirled like a tornado. The few elderly early-morning beachgoers stopped to watch the display, unsure of what they were witnessing, but appreciating the contest for pure entertainment value. By the time the men had returned to Westhead's porch, Adam was ahead by a full length.

"Cheating son of a bitch!" wheezed Westhead, spearing him with a dead-sprint tackle. They went to the sand, rucks and all, fists and elbows flying. It wasn't until each was completely spent, unable to move, that the battle finally ceased.

After a moment, it was Westhead who finally panted, "So let's check 'em."

Adam straightened. Delicately, they hoisted themselves and their packs onto the porch.

"Thirty-two point eight," said Adam.

Westhead gritted his teeth, nodded confidently. He waited for Adam to remove his pack from the scale, then stepped forward and flung his down.

"Thirty-eight point one. Boom!" yelled Westhead, shoving Adam into the railing. "Run laps around the football field with the JV track team if you wanna dog a workout!"

A rumble whined loud above them. Their heads aimed skyward. A formation of F-18's roared past, conducting exercises over the Atlantic. Within seconds they were gone.

Adam looked back to Westhead, seething, but only said: "Ready to swim?"

Westhead acquiesced. The victory was short lived.

The hardest part of an operation is after it's over. We analyze every step, every action taken on successful missions. After a failed one like Operation Atlas Revenge where we lose a man, that dissection and second-guessing is ratcheted up tenfold. It's not easy to flick the off switch and dial back the adrenaline just because an op is over—that's why we have beer. But when the beer and pills, the fighting and jumping out of airplanes and chasing women and fast motorcycles, when that doesn't work anymore, we have to find a new outlet. That's why I stopped off at JOE-CAG headquarters after morning PT, taking more RDX-X for the next phase of this op. *My* op. This is my outlet. My mission. FBI investigation be damned.

The experimental version of RDX that we use is a malleable soft explosive that can be segmented like putty. Not only drastically more powerful than more common plastic explosives, it's harder to detect, and blast size easier to calculate. Even with the extra scrutiny on our supply, it's so powerful that I only need to shave tiny pieces off existing four ounce blocks—pieces that will never be missed.

Before I leave the otherwise empty compound, I also grab an extra pack of the new, more flexible and secure flex cuffs the head shed just approved—you never know when flex cuffs will come in handy. As I pull off base, I can't help but check my rearview for signs of the FBI agent.

The team is meeting at Chick's, a bar on the Wolfsnare Creek featuring bright views of the Lesner Bridge, the bay and ocean beyond that. Chick's is well known for cheap beer and Frog Hogs, making it a regular haunt for the guys. At least half the team is single, a friendly mix of divorcees and thirty-year-old Peter Pan types who leave sick call every Monday morning with a prescription for antibiotics in tow. The team needs this, after the failure of Atlas Revenge. To mourn Darby in the best way we know. A little day-drinking to bond off the battlefield, without worrying about your buddy getting blown up.

For me, I plan to use the opportunity to find out who has talked to Agent Kopen. I need to see how close he—or anyone else—is to uncovering my mission.

Both men were still jacked from the failed mission and intense PT session when Westhead picked up Adam at his place after breakfast and showers. They were meeting the team at Chick's, a favorite watering hole.

Westhead's ranting during the ride was especially animated that morning. It was becoming an activity increasing in frequency and duration as the years passed. While he had grown grumpier with age, he had been a model of joviality and source of overactive energy as a younger operator. There were great stories about him from BUD/S, when youthful indiscretions and risky hijinks would regularly land him on the Goon Squad. Never content to be the "gray man," Westhead had been a regular selection for generous amounts of extra PT, usually for opening his mouth.

Adam, while trying to distance himself from the class screw-up, had been convinced Westhead just liked the attention. During Hell Week, Westhead never even made it to the chow hall. Just after Breakout, he had left his swim buddy to take a dump and left his swim fins in the head. For the rest of the week the instructors made him run the mile to and from chow with the rest of the class, 265-pound inflatable boat, small (IBS) bouncing on their heads, but while the class scarfed a hot lunch or midrats in the chow hall, he was outside doing push-ups and flutter kicks. After the class had eaten, he'd get to ingest a wet beans and motherfucker MRE (also known as Five Fingers of Death) while standing in the surf zone, belting out 80's sitcom theme songs at the top of his lungs. The instructors were sure he'd ring the bell, but they didn't yet know Seaman Dan Westhead. He would have died first. In the Teams, your reputation follows you your whole career, and it starts at BUD/S. That Hell Week story solidified Westhead's: He may screw up, but he won't give up. And he will make it right. For the most part, experience and discretion had matured him in his old age. The pranks and shenanigans had been replaced with letters to the editor and political blusterings.

Adam leaned back in his seat, fiddling with his wedding ring, enjoying the discourse. It had been a while since his buddy had been this worked up.

"It's the vocal minority, man, that are ruining this country," Westhead complained. Adam stared out the passenger's window of the Jeep, watching the traffic fly by, just barely flinching when they came *this* close to sideswiping a green Subaru. He did a double take when the old lady driving it shot them an energetic middle finger, but Westhead was too amped to care even if he did notice. Two pedestrians looked up sharply when the Jeep swerved onto the shoulder to blow past an SUV.

"The Internet, man, it's the fucking Internet that is ruining everything."

Adam had heard this speech before, at least versions of it. He smiled slightly, listening with a mix of amusement and agreement.

"Social media. Twatter and Snapface and shit. You see these Pokémon morons walking around now like zombies? The Internet allows the weak to sound strong. Darwinism is dead, man. Social media gives these lunatics, these outliers, an anonymous pulpit that legitimizes their bullshit whining. The land where there is no accountability. Keyboard commandos who can say whatever they want because there's no chance to get a punch in the nose. And they all want to play the victim card. Who refuse to be held accountable, who want to blame their problems on everyone else. And the rest of the lemmings, they don't know any better. Hell, it's easy to say, 'it's this group's fault. If it wasn't for them, I'd be rich and happy and good looking and the cheerleaders would want to bang me,' so they go to battle with anyone excelling in life, 'cause *they're* the ones to blame. And they tell each other that, and they blame everyone else. They tell each other, 'yeah, man, you have a point. I *should* be offended by that. And worse, because *I* am offended, *you* have to stop saying that.' Forget about the First Amendment. Freedom of Speech is dead. It's Freedom of the Loudest, Whiniest Voice now. They're all for inclusion, unless you don't agree with them."

Adam rolled down his window, hocked a loogie.

"And don't get me started on the pansies we're churning out in college. My God, these little weak-kneed turds think the world *owes* them something. That they deserve a 'safe space.' Holy shit, wait until they get into the real world, and need a 'safe space.' It'll be the unemployment line, which means we'll have more able-bodied Americans on the government teat."

Westhead was so riled up Adam wasn't sure he remembered he had a passenger. It was like a vocalized inner monologue. They whipped around a black sedan, somehow managing to avoid trading paint with it.

"You're right about that," Adam offered, mostly as lubricant to keep his buddy going. He wanted to tell him, "Get off my lawn!" but was afraid the joke would risk ending the diatribe.

"I mean, people are so afraid of offending that they're paralyzed, and it actually gives credibility to these PC nuts. It's enough to make you wonder who you're fighting for."

Wind raced through the car when Westhead lowered the window to scream at the sedan's driver, whose own face was sticking out his window, snarls and curses hurled in their direction.

"Can't look at it like that," said Adam. "Yeah, we're fighting for country, of course, but—"

Westhead cut him off. "Yeah, yeah, I know, 'fighting for the man to my left and right,' I know it, I'm not saying that."

"Besides, what else are you going to do? Get a job?"

Westhead's focus moved from the windshield to his passenger, shaking his head and shrugging simultaneously. "I don't know, man. I don't know. That's the problem. But something. Something else, sooner than later. Between you and me, man, it's all taking a toll. Can't do this forever. I'll tell you what, I wish I was either a little smarter or a little dumber." Adam chuckled.

"I mean it. I'm the exact wrong level of intelligence. Smart enough to understand the problem, too dumb to do anything about it."

"So where does that put me?"

The engine roared. Westhead grinned. "You want me to answer that?"

"Please don't," Adam answered. "So did Kopen talk to you yet? You believe this? He actually pulled me over as I left base yesterday. Said he's going to interview everyone in the unit even if he has to do it on the side of the road. Said if we keep dodging him, he's going to get subpoenas."

Slowly, Westhead turned, looking at his best friend intently. Clearly, the news had intrigued him.

"Are you kidding me? Subpoenas? Pulling guys over? What, did he give you a speeding ticket?"

"No infractions, but he grilled me pretty good."

"Incredible. Man, this guy is really in our shit. Yeah, I met him. Honestly, he doesn't seem like a bad guy. I mean, Stevens and Hagen are none too happy he's poking around. And that little stunt isn't going to gain him any friends. But he's just doing his job."

"Just doing his job? Forget that. He's basically accusing us of being terrorists."

"You gotta admit, there are certainly enough indicators pointing to a Tier 1 JSOC group. And everyone we know has a reason not to shed any tears for the Basting Group."

"I don't have to admit anything," Adam said, a little more hostile than was his custom. "Which is basically what I told him, and would expect everyone else to as well. We don't need to be giving that guy any information that could lead to publicity of our unit. Little weasel with his hair gel and cheap suits. Let's see what happens I got blue-and-reds in my rearview again."

Westhead gave him a sideways glance, a little stunned but also amused at the uncharacteristic venom. Despite the rosy exterior, you didn't want to get on Whitey's bad side. He had little bark, but his bite could be deadly.

"You know what else isn't good for our unit? Interfering with a federal investigation. Or worse."

Adam sighed. "Of course. I'm just saying we don't have to welcome him with open arms. We'll all be better off after he moves on."

"You got something to hide?"

"Screw you, Dan." Adam's demeanor had darkened. "You accusing me of something?"

"Whoa, dude. Take it easy. I was kidding. Just surprised you're taking such offense to the FBI conducting a thorough investigation. Our country was attacked."

"And I've served that country with distinction for a long time. I've sacrificed a lot. We all have. I don't appreciate having my credibility called into question. And definitely don't appreciate an unmarked Ford lighting me up in the middle of Shore Drive."

"I don't blame you. I just think the FBI, and Kopen by extension, is doing their job. The fact that it was RDX-X is definitely significant. You don't think there's any chance the attacks actually could be internal?"

Adam seemed to be thinking about it. "No, I don't," he finally said. His normal animated, happy face was anything but. "You do?"

"I don't know. But you're right about Kopen. And you don't gotta worry about him. He ain't getting shit from us."

"Good to hear. Someone needs to be the quiet professionals."

"If anything, we are that. The polar opposite of the rest of this country, all the PC warriors caught in their social justice circle jerk, whining and getting butt hurt by everything. Worried about offending the few at the detriment of the many."

Adam smiled, debating whether or not to wind him up even more. The decision was easy, and he asked him what he thought about the new call for a ban on assault weapons. They arrived with Westhead still fuming about the perceived attack on the Second Amendment.

I watch the scene at Chick's with a detached interest. Shots passed out, loud toasts, each man trying to cope with their feelings of loss, reconciling it with their need to stay hard to do this job at the highest level. My head pounds. My fingers knead tiny circles just above my ears. I watch.

I'm here only because I have to be. Socialize because it's part of the job. Every conversation forced. I feel like an actor. I feel disconnected from my teammates, from everything. Another tragedy that doesn't seem to be affecting me, which no longer even tightens my throat. The truth is, Darby's death barely fazes me. My mind is on my mission, and that's the only thing I can focus on.

The guys drink, toast Darby again, then toast Mo, toast Bull and Spencer and all of them. Drink more. I try to stay involved strictly for appearance's sake. They get louder the more they drink, and it's interesting to see how the other patrons in the bar react. They're not sure what to do, don't know what we are—all they see is a group of loud, muscular men who don't seem to be the least bit concerned with societal decorum. We don't necessarily look military, what with the beards and longer hair, but certainly not run-of-the-mill civilians either. A crazed hockey team deep on a playoff run, maybe. You can tell they want to witness the spectacle, but from afar. I smile to myself; that's what it all boils down to.

"New Guy, beer and a shot!"

McDonald offered Thor a thumbs-up and leaned in to the bartender.

"You guys seem deep in it," Westhead said, looking over his teammates. At least half of them were belly up at the far end of the bar, empties scattered throughout. There was a disarray to the gathering that surprised him, though the melancholy did not.

Jud answered, reaching across the bar: "We do what we can with the time we have."

McDonald's round of shots disappeared in Jud's huge paws like thimbles. He distributed them with a sacredness, like a priest with the Eucharist. Adam, who didn't drink, and Nailer, who had watch later that night, declined. Everyone else held them aloft delicately, patient, while Jud's voice rose in volume and pitch, as he lifted the last one high above his head, the pain and confusion on his rugged face unhide-able:

"To Darby, long-boarding that eternal wave, neck-deep in hula poon!"

A deep "Hooyah Darby!" rang out from the group, shot glasses slamming, beers chugged. The boys were in full-throttle mourning; they didn't have much time to get it out, so they would have to accelerate their grief, display it for one night then push it back down to reflect on later. They still had a job to do.

"Where's everyone else?" Westhead asked. He skimmed the crowded bar to see who was missing. Jud stood up and waddled toward the bathroom on unsteady legs. His mass seemed to expand and swallow the room. Behind him, someone started handing out bottles.

"A few guys went to pick up Darby's parents at the airport and some are at his apartment pinning his Class A's," Nailer said. "Me and GQ got his DD-214—never knew how many medals he rated."

"Gonna need a second casket for all the chest candy. Rack's filled." The expression on GQ's olive face hinted at how impressed he was, not just at the laundry list of awards and medals, but the fact that Darby had never mentioned them. He smoothed a colorful, button-down shirt with both hands. "We gotta stop at the NEX later. Three Purple Hearts. Four bronze stars with Combat V. *Four*."

He shook his head with jealousy while continuing to survey the crowd. It was something they all did instinctively, although with GQ there was a good chance he was scouring it for women just as readily as unfriendlies.

"Friggin' war hero and all."

Westhead lowered his face, stared into his beer. "Who's standing watch?" Darby's body would not be left alone for even a minute before the funeral tomorrow.

"Mountain Man and Red from Team 2 are at the funeral home with him now," Nailer said. "Me and McDonald are relieving them at midnight." Off Westhead's concerned look: "Don't worry, we're staying sober. Ish."

"How's Mutt doing?"

GQ grimaced.

"That bad?"

He nodded, lowered his voice. "He packed Darby's stuff up for the family late last night. I heard it did not go well. Some new holes in the drywall." Darby and Mutt had gone through BUD/S together and had been in the same SEAL platoon their whole careers. They had been recruited to JOE-CAG together, completed The Dump together. Still roommates in a beachside bachelor pad, they had been inseparable for the better part of a decade. As a California surfer bro, Mutt had immediately connected with the Hawaiian over their love for the water and similar laid-back dispositions.

"Any word on when we're gonna get some payback?"

"Ask him." Jud motioned to Stevens, weighing down a barstool alone at the far end of the bar, full beer at his elbow.

"What's that all about?"

"Probably blames himself."

"That's not gonna help anyone."

"Nope. Buy him a shot."

Louder: "Blade! Shot?"

Stevens looked up. He declined. Thor and Jud exchanged glances.

"He's fucked up."

"We all are."

"Yeah, but we don't show it."

"Not yet we don't."

"True that." Thor raised his glass at Stevens and finished it off.

"Moby, play it!" I yell. Moby, the bartender, pauses, pensive, rotating from me to my crazed teammates. He doesn't want to play it. He doesn't have a choice.

Demands of "Play it!" increase, and they aren't going away. The requests' volume grows. Soon, we're in an uproar, beer and chants thickening the air. Moby unfreezes himself, turns to the stereo, resigned. The soft rock that I hadn't noticed playing stops. For a moment, the bar seems quiet—the proverbial calm before the storm, no doubt. With one more glance over his shoulder, Moby takes a deep breath, hits Play.

The first two bell strokes ring out across the suddenly hushed audience. They echo ominously, as if someone had hit an unseen gong. When the guitar intro rips across the crowd, all hell breaks loose, the guys moshing and head banging feverishly to Metallica's "*For Whom the Bell Tolls.*"

It's a frenetic scene, and I immediately find myself caught up in it. I smash into Westhead, whose forehead is jutted out in emotion while he bobs his head up and down with the beat. Most of the guys are singing along, crashing into each other, and it escalates quickly as bar stools are knocked into puddles of beer and Jack Daniels wets my shirt and I can smell the sharp odor of alcohol on me so I take the shirt off, throw it behind the bar to continue whatever it is you would call what we're doing, bare-chested now, the violence and booze soaking into me and numbing whatever pains I may have, singing out loud,

"... *Gone insane from the pain that they surely know,*

"*For Whom the Bell Tolls* ..."

and I'm getting winded, a light-headedness that can only come from the combination of deep, powerful emotions, lack of sleep, and intense activity. The same sweat that beads my face, my chest, tells an identical tale across my brothers' bodies as they slam each into each other, men hitting the deck, sliding, falling, hitting with an anger and rage built from the ashes of so many crumbled sorrows.

"... *Take a look to the sky just before you die,*

"*It's the last time he will* ..."

We're crazed. Many of the bar's patrons have left in near panic. Those who haven't cower on the side far from us, frozen. I grin—mad, excited with the tiny piece of mayhem we have brought to Chick's.

I don't know when it was that Moby had turned off the music, but it no longer matters. Auditory fuel is no longer necessary. The emotions powering us don't have an off switch. Someone had grabbed a bottle of Jamison, and each man takes a long, unflinching pull, hoping that it will dull whatever pain they are feeling. I know it won't: For me, there's only one thing that accomplishes that. My teammates are more like me than they know.

When things finally slow back to their normally scheduled pace and I am again able to view the scene from an impartial perspective, I can't help but laugh, and it's a loud, teeth-showing, lips-curled, head-back, bright-eyed cackle. The carnage is superficial, more intimidating than actually destructive: a couple of broken glasses, overturned bar-stools, some discarded clothing including a pair of jeans spinning from a ceiling fan, wet and sticky floors. Any remaining patrons, enthralled, petrified. The dozen or so of us are soaked in sweat and spilled beer, faces red and chests heaving. We know we're thrown out, but it's not until the magical words are yelled, by who I don't know, that we take off: "The MPs are coming!"

"Born on a mountain! Raised in a cave! Fighting and fucking is the life I crave! Drink my beer from a gasoline can, I'm a mean motherfucker, I'm a Naval Special Warfare man!"

Westhead was part of the group who had spilled onto the board-walk, unsure if the MP announcement was just a threat to get them to leave but not wanting to find out. He was arm in arm with sever-al other SEALs, chanting proudly. The former soldiers and Marines walked ahead, loud with their own cadence:

"C-130 rolling down the strip,
Airborne daddy on a one-way trip.
Mission top secret, destination unknown,
Don't even know if we're comin' home.
Stand up, hook up, shuffle to the door,
Jump right out and count to four.
If my main don't open wide,
I got a reserve by my side.
If that one should fail me too,
Look out ground, I'm a-comin' through.
If I die in the old drop zone,
Box me up and ship me home.
If I die on an Afghan hill,
Box me up or the Taliban will.
If I die in the Iraqi sand,
Honor me with the army band.
Pin my medals upon my chest,
Bury me in the leaning rest."

Westhead had the awareness to take in the oddity of the scene. Two different groups of wild men marching the boardwalk, shouting over each other, completely uncaring as to the scene they were making. It was broad daylight. It would be easy to blame alcohol, or loss, or hell, the traumatic brain injuries each of them had suffered over years of constant war, but he knew better. It wasn't just ego, or their type-A, uber-aggressive personalities that allowed them so much success while at the same time making them particular kinds of assholes. It was the real knowledge that any day, at any moment, their life could very readily be snuffed out, and they didn't have time to worry about who they offended in the meantime. So they lived for each day, happy to wake up every morning and maybe a little surprised to be getting into bed each night.

Westhead smiled through his pain, the realization liberating, then pulled on GQ. GQ had first dropped into Afghanistan in the fall of 2001, his Special Forces ODA already beginning to organize and arm the Northern Alliance while the rest of the country was still figuring out how momentously their world had changed. He had seen it all, done it all, and wore those experiences in his nervous, high-strung demeanor. GQ struggled with the nuances of daily life. Things like paying bills, grocery shopping, or casual conversations were great chores for him. It was as if he could not operate outside of an adrenaline rush. But at that moment, he wore a big goofy smile, seemingly as content and collected as one can be in the face of such absurdity.

"Chief," he breathed into Westhead. "I'm hammered." He grabbed Westhead's arm and pulled him into a well-lit, half-full bar. "Let's get a drink here."

Westhead readily followed his teammate inside, slightly more sure than he had been a minute earlier. GQ ordered two beers, and they leaned against the bar waiting for them, taking in the scene.

The other patrons viewed the newcomers with interest, like they were the point of a story that's in the middle of being told. Their attention piqued Westhead's interest, and it wasn't long before he was privy to the inside joke.

"I can't tell you when I was in Syria or what I was doing there," a younger, muscular guy was saying. He was smooth-skinned and tan, with bright teeth and a million-dollar smile. Quite sure of himself. His comment, directed at a semi-interested blond girl sipping a clear drink next to GQ. She didn't seem to be completely sold yet.

"I thought we only had troops over there to train them," she said wearily.

"That's what they want you to think. When you're in the SEALs, mission secrecy is non-negotiable. Let's just say I saw, and did, some crazy shit over there. Shit our government isn't telling the public about. I can't say any more than that."

If you weren't looking for it, you never would have noticed the perceptible change in Westhead and GQ's dispositions. But to be sure, a flash of darkness ripped across each of their faces, if only for a second. Westhead thanked the reluctant bartender, passed over two bills and a friendly grin (his attempt to assuage, the bartender clearly having an ominous premonition as to what was about to unfold), and handed GQ his beer. Their eyes met, just briefly. Casually, Westhead turned to the kid. GQ placed his bottle on the bar top.

"What did you say your name was?" he asked him.

The kid turned away from the blond, did kind of a double take. Something like fear supplemented, if not fully replaced, the confident demeanor.

"I didn't say."

"Well, why don't you." It wasn't a question.

For some reason, the kid answered, shakily. Words seemed to be harder to come by. "Paul."

"Paul?"

He nodded.

"You don't look like a Paul. A Martin, maybe. Or a Connor. Aren't all you millennials named Connor? Paul what?"

"I can't say. Um, we're not allowed to give out our last names."

"Because you're a SEAL, right?"

The young man swallowed. "Yeah. ISIS and shit, they try to find us online."

"ISIS, yeah, you should definitely be worried about ISIS. Now, for your sake, I really hope you can answer these next questions satisfactorily. I know you won't be able to, and then it's going to be a whole different conversation, but for right now, let's just say I'm rooting for you."

The guy went an even paler shade of beige while attempting again to swallow. His mouth started to open, but no sound come out. The girl backed up. Westhead began his challenge.

"What BUD/S class were you in, who was your indoc proctor, and what is your NEC code?"

Paul's head turned, spinning around the bar, face pleading for help. A large group of similarly fit, good-looking college kids got closer, but even with their superior numbers they didn't appear much more confident than their friend. A frat or rugby team, maybe. Westhead leaned closer, speaking now into the kid's ear at just above a whisper.

"Here's what's going to happen, you Lambda Lambda Lambda douchebag. Two choices. One: you drop your trousers, underwear and all, and pull your shirt over your head. Then, you start sucking your thumb, and shuffle through this bar and onto the boardwalk yelling, 'I am a stolen-valor piece of shit and will never claim to be anything other than such,' until I tell you to stop."

Paul gave a last-minute appeal to his frat buddies for assistance, for some bolt of inspiration. Westhead was surprised, even slightly impressed, when he seemed to find it.

"And what is option number two?"

Westhead chuckled. GQ stiffened.

"I prefer not to talk about option two. Let me show you instead."

Westhead placed his beer on the bar, but before he could turn back to the surging group, something smashed into him from behind. A flash from over his shoulder collided full speed into the kid's face. Paul hit the ground, his buddies lunged forward, and soon breaking glass, thudding fists and yelps of pain monopolized all sound.

Amid the chaos, Westhead realized he was fighting next to several of his teammates, who must have come into the bar and witnessed the interaction. The fight carried outside onto the boardwalk. From the corner of his eye, he saw Adam body-slam one of the youths. Nailer had another by the collar and threw him roughly to the side, discarding a nuisance more than a malicious act. Jud and Thor were soon running toward them, their presence felt as they eagerly leapt into the pile. Instantly, the two were swallowed by the younger men, a swirl of punches and stomps engulfing the boardwalk. They both emerged from the center of that mass, faces electric, scanning for additional targets. Within seconds, the rest of the team was on the group. The college boys began rising slower with every tumble, less willing to re-engage after each interaction. By the time Hagen started pulling his men off, it was over. Ten or so JOE-CAG members stood over double that many stunned opponents. The reality was, it had been more of an intense wrestling match than a violent beat-down, but the military men had undoubtedly left their mark. They were panting, not quite incensed, even slightly more tranquil now with this small release of violence. They began to laugh and pat each other on the back. Jud spit out a tooth proudly.

When Stevens yelled, "Fall back!" they did so, scattering. Now there *were* sirens in the distance, and each man knew an arrest could mean the end of his career. Everyone took off with a not-so-graceful urgency, finding alleys and bars to duck into to avoid eager law enforcement.

I threw the first punch. It was impossible not to. I had heard everything Dan had said to that frat boy and how he had responded. It had been a relief when he concluded, with the youthful invincibility characteristic of that age, and of course aided by intoxication, that his buddies would be enough backup to consider option number two.

When someone yells to beat feet, we do, and in a hurry. It's early evening, and my head feels slightly wobbly, my thoughts coming a little too fast. The ground seems far away, the clouds touchable. I stumble down an alley, my whole body tingling, and vomit behind a dumpster. It's an exhilarating feeling and brings a rush of euphoria that warms my face. Laughter becomes uncontrollable, and finally, *finally,* the headache is somewhat muffled. Like a shark that has smelled blood, I'm frenzied, and know what I have to do.

A figure in the distance draws my attention. It's a silhouette, really, a dark outline against the setting sun. But this outline is carrying itself in a manner unlike the rest of the bustling boardwalk crowd, their lumbering movements carefree, activities supple and jovial. Mouths are wide with laughter and importance. But no, this outline is stiff, rigid, facing the wrong direction. Too much interest in our merry band of brothers, without any of the fear. It's wearing a suit, despite the heat and setting. I lower my sunglasses and duck out of sight, searching for the rest of my teammates.

Westhead grabbed Adam, who had just finished putting one of the students' shoulders back in socket. They took off down a side street and ducked through the first door they saw.

It took Westhead a moment to adjust to the quiet and dark of the nearly empty bar. Country music played softly, just over the occasional clinking of glass and throat-clearing. The four customers sitting alone at the bar had the air of regulars. They didn't acknowledge the interlopers. No visible bartender.

"Looks as good a place as any," Adam said, stepping forward into the smoke. He had a Gerber tool in his hand and was flicking open the various utensils absentmindedly. The hand was slightly swollen, knuckles skinned. He didn't seem to notice.

Westhead pulled up a stool next to him, politely offering the old man nursing a draft beer to his right a "good day."

"If you say so," the old man growled back. Westhead swiveled back to Adam, eyebrows raised, amused.

"Might as well let things cool off out there before heading home," Adam told him. "Tomorrow's gonna be a hell of a day."

Westhead agreed, murmuring, "They never get easier, do they?"

"No, they do not." Then, spotting an older, balding man who, even though he wore no uniform, no apron, had the appearance of the proprietor: "Sir, can we get a Coors and Pellegrino down here?"

The man looked them over through thick glasses and deliberately picked his way behind the bar without uttering a word.

"Guess that's a yes."

"I have Darby's Just in Case Letter," Westhead announced.

Adam turned with a blank expression. "Who's it for? He didn't have kids."

"Same people it's always for. For us, his parents. He had a sister and nephew in Hawaii he was close to. He left his Trident and drone for him."

"Drone?"

"You never saw him fly that thing? He'd attach a Go Pro and film people surfing and crap. That's where the footage came from when him and Mutt greased the Dirty Name. Guess the nephew loved it."

"Haha, I heard about that! When they were Brown Shirts, they snuck on the O-course and covered the logs with Crisco, right?

"Indeed. And filmed the First Phase candidates sliding all over the O-course the next morning. I think Instructor Gutierrez made those two carry Old Misery all the way to Tijuana."

"Definitely worth it. So you already read it?"

"Last night."

"I hope you haven't read mine."

"Nope. Not unless you eat it."

"I don't plan on eating it, brother."

"Darby didn't either."

"Guess Darby was wrong. Don't read mine."

"It's in the safe in my bedroom. I look forward to giving it back to you when we retire. And you can do likewise with mine."

"Roger that. I look forward to burning both."

The round bartender put two bottles down, one brown, one green. He watched them intently. It wasn't with alarm, just a leery attention. Adam tipped his toward him as a friendly gesture before taking a sip. Then, "One more to Darby," raising the bottle again.

"One more to Darby. But I'm not cheers'ing with that water."

Adam smiled knowingly and sipped his Pellegrino. They sat. It was hot in the bar, the air sticky and thick. The adrenaline from the fight had dissipated, the only evidence some scratches and ripped clothing. Adam's attention seemed monopolized by a dusty overhead fan, spinning crookedly round and round. Westhead drank, they sat, they contemplated. Someone played Billy Joel on the jukebox. *"Piano Man."* The bartender turned it up. Then back to country. There was a clatter when someone started a pool game. Westhead ordered another beer. He turned to Adam.

"You think religion helps you with shit like this?"

Adam thought about his answer. He selected each word with the care he would use to map out an exfil route.

"I think it brings a small semblance of order to the chaos of life, and certainly the chaos of our lives."

"What if there is no order? No rhyme or reason, no genie pulling the strings? Life just happens, shit just happens, and we gotta deal with it at face value. Is that too terrifying for people? Too difficult to go through life with the realization that it might all just be random and meaningless? What if life is just a series of arbitrary events happening to organisms made up of carbon and cells and when that life is over those compounds turn to dust and that's it?"

"I don't believe that."

"What evidence is there otherwise?"

"None. That's why it's called faith."

"I don't know how you can do what we do and believe that."

"I don't know how you can do what we do and not believe it."

"Look at Phil. What should he have faith in?"

"You'd be surprised about his faith. Phil used to go to church with me. Bet you didn't know that. He wasn't sure if he believed, but he had an open mind. That's a start."

"And now he has no arms, nose, lips, or eyelids, seventy-five percent of his body covered in burns. If he *did* believe in God, I would imagine he would be pretty pissed at him."

"And I wouldn't blame him. But that's a good start, just having a relationship with Him. You been to visit Phil lately?"

Westhead lowered his head before answering in the negative.

"You should. I'm going next time we have some downtime. He'd like to see you. Asked about you last time I was there."

"I don't know, man. I know it's ... I don't know, I guess it's selfish, but I hate seeing him like that. Not Phil. Anyone but Phil. I know it's ..."

"Heck yes, it is. Selfish as all kind. It's not about you, Dan, about your comfort. The life we chose isn't easy, but you're the last person I would expect to shirk from that duty. Leave no man behind, right?"

"I know it, Whitey, I do. It's just—look, when I was a kid we had this dog. Pepper. I loved that fucking dog, and she loved me. Boy and his dog, all that crap. Well, one day I come home from school, and Pepper doesn't come to the door. I call her, she doesn't come. I finally find her lying under the coffee table, whimpering, barely able to move. Turns out, my parents never told me that she had cancer. Tumors were eating her alive. My mother had been trying to get my dad to put her down, you know, so she wouldn't suffer, but he was too afraid of what it would do to me. So instead I had to find her like that, barely breathing, near death, suffering. I never forgave my dad for that."

Adam's leg shook involuntarily, wobbling his barstool while he listened. He stood, ran his hands through his hair, sat back down. "Who is Pepper in this story, bro? Just what is it you are trying to say?"

"No one is Pepper, I'm not saying that. Hell, I don't know what I'm saying." He peeled the label off his beer bottle, rolling it into a ball. Adam took a deep breath before speaking again.

"I think we take it for granted, man, but life is a beautiful thing. I don't mean just being alive, like, the fact that we breath air and shit. I guess I mean the world. It's beautiful, man, and it's easy to forget that. I think we do it on purpose. If you don't have any bad, how can there be good? So we make bad, in the hope that we can really appreciate the good. But the truth is, even stuck in traffic, that shit is beautiful.

So many people are just looking to be on that permanent beach, their vision of paradise, they're only focused on what can be better, thinking that's the only time, place, they'll truly be happy, and they forget about what's in front of them. And yeah, it may be a desk and computer and freaking email, but it's still beautiful, man. So I can't believe that it's just random, that God isn't watching over us all. Come watch the sun rise on Lake Hamilton and tell me you don't believe in God."

"So, what, your whole point is to be happy with what you have? Live today?"

"Something like that, I guess."

"Sounds like a bunch of happy horseshit to me." Westhead drained his beer and swiveled back to the bar.

"Maybe it is."

"This seat taken?"

They both turned to the voice. An unremarkable brunette stood before them. Immediately, Adam stood. He was doing all he could to stave off divorce and wanted nothing to do with this scene.

"I know where this is going. That four-ten-four Desert Queen is all you, partner. Bus to Arlington leaves at 0600. See you on base." And with that, he placed his bottle on the bar, clasped Westhead on the shoulder, and moved toward the exit. Westhead called him back.

"Whitey?"

He paused in the doorway.

"You want to know what happened to Pepper? It was me. I was the one who had to put her out of her misery. I had to shoot my own damn dog."

Adam nodded like he already knew, entered into the night.

Westhead spun back around on his barstool. "Guess you can have his," he told the woman, motioning to the stool. "He had elsewhere to be."

"Thanks. Base, huh? Oh-six-hundred?" She sat down.

"Excuse me?"

"Military talk. You guys in the Teams?"

He shook his head. "The Teams? Nope. Just a lowly civil servant. I polish medals for war heroes and generals."

"That right? 'Cause I've known a lot of SEALs, and you got that look."

"What look is that?"

"You know. Jacked, but from actual activity, not just pushing weights around a gym. Rugged, like you could build a log cabin with your bare hands. And those eyes. They see something the rest of us don't, that's for sure.

Westhead couldn't help but smile. "That's mighty kind, ma'am, but nope. Told ya, just polish medals. It's important to generals that you're blinded when looking directly at their rack of ribbons."

At some point, he turned to gauge her. She was typical of a certain group of women who roamed these Virginia Beach bars: better looking in their dim settings than out in the light of day. A healthy heaping of makeup didn't have its intended result; namely, to pull off twenty-eight rather than thirty-eight. There had been a time when Westhead would have been all over this opportunity. Not anymore. When she leaned forward, Westhead breathed in Dolce and Gabbana, vodka and cigarette smoke.

"Ma'am, this probably ain't gonna go the way you're expectin' it to," he said softly.

"Texas?"

"'Scuse me?"

"That accent—what part of Texas you from?"

"The part with lots of scrub oak and steers."

"Don't all parts of Texas have steers?"

"Couldn't tell you, ma'am, I've only really spent much time in West Texas."

She scrunched her face, beaming in what he could only assume was an attempt to look cute. He knew what she was going to say next, and he sighed in resignation.

"So is it true?"

"Ma'am, don't ask me that."

"You don't even know what I was gonna say. You SEALs all think you know everything."

"I told you, I'm not a SEAL. But I do know what you were going to say. And I'd rather you didn't."

"And why's that?"

"Because if you, do I'm going to have to answer honestly. And if I answer, later tonight you're going to end up liking me, probably a lot. Followed by *not* liking me even more tomorrow morning. And then in a week, maybe two, I'm going to bump into you at Fran's or Calypso after you've have had a few shots of Fireball and decide that you want to scream that I'm a lousy no-good piece-of-shit squid limp-dicked SEAL who can't screw for a damn, and maybe you'll even tell me that you hope I get my balls shot off by some raghead in Afghanistan. So why don't we skip all that, finish our drinks in peace, and you don't ask me if everything really is bigger in Texas."

When she finally stood, it was in slow motion. Westhead wondered if the contents of her glass were going to end up in his lap.

"Maybe you are a limp-dicked piece-of-shit SEAL who's lousy in bed. Guess I'll never know." And with that, she shuffled off.

"Maybe I am," he said, turning back to his beer. "Probably, in fact." A moment later, he felt a presence close.

"Listen, I told ya, I'm not interested ..." he started.

"Is that any way to talk to a lady?"

Westhead turned to the voice. Agent Kopen stood before him.

"You've got to be shitting me."

"I shit you not, Chief," Agent Kopen told him, getting the bartender's attention. "Two Glenmorangies, please. Rocks."

"The FBI must have a generous view on expense accounts."

"This one's on me." He handed Westhead the drink, clinking it against his own. "Cheers."

"I won't turn down free booze. Cheers."

Kopen lowered himself onto the stool just vacated. "Interesting way you guys mourn, I have to say. I wouldn't have pegged you for such ... such, *theater*."

"Is that how you see it? You don't know the first thing about what we go through, sir. You sit back, in the shadows, watching us for one afternoon after one of our brothers makes the ultimate sacrifice, and *that's* your conclusion? That we're dramatic? Screw."

Kopen gulped scotch, ordered another. "I know more about what you guys go through than you may think, Chief. You really think I've just been watching you for one afternoon?" He leaned close. Westhead could smell the liquor on his breath. "The Basting Institute was the worst act of terrorism on American soil since 9/11. There's forensic evidence pointing toward it being perpetrated by one of the Special Operations groups under JSOC, which your unit serves under. I don't think you guys are taking this seriously enough."

Westhead sipped his drink, thinking. "I'd be hard pressed to find another group of men that take terrorism more seriously than we do."

"I'd also be hard to pressed to find a group of men more capable and with more motive to take out the Basting Group," he countered.

"Unless you have some real evidence of that, Agent Kopen, I would keep it to yourself. This team does not take kindly to unfounded accusations, especially after what we just went through. I would advise you to not poke a rabid dog."

"The last thing I want to do is make your already-difficult job any harder, Chief, but I have my own job to do." Agent Kopen stood and placed his card on the table. "If anything doesn't seem right to you, give me a call. Something tells me you wouldn't stand for a terrorist operating on your team."

Westhead looked at the card with disdain but picked it up. "Thanks for the drink."

NORFOLK, VA

The night air cools me, eases my mind. The truck's windows are down, the wind salty and fresh on my face. I sing along to the Dropkick Murphy's "The Warriors Code" thumping the cabin. Below me, water under the Lesner Bridge is black and invisible. I'm confident of its existence strictly because of past experience.

"*You're the fighter, you've got the fire, The spirit of a warrior, the champion's heart ...*"

I'm electric, still alive from the fight that afternoon, now rabid with anticipation. I pull into a gravel parking lot, the shabby hair salon and convenience store at its edges both dark and empty. The parking spot has been selected carefully, against the far tree line. It's not visible from the building's single security camera, which I know only films the entrance to the store. The lot's single floodlight had been shot out on an early recon visit and I'm not surprised to see it still hasn't been fixed.

After shutting the truck off, I wait in silence, dim lights from the Crescent Islamic Center pulsing on the other side of a hedge of pine trees. Once I'm sure my truck hasn't been detected, I reach into the gym bag on the passenger's seat and take out a burqa, deftly throwing it on over my clothes and exit the vehicle.

I breeze through the tree line and crouch in the shadows on the edge of the mosque. It's partially blocked by tall shrubs, the ornate building purposefully hidden from the road and adjoining strip mall. The robes of the burqa flutter just slightly in a light wind, and not for the first time I appreciate how operationally efficient the outfit is. All black, my face covered, legs and arms unencumbered, I wait, attuning myself to the surroundings.

When accented English comes closer, I bounce on the balls of my feet. Under the robe, I press-check the Sig Sauer P226, now suppressed. Through the slits in the mask, my eyes dilate with anticipation. Each sense is heightened, everything registering amplified and clear.

"Thank you, Imam Shami. The sisters of the American Arab Women's Group are extremely excited for your talk tomorrow. I expect it to be standing room only."

"It will be my honor, Noor. Your organization has been doing great work, and the executive committee was beyond impressed with the coat drive for the homeless you organized last winter. That type of public outreach is invaluable."

Here they stop on the sidewalk, facing each other. Around them, darkness and quiet. When I step from the shadows, my arm is already extended. They turn. No expression of alarm registers on either of their faces.

I don't speak, just shoot once. A pink mist sprays from the woman's head, her hijab flying from her shoulders. It comes to rest in a clump next to the disjointed body, crooked and lifeless. I put another bullet into her chest, turn to the man. Imam Farouk Shami is small, fragile-looking, wearing a meticulously kept beard. Tiny eyes glisten against the dark, staring into me. Not with shock, not anger. More of a captivated interest, like he's watching an enigma. I move forward.

"What are you thinking right now?" I ask, genuinely curious.

He takes his time, squinting into my figure, an attempt to see inside my mind.

"I am thinking, 'Is this man who is dressed like a woman, who for some reason is wearing a niqab, is he going to kill me as he has this innocent sister?'"

"That's it? I thought it was a burqa."

"It's a niqab. And yes, that's it."

"Ah, I didn't realize there was a difference. They say it's important to learn from your enemies."

"I am not your enemy."

"Maybe you are, maybe you aren't. We can come back to that. There should be plenty of time to chat. But for the time being, if you would be so kind, please turn around, walk backward, and get on your knees."

"I get on my knees for no man."

"I can respect that. Let me help you." I step forward. The deliberate kick to the side of his knee folds him to the sidewalk. My hand immediately goes to his face, finger pressing down on a fogger that sprays 3methylfentanyl, a potent opioid, directly into nose and mouth. The struggle is short, and it's not long until his grunting ends, legs stop kicking, and we are alone with the sweet, ethereal smell of the chemical. I move quickly now, using flex cuffs to secure his ankles and wrists, placing a balaclava over his head. He's shockingly light, and I have no trouble hoisting him over my shoulder while retreating through the trees, Sig at the ready.

Once I have the unconscious body secured under a tarp in the back of the pickup, I grab my bag and head back to the mosque. It's deserted, and I do my work quickly. I'm back in the pickup within minutes, having set the timer for nine hours, putting the explosion right in the middle of morning prayers.

That should keep the FBI busy for a little while.

VIRGINIA BEACH

Porch lights led Westhead through his quiet neighborhood, long since asleep for the night. He turned the radio off, leaving him alone with harsh, muddled thoughts. The hand that reached into the glove box for a prescription bottle seemed like someone else's, only growing familiar after tossing two Xanax into his mouth. He was all too aware that the only way to find rest tonight would be with assistance. There were not many hours left before the team would head to Arlington National Cemetery for Darby's funeral.

It would be a large affair, attended by every East Coast–based SEAL not deployed overseas, as well as his JOE-CAG teammates. SEAL funerals generally drew crowds of curious civilians and media, the death of an elite commando qualifying as front-page news. Westhead sighed to himself as he drove home, having attended too many of those services over the years.

When he pulled up to his house, the illuminated kitchen alarmed him. He knew he hadn't left the light on that morning. Instead of pulling into the driveway, he passed his home, parked a block over. Holding a pistol close to his chest, Westhead crept through the yard running along the side of his house. A dog barked in the distance, and he slowed his gait. *Slow is smooth, smooth is fast.* At the kitchen window, he saw a shadow. He peeked inside, gun drawn.

"Son of a bitch."

"I can hear you out there, Chief. I hope that's not how you patrol to an ambush site."

Westhead straightened up and flipped off the figure standing in his kitchen, back to the window.

"We can see that too, can't we, Tex? Can't we?" Nate Butler met his mentor on the back porch, palm resting on the dog's head. The dark silhouette framed the doorway, blocking his view into the house.

"Took a hop back for the funeral," he explained before Westhead could ask. "We're on stand-down now, so the CO asked a few of us who were on Atlas Revenge to come back to fly the Team 2 flag at Darby's service."

Westhead consented, tired, a little drunk. He took in Nate's young features. He seemed just a kid, especially in civilian clothes. He had to remember that Nate should be in college, another hungover slacker on a meal plan partying through fall semester. Instead, he had decided to put his safety, comfort, and life on the line. And for what? Westhead didn't bother answering the question. They all had their reasons. He was happy to see the young SEAL. Surprisingly, he was happy to have someone to talk to. He placed the Glock on an end table before slumping into a recliner. He glanced around his old but perfectly adequate home. It was dated and on the small end, and at any given time usually had a Team buddy in between duty stations on the worn couch, but it was his, and you couldn't beat the location.

He couldn't help but notice that something about the room looked different.

Off his confused look: "I picked up a little bit," explained Nate.

"You cleaned?"

"If I'm going to be staying here, I'd rather not live in filth. No offense."

"None taken. I'm not here long enough to clean. That means you're staying here while stateside?"

"If you don't mind."

"Glad to have you. How you doing with everything?"

Nate handed him a beer without taking one for himself.

"Doesn't matter, does it? Still have a job to do. Darby's death doesn't affect that."

"No, it doesn't. But you learn a lot about yourself after your first combat. Headshrinker get to you?"

He shrugged. "They made me sit with one in Kuwait. Told 'em I wasn't going to eat my rifle or massacre haji families, so they gave me a clean bill."

"Ask you about dreams?"

"Yeah, I guess. Asked all kinds of shit—I kept my answers to one syllable grunts, nods, and headshakes. Wasn't going to say anything that would let them take my Trident."

Westhead drained his beer.

"Good. You need to talk, you got brothers, Team guys for that. You got me."

Nate paced through the living room, rubbed Tex's head. He didn't sit.

"I know, I know. I'm—I'm, I don't know ... Between you and me? I'm a little fucked-up man, I really am. For a minute, I froze. I froze in battle. That was the longest second of my life. Our biggest fear, and it happened to me."

"Yeah, you were cherry, no doubt about that. But you unfroze, and that's what's important. I saw you in that firefight, Nate. You're good to go. You saved my life. You have nothing to be ashamed of."

He looked up, seemed grateful for the words. "I keep seeing that muj's head explode. I did that. And Darby, Darby in the chopper, bleeding out right in front of me. There wasn't fuck-all I could do. That's a lonely feeling."

"Believe me, brother, don't I know it. But that's to be expected. I wish I could tell you those images will go away. The sounds, the smells. But they don't, or least haven't for me. Yeah, maybe for a little while they do, for a spell. And when they do, for those rare moments"— he smiled here, like drawing on a fond memory, a sexual encounter, a beachside beer, maybe—"it's a nice reprieve, a momentary bliss when I forget about the shit I've done, what I didn't do. Couldn't do. What I've seen. But when it comes flooding back, it's almost worse, because at least when you're always thinking about it, you forget that there was a time when you didn't. For me? I know that for me and some of the other guys, it's only when we're back in battle, only when that adrenaline is going, that we're really at peace. That's why I keep re-enlisting, keep going out even if maybe I've lost a step. And that's a sad, scary sentiment. Because, like an athlete, you're always the last to know when your time has passed."

Nate finally stopped in place, sat on the couch opposite Westhead. His head was in his hands, listening, trying to get his mind in order. Westhead leaned back, eyelids beginning to droop. The words came slower.

"I don't know, maybe one day we will be able to put it all to rest.

Reconcile it all in our heads. Maybe after this war is over, or the next one, or at least when they're over for us, maybe we can forgive ourselves for what we did, for what we didn't do."

Nate looked over. "You still beat yourself up over my dad?"

Westhead's eyes jolted wide. They stared at each other, into each other. "You know I do. Every fucking day. Him, Bull, Spencer. Now Darby. Many more. I lost thirty brothers in Operation Atlas. They all haunt me, every one. And the only way I know to sooth that pain, to kill that beast, is to get the bastards back who did it. That's why I keep doing this, and will until the day they put me in the ground."

Nate's face got even harder, more determined, his jawline extended. "There was a guy from your team on the chalk I exfil'd with."

Westhead leaned back, suddenly calm again. "Yeah, who?"

"Didn't get his name. Strange guy. But he told me something, something I guess I already knew, deep down, but hadn't yet fully realized. He told me not to forget the image of Darby, of my brother bleeding and dying. He told me to *taste* it, to use it as fuel every time I go into battle." His eyes hadn't left the far wall as he spoke, a blank stare across his face. The words were careful and monotone. "And believe me, that's what I'm gonna do. I can't wait to get back out there."

The response was a cross between chuckle and snort. Westhead's words were sluggish with fatigue. "Damn right, son. Yeah, you're good to go. Pipe-hitting meat eater." He reached for a blanket, pulled it over himself. His breaths came slow and heavy.

NEWPORT NEWS, VA

By the time I cut the imam's flex cuffs off, he's nearly awake, moaning slightly. I'm sitting in front of him on a milk crate, grinning, appreciating the terror that flashes across his dark eyes as he takes in the surroundings. I wave the ammonia inhalant under his nose again, jolting him into sudden alertness.

"We're in the basement of an abandoned house," I inform him, standing up. His gaze follows me, intent, trying to wrap his mind around what is happening.

"You're probably noticing that you are not muzzled. In fact, you are welcome to be as loud as you want. Scream, please. As you can see, no one will hear you." At this, I open my palms and spread them before me, showing him the soundproof foam coating the walls. When I suddenly release a blood-curdling shriek in his face as proof of the fortification, he pulls his knees into his belly, shuddering. The pose makes me happy.

"And I mean that. Please—scream as much as you would like. There's going to be a lot of pain."

I make a show of putting on latex gloves while circling him. He tries to crawl away, not yet realizing that his ankle is chained to exposed pipe. The scraping of metal on metal adds to the environment. Like always, I talk the whole time.

"The ties that bind us, huh, Imam?" WHACK. I club him across the face with an ASP baton, just to get the blood flowing. "Don't worry, you'll be with your seventy-two virgins soon." WHACK. "Well, not too soon. I have a few free hours, and plan to enjoy them. Let's start with your fingernails. I know that is a favorite of your people."

I stomp on his left wrist, probably breaking it, reach forward with pliers.

"No!" he screams, amazingly loud and lucid. "No, stop! Please, I beg of you! I've never hurt anyone!"

I try to rip the nail off his index finger, but he squirms, and only half comes off in the pliers' teeth. Oh well, I think. Just as painful.

"Those killed in the Twin Towers had never hurt anyone either. Those in San Bernardino, Orlando, Boston. Nice, Paris, Berlin. Manchester. London. All of them, truly innocent. It's a war with Islam, isn't it? It's your religion's leaders who say so." I kick him in the face with the toe of my boot, leaving his nose twisted and pouring blood. He cries out again, more muffled than before.

"That is not my religion!" he pleads. "My religion is one of peace! OF MERCY!"

Putting my boot once more on his wrist, I squat before him, the pliers working to grip a thumbnail.

"I don't know, Imam. It's going to take some convincing for me to believe that. I've spent a lot of time in the Middle East. I haven't seen a ton of mercy from your people."

This time, the entire nail comes off and the blood oozes upward swiftly, covering his hand. The screams are unintelligible now, naturally.

The next three nails splinter and rip out in pieces, which I imagine is more painful, so I'm okay with it. During this time, we have a mostly one-sided conversation about religion and its place in politics. I think I'm winning the argument, but one can never tell for sure.

"How's that feel? I hope that wasn't your violin hand." He's curled in the fetal position now that I've taken my foot off his wrist. I'm sweating, spit is flying, and I feel alive. Any headache, pain from my sprained ankle, long gone. I pause, relish the rare freedom from discomfort.

His groan is barely audible, chin covering the injured hand. "Please, enough. You've made your point. It's not too late to stop this now. I am not your enemy—my mosque is one of benevolence, you must believe me." It's a whimper, really.

"Must I? Benevolence toward those fighting against us, I believe that. Isn't that what you and Dick Basting believe? That bitch from the ACLU? What your committee convinced the president of? Forgive me for saying so, but maybe your benevolence is misdirected, Imam."

"The Basting Institute study? Is that what this is about?" He's crying now, moaning really, which only electrifies me further.

"Could have something to do with it." WHACK. "Did you ever think that asking the president to change our rules of engagement would put American lives at risk?" WHACK. "That war is not pretty, and the men risking their lives, spending months away from their families, that they deserve more than politically correct kowtowing to the heathens who are responsible for putting them in harm's way?" WHACK.

He's just this side of conscious, but it finally hits him and he murmurs "Operation Atlas," like he finally understands why we're here.

"One of the many operations where my brothers were killed because our own government tied one hand behind our back. You know, if it were up to me, I'd just nuke the whole damn region and be done with your backwards religion and antiquated view of the world." WHACK. "But since it's not up me, here we are. You do what you do, and I ..." Here I trail off, letting the insinuation hang in the air.

Since this began, through the pain, I can tell he had held to an irrational hope that at the end I would simply let him go. That he would survive this, whatever *this* is. I had read it in his eyes, even while beating him, through the blood and shock. But with the mention of Basting and Atlas, it's obvious he now knows that he has no chance of coming out the other end.

He looks away, resigned, but I see a defiance in his posture, the angle of his head, and I almost respect it, but want him to turn back to me, because he doesn't yet notice the drill in my hand so I point it airward and squeeze the trigger and it lets out a shrill, terrifying skirl, which immediately makes his bowels open, the pungent smell everywhere, covering the room in a vile, antisocial stink that I have smelled before.

"You recognize that sound, don't you? Another favorite of the jihadists." I spit the last word, and the volume of my voice continues to rise so it can be heard over the whine of the drill. "Now you're going to know that same fear, the same pain!"

I pounce on him, sinking the drill into his chained leg. Immediately, a geyser of bright, clean, almost fluorescent red shoots into the air, catching me directly in the face. I wrench to the side, sputtering, feeling the warm liquid in my mouth, eyes, my ears. It collides with the other smells of the room, until the fear, the blood, the feces, the sweat comingle into a hopeless bitter jumble. I am frantic now, raising the drill up above my head then back down, the imam dodging some of the blows, others digging deep into flesh and causing fresh rivulets of blood until we're both covered in it, sliding along the slick floor as the owner of the yelps, shouts, and prayers loses all semblance of reality in the explosion of senses, and I feel disconnected from all this and wonder what time it is and if I'll be able to get any sleep on the bus ride to Arlington in the morning.

When the drill bit finally breaks, I lean over the whimpering, bloody, shit-stained man and hiss at him that all this is his fault and he only gasps slightly, eyeballs bulging, when I slit his throat with my custom Half Face Blade.

I realize that I forgot to tell him that I was going to blow up his mosque in the morning, and that pisses me off enough to kick the corpse on my way out, just before I light a cigarette mostly to stare at its ember, glowing alone in the dark. When it burns to my fingers, I finally drop it, and put in a wintergreen dip. Let this be a message to Agent Kopen.

VIRGINIA BEACH

It was still black outside, but the sensation of morning's imminent arrival enveloped the home. Westhead wasn't quite awake, yet not fully asleep. Lost in an all-too-familiar purgatory of helpless terror, it was a blood-curling shriek that shocked him into consciousness. When his eyes were able to focus, he found himself squatting in the corner of his living room, naked, covered in sweat, pistol in hand. The scream had been his own.

"Dan, what's wrong?" an urgent voice called out from the dark.

Westhead stood, wiped his face, chest heaving. He noticed the gun in his hand and set it down.

"Nothing, go back to bed. I'm fine." His voice cracked. He had to repeat the second part.

Nate stepped from the shadows, sleepy and concerned. "You sure, man?"

He didn't respond, just lowered himself to the sofa. The dreams were coming back to him, at least pieces of them. He knew he needed to embrace them, to acknowledge them before he could let them go. At least that's what the therapist had told him after Atlas. But he couldn't put them fully out of mind until he could remember them.

The words came faintly, a gentle breeze on the back of his neck. "There was smoke ... and flames. Fire. Flames shooting straight up, through the helo floors. Bull, Spencer, Mikey ... Hatchet, Guzz ..." He paused here, closed his eyes, in something more like a trance than thought. "And God, their screams. I know I was hearing their screams as they ... I'm just glad dreams don't include smells."

He thought about it. "Or maybe they do, I don't know."

ARLINGTON, VA

"Shit. Dan. Psst. Dan."

Westhead twisted in line, trying to get a glance at Nate over his shoulder. The young SEAL's eyes had gone wide and nervous. His face, pale. He hissed again.

"Dude, what am I going to do?"

They were standing rigidly with the other SEALs in attendance. Two solemn, stately columns of military excellence, one on either side of Darby's casket. The collection passed slowly, each SEAL removing the Trident from their left breast, placing it against shimmering wood, and sending it home with a sudden, violent slam of the fist. Westhead and Nate's turn was advancing.

"What is it?"

"I can't do it."

"What do you mean you can't do it?"

"I mean, I can't do it. I'm wearing my dad's Trident."

The significance hit Westhead. The Trident his father had worn, had left him after he was killed.

"Oh, shit. Just fake it then."

"I can't. Someone will notice."

The line shuffled closer. They were almost to the head of the casket. Westhead's fingers went to his collar, nimbly removing the backings to his pin. Nate's did the same, albeit clumsily.

"No one's going to notice. Take it off, slip it in your pocket, and just punch the casket like everyone else. No one will notice."

Nate wiped his neck under the hot sun. Westhead snuck a glance at him, could see his face growing red. He smiled, amused at the boy's uncomfortableness.

"I mean, it is a sign of complete disrespect to Darby," he whispered. "But I'm sure he'll get over it."

"Fuck you, man," Nate hissed. He slammed his fist on the casket and the train kept moving.

It's right around the time that "Taps" begins to play that my watch lets out a series of tiny beeps. I look down. 10:38. I mouth the word *boom*, or maybe I actually say it out loud, I'm not sure, the bugles carry their mournful sound over everything, and who can think or hear above them?

I wonder if it really is as hard for the guys as they make it seem. Or are they simply spilling crocodile tears, putting on a show because they have to? For me, I know it's the latter. I guess you can call it a numbness, something resembling apathy, which I grew accustomed to some time ago. If anything, I am jealous of Darby, of not having to deal with this shit anymore, of being buried a hero. The closed roads and honor guard, streets lined with curious citizens. Facebook posts and news articles, the fashionable support for our country's heroes. All the nice things people said at his funeral, all the time they took off from work to watch him being lowered into the ground. Bagpipes and toasts, remembrance plaques and medals. When my time comes, it won't be with those kind sentiments, I know that. Not for many years after will I be appreciated for what I have to do.

It's a beautiful day at Arlington, an Indian summer. Not that I care.

I'm bored: Bored with the strong words from our leaders describing Darby's heroism, his strong character. Bored with the tears his parents cry as ADM Bradley takes a folded flag and kneels before them in their dark dress and suit, sunglasses hiding puffy eyes, faces set in a pathetic attempt to appear strong, jolting just slightly three times as the honor guard, seven shoes in baggy uniforms who look as if they have never fired a rifle in anger, complete their salute just before the SEALs in attendance, of whom there are many, walk by the casket slamming Tridents into it until it is covered in gold, and I think what a pretty picture it all makes: **Come die for your country and enjoy the pageantry.**

After the ceremony, we're gathered around our bus, parked at the edge of Section 60, our duty fulfilled, at least for this day. My distemper is broken by an exclamation from within the group.

"Holy shit! Someone blew up a mosque in Virginia Beach this morning!"

I turn, suddenly interested.

"Sounds like a lot of people dead." He's reading from his iPhone, scrolling for information. "During morning prayers, they're saying. The imam is missing."

"How"—my voice gives out, and I start over—"How many dead?" I hope I sound concerned rather than excited.

"They're not sure yet. But they're already saying it might be the same people who attacked DC last week. 'Domestic terrorism,' they're calling it."

Another round of murmurs ripples through the assembly. Everyone is concerned, even if they're not sure why. For us, any piece of terrorism perpetrated against Americans usually means a quick trip to some faraway hellhole, but since this one is on home soil, no one is sure if we'll get the call. That thought intrigues me more than most.

"Wonder what this means for us? We gonna be pulling overwatch on mosques now? Security detail for imams?" The questions come rapid-fire; of course, no one has any answers.

"Probably can expect more FBI scrutiny," Hagen says with regret.

"Crazy, huh?" Westhead says to me. "The States are starting to feel like Kabul."

I lower my head in the affirmative, happy this phase in my op is complete, obsessed with finding out my kill total. The chatter slows as we all begin to reflect on the news, consider how it will affect our mission. If it will again tie back to us, to a JSOC group. I'm the only one who knows the answer to that. We stand around the bus, in the heat, not sure what to do next.

"How you doing anyway, man? You've been quiet since we got back. Ready to get some payback for Darby? We can't let these attacks distract us from al-Baghdadi."

Aloof, I turn to face Westhead. He's ramrod straight, tall and clean in his dress whites. Gleaming markers of our nation's heroes dot the background, slow-walking, darkly dressed mourners intermixed. I can't tell whether it's interest or concern or suspicion painted across his face. Analytical eyes probe me, searching for something. I tell him yes, slowly, softly, then say it again, firmer now, agreeing, hoping he will take the half-hearted response as shock rather than exhilaration, or worse, callousness. I focus on my breathing. There is no mistaking suspicion in his mien.

"Good. Stay frosty. If you believe the president, we'll be going back in after alBaghdadi."

I nod, feeling the sun on my face. "If I believe him."

The bus door opened with a hiss, the weary men of JOE-CAG crowded around it, anxious to get home. But before the first man could board, a shout rang from their ranks. Hell, pushing through his teammates, pointing angrily at something on the other side of the bus.

"Get the fuck back!" he yelled. "Don't you dare snap another picture!" He started running toward the edge of the cemetery, down a slight incline, where a narrow road ran along the edges of trim, sacred grass. A cluster of American-made sedans and SUVs were lined inconspicuously, though not inconspicuously enough.

"Show some respect! There are people mourning here!" Hell bellowed at them. The group of men sitting in the cars, leaning on them, dark suits and aviator sunglasses not as out of place here as elsewhere, paused, taken aback by Hell's aggressive movements but loath to acquiesce. Cameras and notepads eventually lowered. Behind Hell, the rest of his team saw what he had. Incensed, they followed him toward the federal agents. It was Kopen who stepped from their midst, their apparent representative for this confrontation.

"Gunny, take it easy, sir."

"Don't tell me to take it easy! You and your men need to pack your shit and get out of here. These are hallowed grounds, and I won't have you injuring the memory of this man. Leave. Now."

Kopen stepped closer, arms raised in deference. Hell's already ruddy face was a new shade of scarlet, spittle dotting the corners of his mouth. When Thor reached him, only coming mid-chest, he placed an arm across him for fear he would strike the FBI agent.

"Get. The fuck. Out of here." Hell was hissing now, struggling against Thor. Hagen was the next JOE down the incline, and he sharply admonished both parties upon arrival.

"Get him on the bus!" he instructed Thor before wheeling toward the FBI contingent. "And you, Agent Kopen, shame on you and your men. Have you any decency? After what these men have just gone through, you pull this? I would respectfully ask you and your men to vacate this area immediately, for the good of all of us." Over his shoulder, Darby's parents were visible, confused and unsure if they should be horrified or intrigued by the display.

"Commander," Kopen said, his tone conciliatory, "We meant no disrespect. The entire bureau is sorry for your loss, and for any additional strain we put on you here today. But we are—" He paused here. Instead of finishing the thought, his hand went into his pocket. He apologized to Hagen for the interruption and turned his back, cell phone to ear. A muffled "Yes, sir," was all they could hear of the call. When he lowered the phone, Kopen addressed his fellow agents with urgency. "Men, clear the area. That was the director. I'm being recalled to headquarters." He turned to a younger, nervous-looking agent. "Neil, drive me into DC. The rest of you, back to Norfolk. You have a new crime scene to investigate. Commander, again, my apologies for the interference." And with that, he rushed to the first SUV in the line, a black tinted Tahoe, and hopped into the passenger's seat. Slowly at first, then quickly, his men followed and the gathering dispersed, this time with emergency lights flashing. Several of the feds offered pointed glares at the posturing JOEs as their caravan departed. Hell spat heatedly onto the pavement, involuntarily flexing in the direction of retreating taillights. The rest of the team shuffled feet, traded confused glimpses on their way back to the bus.

"Do you mean to tell me that we knew about the mosque bombing before the FBI?" Pos asked, incredulous, as they boarded. "How is that possible?"

The disbelieving look was shared by his teammates as they took seats. Most were checking phones for more information as the bus departed.

LITTLE CREEK

JOE-CAG's bus eked out the last leg of its trip from Arlington to Little Creek with most of its passengers in various stages of hungover and sorrow, eyes heavy, undershirts soaked. The initial excitement around the mosque bombing and FBI surveillance had subsided, and the past week was catching up with them. A few SEALs from Team 2 had bummed a ride, including Nate, who dozed peacefully across from Westhead and Adam.

He stuck out amongst the gnarled men ten, twenty, hell, some thirty years his senior. Many had been operating since before he was born. Nate seemed especially fresh, even out of place, in the bright-white Cracker Jacks of a lower enlisted man. The differentiator being, of course, the flash of his still-new Trident upon that uniform. He wore a fresh regulation haircut and shave, and with chiseled shoulders and angled features, was the very image of a SEAL. Just a young SEAL.

At times, Westhead still saw the thirteen-year old Nate, the determined young man at his father's funeral some seven years prior. A young man whose destiny had been set before he even knew it. That of a warrior elite.

Westhead had spent some time in Coronado while Nate was in BUD/S, and from day one of indoc he knew the youngster would make it through. The instructors knew who he was, who his dad had been, and they treated him no differently than any other student: namely, like shit. And in the end, he graduated as Honor Man, as his father had twenty-plus years before him.

"Now that's a sight for sore eyes." Despite his exhaustion and frustration, Hell sounded about as excited as he got. He rushed to the front of the bus as it slowed before the JOE-CAG headquarters.

More smiles pressed against the bus's windows. A small group of family members was waiting in the fading sun, appearing like optimistic refugees behind the barbed wire fence. They raised a few colorful "Welcome Home Heroes" signs, created lovingly by small children undoubtedly with an assist from Mom.

"Mikey!" clucked Hell as he hopped into the warm afternoon. Grinning widely, he crouched in his uniform, arms outstretched for his son. Time slowed. Mikey stood tentatively, tiny fingers gripped around his mother's index. The tall, dark-haired woman leaned down, whispered to the boy. Large, almond eyes went skyward, catching hers, then his father's. A recognition finally hit him and he dropped her hand, rushing forward with glee, exploding into Hell's leg at full speed. He lifted Mikey high into the air, and they spun around happily. Westhead watched the display with something like wonder, before noticing Nate off to the side. Nate caught his fleeting look.

"I remember my dad doing that to me and Cheyenne when he'd get home from deployments," he explained. "We came to pick him up no matter what time he got back."

"I remember."

"Seems like so long ago."

The comment again made Westhead recall that broken-hearted but brave thirteen-year-old. "It was, I suppose."

Nate smiled, smoothed the knot on his Cracker Jacks. Around him, the other men greeted their families, embracing wives and girlfriends, reintroducing hesitant children, swallowing any sourness for a chance at momentary contentment. McDonald's wife squealed next to them, her hands resting on a swelling stomach.

"Baby, get over here and give me some sugar," she cooed, face wide and flushed. "And then give your little girl some sugar. Ella misses you! She's been kicking like Bruce Lee in there!"

They fell into each other's arms hungrily. McDonald kissed his new wife, then her belly.

"Watching that makes me feel like it was just the other day. Funny how that happens," Nate said.

Westhead let the silence hang in the air. They watched Hell and Mikey play. Then, a tug at Westhead's pant leg. He looked down, a new grin plastered wide. A young boy glared up, his face contorted in an attempt to look tough.

"Stinky Uncle Danny!" the boy giggled. Bold, with a nerve-filled confidence through big unblinking eyes.

"Jack! My man! Give me five!"

The toddler looked him over with suspicion, staring at Westhead's outstretched hand like it contained electricity. He sought advice from his father, but Adam remained stone-faced. Finally, carefully, he brought his own hand up, then slapped it down quickly. Westhead pulled his back before they could connect.

"Too slow!"

Jack hollered, took a swipe at Westhead's knee.

"You're a dick, Dan." It was Mary Anne, standing to the side, arms crossed. She was short but mighty, capable of going against—and beating—her husband and his crazy friends at whatever challenge they may present. "Stop harassing my child."

He gave his best *who me* face and stepped back to let Adam and

Jack have their moment together.

Again, Nate watched from afar as father returned to son. Jack didn't know where Dad had been, what he had gone through, only that he was home. And that was enough for them both.

"I wonder who's happier when a soldier comes home, the father or son," Nate said.

"Probably the mother," answered Westhead. "Gonna stay at my place again tonight?"

"If it's okay with you. Tammy is still in my apartment. Didn't tell her I was back and don't want to deal with it. I wouldn't be all that surprised if she had some guy already moved in."

"When is she moving out? After the divorce is final?"

Nate grimaced. "Yeah, right. She's never leaving. The lease is in her name, not that it would matter. Pretty much everything is going to her. What little we have, that is."

"At least you got your dog." Westhead paused, then off Nate's pained expression: "Right?"

"You would think. She's fighting me on that, saying he's half hers. No heart on that girl, I'll tell you what."

"Guess you shouldn't have kicked her brother's ass."

"Guess he shouldn't have come at me! What was I supposed to do?"

"Not sure, but knocking him out wasn't it. Fuck the house, fuck the car. But you gotta get Spence back."

"Damn right I do. I got a plan."

"Yeah?

"Yeah."

"Want some help?"

"Hell yeah. Two-man entry team?"

"Distract and extract."

"Let's do it."

"Just let me know when."

"After you get tested."

Westhead winced. "I know. I will. I am."

"What the hell are you waiting for? Cheyenne's leukemia isn't going to wait."

"I know, Nate, believe me, I know. We were actually just talking about—"

"What?"

"Nothing, never mind. Just haven't spent enough time stateside to get tested yet."

"Don't give me that shit, Dan. Get it done."

"You think I don't want to? You don't think I'd give anything to be a match? That I'd do anything to help your sister? Soon as we're back for a few days, we're all getting the blood test. And then we'll get your dog back."

"Deal. I just can't stop thinking about it, and like Master Chief says, you can't bring your personal life on the battlefield. You have to check that baggage at the door. That's how you get dead. Or worse, get your teammate dead."

A terrified cry interrupted Westhead's concurrence. They both spun around to find Mikey wailing in fear. The boy was frozen, staring at a large, bright-yellow butterfly. It sat loftily on his shoulder, perched majestically, wings slowing pulsing.

"Look how pretty it is! It's just a butterfly Mikey, it won't hurt you," laughed Hell. He went to one knee, enjoying the company. Mikey yelped again, violently smacking at his shoulder. His tiny palm landed flush on the butterfly, and it fell, flailing, spiraling slowly downward. For a moment, it seemed as if the butterfly would fly away, that it was searching for a suitable landing spot on the pavement, maybe. Mikey's face changed to amusement, laughing, watching the fluttering descent. Soon he realized it wasn't flying away. The butterfly came to rest upside down, its black splotches vibrant against a lemon background. It didn't move. Mikey's big eyes rose up to his dad with horror, comprehending what he had done. Hell scooped him up just as the sadness overtook his tiny body. The boy was apocalyptic.

"Shh, shh, Mikey, it's okay, it's okay." His dad's words did not soothe him. Finally, he handed the boy over to his mother, where he began to calm. Mikey didn't look at his father, his head buried in Rosemary's thick hair.

"I'll take him to the car," she said, giving her husband a resigned look. Hell stood, watching his family walk away, as lost as his little boy.

Afraid of embarrassing Hell, Westhead turned back to Nate. "I've already talked to Doc Soto, and he's setting up a clinic so that we can all get tested. One of us is going to be a match, Nate—everyone wants to win that bet." Here, he smiled. "I'm still hoping it's me who gets to walk her down the aisle one day." He held up crossed fingers, then ringed his hand around Nate's neck. "Let's go get a burger somewhere. I'm friggin' starving."

FORT STORY, VA

The church was smaller than Westhead had expected. Barely a chapel, really, with bright green doors to welcome. Severe slants were reminiscent of a prairie home. A single square room, the lined stained glass allowing in as much light as the sun would afford. Pews, floors, altar, intersecting beams high above the worshippers—all unadorned wood, bare, as close to a natural state as saws and hammers and deliberate labor allow lumber to remain. The chapel seemed to Westhead a part of nature, as if this structure had grown from the earth into this shape rather than assembled by human effort.

"Ave Maria" echoed throughout the warm building while they took their seats. Westhead contemplated the melody, wondering when it had begun. Had the choir been singing so softly when they entered? The organ spewing those ghastly notes as Adam led him to an empty row in the middle of the chapel? He couldn't remember; in fact, Westhead couldn't remember walking into the church, and that realization sent him into a panic. He reached into his pocket, feeling for the tiny discs, and casually put two in his mouth, swallowing discreetly.

"You all right?" Adam whispered.

"I'm fine. It's just, well, it's been a while."

Adam placed a hand on his arm. "Jesus doesn't judge."

Westhead looked at him, genuinely confused. "I thought that was exactly what He does."

"Not like that. It's not judgement, it's forgiveness. For anything—there are no exceptions. As long as you're truly sorry, He doesn't judge, He forgives."

"That's good, 'cause I've done a lot of bad shit. Oh, shi—. I mean, sorry, didn't mean to say that."

Adam smiled. "He's heard it before. Just take Him into your heart, and you'll be free."

"Let give and let go, and all that crap?"

"Yeah, and all that crap."

Two altar boys filed past their pew, one holding a liturgical book high overhead, the other a cross. A looming, powerful-looking priest, singing loudly, followed closely behind. As he drew level with them, the priest paused his song, reaching out to shake Adam's hand, imparting a familiar look.

"Father," Adam murmured. The deference impressed Westhead.

"Adam," the priest monotoned as he passed. "See you in theology study this week?" He possessed that reverent, hollow-sounding voice which all men of deep faith seem to share. Like they were absolutely sure of something, when you were just hoping.

A tight head bob gave the priest his answer, and the procession continued. It paused at the altar, each member bowing deeply in unison in the direction of a large crucifix, before taking the single step up.

"Let us pray," the priest intoned, accent vague, arms outstretched toward the few early-morning worshippers. Westhead looked around, greatly impressed. He took everything in with fascination and more than a little awe, finding Adam and the other worshippers with lowered heads, hands respectfully clasped in front, eyes closed. He did the same, awkwardly, feeling a spotlight glaring on him, but maybe it was just the sun pouring through those stained-glass windows, seemingly brighter and fresher than he had ever before noticed, warming him from the inside even while goosebumps took over his arms, sending an unexpected peace through him, and in that moment he was happy, or even better, content.

VIRGINIA BEACH

"What are your thoughts on McDonald?"

Westhead shrugged, noncommittal. A midday sun glistened off wet hair, shoulders. "Good operator. I think he still has a little learning to do about the JOE-CAG way, but the intelligence skills he brings from the Agency are second to none. He stayed in Ranger Regiment rather than go SF or Delta, so he doesn't have as much direct action experience as some of us do, but he makes up for it in other ways. Why?"

Adam paddled out a few strokes and coasted, bobbing with a listless wave. They were alone on the water, straddling surfboards against a blue expanse.

"Just curious. I haven't gotten to know him as well as I would like. He completed The Dump over a month ago, and I still haven't cracked him. With all this extra scrutiny on us now, I just want to make sure he's squared away."

Westhead splashed water on his chest before responding.

"You think it could be someone on our team? Doing all this?"

The length of time it took Adam to deny the contention made Westhead think he did.

"Maybe not on our team, but known to us. It's a small community. Whoever it is, they had to have extensive military training. Not just a regular grunt. And of course have access to RDX-X and the know-how to use those initiators. I'm not saying I think it's a JOE, I'm just saying I don't like it pointing toward us. The existence and mission of JOE-CAG is in real jeopardy with the FBI investigating us." Whitey turned to paddle into a wave, but missed it. He shook water from his head.

Westhead agreed. "My guess is an ex-DEV or Delta guy. One of the ones who could never come back down. Once they got out couldn't assimilate into civilian life. It's not uncommon."

"I know it isn't. Heck, I can almost understand. We're getting to the end of our operational lives, and I don't see either one of us doing well behind a desk."

Westhead squinted into the horizon. "At least you have the ministry. What other skills do I have? Maybe we'll get lucky and bite it on our last mission. The big mish, getting al-Baghdadi and going down in a blaze of glory."

"I would be more surprised if I didn't go out that way," Adam admitted. He turned into another wave. "Can't believe I've made it this far." This time he was right on it and paddled once, then quickly a second, deeper thrust. The wave, a head-high left, started to break at his feet. In a singular smooth motion, he raised his chest and pressed down with his hands, hopped to his feet. He rode the wave skillfully down the line. After a quick cutback, he carved the rest of the face expertly, then dove over the whitewater. Westhead hooted a victory salute, arms raised high overhead. When Adam paddled back out, teeth and grin sparkling against the water, he suggested they grab one last wave or they would be late.

On shore, the two men dried off with an air of satisfaction. A rare contentment, the kind most often known to babies and dogs.

"I guess it doesn't matter, really. Whether it's someone we know or not. I mean, I've given it a lot of thought, and I could come up with a list of twenty guys crazy enough and pissed off enough at Atlas—or any number of other FUBAR ops—to start taking people out. But I'm just going to shut my mouth and follow orders like I always have."

"The Frogman way," Westhead agreed while pulling on a t-shirt. It struggled over his arms, causing the tattoos to contort in a way that made them come alive.

"So you wanna be a Frogman," Adam laughed. They walked through the sand, boards under arm. "Where'd you buy that shirt? Get a gift card to Baby Gap?"

Westhead feinted toward him, but it was half-hearted at best. Maybe due to the residual peace from the ocean, maybe because of their next stop, the attack was quickly abandoned. They loaded the boards onto the roof of the Jeep and headed down General Booth Blvd. toward Christopher Farms.

Westhead parked at the end of a small cul-de-sac where the homes stopped ingloriously in a tight semi-circle, the yards clean and stately with modest but proud landscaping. They approached an unassuming two-story rambler. A large American flag billowed off the front porch overhang. Cars, trucks, and motorcycles were scattered in the driveway and along the street. From the backyard, the animated voices of adults and children alike reached the men coming up the front walkway. The box Adam held, wrapped in silver paper, was big enough that he had to follow close behind Westhead so as to avoid any obstacles.

"Daddy! Stinky Uncle Danny!" Jack raced at his father and godfather. He smacked each of them on the leg, hard, and without slowing, ran back toward the other kids. The birthday hat covering his ears was too big and slightly off center, as was his smile.

"We were wondering when you two would make it," Mary Anne said. She leaned forward to kiss her husband on the cheek, even giving Westhead a sincere hug. "Two spiritual activities this morning, huh? I guess the gospel and waves were good."

Adam scooped up Jack, throwing him high in the air. "Not good enough to miss this! Where's the birthday boy? Jack, did you wish Mikey a happy birthday?"

"Uh huh, and he got a lot of presents too! He got a Nerf gun and a remote helicopter and a robot too." Jack lowered his voice into what passes for a child's whisper. "But the cake is yucky." His face contorted at the remembrance.

"Some gluten-free, vegan recipe." Mary Anne's face mimicked her son's while she explained. "You know how Pete is, he wouldn't let Deirdre use eggs or sugar. Tasted like cardboard."

"Why don't you go give him our present," Adam said, offering the giant box to his son. It was taller than the boy. Jack stared, unsure if he should attempt to pick it up.

"Daddy, it's too big!"

Mary Anne interjected. "It's okay, honey. Daddy can take it to him." She glared at her grinning husband and sent him on his way. "Not so fast, Daniel. I want to talk to you."

Adam gave his friend an empathetic look but made no attempt to assist. Westhead remained while Adam joined the party.

"Want to tell me what the hell happened with Sara? You just drop her like that? I thought you two really hit it off. It sure seemed like you were getting along well."

"We were. We did. I mean, she's a nice girl, I just don't know that there is a future there." He took her hand, batting eyelashes. "I can only be in love with one White woman at a time."

She dropped his hand, rolled her eyes. "Spare me. I've had my fill of SEALs and then some. All brawn and no brain. In my next life I'm taking a nice insurance adjustor who's home for dinner every night. Or at least a Marine."

Westhead's face darkened. "You don't mean that, Mar. You're too delicate for a Jarhead."

"Am I?" She started into the backyard, where Mikey and Jack were hitting a fire truck with whiffle ball bats, leaving Westhead to stand alone. He stared across the lawn. A long sign ran the length of a chain link fence. HAPPY BIRTHDAY MIKEY, in bright red lettering. Westhead looked closer and shook his head when he noticed the sign was attached by flex cuffs.

"Mary Anne still giving you grief about her sister?" Westhead turned to find Mutt standing next to him, two beers in hand. He took one.

"Something like that. Nothing compared to what she's doing to Whitey though. Unfairly if you ask me. She knew what she was signing up for when she married him. They all do."

"Yet somehow they always seem to forget. Funny how that happens. The muscles and excitement are cool when they meet us, but quickly get forgotten when we're gone nine months a year. You won't catch me getting on a knee again while I'm still operational."

Westhead looked at him, smirking. "You? Get married again? Shit, you'd have to replace your wife's birth control with penicillin."

"Probably so, brother, probably so." Distracted, he rubbed his cheeks. Mutt had shaved for Darby's funeral and was growing his beard back. The short blond whiskers looked funny, unnatural against such tan skin.

"By the way, can you believe this?" Westhead pointed at the birthday sign.

"What's that?"

"That sign, on the fence. You see what's holding it up?"

Mutt considered the display. "Yeah, so?"

"Yeah, so? The new flex cuffs. Hell clearly took those from headquarters. In case you haven't noticed, the FBI is up our ass and trying to inventory our equipment. We don't need more shit to come up missing."

Mutt, usually a model of nonchalance, had bulging veins in his neck when he spun toward his teammate. "Screw the FBI. Big difference between flex cuffs and RDX. You telling me you don't have a SOG tool laying around your house that you 'accidentally' left in your gym bag? No scopes reported lost in training that ended up on your .30-06 when you went elk hunting last fall?"

Westhead was taken aback at the venom. "Jeez, Mutt. Not saying that. Just that it's not the best idea to be taking equipment in this current environment. That's all."

Mutt looked pissed. He paused before walking away. "Thanks for the warning, Chief. But be careful talking like this. You don't want people to start wondering who you play for."

The day is hot, sunny, the backyard full and loud. Kids run under foot while parents drink beer, talk closely with each other. Conversations are more subdued than normal and skirt the real issue at the top of everyone's mind—namely, the danger that every man here faces, and the real possibility of a violent death that would change their family forever. There is less laughter, fewer antics at this gathering than normal. Darby's death weighs on all, bringing the reality of our job back to the forefront, as much as we like to ignore it. Our families, not so much. There's still the standard amount of drunkenness, but it has a morbid restraint to it. We're on Alert 60 so the bourbon stays on the shelf, but there's not a man here who isn't looking longingly at that liquor cabinet. The birthday boy is only peripherally aware of the somber undercurrent and enjoys the day like singular-focused children do.

The vibrating of my phone is a welcome interruption. Excusing myself, I walk to a corner of the yard and answer. When I look up, it's the wedding scene from the movie *Navy SEALs*. The women are frozen in place, visibly upset, hands on hips, watching their men stare at cell phones. It takes a moment before the children notice the change in dynamics, but the older ones, having been through this so many times, suddenly realize what's happening. Within seconds, we're rushing goodbyes to crying kids and angry women. The single guys organize rides while the married ones hand their better halves car keys. As if the wives didn't already know it, the men explain that they're not sure when they'll be back. Reminders about trash day and gas bills on the way out, disappointment about nonrefundable *Death of a Salesman* tickets, a dentist appointment. If they're lucky, wives and girlfriends get quick, distracted kisses goodbye. Kids, ruffled pats on the head. Minutes after the recall comes, we're flooding out the backyard and parading back to base.

LITTLE CREEK

"Hey, Blade, you got something against Mikey?" Hell yelled as soon as they were all in the team room. There was an anticipatory buzz and lively din that he had to shout over. "That's twice now. The kid's going to start hating his birthday."

"Cry me a river, Hell. You know how many of my kids' birthdays I was home for? 'Tis the life we chose."

McDonald looked surprised. "Colonel, you have kids?"

Stevens was offended. "Yes, New Guy. Is that so hard to believe?"

Thor took advantage of the opportunity. "I think he's just surprised that a woman would let you touch her, Blade. We all assume it was artificial insemination."

"I had no idea," McDonald said.

"Two daughters. The oldest is a surgeon in Baton Rouge. I was young when we had her. Why do you think I joined the army? My ex-wife took her to California when she was eleven. My youngest is in grad school at Stanford now. She takes my tuition checks, but not my calls."

GQ was pacing in the back of the room, hands running through thick hair. "That's a tragedy, Blade, really it is. But I'm guessing we didn't get recalled so you could give New Guy your family tree. You going to tell us what's up?"

Stevens looked his troops over with an unfriendly eye. "It's the proverbial good news, bad news, boys. Which do you want first?"

All sixteen men shouted their preference at the same time. Stevens and Hagen leaned back, enjoying the chaos. Like usual, the loudest argument won. It belonged to Thor, who stood on a chair, hands on Jud's shoulders, red-faced and screaming over the top of his head for the bad.

Stevens waited until they had calmed. "ADM Bradley just informed me the president is putting us on stand-down until further notice."

A collective groan rippled through the room. Any ensuing complaints were muttered or muted out of respect for the JSOC commander and his position. Follow-up questions came rapid-fire.

"Is this because of the attacks and suspicion on Tier One Special Operations Groups?" Nailer asked. "The failure to capture or kill al-Baghdadi? They blaming us for that? It was an intelligence failure! A dry hole!"

"I was given no additional information, gents. Sorry, but for now, that's all I have."

The grumbling continued as the men moved about. Hagen finally spoke, bringing them back on task. "Gentlemen, aren't you forgetting something? Colonel, you mentioned there was also good news ..."

Suddenly reinvigorated, interested eyes darted back to the front of the room. Stevens's lips curled back, in what for him passed as a smile, his teeth small and unnatural, the first time his men could remember seeing them in some time.

"You're being secured for three full days," he announced. A roar lifted the room as the men thought of resting tired bodies and spending time with families or the opposite sex. He held his hands up and got silence. "After you head on down to Hell for a little PT, that is."

Hell clapped his hands once, popping to his feet with a sadistic grin. "This one is for Mikey. I think we can find some interesting evolutions today, boys. What do you think?"

The ensuing Monster Mash is a fast-paced run/swim/run/obstacle course with habanero peppers ingested before each leg, followed by a game of underwater rugby that results in only two bloody noses.

Afterward, we lounge casually in the team room, hydrating, still talking shit about slow times and not putting out. Most of us are still in PT gear—dark UDT shorts and New Balance Tactical Abyss II boots for the navy guys; the soldiers and Marines, olive silkies and Salomon boots, for the most part. The OGA guys have their own style, but the common theme is skin, and lots of it. Most guys are shirtless, with no one's shorts making even the slightest attempt to reach a knee.

"Man, you guys look like the entertainment for a bachelorette party," Hagen says, shaking his head. "The only thing missing is a kiddy pool full of Jell-O."

"Sorry, Commander, but NSW Group 2 cleaned out the commissary of all gelatin-related products. Something about a team wrestling match," one of the army guys calls out from the back, earning a smattering of threats and insults from the SEALs in the room.

"Well, I'm sure they would have used lube for the event if Delta hadn't cleaned out all the KY," he replies, half-heartedly at best.

"Jerk-store!" someone yells at him. Then, shocked: "Man, I can't even believe he knows what KY is."

"Okay, okay, my jokes are lame, I get it." Hagen runs his hands through sweaty hair, standing in front of a podium embossed with JOE-CAG's unofficial seal: "We don't decide who lives or dies, we just make sure the order is carried out," over a ghoulish-looking skull wearing a black hood and holding a scythe. The figure's head is lowered, to represent humility. The scythe, razor sharp, to symbolize our readiness. In the background is a dark beach with mountains and a sky full of stars, but no moon. We are lethal anywhere, and you'll never see us coming.

"Unless the colonel or team leaders have anything else, you're secured until 0700 Monday." He raises his voice as everyone begins to stir. "If anyone doesn't find themselves wobbling a barstool or in a strange bed, I would suggest visiting Phil in Bethesda. I know that not everyone knows Phil, but I can tell you he would appreciate any and all company from like-minded men. That's it for me—Colonel, you have anything?"

"Yes. Most of you got a cut and shave for the funeral, but let that shit grow back out. We may be on stand-down right now, but don't be surprised if we go indig on the next op. And don't forget, you're on Alert 60 and six ring status. That's it. See you Monday morning."

It's as if someone yelled "Fire!" Everyone begins to scatter, anxious to unwind during the rare downtime. We spend most of our waking moments together, and a lot of our unwaking ones too. Nine-to-fivers we are not. But every once in a while it's nice to get a break, and as I look around at tired faces, I know the team needs it.

I'm looking forward to the three days off as much the rest of the guys, albeit not for the same reasons. While they'll be content drinking, fucking, and fighting, I have preparations to make. And more supplies to procure.

The hot afternoon sun warmed Westhead's face. He squinted into it, sunglasses off, pausing to appreciate the moment. It was one of the good ones, and he was never sure if they would last a minute, an hour, a day. So he simply enjoyed it, until realizing he had left his phone in his locker.

He retraced his steps through the now-empty JOE-CAG parking lot, smiling to himself, amused that his moment of Zen had—of course—been broken just as quickly as he had found it.

He waved his badge at the reader on the front door and walked onto the unoccupied quarterdeck. The duty station officer looked up and nodded as Westhead made his way past him and into the team room.

"Hey Chief, w-what are you still doing here?"

The voice surprised him, and he wheeled around to find McDonald standing there, latex gloves on, a bottle of bleach in hand.

"Forgot my phone." Then, "Don't tell me you're cleaning heads when we actually have a few days off."

If you glanced around a crowded room, say, at a party, you probably would look right past McDonald. If you didn't know what you were looking for, you'd think he was just a normal-looking fit guy in his late twenties. An Ivy Leaguer or shy personal trainer. Not particularly remarkable. A little shy. Not tall, not short, he wasn't the best swimmer in JOE-CAG, wasn't the fastest runner, and wasn't particularly funny, a trait that always went far in SpecOps. He wouldn't be chosen first for a pickup basketball game, and he certainly wasn't the strongest guy in the weight room. But what he exemplified was the SpecOps maxim "a common man with an uncommon desire to succeed" and had converted this commitment and work ethic into a fierce reputation as a warrior on and off the battlefield. McDonald was well on his way to earning the universal respect of everyone in his new unit, something not just handed out. That reputation had begun during Atlas Revenge. He always did what needed to be done, never complained, and never questioned the task at hand. He just got it done right, the first time, with a never-quit mentality. Westhead knew he was solid.

Now, a little embarrassed, like he had been caught doing something wrong, he was giving off some soulful, puppy-dog eyes.

"Yeah, man, after the food Pos brought in, they're looking a little rough. D-d-didn't want Stevens or Hagen to come in over the weekend and find them dirty."

Westhead shook his head. Another one of Horrigan's pranks to screw with the new guy. "You do realize he brought in Taco Bell just so we'd destroy the toilets, don't you?"

McDonald's expression implied legitimate skepticism. "No way."

"Way. Does it to all the new guys. Guarantee you'll find a few toilets that haven't been flushed. You can probably thank Thor for that. Or that little weasel, GQ."

He shrugged. "Part of being an FNG, huh? After I completed Ranger School and got assigned to Battalion, my platoon mates taped me from head to toe with just a slit for my mouth. They st-stuck a pen in it, and told me I had to complete a New York Times crossword puzzle before they'd free me."

Westhead chuckled. "The night I got my Budweiser, my new platoon LPO put my cell phone in a waterproof bag and gave me the co-ordinates for the buoy chain he had attached it to two miles off the coast. Hell, I would have just gotten a new phone, but Senior Chief had texted me my job. That was a long, cold swim."

"Medieval bastards."

"Yeah. I won't tell you what we had to do to reach the second deck after getting assigned to our squadrons in DEVGRU." He reached for the bleach. "I remember what it's like to be a new guy. I'll give you a hand so you can get out of here. Pregnant wife at home and all. We don't get too many days off; I'm sure she could use her husband for a little."

McDonald looked suspiciously at the senior operator, all too aware of potential treachery. Only last week Thor had offered to help him empty the building's trash, then had promptly dumped all the cans on the quarterdeck. Once he realized Westhead was serious, the offer was respectfully accepted and the look changed to appreciation. Holding their breath, the two operators backed into the bathroom.

"Good God!" McDonald called out as the stench hit him.

"You gotta look everywhere. Pos often hides surprises for new guys. I'm guessing he thought that you wouldn't come clean until Sunday, when it would be *really* ripe."

The two began to scour the half dozen toilets, showers, and the bright-white tile floors of JOE-CAG's bathroom. Their mood was light considering the exercise, the retching and mutual disgust motivating some very specific revenge plans for Pos and Thor.

While Westhead didn't enjoy the work, he appreciated the opportunity to get to know McDonald better. It was imperative that in an elite unit like theirs every man know and trust the other operators he went into battle with. Although they had each graduated from JOE-CAG's training course, they had come from markedly different fighting forces. SEALs and Rangers had disparate missions and as such operated quite differently. The Dump, not subtly, hammered home the tactics, tech-niques, and procedures fundamental to the way JOE-CAG operated. It was designed to do two things: find the best of the best, then get them on the same page. They practiced close-quarters combat until breaching all types of structures was an automatic, choreographed dance. Explosives, escape and evasion, ship-boarding, HAHO and HALO jumps, water insertions, even how they stacked on a door and cleared rooms was all perfected the JOE-CAG way. Naturally, training didn't ease up after The Dump. Limits were always being pushed, living by the SEAL mantra, "the only easy day was yesterday."

Still, there were philosophy and personality differences amongst the services, especially within the ultra-aggressive, type-A characters intrinsic to Special Operations Forces. And no better way to bridge those than by kneeling shoulder to shoulder and gagging over a clogged toilet.

After an hour, Westhead took inventory and straightened.

"I think that'll do it," he said, wiping his scalp with a forearm.

McDonald rose, but quickly lowered himself back to one knee, toilet brush still in hand. He pinched the bridge of his nose in pain.

"You all right?"

He didn't answer, face scrunching tighter. Westhead took a step in his direction, footsteps reverberating loudly across the empty bathroom. When he reached him, McDonald unstiffened and smiled.

"Sorry, just these damn headaches. Probably was all the bleach. I'm fine."

Westhead stared with concern, but left it alone. "Okay. You're all kinds of banged up, huh?"

McDonald looked at him, confused.

"Your knee? You were limping on the way over to the sandbox."

McDonald reached to his leg, patted it. "Oh, that. Yeah, the n-n-n-knee's fine. Good to go. Forgot all about it."

The pause, the space between them, felt clumsy. Westhead put his hand on the younger man's shoulder. "Good to hear. Now let's get out of here. I'm sure there's a beer and a shot somewhere with your name on it."

Together, awkwardly, they exited the bathroom.

"Wait till the guys find out a team leader helped a new guy scrub toilets. No one's gonna believe it."

Westhead made a face at his new teammate. "No need to tell them anything. We help each other—that's what we do. Recognition not required."

"The deed, not the glory, right?"

"Something like that."

"Either way, I appreciate it. How about I buy you that shot and beer?"

Westhead started back through the hallway toward the team room, shaking his head. "Thanks, but I gotta grab something from my cage and head out. You go. Enjoy. Get some rest. I have a feeling our op tempo is going to pick up after this stand-down is over."

"Yeah? What are your thoughts on the DC attack and mosque bombing? You think we could actually be tasked with something domestic?"

Westhead thought about it before turning back. McDonald had reached the main door and was holding it open. The outside came in, humid air and brilliant light clashing with the industrial air conditioning.

"There's not much precedent for it, but I'll tell you this. We weren't formed to stand down during the big missions. If the president thinks we can stop whatever is going on, then he's going to use us. I for one welcome the chance to put down the son of a bitch killing Americans on our own soil, no matter who it is. And, as much as I hate to say it, clear this unit's name."

"It's crazy, all the ties to the Basting Institute. I heard the missing imam from the Crescent Islamic Center went to Harvard Business School with Dick Basting."

Westhead confirmed. "Imam Shami was the lead on the Basting study that convinced the president to change our ROEs just before Atlas. He thought SpecOps engagements and CIA interrogation techniques were responsible for too much collateral damage and turning the population against us in the Muslim world. He doesn't have too many fans inside this building."

"Not where I came from either. No way these attacks aren't related to that study."

Westhead seemed to remember something. "You were in Iraq for Atlas, weren't you?"

McDonald wagged his head. "Sure was. I guess I can talk about it now that we all have the same clearance. I was still with The Agency's Special Operations Group, and did a lot of the intelligence gathering for the op. I was part of a two-man recon team inserted in the days before you guys were ambushed. When the operation went sideways, me and my partner had to E&E in the desert for a week before finally making it back to Camp Fallujah."

"I knew paramilitary guys from SAD were calling in coordinates during our infil. Didn't realize that was you."

"Yeah. Us and a small Delta attachment situated on the opposite ridge. We radioed The Activity guys and told them the HLZ was hot. For some reason that intel was never passed on to your pilots." He paused here, his demeanor shifting. "I watched that helo get shot down, Chief. If the mission planner had gotten approval for Apaches on station, we would have had the air support earlier and could have saved those guys."

Westhead felt McDonald's anger, saw the venom in his eyes. "Still pissed about it?"

He didn't hesitate. "Of course I am. Aren't you?"

"What do you think?"

"I'm sure you are. We all are."

"I just wonder if someone is pissed enough to be killing citizens and blowing up buildings because of it."

McDonald shrugged. "Someone is. Doesn't mean it's one of us."

"No, it doesn't, despite what the FBI thinks." Westhead considered something. "If it weren't for you guys calling off the second Chinook, it would have gone down too, with me in it. So thanks, I owe you one."

McDonald motioned back toward the bathroom. "I think we can call it even."

Westhead smiled and continued down the hallway. It dimmed when McDonald let the front door close, then fell silent.

Fluorescent lights buzzed over Westhead as he moved through the team room flicking switches. He retrieved his phone, but as he made his way to the exit, animated voices coming from the OIC's office stopped him.

"You see that? That's a goddamn subpoena. You can tell me to go fuck myself, but you can't tell the US District Court to go fuck themselves." Westhead recognized the angry voice. It was Agent Kopen.

"I can't?" snorted Stevens. "US District Court, go fuck yourself."

"You have fourteen days to comply, and then you will be held in contempt. I'll be the one holding the handcuffs."

"And I'll be the one with my foot up your ass. Get out of my office."

"Let me find out you are withholding evidence that could stop a terrorist attack, Colonel, and top-secret black ops bullshit League of Nations organization or not, I will have you arrested, tried, and convicted. Whatever shadow group you operate under does not have authority to skirt federal law and has no suction with the FBI or United States Attorney, that I assure you."

"Thanks for coming by, Agent Kopen. But don't be so sure about that last part. I have friends in high places. If you're smart, you'll spend your time elsewhere."

Westhead continued to listen as the voices rose. Then, they stopped altogether. Soon, Kopen strode out of Stevens's office, nostrils flared. He marched briskly down the hallway, brushing past Westhead without a glance in his direction.

Westhead bristled toward the man but did not speak. Kopen stopped, shifted a briefcase from right hand to left, smoothed back rumpled hair. The pale eyes glistened with anger, but they didn't break from Westhead's glare. Like this they stood, long enough that no dominance could be affirmed. At least not with this interaction.

"Dan, shouldn't you be off enjoying your long weekend?" Stevens's rebuke from the doorway broke the tension between Westhead and the FBI agent, and the two men stepped away from each other, wordless.

WASHINGTON, DC

Sweat runs down my chest, my back. I wipe my face as casually as I can, but the truth is, this recon exercise is one of the most difficult of my career. And I've done them on six continents, while being shot at, bombed, as fire ants attacked my groin, circled by sharks, disguised as a woman, in sandstorms, blizzards, monsoons, and every other type of weather and environment imaginable. Just never a real world op on a busy American street crawling with law enforcement agents I've trained with.

Furthermore, my bombings are having unintended consequences. The sidewalk on the White House side of Constitution Avenue is now cordoned off, and there is even less accessibility to the adjacent streets previously open to pedestrians.

I'm thankful for wrap-around sunglasses hiding fixated pupils, focused intently on the famous swath of bright green grass before me. My goal is for none of the hundreds of uniformed, plainclothes, and hidden Secret Service agents or Capital Police to notice me taking more than a tourist's interest in the White House South Lawn.

I squint over the White House roof, also taking in the Eisenhower Executive Office Building that overlooks the Oval Office. We've conducted exercises with Secret Service snipers and Counter Assault Team, and I'm quite familiar with the skilled marksmen perched on the rooftops of both buildings. It's not lost on me that they are the same people who ultimately kept me from killing the president in Virginia Beach.

This is the first reconnaissance I've ever done without a weapon, and that nakedness gives rise to an anxious, exposed sensation. DC's concealed-carry laws are beyond invasive, and it's not worth the risk of explaining to my command why I was illegally armed at the commander in chief's front door. Being the end of summer works in my favor, and I do my best to blend in with the thousands of tourists converging on the National Mall. Even with the recent attack a mile away, they still come to the city in droves. Little do they know they're licking ice cream cones and posting photos from what will soon become ground zero in this war against the politically correct. And make no mistake, it is a war.

I cut in and out of those tourists in an effort at anonymity, unable to shake the feeling I'm being watched. I conduct a few casual-enough countersurveillance maneuvers, stopping short to tie my shoe, checking my reflection in cars, but can't pick out any agents for certain. After walking briskly up 15th Street, I pause at the brass foot of Marquis de Lafayette. A bare-breasted woman reaches toward him with an offer of a sword, that sculpted emblem of independence and friendship representing an unselfish sacrifice for the birth of a free nation.

When I spin 180 degrees at the base of the statue, a dark suit blurs amongst the throngs, catching my attention. A flash, then it's gone. I squint, searching. For what? Slicked-back hair, glacial eyes? I crane my neck, anxious, wheeling in and around engrossed tourists, making every effort to recapture the image, the form, but it's gone. I shoot into the crowd, eliciting complaints as I bump into pedestrians, but can't find the figure. Did I really see the pockmarked face, the suspicious glare? Was that really the flash of a gold watch? Even a toothpick completes my vision.

I scan the crowd further, sweating, chest heaving, but no sign of Agent Kopen. Was it my imagination? Is guilt manifesting itself in paranoia? No, not guilt, that isn't fair. It's not guilt tearing at my emotions. What is it then? Fear? Fear of Agent Kopen? No, not quite. Fear of being caught, of not achieving the end result I so desperately require? Closer.

I spin around, resolute, no longer expecting to find my adversary, but more convinced I must do something about him. I've always trusted my instincts, and they are now manifesting themselves into this terror I just experienced, that terror taking the form of FBI Special Agent Seth Kopen.

Again wiping sweat, it suddenly occurs to me how best to hide in plain sight in the nation's capital. Usually, on a sniper mission like this I'm concealing myself in the middle of a war zone, doing everything in my power to go unseen. In this case, I can drive right in, park 1,000 yards from where Marine One takes off and lands. Hide in plain sight. The trick, as always, will be the extract. I've been more than willing to give my life for my country since I took the Oath of Enlistment so many years ago, but if I can delay that culmination and continue the mission, so much the better. I consider what type of vehicle would be able to get in and out of our nation's capital during an attack on the White House. It occurs to me that an emergency vehicle with screaming lights and siren—say, an ambulance—would do the trick.

LAUREL, MD

Each time the cluster of balloons drifted to the front of the Jeep, Westhead would gently flick them back. This episode had played out more times during the four-hour drive than his nerves could handle, and the balloons—their positive messaging notwithstanding—were in danger of getting the spike blade sheathed to his ankle sliced through them. When he finally realized that instead of a rogue air current it was his passenger continuously pulling the balloons forward, he punched a giggling Nate in the arm. They both sighed with relief when the Jeep turned into a quiet, tree-lined subdivision.

Driving down Claflin Street was warm and familiar and intense, and provoked certain emotions, both good and bad, for each man. They moved slower than necessary through the well-ordered suburban world, taking it all in: An older man struggling with a lawnmower. A young boy chasing another with a stick. A fat cat nosing around trashcans.

"Your mom has no idea we're coming?" Westhead asked again, glancing at Nate. He seemed to raise higher in his seat with each modest home they overtook.

Nate shook his head. "Nah-uh. Wanted to surprise her."

"Cheyenne neither?"

Again, a slight shake. "Nope. It's her last day of chemo, and I thought this would be a good way to celebrate."

"She lose all her hair?"

"Nope. Didn't give it a chance to fall out. She shaved it all off before the first treatment and donated it to Locks for Love."

"Attagirl."

Westhead stopped the car in front of a simple white two-story house.

"Here we are."

Unhurried, they both arched backs and cracked knuckles as they stood on the sidewalk, Nate with the balloons and Westhead clutching a bottle of wine. They picked their way up the stone path, oblivious to the humidity, the chirping insects, the staunch seasonal air. By the time they stepped onto the porch, the screen door had swung open. A pretty but weary woman stood in its stead.

"I was wondering when I'd see my SEALs again," she said with a tired, honest smile. "And they even brought gifts." She stepped back to let them enter. "Come in but be quiet; Cheyenne is lying down.

"I guess it would be asking too much to expect a phone call so I could clean, put something in the oven?" she asked once they were inside, not really surprised and not the least bit offended. "Different generation be damned, that's just what Team guys do: fall from the heavens."

Westhead spoke softly, offering the bottle. "Gayle, you know you don't have to prepare anything for us. We got an unexpected couple of days off. Nate thought it would be a nice surprise for Cheyenne."

She smiled again, bigger, fatigued but pleased. "Oh, don't mind me. It's been a rough day. You would think I'd be used to it." She reached up suddenly for Nate, like she had just noticed him, wrapping her son in a fierce hug. The top of her head didn't quite reach his chin. Her thin frame stretched his circumference. Even so, there was no mistaking who was in control of the embrace.

"It's a lovely surprise," she murmured into him more than once, pulling him tighter. After a moment, she released her son, took a step back, smoothed her tank top and wiped glistening eyes.

"Let me look at my boy. I know, not a boy anymore, I know that." She reached up, rubbed his chin. "Nathan, you need to shave." She smiled then, like she was remembering something, and lowered her hands to his wide shoulders. "I won't say the obvious …"

Nate's breath came out of his nose sharply, the tilt of his head its own reproach.

"I know, I know," she said, taking another deep breath. The color flooded back into her face, joined by a countenance of content. She turned to Westhead. "He hates when I tell him that. Come in, guys, sit down. Dan, give me a hug. It's been too long. What can I get you? Dan, a beer? Nate, soda? You must be hungry. That's a long drive."

They sat in the living room while she fussed over them, Nate childlike and comfortable on the couch of his youth, Westhead stiff and respectful. They made small talk, avoiding the topics Mrs. Butler wasn't yet ready to broach.

When a slight movement caught Nate's eye, he spun to the hallway. Immediately, the blood rushed to his head. He stood, gave his strongest smile.

"Chey! How are you, sweetie?" He walked toward his teenage sister, taken aback at how small she seemed.

For a moment, they couldn't be sure she wasn't sleep-walking. She stood before them flat-footed, with heavy eyes and a blank stare. Slowly, her lips parted. She stepped forward.

"Nathan!" she slurred, burying her head into his ribs. "You're safe!"

He could only think to chuckle in response. "Of course I'm safe, Chey. How are *you? You're* the one we're worried about."

She raised her chin, indignant. "I'm fine, and I'm going to be fine. This leukemia doesn't have any idea what it's in for. Four weeks of chemo down."

"I'm so proud of you!" He knelt in front of her. He was shocked at how easily she now fit into his arms. He scooped her into the air, unaware of the wincing grimace.

Mrs. Butler said, "Okay, okay, let's put Cheyenne down. She's had a long day. We need to get you an orange juice, honey. Keep those fluids moving through you."

"I will." Then, looking around: "Where's Tammy? She didn't come with you?"

The shared expression on each adult's face was all the answer she needed.

"Nate!" she exclaimed, but didn't know what to say next. So she shuffled over to the couch, taking the cushion next to Westhead. She watched him, serious.

"Hi, Uncle Dan. It's good to see you," she told him.

"You too, Cheyenne. I'm glad to see you're doing better," he said.

"I'm not doing better. Not yet. You know I still need to find a marrow match, don't you?"

He nodded, shifting in his seat. "I do. Everyone on base is getting tested. You remember Doc Soto? He's working with an oncologist at Naval Medical Center Portsmouth to host an open clinic for all sailors stationed in the area to get tested. In fact, he's organizing a donor registry drive for when we get back. We'll get you a match, Cheyenne."

Her big blue eyes scrunched in thought. Then, realizing something: "I notice you didn't say 'I promise.'"

Westhead's seat seemed uncomfortable. He fidgeted, re-crossed his legs. Where words should come, his mouth open but empty. Finally: "Honey, I would give anything to be able to promise you that. But that's not my place, and we both know it's something I can't promise. What I *can* promise you is that we are going to do everything we can to find a match. That Nate and I are going to make sure every sailor and solider in Virginia Beach gets tested, and if there *is* a match, we'll find them. And make sure they donate. Deal?"

He offered his hand. Stone-faced, she stared at it, contemplating. When she did take it, it swung up and down vigorously, her pale, delicate fingers swallowed by the calloused mitt.

"Deal. We shook; you can't go back on that."

"I know, honey. I would never."

It was later that evening. The four of them sat in the dining room, takeout sushi, soy sauce, drinks, elbows, and jovial conversation covering the table. An uninformed observer could assume a model family, two good-looking parents with a completed brood. For this night, at least, they could play the part, the suggestion of loss and pending danger only skirting the edges of conversation and mood.

"This is amazing, Gayle. Great idea. I couldn't tell you the last time I ate sushi." Westhead's mouth gaped over unsteady chopsticks, struggling to get a dripping roll to his mouth.

"I think that you guys didn't tell me you were coming because you didn't want me to cook, that's what I think," she replied. She put some more edamame on Cheyenne's plate. "Eat, honey. You like these."

"Ugh. Raw fish? What makes this a delicacy?"

"You gotta keep your energy up, Chey," Nate told her. "It's going to take a lot of strength to get through this."

"And she has it, boy, let me tell you," their mom said, proud. "You should have seen her every Friday in that hospital, getting pricked and prodded through those chemo treatments. Not a complaint or tear the whole time."

Cheyenne shrugged, nonchalant. "Whining won't do any good," she said.

Westhead laughed. "I know some guys who think they're pretty tough that could use that advice."

She shrugged again. "Besides, there were lots of kids in there younger than me, who were in a lot worse shape. I had to be strong for them. Seeing what they were going through, seeing what Monique went through—" Here she stopped, turned to her mom with a wobbly jaw. Nate and Westhead watched the interaction, concerned.

"Monique was a friend of Cheyenne's. A good friend," Gayle explained.

"Acute lymphocytic leukemia. Same as me. We were diagnosed a week apart. And now she's dead." She spoke matter-of-factly.

The silence one would expect when faced with such a statement followed. Westhead broke it.

"You know, honey, we just lost someone too. And what's important, what that person would want us to do, is to move forward. To fight harder, to never give up. Because you know what it would mean if you gave up, if you quit?"

She surprised him by having the right answer. "Yeah, that they died for nothing. Well, I'm not going to let Monique die for nothing. I'm going to fight."

He was impressed. "That a girl." Westhead took a careful look around. "You Butlers, I tell you what. There's something in your DNA that makes you stronger than most."

Gayle snorted. "That's because we have no choice. Strength is found when it's needed the most. That's what Steve always said, and this family has needed it in spades over the years. But we're certainly proud of Nate and Cheyenne's strength, both when their father was killed, and the challenges they are facing now. I have no doubt they'll overcome whatever God puts in front of them."

"Next week I'm going to get another lumbar puncture," Cheyenne stated. "Depending on what it says, I'll probably need radiation after that. All I have to do from there is not get any infections and then find a blood marrow match and have that surgery. If all the post-induction therapy goes well and there's no relapse, I'll be good as new."

Westhead's eyes went wide. Cheyenne smiled at him, head held high. She wasn't after sympathy, and he knew it.

He raised his wineglass. "Is that all? Well let's drink to Cheyenne overcoming this terrible disease, and to Nate not screwing anything up that's going to get his eyebrows shaved."

"I'll drink to that," Gayle said, finishing the toast. She leaned back in her chair, taking in the surroundings. Then: "Nate, I almost forgot, I found something you might want to take back to base with you. I left it in your bedroom."

He scrunched his face, both surprised his mom had something for him and that she still referred to it as *his* bedroom. The chair squeaked on the hardwood floor when he stood, uncertain.

"Go ahead, it's laying on your desk. I found it in an old box. Thought you might want it before it gets misplaced."

Westhead watched Nate go, reaching for his plate once he turned the corner. Westhead went straight for the California rolls, sticking one of his chopsticks through the middle. Avocado, green and mushy, came out the other end. He scooped a wad of wasabi from its container and jammed it back into the roll. Evenly, smoothly, he repeated the chore, replacing each roll on Nate's plate. Upon completion, he leaned back without a word, calmly sucking out the seeds from pieces of edamame. Cheyenne and Gayle traded glances, initially hesitant, but barely able to contain their giggles by the time Nate returned to the table. He carried a tan piece of cloth.

"What do you got there, dude?" Westhead asked. The innocuous tone, undoubtedly meant to disarm, had instead the opposite effect. A mask of suspicion enveloped Nate's face. He inspected each party, searching for evidence of wrongdoing, but could find none, even in the tight lips and wide eyes of his sister.

"Spencer's Trident," he answered slowly. "You remember giving it to me, Dan? He left it for me in his Just in Case package."

"I remember it like it was yesterday," answered Westhead. "Who would have thought you'd end up earning your own?"

Nate looked up. "I did."

Westhead winced at the reprimand, not for the first time forgetting Nate was no longer a kid, was a Frogman just like him.

"Do you still wear Daddy's?" Cheyenne asked him.

Nate's chin rose and lowered sharply, vehemently, a single time. He had been pinned with that Trident by CDR Hagen after SQT and being assigned to Team 2's Echo Platoon, his dad's old platoon. The same pin that he had held so delicately as a child, even as a youngster understanding the great weight that it carried.

"So who wants more? Nate? You have a few California rolls left." His mom's words shifted the mood, and just like that, shoulders relaxed, breaths exhaled, faces lifted.

"I can always eat more."

He lifted his chopsticks. If he was aware of the onlookers, he didn't acknowledge them, dipping the first roll in soy sauce. If he heard his sister's gasp when popping it into his mouth, there was no reaction. And while his eyes may have immediately gone red and teary, his nose starting to run, he didn't so much as peek in the direction of his now-howling tablemates, each sputtering with laughter while he chewed deliberately and tried not to gag. Without a word or eye contact, he choked down the remaining four rolls and gently placed his chopsticks across the empty plate. Although eying his water glass, he didn't drink from it.

Westhead reclined in his seat, face beaming with satisfaction as he enjoyed his handiwork. He had a feeling he wouldn't need any help sleeping.

BETHESDA, MD

It's nice to feel good. Rare, but appreciated. And right now, I do. There's no headache, a more-than-welcome reprieve. I feel accomplished, one of those occasions when you trust that you've used your time well. I feel ... productive. I've stopped looking over my shoulder, and that helps.

There's one more stop to make before I leave DC. It's a short walk to Metro Center from the White House, and I use the time to monitor alternate escape routes and take note of jammed arteries, all while appreciating the clean light on my head, the fast-paced, civilized sounds of the capital.

This city reminds me of my youth, even if they feel like the memories of someone else. Maybe a film I saw a long time ago.

It's the angles of an intersection, the smells of the city. The way a siren echoes off the buildings that really brings me back to that day. Fourth grade, undersized, shy, anonymous in the back of the line bouncing from museum to museum. A class trip to the nation's capital. It was intentional when I let go of the girl's hand in front of me, I remember that. I had watched with something like fascination as the class crossed the next street. It grew smaller and smaller. On one of these streets right here, right on this busy block in the cradle of power, rickshaws and cabs shooting past, suited pedestrians and sidewalk musicians. I had watched that girl shrink, the teacher, the chaperones separating two fighting boys, the group shriveling as they got farther away. No one looked back. And I stood, not frozen, but exhilarated, free. Alone and unafraid.

I had gotten a beating after we returned home, one of the first bad ones. I swore that I would kill my stepdad but had to endure many more before I was big enough for that.

If it weren't for the first-person nature of those recollections, the tug of familiarity at the honking horns, the pace of the foot traffic, the anonymity of packed sidewalks, then I'm not sure I could be positive they were my own, that I hadn't read them somewhere, been told by a friend about the scenes of their own childhood, or experienced them in another life. But no, it is my memory, one of those indelible moments that had shaped me, an unavoidable experience of my youth, now faded but lingering stubbornly.

The Red Line is packed; muggy and claustrophobic. The train creaks and rattles around each turn. My arm, extended high to grip the metal railing, starts to numb. I switch arms and let myself bob with the car's motion. I can't help but scan faces, on the lookout for the man I now consider my enemy.

At the Medical Center Station, I cross under Rockville Pike. The sprawling series of boxes that is the rebuilt Walter Reed National Military Medical Center looks like a modern-day fortress. Light-colored stone, severe right angles, the building blocks jutting out of the earth to catch the sun's glare in an antiseptic illusion of care. It didn't look like this the last time I was here.

Phil has a room by himself. He's lucky. Many of the wounded, including him, used to be packed four and five at a time into rooms meant for two. Holes in the walls. Rats. I should know. It's better today. Even so, anger rushes to my face whenever I enter this hospital, every time.

Mechanically, my hand moves to the back of my head, rubs the lined scar hidden under thick hair. Three spherical scars decorate my upper chest, circular ones with corresponding circles in the back. Results of the contact which sent me here as a patient for two long months. A journey with Phil, similar to thousands of others' during our country's longest wars.

Our trip here began in Ramadi in 2006, where our team was conducting anywhere from one to four direct action raids on high-value targets every night. One of those nights, it was our night. Our turn. From the dusty battlefield it had been a hurried Blackhawk CASEVAC to a small FOB, a MEDEVAC to the Green Zone, then a CCATT flight to Landstuhl. After a month in Germany, I had improved enough to be sent here. Phil had never left.

Our journeys, luckily, had not stopped in Dover. A year later, I was back in Ramadi, fighting the same insurgency that al-Baghdadi later transformed into ISIS.

That night, at least up until the IED, is still crystal clear in my mind. I couldn't tell you if it had been a Tuesday or a Saturday, but then again the characteristics inherent to days of the week fall away in war. There is no TGIF, no hump day, during combat. That day had felt like all the others, even if it didn't turn out the same.

Each deployment has its own pace, its own mood. Some, you're positive you're not coming home. Others, you feel invincible. I've had both, and learned that those feelings don't mean shit.

Abu Ayub al-Masri, code-name Caterpillar, was the target that night. The Egyptian-born bomb maker was responsible for so many of the IEDs killing our soldier and Marine brothers. Definitely a high-value target, and we were psyched to have gotten the mission.

By nightfall our squad was jocked up and loaded onto two MH-6 Little Birds. SOAR pilots flew the small, agile choppers blacked-out, using night vision to navigate, skimming so fast over and between the three- and four-story buildings which dotted Iraqi cities like jagged teeth that by the time you reached a building, it was gone. It always amazed me how low we flew, so close you could lean out and brush gloved fingers against the homes' satellite dishes, those technological symbols contradicting the insurgency's medieval philosophies, crying out, at least to me, "Hey, we just want to watch TV like everyone else."

I remember I had felt particularly at ease that night. I realize there's always the possibility of revisionist thinking, that it's the results making the memory, but that's the way I remember it. Wedged on my bench outside the Little Bird, feet dangling, I could lean forward and achieve the sensation of riding a roller coaster as we raced through the night, cutting the thick air, twisting and sliding like a racecar in the rain, nothing between my boots and the Iraqi earth below. I remember simply enjoying the night scenes and rhythmic pulse of the helicopter's blades. The small, agile bird sounded like a lawnmower and tended to put me in a trance.

My thoughts were calm, but back then that was more common. I wasn't particularly worried about getting shot down—the reason we flew so low was because by the time anyone heard the chopper, it was already past—and the raid was the same as hundreds we had conducted in both Iraq and Afghanistan. We trained for this over and over. My squad would insert on the roof of the target house, the second fire team would land in the courtyard, we'd breach, and meet in the middle. After the house was cleared and the bad guys killed or captured, we'd secure any intel we could find, bring it back to the OGA guys at Monsoor, and wait for the intelligence we'd collected to give us our next mission. Easy-peasy.

That was how it was supposed to go. Of course, in war nothing ever goes exactly as it's supposed to. And that was fine—improvising was our specialty. But everything went wrong that night; it was a perfect storm of tiny fuckups that left one operator dead, me close to it, and Phil wishing he was.

Everything was fine on the ride in.

"First guy with a tango kilo gets a surf-and-turf dinner next time we get the good chow in the Green Zone." The announcement in my earpiece came from Hub, our team leader, on the second chopper. "Lobster if you use your knife."

I keyed my throat mic. "Roger that. Powder's the only one without a knife kill, I believe. Maybe that pacifist hippy will get a little blood on his kit tonight."

Powder sat on the opposite bench, on the other side of my helo, preventing me from viewing the middle finger undoubtedly aimed in my direction.

Fifteen minutes later, the target city opened up below. As we approached the X, the AC-130 Spectre gunship flying above sparkled the target compound, bathing it in a white light that shone through our NVGs. At first glance, the three-story, dingy-white stucco building blended in with the rest of the neighborhood. But as we approached, we could see the roof was heavily fortified. Insurgents scrambled behind a Russian-made PKM, the light machine gun easily capable of shooting down our choppers. No one spoke as we approached, just raised our weapons and coolly began engaging targets from the circling choppers. Our minigun's violent buzz gave us all a confident rush of adrenaline as it ate up chunks of roof and building. Immediate return fire began sparking off the sides of our lightly armored helo.

I cinched down on my gunner's belt just before the pilot banked hard over the neighborhood, our nose aimed straight down, my body extended forward like an Olympic diver. I was strapped in securely, but that didn't stop my stomach from leaping into my throat. After a few evasive maneuvers, the pilot quickly brought us back on station, hovering just feet over the target roof, still taking fire. As point man, I hopped off the skids first and peeled left, M4 shouldered. Mini sonic booms snapped around me as I registered the cracks from half a dozen AK-47's. It's funny, when the bullets are close, they aren't that loud. More like someone snapping their fingers in your ear. These rounds were close. Their PKM sent 7.62 fire at the chopper at 855 meters per second. We needed to neutralize that weapon, and fast. My PEQ-15 laser found a target, and I fired two concise shots into the throat and chest of a thick middle-aged man wearing a white skullcap. He never had the chance to register surprise. The RPG launcher he had been raising toward our chopper clattered to his feet.

My focus went back to the PKM and the danger it posed to the Little Birds. Taking out the machine gun became my priority. Indeed, it was still sending fire at the departing helicopters' tail rotors. One pilot banked hard between two buildings, then dove steeply in a hair-raising evasive maneuver. For a second, it disappeared. I spun toward the sandbag cutout holding the belt-fed machine gun and two insurgents operating it. While calmly taking a knee, I reached over my shoulder for my Thumper and sent a flechette round directly into their nest. The explosion launched the men into the air, actually blowing one off the side of the roof. The volume of his scream faded as he fell to the ground. I could feel the blowback, smell the burnt flesh. Staring in awe, I turned to my buddy.

"You see that shit, man?"

Talon grinned, awed, and gave me a thumbs-up. Behind us, the Little Birds banked again to avoid what was left of the small-arms fire. Within seconds, they were gone. Now we were in the fight.

AK fire still sprayed through the air, gashing the roof, outlining me in shrapnel and small poofs of dust. Snaps. We spread out tactically, calmly and efficiently engaging targets until the AK fire ceased and

I heard the soft calls of "clear" coming down the line. I answered with a "clear" of my own and slammed in a fresh mag, eyes skimming the rooftop for threats. We stood upright, reengaging each of the downed tangos by shooting them in the face. Just to make sure. Wordlessly, we stacked at the roof door. I was first in the train. Powder squeezed my shoulder. Slowly, I placed my hand on the door handle. Unlocked. Everything was oddly quiet. No screaming mothers, no gunshots, no explosions. Just wisps of smoke, acrimonious smells telling the firefight's tale. A deep breath, the handle creaking as I rotated it down. I stayed behind the wall, gently pushed the door in. Nothing. Blackness, even through my night vision. Powder crossed in front of me. Entered. Moving. Filling the open space. Clearing the fatal funnel. Single-file, we slithered inside, eight green lasers urgently searching for work. Nothing. Stillness.

"Alpha 1, first floor secure." Hub's voice came through my earpiece, confident and steady, barely above a whisper.

"Roger that, Alpha 1. Roof and third floor secure. Alpha 2 coming down."

"Come down."

We progressed down the stairs, meeting Hub's team on the second level. Spreading out, clearing each room. Soundless. Empty. The team continued through the rest of the house until everyone ended up on the first floor. Bare and still. Our pucker factor eased, I took a knee on my helmet to suck on an energy gel and debrief.

"They must have all converged on the roof when they heard us coming," Powder said, cocking his Yankees cap sideways to run a sleeve across his forehead. "No joy on primary target. Another dry hole. Fucking intel retards." He spat the curse, Brooklyn accent thick. The dirt on his face turned dark and muddy after a shot of water from his Camelback. He scrunched his eyes and shook the water off like a wet dog, pissed. We all were.

Hub paced, bright eyes wild, slightly parting the front window's curtain with his rifle. He peeked out onto the street. Nothing. We all watched him, waiting for a reaction. For direction. Short, with especially dark features, he could have passed for a local with his unkempt hair and black beard. The curtain gently swished twice, back and forth, after he turned from the window.

"TOC, this is Alpha 1. We have six tango kilos on the roof. No sign of Caterpillar. The rest of the house is completely empty. Search turned up no intel, not even a thumb drive. Over."

He listened, staring blankly into a wall. Then: "Roger that."

He turned to us. "Move out. The Marines have the block secure and will give us a ride back to Camp Ramadi in MRAPs." Then, troubled: "Quiet out there."

Pops, a wily operator with more than twenty years in, spoke. "Yeah, it is. I don't like it. Too quiet. Our entrance would have woken the neighborhood. Where the hell is everyone?"

He was right. We should at least be getting hit with pot shots from neighborhood punks, if for nothing else than to score points with the real insurgents. The tranquility of the neighborhood was absolute, as if no air was getting in or out. It didn't make sense.

"If they're smart, they're huddled in their bathtubs quietly, afraid to let so much as a fart squeak out, lest the fire superiority of the United State of America rain hell upon their location." Powder paused here. "If they're smart, of course."

Hub shot him a glare, still pacing. Something caught his eye and he strode across the room, dropping into a squat against the far wall. Soon, scraping and scratching from his KA-BAR filled the furniture-less room.

"What you got there, Hub?" I asked, walking over. He had flaked away some of the glue holding the floor tiles together. After brushing debris, he lifted the tile with a piqued focus. Bright light shone back.

"Trapdoor," he muttered. The rest of the guys hustled over just in time to dive for cover, as a series of automatic fire from below shattered the loose flooring.

"Incoming!" someone yelled just as we hit the deck.

"No shit, Sherlock," was Hub's response. I made eye contact with him. He raised his chin, head motioning at the hole in the floor. I nodded once, then reached again for my Thumper.

"Grenade out." I chambered a close-range 40x46 grenade, which would spray buckshot upon explosion, and aimed for the hole. *BFOOOOT*, followed by the muffled thump and vibration of an explosion in tight quarters underneath us. Then, only the sporadic crinkle of plaster and pieces of the house falling to the ground. Silence.

Hub spoke softly into his collar.

"TOC, this is Alpha 1. We found a trapdoor and are taking fire. Hold those Marines. Over."

He slammed a new mag into his rifle, standing slowly. We all did the same, fanning out around the hole. Smoke still drifted upward, but a crude set of wooden stairs was visible. Hub and I again traded glances.

We moved toward the trapdoor. I took a breath. My foot gripped the top stair, and I stepped into the void. My ears rang enough that I couldn't hear my guys behind me, but I knew they were there.

Movement down the staircase was careful but quick, each footstep calculated, weapon raised. Drifting smoke made the scene dream-like. I couldn't see my feet, let alone hear my steps over the sirens in my head. When I reached the bottom I stopped. A horror shop awaited.

Even today, standing in the hallway outside Phil's room, the smell of that basement singes my nostrils, makes me dizzy. Blood, burnt flesh, brain matter, all come back to me. The stench of cordite, gunpowder, smoke. Above the disinfectant offense of industrial cleaning supplies, I smell it today. Under the glare of hospital lights reflecting off shined linoleum, I go back to that place. I now realize that what I saw changed me forever. One of the tiny imprints that make me the convoluted, fucked-up specimen I am today.

The basement ran the length of the house. Three industrial lights hung haphazardly, casting gloomy shadows in corners, on the walls. And there, chained to the ceiling so his toes just barely reached the floor, hung a man by the wrists. I squinted, took out my Maglite, and shined it on him. He was white, wearing what was left of a digital camouflage uniform. A Marine uni. As I got closer, I was aware of my teammates' movements behind me, but didn't acknowledge them. The face was distorted, puffy and bruised. Both eyes were swollen shut, and his jaw hung loosely. Dried blood clung in each ear.

My brain struggled to acknowledge what it was seeing. I inched forward through swirling smoke as if in a trance. Closer, closer, the image getting clearer and clearer. Soon I was inches away. The fog cleared and there was no mistaking that this was an American, a young Marine.

Hub went back on the radio.

"TOC, we have one US casualty. Request MEDEVAC."

Hub stepped forward. A spotlight attached to his rifle cut through the mist, a cone-shape beam illuminating his path. A camera was set up on a tripod, a black sheet hanging from the wall across it. That familiar, evil white script. I remember the Marine's morale patch stood out in my peripheral vision. His hands and fingers were angled in ways human hands and fingers were not meant to bend. Black holes spotted his bare feet. The torture he had endured was incomprehensible. He groaned, just barely. He was alive.

Movement flickered against the back wall. I wheeled toward it. There, a young insurgent, his first attempts at growing a beard having failed, lay sprawled on his stomach, trying to crawl away. His legs didn't appear to work. Everything below the waist was covered in blood from my grenade. Wide, angry eyes met mine. I'll never forget the hatred plastered across his face. There was no fear, only disgust. His arm stretched for an AK-47. He was far enough away that it wasn't within reach, but I shouldered my M4 anyway. The green dot painted his forehead. My finger slid to the trigger guard just as—

Hub's hand clasped my shoulder. At first I tensed, only easing when he firmed his grip. The boy had frozen, but was not afraid. His glare willed me to do it.

"Doc, take a look at that Marine," Hub called out, eyes still on the insurgent, his hand not leaving my shoulder. "See if you can make him more comfortable. Someone patch up that kid and flex cuff him.

We're double-time in five."

Everyone stiffened, knowing that it was our duty under the Geneva Convention to aid any wounded, even if he had been part of a terrorist cell that had tortured a United States service member. The thought of helping him made me grit my teeth, clench the rifle that much tighter.

"Easy," Hub soothed. "You don't want to spend the rest of your life in Leavenworth over this piece of shit."

He was right, but that didn't mean I was ready to let it go. Then it hit me who the Marine was: A patrol had been ambushed the prior week, and one of our casualties had not yet been recovered. Other SpecOps groups had been tasked with his recovery, but had thus far come up empty. This had to be him. Just a kid, nineteen, from Falls Church, Virginia, had graduated high school and shipped right off to Paris Island. Now he was here.

"Better to be judged by twelve than carried by six." My voice was cold, detached. Even I recognized that.

Hub was at a whisper now, trying his best to disarm.

"We need to get intel from him, brother. How else are we going to go after the people responsible for this? We're gonna patch him up, evac him out, and interrogate the shit out of him, and we're going to do it because it's our job. Roger?"

Me and the kid still had eyes locked on each other. I saw more in him in those thirty seconds than in people I had known my whole life. The rest of the squad stood around, half hoping I'd do it, the other half looking away so they wouldn't have to report it if I did.

My gun started to feel heavy, the metal electric. My grip tightened. I flexed my back, trying to get the blood flowing. Then, with an urgent scream, I lowered my weapon. Spat on the floor, chest heaving. Violently, I shrugged Hub's hand off, turned back to the ladder.

I waited upstairs, peering out a front window onto the empty street, brain rattled. The heavens carried no stars, no moon. The power had been cut to the neighborhood, and there wasn't a lot to see even with night vision. A white noise seemed to screech omnipotently over it all, or maybe it was a complete and absolute silence, I don't know. I was numb; in fact, the only sense being stimulated was from the standard Iraqi stench, unsympathetic and ever-present as an unrelenting apparition. The whole scene felt overly unnerving. I was ready to call it a night.

"Coming out," Hub said over the radio, and then we were all out the front door, jogging through the streets, headed for the Marine QRF. Other than a barking dog and our crunching footsteps, it was quiet. The insurgent was flex cuffed with a hood over his head, slung over Hubs's shoulder. He was out cold after the butt of a rifle prevented him from biting anyone else. Pops had the Marine in a fireman carry. We moved toward our extract a few blocks over.

I had been sure something was going to happen during the exfil. The feeling of impending contact wasn't just strong, it was unquestionable. I could feel it in the base of my neck, in my balls.

I remember seeing the Marine platoon a block ahead, standing around an MRAP, one of the young Marines smoking a cigarette. I remember thinking how dumb that was, which was right about the time the first explosion hit. Its roar sucked the air from the neighborhood like a vacuum. I'm told it was the first of many eruptions, which seemed to be coming from all sides. The ambush was on. A rocket landed in the middle of those Marines, scattering them and body parts. The next RPG landed no more than ten meters in front of me, sending me flying, a cloud of dust and frag speeding across my vision, crossing with images of shredded limbs, rivulets of blood muddying the dirt. Then, blackness.

When I came to, I was sprawled under an MRAP, the beefy trucks the Marines had driven in that were designed to withstand IED blasts. My body was under its rear, feet just dangling out the back. Black smoke hung like fog, making it impossible to tell what was going on. I tried to raise myself up, but my helmet smacked the vehicle's undercarriage. I had no idea where I was. There was so much gunfire it was hard to identify its direction, only that it was close. I crawled out the best I could, my hands frantically grasping around me. When they finally found metal, a wash of relief came over me. I gave my rifle a quick dusting, then thumbed the safety and loaded a new mag. I tried to stand, but dizziness and nausea felled me. The whirl in my ears was now deafening, a locomotive screaming through my head. I steeled myself and tried again.

A muffled yell sliced through the smoke and explosions, an arm wrapped around me.

"You all right, brother?!"

It was Hub. He helped me to my feet.

I rolled my shoulders and head, trying to clear the cobwebs. "Yeah, good to go. What's the SITREP?"

"We're pretty much surrounded. They were waiting for us, man. They moved in when the Marines set up, and just let us walk into the kill zone."

"Air support?"

"Danger close. A second QRF is en route, but we're going to have to fight our way out. Our squad is coordinating with the Marines. I could use another gun."

"Roger that," I said. "Where do you need me?"

Crouching, we left the safety of the MRAP to join the fight. The tortured Marine lay in the back. I couldn't tell if he was still alive. There was no sign of our prisoner.

When Phil finally stirs, I lean over the bed. I want to touch him, but I'm unsure where. He has no arms, and the burns from his chest up make any contact unbearable. I squeeze his foot.

"It's me. I'm here."

His face is badly scarred, leaving expressions to interpretation. A loud exhalation tells me he's aware of my presence.

His voice works, barely. It's scratchy and just above a murmur, but with some effort, he finds it.

"Hey, fucker. You bring any strippers?"

"Only if you're looking for me to get naked. I can pop in some "Salt Shaker" and rock your world if you want."

What's left of his lips form in a passable grin.

"If I had hands I'd flick you off." Because of catastrophic scarring, prosthetics are not an option for Phil.

"If you had any hands you wouldn't need a stripper."

The goggles he wears to mist his eyes hiss, sending his face into a grimace.

"Don't think I'll ever get used to that."

"I thought you were getting out of here."

"Me too. Turns out the VA won't pay for the private rehab facility. Says I can get the same care here."

I grit my teeth, turn away. Phil never gets pissed, hasn't once since we got hit. I, on the other hand ...

"Those mother—"

He cuts me off quickly. "Forget it, brother." He squirms, uncomfortable. "Nothing we can do about it."

A deep breath calms me, at least to the point where I can address his discomfort. "You all right? What can I do?"

Turning his head seems like a great effort, but he manages it. The rest of his body just lies there, unmoving, like a lumpy mattress. As best he can, he focuses on me.

"There is something. Come here." The scratch is lower now, just audible. I lean forward.

"Closer." I do.

"Kill. Me." He hisses it. I've never heard a more urgent request in my life. Again: "Kill me. I'm dead already; someone just forgot to tell the rest of my body."

A reaction eludes me, at least right off. I'd be lying if I said I'd never considered that he'd be better off if the IED had killed him. Hell, killed us both, put us both out of the separate but equal hells we've been enduring since. I shake off that last thought, sick at myself for comparing our struggles. At least with mine, I have the ability to fight back, to end it at any time.

"I can't do that, brother, not now," I tell him, apologetic.

He scowls, and even through the burns and scar tissue there is no mistaking the anger. I turn away, taken aback by his request, his reaction. He gathers himself and musters all the energy he can to convince me.

"You're the only one who can save me. You think Westhead would do this for me? Any of the other guys? It's. Only. You. I know you have it in you."

He shakes now, wiggling the stubs jutting from his shoulders. I can't help but imagine arms flailing, and realize he must be doing the same thing.

"I can't do it, Phil. I'm working on something, something to get all the bastards back who are responsible for what happened to you. To what happened to all our guys, the people who through willful neglect, apathy, stupidity, or downright murder got so many of our men killed. Or worse."

"A lot of people fit in that bucket."

"Damn right there are."

To my recollection, the rest of the firefight had been quick. Admittedly, those sentiments are relative, as time has an obtuse way of stretching and contracting during battle. It's often hard to tell the difference between two minutes and two hours while engaged in that level of stress, so it's a subjective observation. But even through the throbbing head pain and vertigo, when I summon the images of close-range warfare from that day, whatever it is in our brains that designates length of time tells me it went by in a flash.

A Ranger QRF arrived on station in two Strykers, scattering the insurgents. These weren't the hardened zealots hell-bent on death—ours and theirs. These were just your run of the mill local punks, happy to take AQI's bounty money for any American deaths. They just happened to be organized that day. When the Strykers showed up along with an Apache show of force, they scooted back down their rat holes.

As quickly as the ambush had started, it was over. While blurry,

I recall being placed in the back of the MRAP with the other casualties. At some point my head had been bandaged, and I was ambulatory.

"TOC, we have one urgent casualty, prep surgery. We'll need to CASEVAC to Baghdad. Have a full trauma team on board. Out copy."

I whipped my head as fast as it would allow, facing the corpsman speaking into a hand-held receiver.

"No, I'm fine, man, just a bump!" I yelled to him, rising up on an elbow, "I don't need to go to Baghdad!" He barely acknowledged me. I started to reassure him again, then got a better look at what he was doing.

There wasn't much light in the back of the MRAP. I narrowed my eyes to get an idea of our surroundings. I could make out my rifle at my side. Next to it, the young Marine. Dead. On the other side of him, the medic, on his knees, straddling someone. He had a freeze dried plasma packet in his teeth and was preparing an IV. It wasn't me he was reporting on. It was Powder, writhing in pain underneath him from a sucking chest wound. I scooted closer to them, sliding when the vehicle accelerated through a corner.

"Hang on, brother!" I yelled over the engine's rumble. I took his hand, dilated pupils locking onto mine. The corpsman continued his work.

"Maya told me that Junior got in a fight on the bus last week," Powder breathed. A lot of energy went into the words.

"Yeah? Well, you can ground him when you get home."

He tried to pull himself up, shook his head. The medic held him back down.

"No. He was. Protecting his sister. Kid put gum in her hair."

"Sheepdog."

He smiled. A lonely, resigned smile.

"Tell my kids—" he started, but I cut him off.

"Don't start that shit Johnny, you're gonna tell them yourself!" It sounded banal and I instantly regretted it.

His mouth opened, wide, sucking at insufficient air. He squirmed under the corpsman's grip, fighting to find my face. His hand searched for mine, clenching it strongly. Not like he needed the support, but like he wanted to show me that it was going to be okay. I leaned closer. We were nose to nose.

He fought to form the words. Slurring but intelligible: "Tell them I'm sorry. Tell them I love them, and I'll see them again real soon."

His hand went slack in mine. His eyes, still open but glazed over. I slumped to the floor.

"Things happen in battle, in war."

"They do."

"You have to let it go."

"Can't do that, buddy."

His head circles clumsily around his shoulders. I can tell he's thinking of something.

"The Basting Institute."

"What about it?"

"Islamic. Crescent Center."

"Yeah?"

"Those—that was you, wasn't it?"

Reflexively, I glance at the door. We're still alone. "It was a good start, wasn't it?"

The MRAP had stopped, suddenly. Through thick blast-resistant glass I saw the two Strykers ahead of us weren't moving. Blocking our path was a burning pile of machinery.

"Fuck," I mumbled, not surprised. For some reason we were taking the same route back. Of course the insurgents would have the road blocked.

The convoy reversed, meaning we were now the lead vehicle. Our driver took the first left, the natural way around the blockade. I started to yell, "No!" to him, but it was too late. It felt like the ground fell from under us, rather than being thrown in the air. The explosion was deafening, followed immediately by a low humming deep in my brain.

When the rear hatch of our MRAP opened, it was in slow motion. Hub stood in the haze. Gripping my rifle, I was just able to slide out to him.

"Set up a perimeter while we get the casualties into the other vehicles. Gotta assault through the kill zone!" He was screaming, I'm sure of it, but I could hear nothing. I didn't need to.

Rocks began to kick up around us, one or two at a time, then everywhere, like popcorn popping. I moved and began firing into the houses where the muzzle flashes were coming from.

A break in the gunfire allowed me to get a glimpse of Hub. He was communicating with the Rangers, who had taken up a firing position in an irrigation ditch along the side of the road. A dull glimmer from a Stryker's headlights illuminated them. That's when I saw the wires.

"Bomb!" I called out, pointing, trying to direct them away from it. Hub turned, followed the wire with his eyes. The IED was smack in the middle of the convoy. Instead of taking cover, he ran toward it.

"Hub, what the fuck are you doing! Get back here!"

I hadn't been able to hear my own yells, so I have no idea if they ever reached him. He never said. A burning house framed his silhouette, kneeling, brushing away mud and garbage to reveal a 155-millimeter howitzer shell. Wires spread out from it like a skeleton's fingers, running through the irrigation ditch and over a mud wall. Four or five Rangers scrambled out of the ditch as Hub lifted the shell, evacuating it like, he would later say, "a turd on the counter." A green glow in a window four or five houses away caught my eye as his arms extended. He heaved the IED away from the Rangers, over the wall, falling backward into the ditch with the effort. I sprinted at him just as a bright flash went off. Shards of metal and ball bearings scattered like bullets. We found out later they were coated in human feces to increase the likelihood of infection. I flew skyward and woke up three days later in Germany.

"Mr. Hubbard, how are we today?"

Phil gives his best attempt at a smile to the nurse, an authoritative, gray-haired lady in worn scrubs. She looks him over, then at me with slightly less affection.

"Another day, another dollar," he says. "Don't worry, my friend was just leaving."

"Good, let's not overdo it, sir," she tells him, but it's directed at me. "You have hyperbaric oxygen therapy today, so it's going to be a long one."

"Aren't they all," he whispers before glowering back at me. "Please."

VIRGINIA BEACH

"Feels like right after 9/11."

"I barely remember 9/11. Just my mom waking me up that morning. She sat on the edge of my bed and told me that some bad men had killed a lot of people and we needed to pray for them, but that Daddy and his friends were going to get them and that we'd be safe."

"Daddy?"

"Her words."

Westhead chuckled.

Nate turned from the window, scenery whisking by. "She told me it was my job to protect the family when he was gone, so I remember putting on these camo pajamas I had and getting my toy rifle. I sat in the living room, watching the street the whole day, waiting for the bad guys."

Westhead considered his passenger, again remembering his age. "It's hard to picture a time before 9/11. For your generation, I guess there never really was."

"Nope. And the dominos keep falling to this day."

"They sure do. More so now than ever. It's like we've backslid and there's a cloud hanging over the whole country."

"I don't know. I feel like there's been a solidarity these past couple of weeks. A sense that we're in this together as a country. Even as a kid, I remember that people were friendlier in the weeks after, said hello at the gas pump. Smiled at each other. It made us realize what was important as a country."

"For a few days at least, it did. This feels different. I can't help but think these bombings are just the beginning. And at least after 9/11 we knew who was responsible, had someone to go after."

"Is your team tasked with finding whoever is doing this?"

Westhead downshifted the Jeep to pass an 18-wheeler. They were headed back to Virginia, stomachs full and bodies rested after some much-needed family time at the Butler home.

"You know I can't talk about that, you don't have the clearance. The organization I work for is an ordnance disposal unit. You ever want to learn more than that, you won't ask about it."

Nate stared out the window without reaction. Even as a SEAL, he knew that JOE-CAG's mission was off-limits to him. "What did I say?" he replied. "Just making conversation."

They sat in silence, listening to talk radio. There were still only theories about who was responsible for the attacks, and a retired general was speaking about the possibility the US military was involved.

"I have it on good authority that the explosives used in the bombings of both the Basting Institute and Crescent Islamic Center were not only military-grade, but an experimental type of plastic explosives in the RDX family that is exponentially more powerful than dynamite. This strain of RDX has only been made available to a few select Special Operations groups. Groups that fall under the secretive Joint Special Operations Command, or JSOC. Tier 1 organizations like Delta Force and SEAL Team 6. Even your normal SEAL teams are not yet using these explosives."

"Bullshit," scoffed Nate. Then, after a moment of thought: "Wait. You guys really using a type of RDX we aren't?"

Westhead looked concerned, ignoring the question. He turned the radio up.

"My sources also tell me that the ammunition used to shoot those innocent civilians in Washington was a developmental 7.62 ultra-match-grade polymer round made by Global Tactical Systems specifically for JSOC. The manufacturer has assured me that this ammo has only been made available to top-secret United States military units. Let's just say, you can't pick this ammo up at your local gun show. Even your traditional military forces don't have access to these rounds."

Westhead bristled at the words. An alarm was going off in his head. "I knew about the explosives, but the ammo is news to me. Did the sniper really use our developmental ammunition? If so, Kopen's hiding that piece of information from us. Why?"

Nate watched as Westhead spoke, aware that the questions were rhetorical. Westhead was trying to piece something together, and Nate knew interrupting him wouldn't accomplish anything other than making him go silent.

"Unless ..." he continued, then stopped, suddenly remembering his passenger. "Never mind."

"What?"

"Nothing ..."

"What?"

"I gotta make a stop." Westhead ignored a yellow, rapidly changing to red, light. "I'll drop you off at my place first."

"I guess there is no chance of convincing you to let me go with you."

"Good guess."

Westhead took his iPhone out of the cup holder and switched to music, ending the general's dissertation. He leaned back, thinking, fingers drumming to The Who. He wouldn't say it in front of Nate, but what the general was saying could be true. He had been right about the RDX. And if what he said about the ammunition ... Was it possible?

He turned the radio up, singing along. "*You better, better, you bet—*"

"Damn, Chief, you're old. What is this crap?"

Westhead scowled. "You don't know The Who? Get your head out of your ass, kid; this is a classic. No auto-tuned, 'make it rain on dem hoes' like you punks listen to."

Nate scoffed, mumbled, "Get off my lawn!" just low enough for plausible deniability. They pulled up to Westhead's house.

"End of the line, kid. Don't drink all my beer. I'll be back soon."

HAMPTON, VA

Westhead walked briskly up Nailer's driveway. The cottage sat on a large lot backing Mill Creek, views of Fort Monroe, the Chesapeake Bay, and Atlantic Ocean past that. The yard was long and tidy, sloped gently until carrying the creek. A ten-foot-high iron fence with ornamental spiked corners medieval-ized the yard; motion-activated lights and closed-circuit cameras that Nailer could monitor from his phone modernized it. Baxter, his ten-year-old Rottweiler, wide-faced and thick-shouldered like his master, raced across the front yard to meet Westhead at the gate. The dog's greeting was contradictory to the philosophies of its owner, appearing angrier and more vicious than it actually was. That owner stood at the water's edge, sand wedge in hand and cigar in mouth, watching his visitor approach.

"Wasn't expecting company, bro."

"Last minute stop. Looking for spacemen?" Westhead asked him.

"Not during daylight."

"How was your time off?"

Nailer's casual gesture implied nothing special. "Stayed here. Slept, mostly. Hung with the wife." He reached down to a cooler at his feet. "Beer?"

Westhead took it. "I'll take one of those Robustos, too, if you got it." Nailer, the cigar aficionado, reached past the pistol holstered to his left hip and pulled out a leather cigar case from his back pocket. He passed over a long, unlabeled cigar. From his other pocket came wooden matches and a silver cutter. Just holding it in his hand, Westhead could smell its sweetness, the dry bite of the tobacco. He put the cigar to his nose and inhaled. "What is it?"

"Nicaraguan. Half Ligero, half Seco. That's what gives it that spicy taste. Oscuro wrapper. Just rolled these this morning."

Westhead put the match to his face, smoke enveloping him. He pushed out a thick, gray cloud and spat.

"Did you end up visiting Phil?"

"Actually, I didn't." Nailer made a face. He swung the golf club, sending a ball plopping into the water. "Stevens called the other night to remind me that we're Alert 60 status and that if I was in Bethesda when we got the call I wouldn't make it." He squinted into the water. "Pissed me off, you want to know the truth. Especially when they *told* us to visit him before we were secured."

"And you listened to Stevens? Doesn't sound like you."

"Believe it or not, I did. To be honest, I'm not sure why."

"An Alert 60 is an Alert 60."

"That's bullshit, and you know it. You were an hour away all weekend? When we have a real-world op, we always get more than an hour, and he knows that. Besides, we're sidelined." He swung again, another splash and ripples. "But more than that, it was just strange the way he told me. It was a strange phone call, all around. Can't really explain it."

Westhead drank from his beer and puffed on his cigar. The breeze was warm off the water. A boat sputtered in the distance. Another beautiful day.

"Don't you worry about running out of balls?" Off Nailer's side-eye, he motioned toward the water.

"I do a night dive every so often, collecting. It's nice to be down there without worrying about getting blown up."

"Surprised you don't have your shoreline mined."

"Who says I don't?" Nailer leaned down and opened another beer.

Westhead started again, gaze land ho. "I'll admit that Blade has been a little off lately," he said. "But I think we all would be if we had ADM Bradley and the president of the United States up our ass the way he does. Him and Hagen have pressures we have no idea about."

"Agreed. Me? Hell, I'm happy to just be a shooter. Glorified knuckle dragger. Tell me who to take out and let me get drunk after I've ended their time on this planet. Save the politics for the politicians."

"Roger that."

They puffed, they drank, they stared across the water. Then: "I don't know. He probably just wanted to bust my balls. I could have gone. Should have gone. What's he gonna do?" Nailer turned to his guest. "Anyway, you're not here to talk about my weekend or Stevens's crazy ass. What's up?"

"Actually, I kind of am, in a way. Just gonna come out with it, brother, and you feel like hitting me, then go right ahead and take a swing. But I'm your team leader, and it's my responsibility to ask."

"Can't say I like the sound of that. Shoot."

"What were you doing with that 7.62 in your locker before Atlas Revenge? You haven't shot that ammo since you were sniping in the Teams."

Nailer's face wrinkled. "What difference does it make to you? Maybe I was thinking about taking a sniper system on that op."

"Don't give me that. I haven't seen you use anything other than an assault rifle in our past four op cycles." Then, quieter: "You know that 7.62 ultra-match-grade rounds were used in the DC attack."

Nailer glared into Westhead, lips pursed, eyes ablaze.

"Are you kidding me, brother? What are you saying?"

"Just what I asked. What were you doing with that ammo?"

"You think I used it to shoot pedestrians on their lunch break in Washington, DC before I blew up the Basting Institute?" He crumpled a beer can angrily.

"Didn't say that."

Nailer took a step forward, then leaned down into the cooler to drop the empty. His breathing was heavy, sending air whistling through his nose.

"Yeah, I took some ammo home for personal use, so what? You've never swiped an extra flashlight from supply? Some batteries for your generator? I spend plenty of my own money on gear, I figured I was owed a few shells. You gonna turn me in to that FBI agent? To Blade? Get me a counseling chit?"

"I'm not trying to burn you, Nailer, I'm trying to protect this unit."

"Worry about your fucking self, Chief. You sure as shit have access to that ammo. As much RDX-X as you want, especially as a team leader. Who's to say it's not you? Or Pos? Or Stevens? Or some shit for brains jarhead who got a dishonorable for playing grab-ass with the CO's daughter and on his way out swiped some explosives from a JTFX with Force Recon in 29 Palms? Or some weekend warrior who has the passcode to a National Guard armory on Fort Dix? You better have some goddamn proof before you come over here, accusing me of that shit, asshole."

"Roger that." Westhead crushed his beer can and headed back up the lawn. "See you at the hospital tomorrow morning?"

"You know it."

VIRGINIA BEACH

A late summer sun was just sliding into the bay when Westhead arrived home. Nate stood on the deck, watching Tex chase gulls on the sand.

"How'd it go?"

"How'd what go?"

"Whatever you went to do."

"Don't worry about it."

"Are these attacks coming from within JOE-CAG?"

"You need to stop listening to the news. I happen to know that general was forced out for leaking classified information. It's a miracle he didn't go to prison. Now he goes on TV and radio and talks out his ass."

"Doesn't mean he wasn't right."

Westhead stared into the horizon. "No, it doesn't. The real answer? I don't know."

They watched Tex run down to the water's edge, jumping off his front paws and biting at the breaking waves. There were few things happier than a dog at play.

"That really pisses me off," Nate said, watching.

"What's does? Oh, that." Then: "I don't blame you, man. Listen, I've always liked Tammy, but you can't let her get away with keeping Spence."

Nate's face reddened, and he spun away from the beach. "You're right. Fuck this. I'm going to get my dog."

The porch door slammed, leaving Westhead suddenly alone with the sounds of an empty beach. "Nate, hold up! We're coming! Tex, come on, let's go! Want a treat?"

The big lab's attention piqued with the prospect of food, he bounded up the stairs, tongue lolling. Soon they were all out front, jumping into an old Ford Explorer that Nate barely slowed to let them in.

"Plan?" Westhead asked, situating himself in the passenger's seat.

"Get. My. Dog. Back."

"I got that part, I do. But what kind of Team guy would you be without a mission plan?"

"Good point. Ideas?"

"I was thinking a classic frontal diversion, with a recon element flanking the target."

"Interesting. Go on."

"I'll go to the front door. Knock. Assuming Tammy is home, I'll ask for you, make small talk when she says you're not there. You know, charm her. We can talk about what a prick you are. I think they call that 'common ground.'"

"Good luck getting a word in."

"Then you sneak in from the back, grab your boy, and poof, vamos, we're gone."

"I can work with that."

The Explorer skidded up to a dull, four-floor, garden-style apartment complex. The evening light was fading, and even this far off the boardwalk, the sidewalks were crowded with tourists leaving the beaches, sun kissed, relaxed, headed to happy hours and family dinners.

"Her car is here, she's definitely home. Probably hasn't left the couch all day. Oprah and bonbons."

"Okay. Go around back. I'll wait until you're in position before I knock." Westhead took out his cell phone and dialed. "Put in your Blue-tooth. I'll call you and leave the phone in my pocket so you can hear in case she goes back in."

"Roger that. But give me a few minutes. The apartment is on the third floor."

Westhead looked confused. "How are you going to get in?"

"I'm going to climb up the neighbor's balcony and pick the sliding glass door. Won't be the first time. Just the first time sober."

"You break your neck I'm telling ADM Bradley I was in a strip club all day."

Nate took off in a hunched scurry into the dusk. After what he deemed a proper amount of time, Westhead spoke into his phone.

"You in position?"

The response came as a series of grunts, scrapes, and a muffled curse. Then, faintly:

"Yeah, I'm on the balcony. The damn lady who lives on the second floor was watering her plants. I had to hang from the bottom of hers until she went in."

"Cry me a river. I'm going up."

Westhead took the stairs two at time until he reached the third floor. He knocked on the second door on the right, 33.

"Dan?" The door partially opened and a pretty young lady's head and shoulders stuck out. "Something happen to Nate?"

Westhead raised both hands disarmingly. "No, no nothing like that. We were supposed to go to dinner and his phone must have died. I was wondering if he was here."

Tammy opened the door wider, suspicious, a glass of white wine in hand. From inside, music played. Someone was on the couch; he couldn't tell who.

"Nate's home? He's supposed to be deployed. I thought he was in Turkey or something."

"He is. Was. I mean, some men from his platoon had to come back for a quick trip."

"Well, he wasn't staying here much before he left. I don't know if he told you, but we're getting a divorce."

Westhead couldn't resist. "Really? No ... never saw that coming."

The severity of her sneer should have alarmed him, or at least surprised him, but it didn't. When the door flew inward, he was just able to get his foot in position to stop it from slamming into his face.

"Tammy, come on, talk to me! I'm sorry, that was rude." He lowered his voice to a whisper. Soothing-like. He hoped. "I apologize. I just want to make sure everything is okay with you. And him. You know the way he is, it's hard for him to talk about his feelings."

"Yeah, and the rest of you gossip girls are open books."

He grinned, sheepishly by design, his best *you got me* face.

A bang came from the back of the house, and he heard a howl. Tammy turned her head inside.

"Spence! Stop that." She turned back to Westhead.

"I don't know what you're up to Dan, but Nate isn't here, his stuff isn't here, and he's not welcome here."

Before a response could be concocted, there was movement next to Tammy. The door swung out wider.

"Dan Westhead."

He felt the air rush from his lungs. Shit.

"Hey there, Mary Anne," he cooed. "Didn't know you were here."

"Don't give me that Texas twang, you prick, I know your tricks. That piece of shit husband of mine with you?"

"Adam? No, no, he's still on base, I think. We're leaving in a couple days for a training op. I think he's prepping for that."

Both Tammy and Mary Anne took sips from long-stemmed glasses, hands on hips.

"Sure you are." Then: "Someone's here you may want to see, Dan. Or may not."

Westhead felt himself shrinking. He braced for the ambush. "Jack? I really hope it's Jack." He had a feeling it wasn't Jack.

She turned her head, but the dancing eyes never left his. "Not Jack.

Sara, look what the cat drug in."

Westhead let a nervous chuckle escape. They had no way of knowing how sweaty his palms were. He wiped them on khaki shorts just the same.

"Sara, how are you? How have you been? Everything good?" The squeakiness of his voice and awkward laugh seemed to bolster this gauntlet of angry females, arms crossed in a united display of feminine solidarity.

"I'll tell you, for such a big tough guy, you sure whimper like a little girl." Again, Tammy spun back into the house: "Spence, quiet down back there!"

"You look great, Sara, you do." He started to backpedal, took his phone out of his pocket. His words came louder. "But I should be shoving off, gotta meet Nathan, I'll tell him you guys say hello." He put the phone to his ear like he was making a call, hearing the hiss of Nate.

"Hold. On. One more minute," he breathed. Westhead could make out a struggle through the phone, the same commotion from inside the house. All three ladies turned.

"What is going on with that dog?" Tammy said, heading inside.

"Tammy, no, wait!" Westhead called out. "Don't, um, go in yet. Do you know where Nate keeps his, um, DVDs? I wanted to borrow, uh, *Tommy Boy.*"

The words trailed off as all parties now realized this most certainly was not a social call. Tammy's gaze alternated back and forth from her living room to the perspiring SEAL on her stoop. Suddenly, she bolted inside.

"Spence!" she called out. "Come here boy, come to Mommy!" Yelling, now: "Mary Anne, don't let that piece of shit leave! I'm calling the cops!"

That statement did it for him, and with a holler to Nate, wherever he was, he took off, leaping from landing to landing, his feet hitting about every fifth stair.

He soon reached the front of the complex, completing his mad dash to the parked Explorer, when a white-and-tan missile flashed by him. Nate passed quickly thereafter, arms working like a windmill.

"Get in the car!" he yelled, ripping open the driver's side door. Spence jumped in behind him. The car peeled out, Westhead only half in.

"Holy shit, that was close!" Nate exclaimed, grinning into the rearview mirror like a successful bank robber. "They don't train us to get a sixty-pound squirming puppy off a third-floor balcony!"

"So how the hell did you get him down?"

"I tucked my shirt in and stuck him under it and shimmied down each balcony. Man, he wasn't crazy about it, squirming and biting the whole time. The lady on the second floor started hitting me with a broom!" He rubbed his head.

"Worth it?"

"Hell yeah." He reached back and rubbed the dog's wagging head. "They don't call them man's best friend for nothing."

LITTLE CREEK

It's a docile morning, a few hours before I have to head over to the hospital. Upon return from the nation's capital, sleep had been impossible to come by, leaving my head weightless even after three cups of coffee. It's only with a hard lift followed by an ocean swim and beach run that my headache dulls to a light throb. I decide to make an appearance at headquarters.

The team doesn't have to report until tomorrow morning, but a few guys are trickling in for PT and mission prep. What else are we going to do? Hang out with friends? These are our only friends. Our families get sick of us pretty quickly if we spend too much time at home. Days off are rarely days off. There's always gear to square away, ops to prep, pranks to fashion. I notice Hagen's car and pop into his office to see if there are any updates.

Tactical boots are propped on his desk, an intelligence report in his lap. I feel overdressed, freshly showered in jeans and a polo. His athletic shorts ride high, a faded blue UDT/SEAL instructor sweatshirt stretching over the powerful upper body.

"Hey there, Commander, you leave the compound at all this weekend?"

He closes the folder. Bags pull tired eyes lower. Creases run deep across his forehead, as if in a constant squint. I think he looks worn, old. Hagen had left his office in Hoboken on that fateful Tuesday morning in 2001, squinting into the sun, dazed, tasting the smoke billowing from Lower Manhattan. Like the rest of the country, he had been dumbstruck at what he was seeing on CNN. The difference was, he did something about it. He was a second year trader at a small firm, two years removed from a Wharton MBA. By lunchtime he found himself standing outside the navy recruiter's office in Jersey City. He never made it back to the office.

"I did. I think my kids even recognized me. I know that Karen did, every insult was dead on."

My smile is forced. I don't care about his kids. "They gotta be getting old now."

"Stephen is eleven, Madison fourteen. Going on twenty-four. Somehow they convinced their mother to let them get a puppy while we were gone. I get to sleep in my bed for two nights, and guess who has to get up in the middle of the night to take him out? If I complain, she just tells me I don't get to make these decisions when I'm never home."

"You're a terrible parent and spouse."

"You would think so. So what's up?"

"Nothing, just checking in. I half expected Agent Kopen to be in here asking about match-grade ammo."

"To be honest, I did too."

"Anything from The Activity on al-Baghdadi's whereabouts?"

He holds up the file. "Actually, there is. The team leads are being recalled and will be briefed this afternoon. I don't think this stand-down is going to last long."

"Good to hear. You headed to the hospital?"

The folder falls to his desk. "Soon as I'm done with this."

NAVAL MEDICAL CENTER
PORTSMOUTH, VA

The hospital seemed tame, on this a day of rest, its subdued atmosphere lending itself to an image of temporary tranquility. The few inhabitants walking its halls seemed actors in a formula film, serious-looking nurses moving swiftly, concerned visitors searching for room numbers. It was either late Sunday morning or early afternoon, the quiet time when most people are wherever they may be: sleeping it off, the parish picnic, a long bike ride, maybe. Westhead and Nate had arrived for the bone marrow drive well before it began and were making an effort to assist Doc Soto while bothering him as little as possible. It wasn't going well.

"Hey, Doc, where do you want the sign-in table?" Westhead hollered. Soto, round, dark, with sleepy eyes and a thin goatee, turned sharply from the group of nurses he was addressing.

"Dammit, Dan, can't you see I'm in the middle of something? Stop acting like a kid on Christmas. I told you, we're all set."

"Just trying to help, buddy." Westhead took no offense. Soto was the type of guy that had no filter, no governor. If he thought it, he spoke it, political correctness or personal feelings be damned. He had one speed, full bore, and you either got on board or got the hell out of the way.

"Well, you're not. You two are a pain in my ass. Go rub one out in the bathroom or something. I don't care where you go, just stop interrupting me."

Properly rebuked, they ambled farther down the bright corridor.

"Nice guy," Nate commented as they approached a vending machine for coffee.

"He is. Best corpsman I ever worked with. At least a few teammates on Team 2 wouldn't be alive, it weren't for Doc Soto. And I wouldn't have these three fingers." He stuck out the first three crooked and scarred fingers on his right hand. His trigger hand. "Humvee flipped in Iraq with my hand out the window holding onto the roll bar. Crushed these fingers. They were hanging together by cartilage.

Doc saved them ... and my career."

"I was wondering why that hand always looked like gnarled tree branches. Thought you were just born deformed."

"I can still make a fist, boy, don't you forget that."

"Any time you feel strong, old man."

"What's with the old man crap? Early thirties never looked so good."

Nate stopped, genuinely shocked to think about that. He had looked up to Westhead since he was a boy. It was hard to believe he had been in the military for only a dozen or so years.

"Jeez, I think I like that reaction even less. Wait until you're my age, whippersnapper. These types of years are hard on a man."

"If I make it that long."

Awareness of their mortality wasn't merely a subconscious given as it was with most people. For whatever reason, the Creator had decided to give Man the knowledge that one day He would die. For men regularly sent to war, that reality traversed a road with considerably less pavement than your average citizen's. Unbounded proximity to death meant their own was a constant and recognizable possibility. For some, it even seemed inevitable. They were fine with that, and had, in general, accepted that truth. But that didn't mean their behavior was not influenced by that acceptance. A sense of urgency, a race against an unseen clock, characterized all that they did, even if not consciously.

The automatic doors swished open, and they emerged into a bright, if not brutal, summer haze. Nothing around them seemed rushed in the heat, no urgency from the scene's players. For the moment, everything just was as it was intended to be. No war, no death, no sacrifice. Periodic lulls in sparse traffic amplified the uneven chirping of birds. Even the wind announced itself in a tangible fashion, whispering through the thick green boughs of cedar trees sprinkled throughout the hospital grounds. They paused, taking it all in, without consideration. It was as if these two men had been plucked from their natural setting and accidentally dropped into this picturesque modicum of tranquility, two out-of-place characters sticking out like ducks in the desert.

They stood in the morning, uninterrupted, for several minutes. Trying to assimilate. Every so often, the glass doors would slide open behind them, the motion a sudden reminder of where they were, what they were doing. Just before it got strange, a deep throttle chopped through the quietude. A large motorcycle holding an even larger man stopped feet from them on the sidewalk.

"Dos, my brother. First to arrive." Westhead shook the man's hand and took him in a bear hug.

He was tall and broad-shouldered, strands of brown-and-gray hair shooting out from under a small black helmet. His face, leathery, used, not from the type of sun exposure that comes from sitting poolside. He raised himself slowly, still straddling the Harley, which somehow looked small and insignificant under him.

Westhead introduced. "Dos, this is Nate Butler, new guy in Echo platoon, Team 2. Cheyenne's his sister."

Dos made no initial motion to greet Nate, no effort at sociability. Rather, he inspected him, removing his sunglasses to fully scan the young man.

"I know who he is. That's my old platoon. Lot of tradition there."

Nate nodded, respectful.

"Well, good bloodline, anyway."

"You serve with my father?"

Dos took him in again with more than his eyes, searching for something. Evidently, he found it. "Someday, we'll have beers. I can tell you quite a few stories about your old man. We'll start with the one about the garter snake, Twinkies, and jumper cables." He flicked his head at Westhead. "Chief, you remember that one, you were there."

Westhead actually went a shade whiter and grimaced. "Another time, another place."

"I suppose you're right. I think there's a rule about telling that one anywhere there's electricity and running water. Certainly sober. Anyway, Butler, pleasure meeting you. Look me up you ever need anything." It was clear he meant it.

Nate gripped his hand and thanked him.

"Check in with Doc, he's harassing someone in there," Westhead told Dos. "He'll take a cheek swab and blood sample. If it comes back a match, her doctor will call to schedule further testing."

Dos nodded and started for the lobby. He turned back. "I'm looking forward to walking her down the aisle one day."

The doors parted, and he was gone.

"Dos?"

Westhead chuckled. "Yeah. As in Dos Equis. The most interesting man in the world. To be honest, no one is really sure of his background. I've heard everything from his parents were Buddhist missionaries to he was an orphan raised in Chechnya. If you ask him, you'll get a different tale each time."

"I thought I heard an accent."

"Yeah, that changes too. Not a guy you want to cross. He wrestles bears. No, really. He's wrestled a bear. All types of wild animals, in fact. We had a workup in central Florida some years back, deep in the swamps. One night after a few cold ones, he broke into the gator house and jumped in the water with a bunch of them. They said the next morning, when the hillbillies came to feed them, the crocs wouldn't even come out of the water to eat. They had to get a whole new batch. Those alligators were so scarred that they wouldn't perform for the tourists anymore."

Nate chuckled. If one had to picture a bear-and-gator-wrestling Frogman, that very image had just strolled through those doors.

"I'd like to see Cheyenne's future-husband's face if that guy ends up walking her down the aisle. Probably would turn and run."

"And who could blame him," Westhead agreed. Then, his expression further brightened, gaze pulled magnetically toward the parking lot. He let out a low whistle. "Not like this pretty face."

Nate snapped to rigid attention when he saw the object of Westhead's remark. The commander of JSOC, his smile welcoming and bright, walked alongside COL Stevens and CDR Hagen. ADM Bradley's starched white uniform and close shave—and of course, gold Trident bright and glistening—levied a dramatic incongruence to the ragged, burly unkempts keeping pace behind him.

First in that pack was Thor, elbows bent to engorge each bicep, closely followed by a line of JOEs posturing good-naturedly behind the brass.

"Maybe because Smurfette and Cheyenne are the same height and have the same hairstyle, he'll be a match," Westhead taunted. He received a good laugh and threatening gesture for the remark before correcting himself "Well, you two *used* to have the same type of hair. Now she more resembles you, sir."

ADM Bradley widened his smile, removing his lid and placing it in the crook of his arm. The exposed head—spherical, shiny, and gloriously bald—tapered down to a sharp chin. Like the rest of his appearance, his dome's condition displayed the same meticulousness he undoubtedly put into everything.

"Dan, good to see you. And on American soil, no less, on a day when the sun is shining and birds are chirping." He took Westhead's hand in both of his. It was a forceful and affectionate embrace, the type forged by shared life-and-death experiences.

"Good day to be an American, sir," he responded. "Thank you for coming." He then gestured to Nate. "Sir, this is Nate Butler, Team 2, Echo platoon. The girl's brother. First deployment, and he's already a meat eater."

The admiral turned to Nate. "I know Petty Officer Butler. I had the honor of securing his Hell Week. I recall you as a young man, Nathan. I doubt you remember this, but I presented the flag to Spencer Detse's mother at his funeral." Nate did. "I know after your father passed, you two were close. You're walking in some large footprints, son, and are a credit to the memory of those with whom you share such a close bond. I read the AAR from Atlas Revenge. I'm aware of how you performed under fire."

"Thank you, sir. Just doing the job I've been trained for. And thank you for agreeing to get tested today."

"Your sister is part of our family, sailor, you know that. I'm happy to do it. And I've strongly encouraged all of Group Two to attend as well. If there's a match in Virginia Beach, we'll find it."

"Hooyah, sir."

"BUD/S is over, Petty Officer. You can lose the hooyah crap. Chief, why don't you lead the way?"

Westhead took the group through the doors and into the hospital, a slightly embarrassed Nate following with the JOEs. Thor gave him a playful shove, mocking him with a few sarcastic "hooyah-sirs!" Two nurses manned the sign-in table. Before long, loudly, hundreds of hardcore warriors were getting stuck and swabbed while making side wagers about who would one day win the bet to walk Cheyenne down the aisle.

Nate was overwhelmed with appreciation, and afterward unfortunately admitted as much in an emotional impromptu speech. The mocking that followed was swift and fierce. He knew that if the rest of his platoon weren't still in Iraq, he'd be facing some type of kangaroo court, with punishments for the public tears that he didn't want to even consider. These were creative men, and they excelled at brutalizing each other. At the very least, he'd have gotten choked out. All in the name of love, of course.

I give DNA samples with the rest of our team, along with what seems like most of the Naval Special Warfare community in town. It's what I have to do to keep up the façade. I can't escape feeling like a wolf wearing wool, mingling with the flock. The absurdity of potentially being a match for Cheyenne does not escape me.

When I force myself to catch up with some of the guys, we bullshit about what everyone did during the off time. There's lots of new ink, tales of barhopping and female conquests, BASE jumps, and bouldering expeditions. A lot of guys wear bloodshot eyes, but all are good to go. An undercurrent of anticipation flows through our group after a rumor gets out that we'll be returned to combat-ready status when the full team reports tomorrow.

A slow, sarcastic clap rings out from one of the regular SEALs in attendance upon hearing that news. "Good for you guys. Now you can go back to blowing shit up on American soil."

I wheel, searching for the speaker. A few pissed-off-looking SEALs are standing behind us, arms crossed, the meathead-looking ringleader sneering at our group. But it's not the SEALs that have my attention so much as a lone figure behind them. It's Agent Kopen, watching it all. I try to catch his eye, to make sure he knows I see him, but the commotion yanks my attention, the differing groups of warriors jostling for position on the sidewalk. When I look back, the FBI agent is nowhere to be seen.

"Easy," Westhead tells us, stepping forward. "Lots of higher ups here. Let it go."

Muttered comments and stiff body language had made it clear all morning that the other teams were either suspicious or jealous of us. There's always a little healthy tension between the specialized units and traditional SpecOps forces. Now, the reports of specialized ammo and explosives they don't have access to has added fuel to the fire. Media reports that the attacks could be coming from a Tier 1 group seem to increase their misgivings.

"You JSOC guys all think you're the duck's nuts," the meathead says, stepping forward. I know the guy, Animal, a petty officer from SEAL Team 8 with a reputation as a troublemaker. Loves to throw fists, a big reason why after a dozen years in the Teams, four platoons and a half-dozen combat deployments he's a must-promote. I consider shutting him up, but a part of me wants to see where this goes.

"Well, I say the GI JOEs are a bunch of cake eaters who forgot what it's like to *really* operate. Who went soft once they got the hot shit gear and glam mishes. And now, with their special ammo and explosives, they're giving all SpecOps forces a bad name."

"What is this, *West Side Story*?" one of our Delta guys asks him, laughing. "Eat a dick, squid."

"Yeah, that's right, keep flapping your gums. And keep failing missions, even with your high-tech gear. When you fuck the dog on the next one, don't worry—we'll clean it up for you."

The young SEAL who organized the blood testing with Westhead and Soto steps forward. I realize that he was the kid I spoke with over Darby's body on the CASEVAC after Atlas Revenge. Part of the SEAL IRF. I saw him take out the haji about to light up Westhead in that battle. The kid who Hagen and Westhead are so close with, whose father they served with on Team 2. I hadn't realized in Syria that was him, that it was his sister who was sick.

"We're on the same team, boys," he tells the room. "No one in our community is killing anyone in our own country. Don't believe the media or FBI's bullshit."

Animal's eyes go wide, then black with rage. He makes a sharp move toward Nate. "What the fuck did you say, Meat? New guys are supposed to be seen, not heard."

"Enough." The statement is authoritative enough that everyone stops in place. "I won't have any of this, not on a day that is about helping a young lady fighting for her life. COL Stevens, CDR Hagen, my thanks for hosting Group 2 this morning. Frogmen, if you have already been tested, see yourself back to your high bays and platoon spaces."

ADM Bradley's shiny patent leather Oxfords clack in the now-silent hallway, carrying him through the hospital exit. I watch from afar as the two factions continue to stare each other down. I can't help but feel a semblance of omnipotence at the underlying tension and electricity pulsating through this group of alpha men. It's like a pack of wild dogs biting at their chains.

Nate finishes his address to the room. He thanks Doc Soto and everyone who came to get tested, even getting a little choked up. His emotion makes me smile to myself, knowing the abuse he's going to get back at his team for not only going against his SEAL brothers in the dust-up with JOE-CAG, but even more so for the public display of emotion.

When the hospital empties, I head back to headquarters for mission prep. There is no sign of Agent Kopen.

LITTLE CREEK

It was late afternoon by the time the marrow drive wrapped up. Nate and Westhead had finished thanking Doc Soto and were headed home when Westhead got the call for team leaders to report to headquarters. The stand-down was over. He gave his passenger a little fist pump and turned up Pearl Jam on the radio.

"This, I know!" Nate exclaimed above the wind rushing through the open top. *"I seem to recognize, your face ..."*

"Haunting, familiar yet," Westhead sang, *"I can't seem to place it ..."*

The mood as they drove continued to be light, jovial even. A cautious optimism, if you really wanted to define it. Considering all that they, their units, and the country had been through in the past two weeks, it was a testament to their fortitude that they were standing at all. But they weren't merely standing: Nate, Westhead, and the rest of their brothers-in-arms were ready to run.

After dropping Nate off at the house, Westhead continued on to JOE-CAG headquarters. He felt recharged and ready to plan and execute their next mission, whatever it might be. There still was no word of whether it would be domestic or foreign, but Hagen and Stevens had called in the team leaders to brief them on an operation that had come directly from the president. In turn, they would brief the full team in the morning.

For a scheduled day off, the parking lot was more full than he would have expected. CDR Hagen and COL Stevens's cars were there of course, but a half-dozen others as well. The team was anxious to get back in the fight; there was no doubting that.

The steel door of the compound creaked open with a groan, and Westhead stepped into the air conditioning. Horrigan greeted him, the same ratty Red Sox hat as always loosely propped on his head, lower lip jutted out with a dip. It was unclear whether the red Solo cup in his hand held coffee or spit.

"Danny boy, so good of you to post. We were about to send out the Boy Scouts."

"Your old lady wanted to go again. You know how she is, Pos, I couldn't say no."

"Sheeeiiit. Better you than me. Just leave a little piece for later, for when I'm drunk."

"Can't promise anything. You guys get started yet?"

"Nah. Still waiting on Hell. Whitey's somewhere around here, taking a dump I think. But something's definitely up. Stevens is being a son of a bitch, won't say anything until all the team leaders are here."

"And now that I am, let the party begin."

A slurping sound followed the announcement, Hellesley smacking his lips. He leaned against the door as if he'd always been there.

"What's wrong with you, Hell? You sound happy."

He scowled. "Never."

"Whaddya drinking there? Toad piss blended with an Amazonian fungus found only in unicorn shit?" Pos pointed at the Styrofoam cup getting sucked down with a thick straw.

"Close. Kale-orange-peach smoothie from my very own organic garden."

"Didn't know peach trees were indigenous to southeastern Virginia." Horrigan offered Hell his cup. Its contents were unimportant—the health freak wouldn't touch tobacco or coffee.

Hell contorted his face. "Lots of things you don't know, Mr. HIV-Positive." He pointed at the cup. "Keep that poison away from me. This body is a temple. Started the day with a five-mile, fifty-pound ruck, followed by a four-mile ocean swim. Then a little yoga, just to find my chi. What about you ladies? Get some mall walking in today? Maybe a Pilates class?"

"Pos's old lady gave me my workout."

"Going back to the well, are we, Chief?" Horrigan shook his head. The insult wasn't arbitrary—Pos's estranged wife was known for spending a little too much time in the boardwalk bars when he was elsewhere. He didn't bother getting insulted, much the same way a younger brother wouldn't take offense at a fat lip.

Westhead shrugged. Pleasantries over. The three of them made their way past the duty officer and into the ready room. Before they entered, Hell clasped Westhead's shoulder like a steel trap.

"Chief, a word?"

Pos didn't slow. His eyes avoided Westhead's as he entered the room, leaving him alone in the hall with Hell. Adam was already inside, drinking a Gatorade, the back of a folding chair between his legs. Stevens and Hagen were posted in the front like teachers waiting for the bell to ring.

Back in the hallway, Westhead turned to his fellow team leader. "What's up?"

"Have a good time at Mikey's party?" Hell asked.

"Sure. He like the poker set I got him?"

"Why? You going to lecture him if he cheats at cards?"

"Uh ..."

"You seem to have become quite the moral shepherd lately."

"You've lost me, Hell. You have something to say, go ahead and say it. You can skip the chitchat. We've got an op order."

Hellesley took a step forward. The two operators were nose to nose. Hell's face was red. He growled.

"Here it is. Don't let me hear about you accusing me, or even insinuating, that I had anything to do with those terrorist attacks again. We clear?"

"Hell, I don't have the energy to even guess what the fuck it is that you're talking about. So quit talking in tongues, or go fuck yourself."

"It's the same shit you did to Nailer and Whitey and who knows who else. Asking questions that are none of your business. Like taking a little too much interest in the signage at my home. You playing detective now, Chief? Someone put you in charge of counting every flex cuff in this building? Maybe you're spending too much time drinking single malts with FBI agents. Oh, didn't think I knew about that? Well, I do. We all do. Quit acting like a junior Gman, or you're going to have problems with the men. I'll leave it at that." Hellesley spun away and walked into the room, leaving Westhead alone in the hallway, unsure about what just happened.

"Shit For Brains, can I start, or are you waiting for the next war?" Stevens called out to him. Westhead collected himself and went in. He caught Adam's concerned-but-knowing eye and took his seat without comment. Why hadn't his best friend warned him that confrontation was coming?

"Thank you. I just got off the phone with POTUS, and we have our work cut out for us."

The rest of the afternoon was spent reviewing mission plans and assignments. By the time they finally exited the compound, the last of the evening light had long since faded into the humidity.

LITTLE CREEK

I make sure that I'm first to arrive the next morning. It's still dark when I do. Not quite night, not yet the new day. My steps leave imprints in the dew walking over the grass, and I have to look back several times, panicked, to make sure the footprints are really there. Relief envelopes me when they are.

As expected, headquarters is empty. I appreciate the solitude. I've always enjoyed being alone. Not just here, but always, since I was a kid. Something about the solemnity of an otherwise empty place. *Your* actions are the only ones that matter in that time and space.

I move quickly through the building, not turning on any lights. My key card and code get me into the armory, where I fill out forms for extra ammo, a new Surefire light, an individual first aid kit, an assaulter belt, and spare pistol mags. I move that gear to my cage. The Carl-Gustaf M4 weapon system and three 84-millimeter anti-tank rounds I take but don't sign for go in a duffle bag, stashed in a trashcan that I cover with cardboard. After checking the parking lot for any other enthusiastic arrivals, I take the can out the back door, and hustle it through the approaching dawn, hyper-alert to the plethora of sounds vying for my attention.

Crickets, early rising gulls, an occasional car on Shore Drive. Nothing that threatens detection. Having secured the duffel bag in the bed of my truck, I drive off. I have a few hours before I need to be back, and I plan to do whatever I can to stifle the splitting pain between my ears.

"Let's go, slacker! The day's a-wastin'!" Adam stretched across the bench seat of his 1968 Ford F250, hollering through the open passenger's window. When Westhead's athletic figure sauntered out his front door, he gave the horn an enthusiastic honk and revved the overhauled engine.

"Dammit, Whitey, don't wake up my neighborhood! Just because you don't sleep, doesn't mean normal people don't." He threw his gym bag on the floorboard and hopped in.

"How about you?' Adam asked. "Need any chemical assistance hitting the rack last night?"

Westhead shook his head vehemently. "Not last night. I was wiped. Was out as soon as my head hit the pillow." The mental aspect of planning a mission could often be more exhausting than executing it. "Didn't even notice Nate's snoring on the couch. I'll tell you what, that kid snores like a freight train. Hope he doesn't ever fall asleep on an S&R."

"You remember my roommate during Phase One? That dude snored like a buzz saw. When the instructors did let us sleep, his snoring wouldn't. I tried everything—bought him a new pillow, a mouth guard, even wore ear protection to bed. Nothing worked. By the time indoc was over, I'd had enough and would just flip him off his rack every time he started with that wheezing and snorting. Three or four times a night. I felt bad at first, but heck, if I can't sleep then he shouldn't be able to either." Adam screwed his face tightly at the memory, shuddering. He was a notoriously light sleeper, meaning of course, that everyone messed with his sleep patterns whenever possible.

"Yeah, I remember that guy. Martinez. Short little Mexican dude from LA. *Flew* through the O-course."

Adam's sideway glance meant he was impressed even if not surprised. Westhead had a near photographic memory. "I'm not sure how you do that. No way I coulda pulled his name. Ever wonder where guys like that are now?"

Westhead shrugged. "Nope. Probably was a mess specialist for the rest of his contract. Maybe one of those guys who sucks the shit out of the latrines over in the sandbox."

"Probably. I think he DOR'd the first night of Hell Week."

"He did, and boy do I remember how happy I was when he quit. Instructor Roberts told us we were staying in the surf until three guys rang the bell. Sowell, and that officer whose dad was a senator, ah ..."

"Littleton?

"No, not Littleton, he got rolled with pneumonia. Um, Devery! Yeah, that was it, Jason Devery, a lieutenant straight from the Academy. His old man was a senator from Montana. Him and Sowell quit right after we said goodnight to the sun. But Instructor Roberts wouldn't let us out of the water until someone else dropped. Must have been about three hours of surf passage with only breaks to get sandy and run over the berms before Martinez finally took him up on that doughnut and coffee. I remember I couldn't feel my fingers, and you were finally able to pee on them. Saved my ass, man."

"Long live the brotherhood. I remember. From surf torture to rock portage. That was not a fun night." A not-uncomfortable gap while Adam looked skyward, fondly reliving the misery. Then, almost an afterthought: "So what's in the bag?"

Westhead smiled, adjusting the hefty white plastic bag on his lap. Its smells had begun to overtake the cabin, and Adam looked over hungrily when his teammate raised it toward him.

"It's not all bad having Butler stay with me. He made breakfast burritos for the whole team this morning."

Adam's eyebrows rose. He was impressed. It was never a bad idea to feed the men you would be detailed with, but he'd need to gather more intelligence before granting full credit.

"Breakfast burritos, huh? What goes in said burritos?"

The animation which overtook Westhead's face offered a proud, begrudging respect. "Not your everyday, runny scrambleds on a stale tor-tilla smeared with Old El Paso. Nope, the boy went above and beyond. Fresh pico de gallo, bacon, eggs cooked over hash browns, avocado, cheese, and a homemade salsa he wouldn't even let me watch him make. All wrapped in tortillas he browned from scratch."

"Someone taught the kid well. The boys'll be happy." Adam paused before speaking again. "There is something I needed to go over with you, brother."

Westhead rolled his eyes, having an idea as to the topic. "Shoot."

"Some of the guys aren't happy you've been poking around about the terrorist attacks, acting like we're under suspicion. It certainly didn't look good that you were seen hanging out with Kopen on the boardwalk."

Westhead sneered. "Yeah, Hell made that pretty clear yesterday. But I'm surprised you're buying into this shit, bro. I wasn't hanging out with him, he obviously followed us into the bar. Which begs the question: How do the rest of the guys know he talked to me in there?"

"I don't have an answer to that, but they do. And they don't like it. I gotta say, I felt a little interrogated by you the other day."

"Whitey, we are under suspicion, as a unit. I'm not accusing anyone, but as team leaders, we can't have any surprises. I wouldn't be doing my job if I wasn't making sure my men were buttoned up. I look at it as protecting them."

"I get it. But that should be more of a reason to circle the wagons. We already have this clown asking questions. All's I'm saying is, it's not a good idea for you to be doing the same. You know the way these guys are. No one wants to have you question their character. Every single one has proven themselves a thousand different times on and off the battlefield. You need to have more faith in your men."

Westhead didn't respond. He seemed conflicted. His focus went to the window, on the scenery flying by. The clouds were low and ashen, darkening by the minute. Conversation over.

Adam drove the truck carefully, having restored it by his own hand.

A tight, proud expression signified the simple satisfaction of conquering machine and the hand of time. Despite any underlying tensions, he and Westhead were for the moment happy, these two rough and tumble warriors simply driving the American streets on an early, already-muggy morning. There wasn't much left to say, so they didn't. All the stories had been told and retold. The truck's windows were down and the heightening breeze felt good. They were alive, and for now, had nothing more to complain about.

The first raindrop fell with a thud, a fist-sized blob that splattered on the windshield. Westhead rolled his window up sharply. By the time Adam had the wipers on, rain and hail were sheeting off the truck, sloshing loudly through suddenly slick streets. He leaned forward, two hands on the wheel, squinting through the storm, inwardly if not willfully appreciative of the insulation and protection the cabin afforded. When his passenger pointed down a side street through the rain, Adam's attention moved likewise; the truck followed suit.

A group of ragged souls in a sad, unmoving array of humanity huddled under loose cardboard and shredded tarps. A cluster of tree branches above barely passed as shelter, allowing a constant stream of water to pour over them. There they sat in the gray beginning of a new day, Virginia Beach's forgotten and unwanted, unable to do more than wait out the storm before drying out in the summer heat and humidity, ever at the mercy of the elements.

Adam stopped the truck before the collection, hopping out abruptly and getting soaked for the effort. Those unfortunates assembled watched the visitors with a kind of detached interest, suspicious but curious. After several recognized them and the truck, spirits improved visibly. With a semblance of modest eagerness, they approached the truck through the downpour. Wearing a friendly smile, Adam went to the truck bed and leaned in, returning with full arms. Sheets of material blew in the wind as he splashed toward the small crowd, handing out camo-colored ponchos. Westhead followed, plastic bag in hand. He nodded politely at a confused, if not wary woman, water and filth running off her chin, and handed her a burrito. Wide-eyed, she took it, a mumble of gratitude audible over a clap of thunder. Covering herself with a new poncho, she scarfed the food down. The others did the same, and soon Adam and Westhead were back on their way. They remained quiet and peaceful for the remainder of their commute, satisfied the way you are in those moments in life when you're fully convinced you are a good person.

Mercifully, the tranquility ended as soon as they pulled up to JOE-CAG. The shower had passed, and they found eight or nine guys standing out front, each one talking with more animation than necessary for 6:30 in the morning. Separate from the crowd, Thor stretched, shirtless, blond mane pulled back in a stubby ponytail.

"What in the heck is going on?" Adam asked, excited at the chaos.

The group faced the newcomers, all talking at once. Nailer clutched a handful of cash, pencil behind his ear.

"Thor thinks he can beat Mutt in a 100-yard dash," he explained. "He's getting two-to-one. Still time if you want in."

Not unlike his counterparts, Thor truly believed that he could be beat in nothing, even a footrace against a former UCLA track star.

"Mutt isn't the only JOE who almost made the Olympics," he was saying to anyone who would listen. "And in a real sport too—like my man Kenny Powers said: 'I ain't tryin' to be the best at exercising.'"

"Is cahverin' yourself in oil and grapplin' with anotha half-naked man considered a real spo't now?" Horrigan asked him, Boston accent thick.

"Eat shit and die, Positive. I wrestled for Dan Gable my freshman year at Iowa. Real athletes don't run from other men, they pulverize them."

"And I played junyah hockey in Canada, Smurfette. That's a real spo't. Believe me, you wouldn't last ten seconds against a real athlete. How fahst can those little legs even move? Yah gonna to look like a cartoon with dust clouds kickin' up behind ya."

"Put your money where your mouth is, tough guy."

"I'm not a big fan of tooting my own horn ..." Mutt said, approaching Adam and Westhead, addressing the former while ignoring the latter. "But this shit sounds like free money to me."

The two team leaders exchanged glances. It did to them, too.

"I got fifty on Mutt," Westhead said, reaching for his wallet. He clutched the bills overhead, offering them to Nailer. The crowd quieted, all eyes on the transaction. When Nailer moved, it was away from Westhead, leaving the money fluttering in his hand. "Anyone else got a bet?" he called out. When Westhead stepped in his direction, Adam put a hand on his chest and took the money from him.

"Fifty on Mutt." It wasn't a request. Adam pushed the money at Nailer, who reluctantly took it and marked the bet down, hard eyes on Westhead.

The shouts picked back up. Most were directed at, and mocking, Thor. Unaffected, the small-statured combatant remained steel-faced as he completed a set of lunges.

"Okay, let's get this kicked off." Nailer surveyed the parking lot. "All bets in?" By now, most of the team stood lining the route. Anticipation and excitement secreted with fidgeting and nervous hyperactivity. Not a spectator among them doubted that they would win the race should they be competing. Most were already considering challenging the winner.

The participants stepped to the starting line, largely ignoring each other. Nailer faced them, his arms extended like a plane handler on an aircraft carrier. Before he could drop them, a voice stopped the start of the race.

"Five hundred on the little fellow." All heads spun to the new gambler. It was Jud, who had somehow gone unnoticed in the raucous crowd. The ensuing hush was temporary; an eruption followed.

"I got that!" someone yelled, more cash coming out, Nailer grabbing it with both hands, trying to mark down bets as they flew in. The flurry of activity lasted a minute or two. Nailer confirmed that all wagering had concluded and turned back to the patiently waiting runners. There stood Thor, unsuccessfully trying to hold back a grin. Westhead watched him wink at Jud, and knew the fix was in. He gathered himself, now excited for whatever was about to unfold, even if it meant losing his fifty bucks. Nailer again raised his arms, shouting, "On your mark! Get set!" When he dropped them with the call of "Go!" the two men took off.

Mutt jumped out to his expected lead. Thor, arms pumping, appeared unworried by the view of his rival's back. Then, just as Mutt really pulled away, a fizzing sound caught their attention. The explosion which followed quickly covered the racers, audience, and entirety of the lot in green smoke and a smattering of harmless debris. Mutt immediately hit the deck, rolling through the fog. Thor remained unflinching, and coasted past the smoky finish line, arms extended to the heavens in victory.

"Thor, the military's God of shit-talking and dodging STD's wins!" Nailer announced more casually than expected, despite having to yell to be heard over ringing ears. He lifted the victor's hand high through the haze.

The bettors, having recovered from the shock, began to display the begrudging mix of protests and impressed laughter of legitimately duped contestants.

Jud stepped forward to a chorus of boos and raining trash to collect his winnings. Thor's victory lap through the men and dust netted him as many kicks as high-fives. "If you ain't cheatin', you ain't tryin'!" he called out with a wide grin.

"Thank you," Jud told a reluctant Nailer, snatching the wad of money from his hand. He used it to fan himself. "I'll make sure to spend this real carefully." He scrunched his eyes in thought. "I'm thinking a keg of Heineken and midget stripper mud-wrestling."

With that, the duplicity was forgiven, and everyone headed into the building. Stevens stood at the entrance, silent, a concerned look surveying his troops. His already-sour face went into a squint, then flashed anger. The bullhorn in his right hand went to his whiskers.

"Get. Your. Asses. Inside. You turds," he bleated through it, loud, the words monotone and robotic. The bullhorn cracked across the lot, eliciting laughter from the men. "That's right. Turds. Turds. I called you turds. Move your turd cutters, turds." His seeming lack of amusement made the address that much more humorous. He finally lowered the bullhorn, foot holding the door open, while his men shuffled past.

"Glad to see we're keeping such good track of our explosive inventory, gents. Not like anyone is monitoring our stock. Keep moving, get inside." He continued ushering them, cattle through the turnstiles. "We've got a full mission briefing in five. Patty-cake is over."

He stayed on the front step after the chaos subsided, but his focus remained in the parking lot. A white sedan had pulled up to the gate and eased into the lot. Agent Kopen appeared from the driver's seat. The crunch of his footsteps across the gravel sounded particularly ominous in the thinning smoke. As always, he was dressed impeccably, gray suit tailored closely, tie bar shimmering in the morning light.

"Good morning, Colonel," he offered, watching the last of the men go through the door. "I really hope that wasn't what I think it was. Keeping a real good eye on that surplus RDX-X, I see."

"Agent Kopen, you're up early this morning. You look tired. We weren't expecting to see you again so soon." Stevens filled the doorway, blocking any chance the FBI agent had at seeing inside the compound, let alone entering with the whole team present.

"Actually, still awake would be more accurate. The missing imam from the Islamic Crescent Center turned up last night. And guess what? He points back to you, to this group. Another piece that fits perfectly into the JOE-CAG puzzle."

"I wouldn't believe everything that an anti-American imam tells you, Agent, but hey, no one likes someone telling them how to do their job."

Agent Kopen wagged his head, slowly at first, but soon it picked up steam, his whole body moving in an emphatic display of disagreement.

"That's where you're wrong, Colonel. It's not so much what he *said*, as what he *didn't* say. Because, you see, he was found dead. Tortured extensively, actually. And the flex cuffs that were used to secure his hands? Well, let's just say you can't pick them up at the Army Surplus. You guessed it. Specifically manufactured for JSOC. In fact, each batch of plastic in those ties varies slightly in its chemical makeup. The flex cuffs from the scene are at the lab now—We're hoping for trace DNA as well as the chemical composition. I expect we'll know soon exactly when and to which JSOC branch they were delivered. Potentially even a DNA composite of the suspect or suspects."

If Stevens had a reaction, it wasn't perceptible.

"Nothing to say to that?"

The colonel remained stone-faced.

"I'll take your silence as surprise. Maybe a slight twinge of concern? That it could be one or more of your guys? If I really wanted to run wild, to read into your lack of cooperation, I might even start to wonder if your whole team, yourself included, is in on it. Some black ops group gone rogue? Payback for a DOD policy change that you blame for a tragic accident in Fallujah?"

A wry smile crinkled Stevens's face, pushed Oakleys higher on his forehead. It was hard to gauge the expression's intent, but Kopen took an instinctive step backward, right hand to his head, running it through stiff hair.

"Accident, huh? What you know about a tragic *accident* outside Fallujah could fit on the head of a pin, sir."

Agent Kopen made a sort of clucking sound, shook his head again. "As you know, Colonel, I was Airborne, 101st before Ranger Regiment. Two Iraq deployments, including dropping into Kirkuk right after the invasion. Spent some time in the Green Zone too, but I won't brag about that. Mostly slept, ate, and lifted. But I was there when Operation Atlas went down. I served with some of those men. And I sure as shit know what it's like to lose brothers."

"I know your record, Agent Kopen. I've seen your DD-214. I know what you did in country. Bronze Star with Valor. Purple Heart."

Kopen's smile was forced, not an indication he was pleased with himself. In fact, it seemed quite the opposite. Modest and reticent. Slightly embarrassed at the mention of his medals. "Just a little scrape. In and out. Nothing like the wounds you've sustained." He stepped closer. "Interestingly enough though, your records are completely illegible starting about six years ago. Soon after Operation Atlas. FITREPS and citations completely redacted. Can't even read them, what with all the black."

"That is interesting. Guess you don't have the clearance."

The smile immediately soured. "Colonel, I'd appreciate the professional respect, from one old soldier to another, to not lie to my face. I know what you do here. I may not know everything, but I'm getting there. And I will. Rest assured. I just hope I'm not back with a SWAT team after those lab results come back. And don't think that I've forgotten about our subpoena. Clock is atickin', my friend."

"Thanks for stopping by, Agent Kopen," Stevens said, showing him his back as he opened the metal door. He let it slam behind him.

Westhead was waiting for his OIC in the lobby. "Everything okay?"

Stevens stared into space. Westhead was surprised at the colonel's appearance. His hair and beard, already long, looked greasy and unkempt. Sunglasses hid his eyes. Even with, or maybe because of them, his face looked pale, sallow. Like everyone on the team, he was exceptionally fit, but Westhead thought he looked thinner than his normal, burly self.

Unsure whether Stevens had heard him, he began again. "Colonel? Agent Kopen again? What was that about flex cuffs?"

Stevens whipped his head toward the voice, seemingly surprised to see Westhead standing there. "Dan. Don't you have assaulters to brief?"

Westhead paused. Finally: "Roger that," and headed down the hallway to find his men.

The curses and jokes inside the building had slowed to a dull roar. Faces were transitioning from laughter to solemnity as the men got down to business. Westhead liked what he saw, but was surprised when McDonald backed out of the bathroom with arms full of dripping wet towels.

"Thor and Pos got in early and apparently were bored, so they decided to flood the head," the new guy explained.

"Who, me?" Thor called from the far end of the hall, hands up in innocence.

Westhead shook his head, continued toward the team room. "You ever get tired of fucking with the news guys, Smurfette?"

Thor snapped his head with purpose, legitimately confused at the question. "You ever get tired of oxygen?"

Westhead knew pressing the issue would be futile. So he didn't, instead continuing his search for Nailer. He found him eating a protein bar in the team room, shaking his head at the cable coverage of the bombings. The tank top he wore was tight and faded, an alien smoking a cigarette on the front below the words "I Don't Believe in Humans."

"Nailer. You're with me on this next op, and it's going to be like nothing we've ever done before. Hope you're ready to get out of your comfort zone."

Nailer spun from the TV, his expression shifting immediately from irritation to curiosity. Excitement.

"Talk to me."

"Grab McDonald and GQ, I'll brief you guys in five."

He nodded, stuck his head into the hallway and yelled. "New Guy! GQ! We got an op!" A minute later, both came flying around the corner, taking seats around Westhead. Waiting as patiently as they were able. Not their most natural state. McDonald, GQ, and Nailer—these hardened, veteran SpecOps warriors, dozens of combat deployments and hundreds of real-world missions under their belts, scarred with bullet holes and shrapnel—sat leaning forward like children at story time, captivated by the prospect of pending orders.

The small lounge was decorated in military chic. Mismatched couches and a faded recliner, brought in from guys' garages, were arranged around a metal desk doubling as a coffee table. The mini-fridge against the wall was stocked with beer, Gatorade, or mold, depending on deployment frequency and tenure of new guys. Framed pictures of decorated operators from various units hung haphazardly. A few rugged-looking laptops sat amid the nudie magazines and crusty coffee cups.

Westhead began. "Intelligence thinks they've found al-Baghdadi. We're breaking into four squads. Three squads are heading to Arizona where our training cell is putting the final touches on a mock-up of al-Baghdadi's compound in Western Syria. They'll put together a full mission plan and dry-run it on the mock-up." He took a breath before starting again. So far, he had only been met with excitement.

"Our squad is staying here for the time being. We've been assigned to Operation Palindrome. The president has tasked us with reconning a local mosque that the FBI believes could be the terrorist's next target. Its sister mosque is the Crescent Islamic Center, which as we know was just blown up. Farouk Shami, the imam who had been missing, was found tortured and murdered in an abandoned house in Newport News last night. Our mission is to ensure the same doesn't happen to the Islamic Community Center of Portsmouth or its imam, Ihsan Bagby."

Nailer looked more confused than pissed. "So we're going to miss the al-Baghdadi mission to babysit this imam? Are we protecting this mosque or investigating it? Either way, sounds like the FBI or Homeland Security's job. Maybe they should do a little less harassment of us and a little more proactive enforcement."

"That's not for us to decide. As for our objective, it's a little from column A, a little from column B. When almost three hundred citizens are killed in two weeks on American soil, the president is going to use his A-team to do whatever it takes to stop a third attack."

"A-team, huh? So does that make you Hannibal?" Nailer was growling now. He had left his seat and was pacing. "Where was his support for the A-team when the Pentagon changed the ROEs before Atlas?"

Westhead's rebuke was sharp. "We're not here to debate the commander in chief's decisions, Nailer; we're here to implement them. I, for one, am honored that he's chosen us for this mission over all the other elements he has at his disposal. Not that it matters what the fuck I, or you, think."

Nailer examined the floor tiles before speaking again. "While we're speaking our minds, I think I speak for all of us when I say we think we're not crazy about working with a rat."

"A rat?"

"Yeah, a rat."

"You're calling me a rat because I asked you *privately* about a certain type of ammo in your locker? Because I cautioned people about taking shit home from headquarters when the FBI is crawling up our asses? You're calling me rat because I'm looking out for this unit?"

"I'm calling you a rat because I don't know whose side you're on. Because you voluntarily sat with that FBI agent at least once that we know of. Because he knows a lot more about this unit than he should. That's why."

"He followed me into a bar, you prick. He was surveilling all of us that day. I don't recall you making him."

"Yet he chose to sit with you. I'm not saying. I'm just saying."

"I gotta tell you, Nailer, it's cause for concern that you're so wary of anyone talking to Agent Kopen. I'll say it again: If this unit has nothing to hide, we shouldn't be so worried about the FBI."

"We're a top-secret unit, Dan. If our existence gets out, we're finished. You should be more worried about protecting that than indulging a bullshit investigation. That's what me, and the others, are concerned with."

"And you speak for everyone?" Westhead looked around the room. "You all wonder about my loyalty?" GQ averted his eyes. McDonald stood.

"You don't speak for me, Nailer. Yeah, Chief may have mentioned inventory control to people inside this building. But as far as I know, he hasn't said anything outside of it. Kopen has tried to talk to almost all of us. You want to call Chief a rat, you better know for sure that he's working with the FBI directly, behind our backs. If not, *I* think the man has earned the benefit of the doubt."

Nailer spun in his direction. "No one cares what you think, New Meat. Not yet." His anger transitioned back to Westhead. "If we thought he was working directly with the FBI, this would be a much different conversation, and it wouldn't be taking place under the lights."

Westhead approached his teammate calmly but with fiery features. "Give it a try, Nailer, any time you feel tough. We can be in the dark with the flick of that switch."

With soft eyes and a wholly composed face, Nailer looked up at his team leader, searching. Finally: "I'll keep that in mind, Chief. We're good. For now."

"That warms my heart, Nailer, it does. Now, can I get back to the briefing or is there anything else anyone would like to bitch about?" They had a job to do, and indulging personal conflicts was not an extravagance they could afford. No one else spoke.

"Good. The FBI thinks both attacks—on the mosque and the Basting Institute—are related, and not just because of the physical evidence. Farouk Shami was a close friend of Dick Basting. Both, good friends with the president. Now, the FBI thinks Bagby could be the next target, along with his mosque for the same reason. Both imams contributed to the Basting Institute's study six years ago that led to the change in ROEs we're so familiar with. We're going to conduct surveillance and gather intelligence, all the while making sure no one turns the mosque into a crater. I need a mission plan from everyone by 1200. GQ, you're tasked with HUMINT. Time to put that olive skin and oobey-gooby you speak to good use. McDonald, need you to tap the Internet and phone lines of the mosque and start capturing cell phone data from the imam. I want to know who he's talking to, who he's meeting with. Nailer, you'll be reconning the mosque. Operations rented office space across the street with good sight lines, you'll set up there."

"Guess ADM Bradley doesn't think we have anything to do with the attacks if he's including us in this op," McDonald pointed out.

"Unless it's just to keep an eye on us," countered Nailer.

There's a bustle to the building after the race, a new energy amongst the men. The long weekend helped, the antics in the parking lot added to the charged atmosphere, and now, pending orders back to war slide our mood over the edge.

The day's previously planned training evolutions—a Command PT led by Hell—are discarded. The festivities were to start with an ocean swim and beach run before running the O-course in full MOP gear. By then we'd be properly wiped out, which was the best time to hit the range. To finish the day, the team leaders had planned a night-drop exercise where everyone would be blindfolded and dropped deep in the woods or out to sea (we wouldn't know which until it was time to exit the helos) and find their way home without compasses or maps. Of course, pays to be a winner.

But with the new ops, the training day is forgotten while mission prep continues in earnest.

I take it all in, relishing the violent undercurrents, the somber air of men ready to head into battle. There's a hatred to our movements: This op is personal, and not one man wouldn't trade his life for al-Baghdadi's. I'm certainly of the same mindset but unwilling to make the trade just yet.

In fact, I don't share the same exuberance at going after al-Baghdadi for a third time, not right now. I'm happy to do so, and yeah, I want him dead, but with or without me, al-Baghdadi will be killed. He has his job to do, and I have mine. It's the others responsible for Atlas and for Darby who will go unpunished if not for me. The men I blame are a lot closer to home, and the more time I spend there, the sooner I can get that payback.

I continue to observe from afar. The activity, the planning. Westhead's squad, detailed to a local mission. Everyone else, off to Arizona. A mock-up of al-Baghdadi's compound awaits, ready for hundreds of full mission profile hits. The team will nitpick the details, running different scenarios on the insert, extract, and everything in between. Perfect practice makes perfect, because hey, like we say, the more you sweat in peace the less you bleed in war. My problem, I am beginning to realize, is differentiating between the two.

That consideration makes my temples throb; kneading them with my thumbs is largely ceremonial, more of a tic than a remedy. I feel out of my body as I view the action from above, everyone animated, everyone moving toward a common goal. It's an interesting perspective, and I float, coasting, taking in the tidy disarray from an atmospheric vantage point, the worker bees fluttering to and fro, creating a hive for the American people, one 5.56 round at a time, and it's easy to spot the dedication in gnarled, enthusiastic faces, men convinced their small role has a corresponding impact, happy that yeah, they'll get some, kill 'em all, making the world safe for democracy and the people of the republic.

I'm not saying they're wrong, I'm just saying I have bigger fish to fry.

"I need constant reports, Dan. I'm briefing the president directly on Operation Palindrome, and he does not want to be embarrassed. Likewise, *I* do not want to be embarrassed. So I would suggest to you—based on the gravitational properties of fecal matter—that you ensure we are not embarrassed."

Stevens's right eye twitched while he spoke, making it all Westhead could do to not focus on the spasm, not react to it. It bothered him more than it should, so he made a point to look away, to pick another feature on the man to keep his mind off that fact that this sonofabitch couldn't keep his face straight.

He was slightly ticked at his CO. Usually team leaders picked their men for ops like this, but Stevens had given him no choice in personnel. All three were strong operators, but it was a matter of principle, of respect. Stevens knew there was tension between him and Nailer and had purposely put him on his team. But Westhead's real discomfort stemmed from not being consulted at all. JOE-CAG was unlike the traditional military where rank trumped all, orders were orders. Here, in the Tier 1 SpecOps world, everyone was more or less on equal footing. And Stevens had cut his legs out from under him.

"Any questions?" It was rhetorical, clear that Westhead should leave his office. "Good."

Westhead floated out of the office, head a little light between the meeting with Stevens and earlier spar with Nailer. He had noticed the glances, the standoffishness of the other guys, but until then hadn't realized how big the chasm was. It had been a long day, and his team would be getting started at the mosque early the next morning. It took a moment to diagnose the vibration in his jeans pocket.

"Doc," he answered. "Gimme some good news. I could use it."

"I'd love to, and will be shortly. But I need to talk with Blade first and haven't been able to get a hold of him. He around?"

"I'm actually leaving his office right now." He glanced back at the OIC. Stevens didn't look up. "He's in a mood, and I don't think I'm his favorite person right now—should I disturb him?"

Westhead had to take the phone away from his ear for Soto's response.

"Roger that." Then, stepping back into the office: "Colonel, phone for you."

The subdued way Stevens raised his head made Westhead think, for some reason, that his reaction was going to be calm. He was wrong.

"Didn't I just kick your ass out of here!" he bellowed. Westhead had had enough.

"Not sure what crawled up your ass, Colonel, but if Doc Soto calls two days after you get tested to be a marrow match for a young girl fighting for her life, I'm going to kick in the stall door if you're sitting on the crapper!"

The two men stared into each other, Westhead planted in the doorway, nostrils flaring. Stevens leaned forward at his desk, seething in his own right. Muffled shouts from the phone in Westhead's hand broke the impasse.

"PUT THAT SONUVABITCH ON THE PHONE!" Soto was yelling, clear and audible. Westhead stepped forward, offered Stevens the phone. Reluctantly, he took it.

Westhead watched the colonel nod several times, grunt, then hand the phone back. Westhead put it to his ear, eyes still on Stevens.

"I just told Blade. His marrow is a match for Cheyenne. We may be able to save this young lady yet."

The grin on Westhead's face couldn't have been removed with a belt sander.

WASHINGTON, DC

I know why I'm doing it. Again. Why I'm taking the risk. If nothing else, I *am* self-aware. In any case, it's not hard to figure out. From a psychological standpoint, I mean. Aside from the obvious, the need for retribution. It's the closeness of regular and recurring death which keeps me more alive.

Only death can do that. Only the finality of that state characterizes the trait, that influence on man. Do you feel especially dry when in the presence of water?

And when the death comes from my own hand, the effect is magnified. This is the reason I just drove three hours north instead of sleeping during quite possibly the only time earmarked for that luxury in the foreseeable future. It's why I'm parked in an alley in Foggy Bottom, a backpack with RDX-X and four digital initiators at my feet on a late summer night when I should be preparing for war. Instead, I'm waging my own.

Intermittent headlights flash past the intersection holding my attention. My focus is singular: the stately, eleven-story building at the corner of 22nd and K Streets. Understated, formed with aged, strong stone so many generations ago, withstanding the pressures of time and politics, as old and static as the union itself. War, depression, dissention could not bring the unassuming, powerful building or its occupants down. But I can.

The truck door shuts behind me with a soft click, dome light already extinguished. I'm a ghost, a shadow gliding through the night. A martyr, a revolutionary, a rebel. Part of something bigger than myself or my unit. Not merely a part of history, a *creator* of history. At the intersection I pause, head down to avoid headlights. A police car slowly cruises the muted streets. I watch the red glow of the taillights shrink before stepping into the street, alone. Ahead, a stop sign, the word "caring" scribbled in black marker underneath.

There is no identifying sign on the building, not even an address. The shadowy pseudo-government organization headquartered here works very hard to keep its existence a secret. Large concrete blocks are staggered protectively on the sidewalk out front, a discrete design intended to prevent someone from driving a car laden with explosives through the front door. Behind walls of glass, a lone security guard sits at a marble desk, bored, an island in the middle of the wide, sparse lobby. Dominick. I know his partner Harold will have just started hourly rounds.

My footsteps echo in the dark, a cliché I realize, but true nonetheless. I hustle up the curb, sidestepping those angry concrete blocks. The backpack feels light but significant. I reach for the glass door, knowing it will be locked, but act surprised anyway. Flash the guard a sheepish grin. Dominick appears annoyed at the intrusion and takes his time pulling himself from his chair. The irritation on his face has an assuaging effect, instantly lessening the guilt for what I'm about to do. My smile is forced but disarming, the false nose and chin rising slightly with my cheeks. He pauses when he reaches the door, some inner voice warning him: DANGER. He doesn't listen to it.

As soon as he releases the lock and cracks the heavy glass door to find out what the reason is for the disturbance, my hand goes to my back. The suppressed Sig Sauer comes out easily, smoothly. A flash of panic crosses his face when he realizes what is happening. Of course, it's too late, and the pistol spits, then again. Dominick crumples to the floor, a small hole in his forehead and one in his chest, two larger ones in the back. His eyes are still stretched with surprise, a shock that will never be resolved. Blood begins to pool under his body in two slow leaks.

Slipping through the ajar door with the gun at my side, I scan the street, the sidewalk. No activity. The lock clicks certainly behind me. I bend down, holster the weapon, grasp the guard by both feet. I purposely don't contemplate his features, a disengaged unconcern that I've perfected. Peripherally I notice he's not old, not young. It's an ugly face centered by a scarred, swollen alcoholic's nose. A divorcee, moonlighting to pay child support, perhaps. His body slides easily to the island, lubricated by the blood. I position him out of sight. After removing his keycard and sticking it in my back pocket, I drag him toward the bank of elevators. A gloved finger hits the down button. A glance at my watch tells me that if Harold is following his normal schedule, I have eleven minutes until he walks the basement.

When the elevator arrives, the DING announcing it seems loud under the high ceilings, the shiny marble. I grab hold of Dominick under his arms and drag him into the car, stabbing at the 'B'. More blood streaks. With a wave of his badge we're moving, one floor down. I'm still calm, heart rate normal, not the least bit unsettled.

The elevator opens. We enter a bright white hallway lined with steel doors. I consult blueprints from the backpack. Stop before the fourth one on the right. Dominick's badge gets us entrance into the electrical room. Control panels, meters, and circuit breakers greet us coldly.

I move quicker now.

The guard has to be stashed where he won't be found in the morning. I position him behind a bank of transformers, ask him if he's comfortable. No reply.

One device will be rigged here, in this electrical room, one in the datacenter across the hall, one in the HVAC closet in the far corner, and one in a room not marked on the building's blueprints. When they detonate at 9:38 tomorrow morning, the building should be full, most employees sifting through email, on conference calls, maybe their second cup of coffee, all eleven stories coming down on top of them. Retribution for their hard work that gets good men killed.

The time indicates that Harold is scheduled to arrive in only a couple minutes. I work fast. The DING from down the hall tells me he's early. I stop what I'm doing and wait just inside the open door.

A pleasant, out-of-tune whistle drifts toward me. Inwardly, I smile. That commentary is not lost on me: the only pleasure I take is in death.

"*Psst.* Harold," I hiss, then again.

The whistling stops. So do the footsteps.

"Dominick?" The question is unsure, the voice shaky. I hiss again. Two more steps, but no response.

I decide not to wait him out. He's more than likely noticed the blood in the hallway. He could reach for his phone, a radio. I step into the harsh hallway lighting already in a shooting stance. Harold is frozen, his face covered in disbelief as he observes what must seem to him like a bad movie. My arms jerks twice, just barely. He falls. Two, three, four quick but unhurried steps, then two more jerks. A red river flows symmetrically away from Harold.

With my sleeve, I wipe sweat from my ears and neck. The first real signs of exertion. Concentrating on slowing my breathing, I examine the body. His forehead is caved in, nose gone, bone and cartilage white and bleached-looking. He no longer looks like a person. Maybe what would be left of a person if he was shot in the face. A hand stretches out, like it's trying to escape him. Just past the pale fingers, a cell phone squawks.

"Hello? Sir? What is your emergency?"

Crouching down, I listen for a moment. The question is repeated. I push "end," put the phone in my pocket, and drag Harold to the electrical room to join his partner. The work will have to go quicker now; time is of the essence.

The phone immediately rings in my pocket. I answer with a soft hello.

"Sir, there was a 911 hang-up by this number. What is the emergency?"

"My apologies, that was me. I have 911 saved in my favorites and must have pocket dialed you."

The pause, long. "So there is no emergency?"

"No ma'am. Sorry for wasting your time."

I hang up, disconcerted. If the police come and find my recently departed friends, even if they don't find the four bombs, the building will be a crime scene and mostly empty when they detonate in the morning. I have no interest in killing cops if I can help it. But my resolve is not shaken; no op ever goes exactly as planned. Time to improvise.

It's a bloody mess at my feet, the security guard uniforms in rough shape. I look down at the two bodies and wonder if a SWAT team could be racing toward this building.

"Dominick? Oh, Dominick ..." I half-sing, staring at his body as if awaiting a response. "You don't mind if I borrow your uniform, do you?" After waiting for what anyone would consider a respectable amount of time, I shrug and start to undress him.

The front of the uniform is in decent shape, save for the bullet hole above the breast pocket. The back, a different story. I undress quickly, alert for any signs of arriving police, changing into dark slacks that are too wide at the waist and too short at the ankles. The shirt, loose but at least clean in front. The blood on the back has partially hardened, and I can feel it, both wet and crusty on my skin as steady fingers deftly close buttons.

Next, I hurry off Harold's jacket—despite the condition of the rest of him, it will hide any blood stains. I adjust my wig, patting down rogue hairs to appear as presentable as possible.

The building blueprint again comes out. One door to the left, across the hall. I step over the gore, waving the badge for entrance. A mop and bucket sit just inside the janitor's closet. I fill the bucket, wheel it toward the elevators.

I have no idea if the police are even coming, but Hope is Not a

Strategy. Operators can easily geo-locate 911 calls and dispatch police if they suspect a hang-up is an actual emergency. I have to be prepared if they are en route.

The blood streaks in the lobby are dark and deep and look as if they were staged by a set designer on a horror film. The wet mop cuts through them, muddying the crimson liquid. Soon there are only diluted pink smudges. From outside, a red flash catches my eye. I look up. Blue strobes reflect against the lobby glass. They're here.

I begin combat breathing, using the "theory of fours" to calm me, to slow my heart rate. It's a technique we use in combat that can be applied to any stressful situation. After several rounds of inhaling for four seconds, holding it for four, then out for four, my adrenaline is controlled and the world has slowed. I roll the mop and bucket around the corner and take a seat behind the security desk. I don't have to wait long.

A rap on the glass yanks my head at the lobby doors. I lower a newspaper, slowly take my feet off the desk. The blood through the uniform feels like drying paint on my back. My pistol is loose in my waistband as I make my way to meet an impatiently waiting officer. He looks tired, doesn't want to be working the graveyard shift.

"You the night man?" he asks once I've turned the lock and pushed open the door.

"That's me," I smile. "Ten to six. This about the 911 call?"

He looks me over, head to toe, considering, using whatever powers of perception he can muster to determine, in seconds, if I'm being truthful or am a threat.

"Hang up from a cell phone at this address." He's still leery, hasn't made a decision yet.

I take the phone out, offering it to him. I know I don't know the code to unlock it. If he asks to see it, asks me to turn it on, I know I'll have to take him out and the mission will be compromised. He remains stationary.

"Yeah, that was me. Was trying to call my girl and accidentally hit 911 on my favorites."

"Nine-one-one is saved as one of your favorites?"

The phone, still being offered for his perusal, is electric in my hand.

"She programmed it for me. Said that if there is an emergency at work, it'll take too long to dial." I shrug, disarmingly, as if to say, *women*.

We're facing each other, frozen, for what feels like a long time. He reaches for his radio. I try not to visibly stiffen. If he calls for backup, I'll send my knee into his solar plexus, followed by an elbow through the back of his neck and two rounds in the head before racing out the door and disappearing into the night. Meaning, of course, mission failure.

"42. We're 10-19 on K Street."

The radio squawks back. "10-4, 42."

He musters a grim smile before backing out the door and wishing me a good night. Just two poor bastards on the graveyard shift. I offer the same in return, head back to the desk. There's an article in the *Washington Post* I want to finish, about the Basting Institute's connection to the president and the Crescent Islamic Center of Portsmouth. The article makes no mention of the influence those two organizations had on a chopper crash leading to the worst loss of life in United States Special Operations history.

It's the middle of the night by the time I've planted the RDX-X and programed the four digital initiators. I certainly expect this one to get the FBI's attention.

It's not until I'm safely outside the Beltway, steaming through the dead of the night toward Virginia Beach that I stick a Wintergreen dip in my mouth.

PORTSMOUTH

The safe house location was ideal, set back from the road but with direct sightlines to the Islamic Community Center across the street. Westhead entered the two-story commercial building from the alley, taking the stairs two at a time. He wasn't supposed to be onsite until 0800, but after too many hours examining his ceiling, he'd headed in early.

He stopped before a darkened glass door, A&T Construction freshly stenciled in white lettering, knocked once, then twice more. Nailer let him in.

The office they would be staging out of for Operation Palindrome was small and furnished sparingly. The bulk of their equipment—a series of laptops, servers, monitors and other electronics, their white, red, and green lights blinking like a Christmas tree—sat on a folding table in the middle of the room. Nailer had positioned a second table perpendicular to the floor-to-ceiling windows facing the street, an ideal vantage point for watching the mosque.

Not offering Westhead any further greeting, Nailer re-stationed himself upon that table, the tools of his trade spread out around him:

A bipodded Winchester sniper rifle, locked and loaded to his right. Thermal binos and night vision goggles to the left. The camera was a digital Nikon D5300 with a telephoto zoom lens. A legal pad of paper, the top page covered with dark, terse lettering. A bottle for Copenhagen juice and another that held water.

A crew from JOE-CAG's support team had prepped the small room overnight, tinting the windows, installing cameras and parabolic microphones aimed at the Islamic Community Center of Portsmouth.

"Anything of interest?" Westhead asked. He scrutinized his teammate while handing him a cup of coffee, interested to see whether their previous disagreement had any carryover. Nailer took the Starbucks—a grande Blond Roast, his favorite—without comment, yawned. His demeanor gave no indication of distemper—or indication of anything, really. Like most large, dysfunctional families, conflicts often arose inside JOE-CAG; due to the nature of their business, the luxury of holding grudges was something they didn't have.

"Not since I set up at 0400." He consulted the yellow pad. "The imam arrived just after 0500, and about a dozen worshippers arrived shortly thereafter for morning prayers."

"GQ?"

"Our boy arrived in his linen tunic and kufi to some hard stares in the parking lot from the true believers. He went in for morning prayers an hour ago and hasn't come out."

"No sign of countersurveillance?"

Nailer sipped his coffee, wagged his head. His voice still had that early-morning gravel to it.

"Nah, all clear. I went up to the roof and did a thermal scan with those new Fluke thermal imagers on all the cars and buildings in the neighborhood. Nothing out of the ordinary. McDonald is reconning the neighborhood and street as we speak."

"Hmphf. Not sure if I give those imagers a passing grade. Didn't find me when I was stalking Whitey."

"But you're an American badass. You're Chief Dan Westhead. Captain America. The Greek God of special operators." The barbs seemed more pointed than good natured. Westhead ignored them.

"Melissa called me last night. Wanted to know if you really were TDY on a training mission. She doesn't trust ya?"

Nailer shook his head. "Sorry about that, brother. Like I'd have time to cheat."

"Hey, we all go through it."

"Those of us dumb enough to marry do. Especially those that stay married."

Westhead forced a smile and reached for the pair of binos. Peering through the dark window into the morning, he couldn't help but find the sprawling white mosque somewhat mystical, floating eerily on the other side of its iron fence. The start of rush hour brought a steady flow of unwitting cars along the road separating it from their position. No signage advertised the mosque, and it was set back from the road, blocked partially by thick evergreens. No activity that Westhead could see.

"Heard there was a match for Cheyenne."

He lowered the binoculars and grinned at Nailer. "Yep. Stevens, of all people. They need to do a few more tests to confirm compatibility, but it's looking good."

"Glad to hear. I got to know her dad pretty well. We had a training exercise in Norway when I was at SDV-1. Dude was the real deal. You know how they tell you in BUD/S that if you make it you're going to spend your career cold, wet, and sandy? Well, I'm not ashamed to admit that it was an honor to have snuggled, nuzzled, hugged, been wrapped in Senior Chief Butler's warm embrace on that trip. Four nights on the frozen tundra."

Westhead chuckled knowingly. "Nuts to butts. He did a lot for me, that's for sure. Taught me what it meant to be a Team guy from the first day I showed up in his platoon. The shit they can't teach you in SQT. Him and Spencer ... Once, as a new guy I fucked up on a training op ..." He looked upward, reflecting on the memory, able to do so fondly only because of the time and growth since. "Boy, did they kick my ass. But I learned from it." He chuckled, resolutely, here. "I'll tell you what, I'll never not dual-prime a charge again."

Nailer nodded. They'd all had their own learning opportunities as new guys. "And his kid seems good to go too."

"Nate."

"Yeah. Way I hear it, saved your ass on the al-Baghdadi mission."

"Something like that. Good kid. Green, but shit, he's been in a platoon a whole three months. Already a meat-eater too."

"Lucky bastard. Took me almost six years before I got my first KIA."

"I was with his old man when I got mine. First deployment to Afghanistan. He made me eat raw hamburger after. Said it was part of the initiation."

Nailer smirked. "Dumbass. I remember, dude always had jokes. And he wasn't afraid to open his mind, either."

"Huh?"

"I'm not saying he was a full blown believer ..."

"Nailer, just—don't."

"... but he had questions, as we all should. He wasn't a UFOlogist or anything, but after he went to the IUC with me one year in Arizona, he started to do his research. We had some long talks about exobiology."

"Can't believe I'm taking this bait. UFOlogist? IUC?"

"Yeah. The study of unidentified flying objects? The International UFO Congress? Biggest UFO conference in the world. Don't tell me you haven't heard of it."

Westhead's mouth opened, but he decided against speaking. It was never worth winding Nailer up on the topic of extraterrestrials.

Mercifully, a sharp knock interrupted any forthcoming elocution. When two more followed, Nailer hopped up to answer. It was McDonald, also with coffee. He placed a thermos on the table.

"Here I was, patting myself on the back for bringing coffee, and you already have Starbucks."

"If your plan is to bribe us with hot coffee and doughnuts, New Guy, you're on the right track," Nailer told him. "Where the hell are the doughnuts?"

McDonald reached down and lifted a plastic bag. "Do bagels get me brownie points with you, Nailer? And the coffee ... That's gourmet—Mutt let me use his French press."

Nailer took the bag, impressed. "You're getting there, Meat. But the one thing operations got wrong with this location," he said, "is the bathroom. It's down the hall and shared with a title company and insurance agent. So it's these when nature calls." He shook a Gatorade bottle that was half full of not-Gatorade.

"Chief, any update from HQ?" McDonald asked.

Westhead shook his head. "The rest of the team should be wheels-up as we speak, en route to Arizona. They'll be training on the mock-up of al-Baghdadi's compound until the president gives the green light to stage in Iraq."

"We going to miss out on that op?" Nailer asked, concerned.

"No idea. That's for Stevens and Hagen to decide. Right now, we'll just do our job here until they tell us otherwise."

"GQ, coming out." Their attention moved from the conversation to the window Nailer was staring intently out of. GQ was just visible in the mosque's parking lot.

"He mic'd up?" asked McDonald.

"Nah, we figured it wasn't worth the risk. He's just feeling the place out this morning. We'd only get morning prayers."

"Looks like he's doing more than feeling it out." McDonald pointed out the window as they watched GQ through binos, looking the part in a flowing white robe. Support staff had dyed his hair a darker black, and using prosthetics and make-up, they'd transformed the former PJ into your average-looking Middle Eastern man. The man he spoke with was shorter, with a manicured beard and black skullcap. He walked easily, hands clasped behind his back, listening intently while GQ spoke.

"Is that ..." Nailer whispered, even though there was no need. He studied a corkboard holding a series of photos and names. "It is. GQ is with Imam Bagby."

"Wish we were listening to this," Westhead said.

Nailer's eyes stayed on the window as he backpedaled to the other folding table, then crouched in front of one of the laptops. Putting on headphones, he worked the mouse, hit a few buttons.

"Got it," he said, unplugging the headphones. Immediately, the computer's speakers came alive with echoic, distant-sounding voices. "Parabolics should catch anything said on the west side of the mosque, including the parking lot." He adjusted the volume, and soon they heard the unmistakable voice of GQ, albeit with his impression of a Middle Eastern accent.

"... time in Morocco," he was saying, "but attended university here in the states. In Pittsburgh. I was just hired by an engineering firm in Norfolk and am in the process of relocating my family from Turkey. The State Department has not yet approved their visas."

The imam held his response for long enough to make the men think their feed had cut out. Finally:

"A man of Allah, a man of the world. The Center welcomes you. Let me know if I can be of any assistance in bringing Sister ... what did you say your wife's name was?"

"Laila," GQ said a little too quickly. "Laila and our twin boys, Rafqi and Tafir."

"Ah, wonderful. Laila and little Rafqi and Tafir. I do have friends in the US government; let me know if there is any way I can assist in the visa process. A difficult business, especially in today's political climate, to be sure."

"*Shukran jazeelan,*" he said gratefully. Then: "I never got your name."

His companion stopped, offered his hand. "I am Ihsan Bagby, the imam for the ICCP. *Assalamualaikum.*"

"*Wa alaikum assalaam,*" GQ responded. "It's an honor to meet you and worship at your mosque."

As Westhead watched and listened to the interaction between his operator and the imam, his cell phone rang. "Blade," he informed the room, walking to the other end to take the call.

"Colonel, shouldn't you be on a plane?" Westhead answered.

"The team just boarded, we're pushing off shortly. There were some last-minute things to take care of this morning. You hear the news yet?"

Westhead thought Stevens's voice sounded hollow, detached. He started to pace, as he often did when talking on the phone. "Unless the news is that GQ has twin boys named Rafqi and Tafir, I don't think so. What's up?"

"Another attack in DC. Someone blew up the building housing Riley & Porter this morning. And—this isn't a secure line, but you know who—what—else is in that building."

Westhead's eyes went wide. He knew well. "The Activity," JSOC's specialized intelligence arm, had several floors in the building. Riley & Porter was technically a private law firm, but had only one client: the United States government. Most of their work was done on behalf of SOCOM and the CIA. The president had been a partner at the firm before running for public office and heading the CIA.

"Holy shit. We had them as a potential target, why wasn't there surveillance?"

"That's exactly what the president just asked me, in so many words. Not a conversation I enjoyed. Which is why I'm calling you. Anything going on at the mosque? He's pissed, and is considering pulling us from this op and turning all surveillance over to the FBI. We need to get him some actionable intel to stay in the game."

"Wish I had some, Colonel. All quiet here. We've had eyes on since before sunup, and GQ attended morning prayers. He actually made contact with the imam and is staying on him. We've conducted countersurveillance, checked the neighboring buildings and parked cars. Task Force Orange and the Special Collection Service are monitoring their Internet traffic as well as listening to phone calls and office chatter. So far, nothing to suggest they are either going to be attacked or are planning anything themselves."

"Don't fuck this up. I don't need another call from POTUS tearing me a new asshole."

"No, sir. You have enough assholes."

There was a pause. Then: "All right, that wasn't bad. Call me with another SITREP this evening. We're pushing off."

The minty tobacco seems to have a particular bite this morning. That, and the success of my latest mission, is almost enough to raise the corners of my mouth. At the least, it's taken the edge off my headache. I lean back, scrolling through my phone for death tolls on the K Street bombing. A Gatorade bottle collects spit.

The guys offer their opinion on who they think is behind it, and some aren't far off. I can't help but notice that stares seem more searching, questions more pointed. Not just toward me, but at each other. No one seems to be especially accusatory, but there certainly hangs an air of suspicion. The public may not yet be aware of the links to JSOC, but we all are. The most popular theory inside JOE-CAG is that it's an element of rogue SEAL Team 6 operators. I'm just not sure that Agent Kopen is of the same mind.

The latest CNN report has the death toll at seventy-seven. It is still unclear how many partners of Riley & Porter were in the building when it exploded, but as of now they have found no survivors. I take a deep breath, exhale loudly, keep scrolling.

The first names and photos of the dead are trickling out—and one picture jumps off the page. "Andy Sullivan, IT Specialist with local law firm Riley & Porter. Former Marine Corps major and Iraq War veteran." I recognize the bald, ruddy-faced man as the intelligence agent called Sully who briefed us in Iraq before Operation Atlas Revenge. Good. Fuck him. More bad intelligence there. I don't even consider him collateral damage.

"That one's for Darby," I mutter. I quickly look up, making sure no one heard me, but everyone is head down, lost in their own tasks. I continue reading, mentally checking off one more target.

By the end of the day, the cramped office space had started to smell the way tight quarters will when occupied by men sustained on processed foods and caffeine. Elevated tensions couldn't be avoided with these alpha males, contained and pissed off at the thought of missing a larger mission. The news of another bombing in DC has them even further on edge.

"Anyone else have a real problem with safeguarding the same pieces of shit making it harder for us to do our job, who had a hand in how Operations Atlas and Atlas Revenge turned out?"

Before Nailer's somewhat-rhetorical question, the room had been mostly silent during the afternoon, limited to requests for tobacco or coffee and mission-specific utterances. The fact that there had been no joking, no insults, highlighted the strain. A three-day sniper mission in a terrorist hotbed or reconning enemy forces in arctic conditions was dangerous and miserable, but at least that was what they had signed up for. What they were used to.

"Does it matter?" McDonald asked, just as rhetorically. He stood to stretch.

Nailer continued. "Listen, I'm all about mission success, and I've followed a lot of orders given by worse commanders than Stevens and Hagen, and yeah, worse team leaders and Chiefs than you, Dan. That's the military. But I'm getting a little long in the tooth to miss my opportunity to get al-Baghdadi. This is my Super Bowl, man, and I want to go out like Peyton. Minus the tea-bagging and HGH scandals." His flat, angry face went serious. "I don't want to miss that mission to babysit a goddamn mosque."

Westhead listened with little concern. Sometimes the men needed to bitch, and sometimes he let them. This was not one of those times, especially when his authority was already being challenged.

"I wish I could properly express how little your 'wants' register on my radar, Nailer."

"You've made that clear, Chief, and as I said, when all this is over, we can have that conversation."

"I'll tell you if and when we can have that conversation! For the time being shut your mouth and keep eyes on that mosque!"

Nailer didn't respond. His gaze stayed out the window.

McDonald stood and stretched. "As fun as it is listening to mom and dad fight, I'm first watch in the morning. I'm going home to rack out for a few hours. Call me if anything comes up." He was headed toward the door when the single then double knock stopped his progress. GQ came in.

"Gentlemen," he said, removing his kufi and peeling off the prosthetic nose. "Hot one out there."

"How did it go with the imam?"

"Good, actually. I followed him after morning prayers, and he made an interesting stop. And I don't just mean the rub and tug downtown."

Westhead's eyebrows raised. "You're not serious."

"Serious I am. He had breakfast with some local business leaders, and from there, straight to a lovely little shopping center back on Euclid Road. Happy Landing Massage Therapy. I Googled the place during the hour he was inside, and confirmed it is an establishment of ill repute."

Nailer scoffed, "Like you'd have to Google it, shithead."

"Classic," McDonald said, suddenly very interested. "Did you get a look inside? H-h-how'd the girls look?"

A glare from Westhead brought them back on task. "But not pertinent to the op. McDonald, I thought you were leaving."

He raised his hands in surrender. GQ continued his briefing.

"*After* his handy is when it got interesting. He deployed some robust countersurveillance techniques, double-backs, going 15 in a 50, then speeding through a residential area. Even used a parking garage with two exits. Luckily The Activity had a dedicated drone on him, so I didn't have to stay too close. But that's when I knew I was onto something. After an hour of making sure he didn't have a tail, he stopped at a diner in Norfolk."

GQ looked up here, gauging his audience. The man was a master storyteller, and he knew he had hooked spectators. He decided to enjoy it a little.

"Dumpy little place back in Rosemont. Glad I didn't have to eat there. I saw a few things scurrying around in the back dumpsters looked like a cross between a rat and a dog. A Drat. Or a Rog. Did I just invent a new word? Maybe." His teammates remained still with a practiced discipline, lest emoted anxiety encourage further delay. "Anyway, I parked across the street while he sat in the lot for a good half hour, talking on the phone."

Nailer reached for the yellow pad, continuing a masterful job of ignoring the superfluous. "What time was that?"

"We arrived at the diner at 1145. He stayed in the car on what looked like a single phone call until 1219 before going in."

Nailer's brow furrowed. He set down the pad of paper, walked over to a laptop.

"I show his cell phone stationary in Rosemont during that time, but don't have a call that lasted that long. He spoke to his wife from 1145 to 1149 about household items, what was for dinner. Then a text to his daughter, "DO YOU HAVE DRAMA AFTER SCHOOL." Her reply at 1159, "NO." Then, no phone activity after until 1304, when he returned two emails to Jennifer Harper."

"Jennifer Harper?" Westhead asked.

"ICC admin. Basic stuff about counseling someone and when his monthly address to the congregation will be ready. Nothing of importance in his emails all day. But no other phone activity during that time."

They all realized what this meant.

"Burner," GQ said, narrowing his eyes. "Means he's hiding something. And I think I know what it is. You'll never believe who it was he had lunch with."

Westhead knew the answer to GQ's question before he even posed it.

"Basting. Dick Basting."

Surprise registered on McDonald and Nailer's faces, but only momentarily. It made sense.

"Bingo."

"Any idea what they discussed?"

He shook his head. "Nope. Remember, I'd already met the imam earlier that morning. If he made me in that diner, I would have been compromised. Had to stay in the lot. But they weren't in there long. Bagby entered at 1219, Basting exited at 1233, Bagby shortly thereafter."

"I bet those bastards are planning to revise the ROEs again," Westhead announced with venom. Each man seemed to find a particularly interesting spot on the wall or ceiling to stare at as the possibility set in. It was as if they didn't want to make eye contact, to witness each other's raised shoulders, balled fists. As if those physical signs of anger would only multiply their own. An air of shock suffocated the room.

"They must be using these attacks as evidence that we are creating more terrorists with our tactics rather than eliminating them," Nailer surmised. "Meeting secretly to prepare some sort of joint recommendation to the president?"

"Feels awfully familiar," Westhead breathed softly. "Whatever they were doing, they didn't want to be seen together."

GQ agreed. "That they did not, given those countersurveillance techniques. And the fact that the imam was communicating with someone on a burner proves just how cautious they are being this time around. If it had been the FBI or another agency without domestic drone access tailing him, that meeting would have gone unobserved."

"Guess we know why the president selected us for this mission. I wonder if he's even aware what they are up to."

A round of weary faces let the news sink in. It was beyond disheartening to think that their job was going to get even harder. Eventually, those not on watch exited into the evening.

Violence is on my mind. It's only been a day since the law firm bombing, but the headache is already back. Yes, we are operational, but that doesn't mean there can't be a little bloodletting during the downtime. I rack my brain for a suitable target. When it finally comes to me, air seems a little easier to come by, the tightness in my chest a little less restrictive. I tell the guys I'll be back later, and head into the afternoon.

The ACLU branch is nearly an hour away. A basic, single-story complex with a tile roof. It's parking lot, nearly empty. Across the street, a park, unused save for two youths kicking a soccer ball back and forth. The heat is stifling. Heavy and piercing. I wonder where their parents are. I sit in my car with the windows up and air conditioning off, allowing the sweat to thicken, windows steamed, the pressure of temperature pushing down, pleasurably suffocating, while I watch the children play, waiting for my target to come out of the flat office building across the street but can't help wondering why these kids, so young, are all by themselves IN THE MIDDLE OF THE GODDAMN DAY?

Clouds dart across the sky with alarming speed, dropping shadows on the children, on their ball, on the jungle gym and freshly planted trees and bike racks and big steel barbeques. Back and forth the clouds go, quicker now, at some points so fast I wonder if they aren't moving in reverse, but then they slow, like *slow*, slow, slow motion slow, and I feel my eyes start to cross and for the life of me I can't figure out where these kids' parents are and yeah, it's more alarming than it should be. A cloud draws my attention. It reminds me of a tank. Like a tank cruising through the blue directly at me. It looks like the old M60s, the ones they had in World War II, not the M1 Abrams tanks we had in Iraq, like the one that crushed a special-needs teenage boy outside of Haditha after he sprinted toward Alpha company, 1st Battalion, 3rd Marines while they were conducting a house-clearing operation. The boy, crying and screaming, ran straight at the Marines, arms extended with what looked like a swaddled baby, but I was overwatch on a roof overhead and could see the wires running from the bundle to the detonator taped to his left hand, that it was actually a doll with a chipped face concealing an IED. When I tried to acquire him, a pickup truck was blocking my shot, so I radioed the Marines' frequency to warn them but couldn't make comms, so as the kid got closer and closer all I could do was shoot into the ground around him which is when they finally looked alive because someone must have radioed the tank driver and he swung the turret in slow motion, the whine of his revving engine reaching me up on that roof while dust kicked out and he accelerated toward the kid, scattering the Marines, and just before the tank reached the kid he detonated and the tank drove through the pink spray, an arm and leg and pieces of human flying as it sped through the explosion, a vile mix tossed into the air with recognizable parts eventually coming to rest in an irrigation ditch and palm trees and an overlooking balcony.

The orange curtain starts to fall under those clouds as I think back to that day. When I look up, the picture I pulled up on my phone is closing the heavy-looking front door of the ACLU. Susan Karpavich takes a cautious step into the glittering twilight. She surveys the lot in what I interpret as a nervous manner, though I could be wrong. Not for the first time, I wonder if people have a sixth sense about impending danger. If she does, she chooses to ignore it.

Ms. Karpavich steps off the curb briskly, swinging a red bag over her left shoulder while digging out her keys. Security cameras outside the office building are obvious, so I let her climb into the older 5-Series BMW while I hum along with The Killers' "Mr. Brightside." She pulls onto 7th Street and fades into the rapidly darkening evening. I follow.

It doesn't take long for Ms. Karpavich to wind her way through city streets to a modest house on Curley Drive. I already know that only Cross and Pepper, her schnauzer and labradoodle, respectively, are waiting for her at home. Widowed, no children, her social media feeds suggest other than the pets, work is her only passion. When she pulls the Bimmer into the driveway, I slow as I pass, collecting the garage door opener's rolling code. The scanner can store and decode the door's signature, allowing me to spoof it at my leisure.

I park down the street, wait for her to get settled while darkness encroaches. Lights begin to pop on behind drawn blinds, televisions flickering against muted walls. The evening news and bath time. Car doors slam shut, young kids greet Dad at the doorstep. The nuances of suburbia. My brain tries to make a connection as it always does, revisionist history drawing parallels where there may be none. I find my eyelids getting heavy. I'm actually at peace, despite the current activity, an unfamiliar sense of security and well-being wrapping my psyche like a warm blanket. As soon as I recognize the sensation, identify the comfortability, my brain immediately jettisons any sentiment of pleasure. This is not a scene that I can ever be a part of, not anymore. Not that I ever really had, despite any contrary surface imagery.

It used to be that thoughts of my childhood would soften me, would make me want to push a child in a swing set, help an old woman with her groceries. They don't anymore, and I can feel my insides harden as I walk up Ms. Karpavich's driveway. Gloves go on tightly, hair net loosely. With the click of a button, the garage door rumbles open. I step from the dusk into the dimly lit garage, ease around the red BMW, try the door to the house. Locked. I take out a lock pick set. It's a thumb turn deadbolt—a rather robust locking system for an interior door, but easily pickable nonetheless. Cautious lady.

When the bolt snaps open, I ease the door inward, gently, silently. I can hear a television. Seinfeld. Just as I get a soft foot inside the house, the door slams back into me, bashing my skull and nearly knocking me to the floor. Shaking my head helps to collect muddy thoughts, although a dull whirl circles my brain. Shards of light seem especially bright, viewed through a narrow tube. A woman's repetitive shriek rises above the barking dogs, then the door slams into me again. My shoulder stops it this time, and I'm able to send it back into Ms. Karpavich with a loud crack. The screaming stops suddenly; the totality of the thud when she crumbles to the floor tells me she's out cold. I step over the limp body, a wash of blood covering her face, her nose pointed in the wrong direction. Both dogs whine and bark, frenzied, but stay in the living room, watching me tie up their mistress from afar.

"Welcome home, Suzi," I tell her. My head rings, but in a good way. I feel alive. I straddle her, securing her hands, face hot and animated, enjoying my work. I use the specialized flex cuffs again. Purposefully. It's a message. To the FBI, to Kopen, to Westhead. I'm here, and you will not stop me. When I'm done, I look over my work, notice the angle of her neck. I lean closer, two fingers on her jugular. There is only a faint response.

With a sinking heart, I know that I won't be able to question her about her lawsuit that publicly named 119 Special Operations Forces, men now being targeted by Islamic extremists through social media and the Internet. Or her last case with the ACLU, when they sued the Department of Defense over electronic surveillance techniques JSOC was utilizing in a joint task force with the FBI. The suit led to restrictions on how we could collect information on suspected terrorists both at home and abroad. Another bureaucrat hindering the people who put their lives on the line to keep this country safe. With no hesitation, I gently place her chin in my palm, the other hand cupping her left temple. With a violent twist, I finish the job. The breaking neck snaps loud enough that it shocks the dogs into silence. I leave her in a jumbled mess, slumped in the foyer like a sack of potatoes. I take a mental snapshot, reveling in another tiny piece of justice. It doesn't completely satiate my hunger, but hey, it's a start.

As I slink out the door, I can't get a wintergreen dip in fast enough.

VIRGINIA BEACH

"Never seen it."

"You've never seen it? Not one episode?"

"Not one."

"You're deprived, you know that?"

"Mom wouldn't let me when I was a kid. I actually think it was per Hagen's orders. He loved it but told her I was too young. And I've been a little busy since high school. Not much time for Netflix and chill."

Westhead sighed, like he was remembering something he should never have forgotten. "Hard to believe you're just a few years out of school. Although at the same time it's hard to believe you're not thirteen anymore, I guess."

Nate got up, opened the fridge. It was empty, as least of anything edible.

"You really gotta go shopping, Dan."

"For what? For the ten days a year I spend here? Dog food and beer, that's all I keep. Call for Chinese. And grab me a Corona."

Nate grabbed two, stepping over Tex and Spence, asleep snout to snout on the kitchen linoleum. He opened the beers, handed one to

Westhead, raised the other to his mouth. Narrowed eyes followed him.

"You're drinking now?"

Nate's shrug as he tipped the bottle was one of nonchalance. "Not a big deal. Just one or two. We only have an O-course tomorrow."

"When you rejoining your platoon in Iraq?"

"Had an email from Chief Kantor this morning. I should be flying out to Turkey with a resupply on Thursday, then'll hitch a ride from there."

"So you won't be here for Cheyenne's procedure?"

Nate drained the bottle, shook his head. "Hoping you will be, though."

"I should be. They'll be hard pressed to do it without Stevens. Generally, I go where he goes."

"Although not now."

"Not now."

"What happens if he doesn't make it back?"

"You mean what happens to Cheyenne?"

"Yeah to Cheyenne."

"Don't even want to think about it." He looked Nate deep in his eyes. "I won't let that happen."

"You going to tell me what you guys are doing?"

"I think you can answer that yourself."

"It's not just curiosity, Dan. This is my sister's life on the line."

"I know it, Nate, I know it. I will do everything I can to get COL Stevens back in one piece for the transplant. I don't like the fact that he keeps going out with us on missions, but there's nothing I can do about that. All I *can* do is have his six when we're downrange. And believe me, I'll have it."

"If he dies, she dies."

"I know that, Nate."

"Are you going back after al-Baghdadi?"

"I am part of an ordnance disposal unit."

"Fuck you."

"As you please."

Nate opened himself another beer, earning another glare.

"Since when do I contribute to the delinquency of minors?"

"I'm not a minor."

"You're not twenty-one."

"So I can—"

"—die for my country but not drink a beer? Yeah, I've heard that one."

"Doesn't make it not so."

"Do I have to remind you of your history? Your issues with pills and booze?"

"You do not. Especially when—"

Westhead cut him off again, angry. "Don't even, Junior. You don't know the first thing about my problems, about what I go through. You're the new guy, you're the one who can barely shave. Fresh in his first platoon. When your resume is a tenth of mine, you can start questioning me."

Nate went silent. They both drank, quickly. Nate was madder than he should have been. He got up, went into the kitchen. Poured himself a Jack Daniels, disregarding Westhead's silent rebuke, body language daring him to say something. He didn't. Nate went back into the living room with his glass, set it down with a thump on the coffee table.

"You pouting now?" There was an aggression to Westhead's question.

Nate ignored him as long as he could, finally shaking his head "no."

"You've seen a lot, Nate, growing up as you did. Maybe that helped you, maybe it hurt you in some cases. But never forget, you're not entitled to shit. You earn your Trident every day. We all do. Any one of us will snatch it from your chest if you're not meeting the standards. I don't give a fuck what your last name is, if I can't trust you, you aren't operating with us. We have to trust each other with our lives. Some guys treat you better because of who your dad was, some worse. For a new guy, you don't have it bad. But you better drop this self-pity." He set his bottle on the coffee table. "Counsel over."

The color left Nate's face. He beckoned his dog with a soft voice: "Come here, Spence. Here, boy."

The wiry hound dog raised an eyebrow, contemplating his master. Tex, his counterpart, jumped up, obediently padding over to Westhead and sitting at his feet. Spence lowered his head, back to sleep. Westhead chuckled.

"They know who the alpha is around here." Tex looked up in agreement, then barked toward the back door. Westhead instinctively reached for an end table, opening the drawer and placing a Glock on top.

"Who is it?" he called out. The cable box showed 10:16. They weren't expecting visitors.

"Osama Bin Laden," a familiar voice responded from the back patio. Nate's milky face perked flush, and he hopped out of his seat, quick to the door as a schoolboy.

"Commander," he gushed fondly before working to gather himself. "Good to see you, sir."

Hagen strode forward, surprised to see his protégé. He stopped inches from Nate's face. His forehead scrunched, eyes flaring before narrowing quickly. "You drunk?"

Nate adjusted the sloppy look from his face even as it rose several shades of pink.

"No, sir. Just—you know, a beer with the Chief."

Hagen eyed him suspiciously, finally nodded, understanding. Then: "How are you, son? Didn't expect you here."

Nate grinned sheepishly. "Been staying with Dan while I'm stateside. A little rocky at home right now."

The older man put his hand on his shoulder, offering a sympathetic face. "Unfortunately, that's not uncommon for men in our line of work, Butler. I told you that when you were a kid—this life should be no surprise to you."

Nate was quick to recover. "No, sir. I know my parents were the exception in the Teams, I'm okay with that." Then, stepping further into the kitchen, "Come in. Chief Westhead's in the living room."

Both Spence and Tex hopped up to sniff Hagen's sneakers and lick his hand. He reached into his pocket, coming out with a treat for both. They whined with excitement as he made his way through the house, leaving the sliding glass door open. The sound of the ocean came in with him.

"Commander, I've been hearing some disturbing things about you," Westhead said, handing his AOIC a beer. Nate pushed the glass of whiskey to the side as discretely as he could. It didn't go unnoticed. "Tell me they're not true."

Hagen did not seem concerned. "What's that?"

"You wouldn't let the boy watch *The Wire* when he was a teenager? The best show in the history of television?" He motioned toward Nate. "That's akin to child abuse."

"Thought it was too violent. Bad language."

"I see."

CDR Hagen took a seat on the sofa. He and Westhead regarded each other silently, ignoring the young SEAL standing in the kitchen with the dogs. No one spoke. Finally:

"I guess I'll take these guys for a walk." Reluctantly, Nate moved, whistled to the dogs. No one tried to stop him.

When he slid the porch door shut, Westhead began. "I thought you were in Arizona with the rest of the team."

"I went up to DC to brief the president, then came back for some additional mission prep." He paused. "And to brief you."

Westhead leaned back, re-crossed his legs. The left knee gave a loud pop, his right hand rubbing it almost absentmindedly. "Don't know if I like the sound of that. Tell me you didn't come all the way over here because of guys complaining that I'm asking questions about specialized ammo and flex cuffs."

Hagen wagged his head, a mix of confusion and annoyance. "Happily, I can say I have no idea what you are talking about, and more so, don't want to know. No, it's about the latest bombing in DC. The administration is officially in an uproar. Operation Palindrome is going to be terminated. The president is pulling your team from the mosque."

Westhead's mouth started to open, but he clamped it shut, wisely. The commander wasn't done.

"After the latest attack, he's under the impression Homeland Security and the FBI are better equipped to run the investigation domestically. They will cover all aspects, including surveillance on targets of opportunity. The administration has drawn up an updated list of people and organizations they think could be viable targets and is detailing federal agents to those locations. It's a brave new world, my friend."

"Does the president thinks that we have inside knowledge? That we could be the ones responsible?"

"He gave me no indication that he believes that."

"Except we have an FBI agent investigating our unit. Agent Kopen's constant presence isn't enough to make you think that?"

"I serve my command, Chief, as do you. I don't bother trying to guess what the president is thinking. Me? I'm just a glorified knuckle-dragger. You're not even glorified."

"The hell you are. What about our rules of engagement? Any indication they're going to be changed again? You know that we reconned a clandestine meeting between Imam Bagby and Dick Basting, right?"

"Those two have known each other for years."

"They met in secret, after doing everything in their power to make sure they weren't followed. Sound like two college buddies reminiscing about fraternity football? We think they're going to recommend changes to the rules of engagement again. The last time Basting conducted secret meetings, that's what happened. Do they have the president's ear again? Maybe we should plan on conducting missions with BB guns, asking terrorists if they wouldn't mind please coming with us and oh, by the way, are you or anyone you know planning on blowing us up?"

"The president has made no mention to us of another ROE update. But again, they wouldn't. It's outside our purview and nothing for us to concern ourselves with. Until—if—it happens. Again, we follow orders from our commander in chief. And you follow ours. That's the way it works and has always worked. So quit yer bellyaching. Dick Basting is the president's oldest friend and his current foreign policy advisor. You start making accusations that they are up to something, the president will have us pulling security for diplomat's wives making humanitarian trips to Africa." Hagen's facial expression indicated the discussion was over. He leaned back, taking up more of the couch before finishing his point.

"Blade has a conference call tomorrow morning with the president and my guess is your squad will officially be pulled at that time. You got another day on the mosque, but after that you're off to Arizona, and if we're lucky, back to Syria with the rest of the team for another crack at al-Baghdadi. We aren't missing this time. Where else would you rather be?"

"Roger that, sir. Another beer?"

"Don't mind if I do." He put the empty on the table and raised his voice. "Butler, you can come back in now."

Westhead was happy when the sliding glass door opened and the warm summer air returned with Nate and the dogs. The fan overhead hummed peacefully. Someone on the boardwalk shouted, a drunken, carefree greeting to a friend. Rushing waves rolled forward like cyclical thunder. A racket as Tex and Spence raced back into the living room.

"Still warm out there," Nate said.

"Not as hot as it is in Syria. I spoke with Chief Kantor, you're reassigned to JOE-CAG until further notice. You'll ride with us to Arizona and then Iraq and on to Syria. All I ask of you is to do everything you're told with absolute perfection, the first time, with no questions or complaints."

Nate's posture straightened. His eyes went wide. "Hooyah, sir. The SEAL way."

"Hasn't anyone told you to knock that hooyah crap off yet? You're not in BUD/S anymore." Hagen stood to leave. "Teams-n-shit."

"Teams-n-shit. Mostly shit," Nate replied.

"Ah, so you know that one?"

PORTSMOUTH

Street lights blanketed Westhead's path with a subdued glare. It had been another night of tossing and turning after Hagen left, and was still hours before normal people woke. The only ones on the placid Virginia Beach streets seemed to be cops and drunks. The old adage your father delivered about not being out past midnight held true.

He passed the mosque slowly, its bright flood lights revealing an oasis among potholed county roads and faded strip malls. When his phone brightened in the cup holder, its shrill ring broke what for him passed as a peaceful moment.

"Whitey, how goes it in Arizona?" Westhead answered. "Must be early there. Or late."

Adam sounded tired but eager. "Awesome, dude! Quite a production. Haven't seen a mock-up like this since Neptune. Wait till you guys get out here."

"Sounds like that will be sooner than later. Hagen came to see me last night. Apparently, the president isn't happy with our work here. Guess his whole speech in the hanger was bullshit."

"You mean to tell me that a politician lied to you? Say it ain't so. You must be devastated. Wait until you hear about Santa and the Easter Bunny."

"What about them? Is the Tooth Fairy okay?"

"She's fine, I saw her sneaking out of Thor's hooch last night."

"So what's up? You just calling 'cause you miss my voice?"

"More of a heads-up. It's a little touchy, but I wanted to read you in on the team leader briefs I've been having with Pos and Hell out here. Especially since, you know, some of the guys aren't thrilled about some of your questions. But this is more about Stevens."

Westhead had pulled up to the safe house but stayed in the car. The dark lot was nearly empty.

"They'll get over it. What about Stevens?"

"We think he's cracking, man."

Westhead picked his words carefully. "Blade has always been a little off, that's what makes him who he is. And what makes him a good SpecOps leader."

"It's more than that now, bro. Things that make him operationally unsafe. He's forgetting things. Mumbling to himself. He disappeared for four hours last night. We had no idea where our OIC was as we're finishing mission prep. Still have no idea where he went."

"He's the boss, Adam. You don't need to know where he is."

"Don't give me that chain of command horse manure. This isn't the fleet. We're only as strong as our weakest link, and right now, me and the other team leaders are worried we have that weak link in our OIC."

"Have you addressed this with Hagen?"

"Not yet. He was still back East when we had our little pow-wow. When you guys get here, we want to sit him down. He has to have noticed himself."

"I noticed when Doc Soto told him he was a marrow match for Cheyenne. His reaction ... His reaction was—not what I was expecting."

"How so?"

Westhead leaned back, staring upward in thought. "He seemed like he didn't really care. I guess there wasn't much of a reaction at all, which is what surprised me. At the very least, I would have expected annoyance at having to go through the procedure, but there wasn't even that. It was just—nothing."

It was some time before Adam responded. "That's what we're talking about, Dan. I just don't know that he can be trusted anymore. Maybe the years and pace have caught up with him. He wouldn't be the first."

Neither of them wanted to say what they knew the other was thinking, but there it was, hanging between them like flaming wreckage, too hot, too risky to touch.

"Do you think—" Westhead began before tailing off.

Adam's voice came quietly through the phone. "I don't think anything. Pos and Hell, they're not saying it either. God, we don't even want to think of that, of what it would mean for our unit. We're just saying the man has been acting funny, and we need to get it under control. Let's use this as an opportunity to regroup, to make sure we're protecting each other. And for you to make nice with the rest of the guys. Because if we don't, this investigation is going to tear us apart."

"I couldn't agree more. Thanks for filling me in. I just pulled up to the safe house. Let me think about how to handle this and get back with you. Sounds like I'll be seeing you soon."

"Looking forward to it."

"Aw, you miss me, don't you?"

"Like the deserts miss the rain."

Westhead pocketed the phone and entered the alley. At its end, where the parking lot continued, a single, faint light caught his attention. He stopped, peering toward it, senses heightened. Something felt amiss. The light suddenly went out, leaving him alone in the dark. Behind him, a footstep scraping the pavement echoed across the alley entrance. He spun around, hand moving to the small of his back, closing over the Glock's familiar grip. He let his right hand swing by his knee, the pistol ready but out of sight. With deliberate steps, he began easing back the way he came. Half-crouching, he kept his head on an even swivel, maintaining 360-degree awareness. Each footstep landed carefully, noiseless, hitting the gravel heel first, then toe. When he made it back to the alley's entrance, he paused once again. No unaccounted lights appeared, no foreign sounds. He looked and listened, soaking in the surroundings. Some early-rising birds began their halting songs, the chirps particularly crisp against the approaching daybreak. A weak breeze blew against his face. A car on the main road. It had rained overnight, and its tires kicked up puddles as it passed. After, complete silence, save for a dripping gutter in the alley. Too quiet.

Westhead took cover against a wall where he could take in most of the parking lot. Across the street, the lights of the mosque continued to glow in a muted haze. His focus landed on a black Tahoe with tinted windows, backed into the far corner of the lot. If someone was watching them, it would be a perfect surveillance spot. Unobstructed views of their team's small office and the ICC across the road.

The SUV was covered with droplets of rain, telling him it had been parked in the spot since earlier that night. It glistened under the few streetlights casting shadows in the parking lot. The light directly above it was out. Could be coincidence, Westhead thought, or the driver could have selected the spot because of that or even disabled the light himself.

The sky was beginning to brighten. He stared into its lightening grayness. Soon, morning would arrive.

Westhead made a decision. Cautiously, he retraced his steps back through the alley, gun still at his side, stopping just before it opened up into the other side of the lot. The SUV was now on his left. From this angle, he still couldn't tell if it was occupied. But he was going to find out.

He lifted the lid off a trashcan and found what he was looking for. Taking a knee, he peeked around the corner. Seeing no activity, he launched the bottle high in the air, retreating quickly back into the alley as it traveled. By the time he reached the other end, a crash had exploded across the lot, the breaking glass echoing off the pavement.

Back in a crouch, Westhead risked a look. He thought longingly of the developmental weapon they were testing that shoots around corners, but was not yet operational. For a moment, nothing happened. Then, a rear door to the SUV opened. A thin man in white shirt and tie, no jacket, sleeves rolled to his elbows, eventually eased himself out, two-handing a pistol. He backpedaled unsurely around the rear of the Tahoe, lips tight, looking back into it as if he had drawn the short straw. Duty urged him forward reluctantly. He continued to where the bottle had smashed, examining shards of glass at his feet.

Interesting, Westhead thought. It had to be feds. But were they watching his team or the mosque? Or both?

He took the opportunity to dart from the alley, reaching the bumper of an unoccupied van without drawing the attention of the fed. From his new vantage point he could no longer see him, but could make out clumsy footsteps shuffling farther from the SUV. He needed to get closer and take down the tag number. That would be the only way to determine who was operating in the area.

Then, complete silence. The man had stopped moving; sporadic traffic on the main road had ceased. No birds called, the wind on hiatus. From experience, Westhead knew that sudden and complete calm usually meant only one thing. His senses amplified correspondingly. While considering the stillness, he suddenly sensed a presence behind him. Imperceptibly flicking the safety off his pistol, the rest of his muscles taut, he prepared to confront. Instead, a voice rang out in the approaching morning.

"FBI. Drop that weapon."

His first instinct was to roll into a shooting position and neutralize the threat. But then he remembered he was on American soil, and engaging an FBI agent was certainly not within his ROEs. Still, there was no chance of him going unarmed. Without so much as a flinch, he spoke to whoever was behind him.

"I have a concealed carry permit for this firearm. I am going to turn slowly toward you. I am not going to raise the firearm."

The voice replied louder. It sounded familiar.

"You will place the gun on the deck and slowly walk backward toward the sound of my voice."

Deck, Westhead thought. Interesting. Only a military man would call it a *deck*. Then it hit him.

"Good morning, Agent Kopen. I think you know that there is no way I am going to relinquish this firearm. You also know that if I choose to engage you, you will go down, and in a hurry. So again, I am going to come toward you slowly, and we can talk. I would ask you to not make any aggressive movements toward me, or I will be forced to defend myself. Understood?"

There was a long pause, which Westhead expected. FBI agents weren't used to being told what to do. While he waited for a response, he continued to turn slowly in that direction. A figure cut into the navy sky, its features not yet recognizable, but Westhead knew exactly who was standing twenty yards away in the dark windbreaker, steady hands pointing a .45 at his center mass.

"Chief Westhead, I am not going to ask you again."

"Agent Kopen, I am not going to tell you again."

They each took a step forward, eyes straight ahead, pistols leveled at each other.

"Drop your weapon."

"Not going to happen."

The twenty yards became fifteen. Westhead could see the man's slight paunch, meticulously styled hair. The pale blue eyes were intense. Alert but not scared. There was no sweat on his brow. They moved closer.

"You know what we have here, right?" Westhead said.

"A Mexican standoff?"

"I was going to say a failure to communicate."

"Some men you just can't reach."

Ten yards.

"You do know that if it comes to shots fired, I'll put you down before your finger ever touches the trigger."

"That may be so. But not him." Kopen raised his head as if greeting someone behind Westhead. A throat cleared from that direction, then a second, nervous voice.

"Sir, drop your weapon."

Westhead smiled.

"Something funny, Chief?"

"The fact that you don't realize you're both covered."

"Morning, Dan." The voice came from further back, behind the second agent. McDonald. "I have target left, you take target right."

"Roger that."

"On three."

"One."

"Two."

Westhead felt the second agent fidgeting to his six. Still directly in front of him, not more than five yards away, Agent Kopen gripped his pistol securely, cold stare locked on Westhead.

"Now it's definitely a Mexican standoff."

"Wrong, sir," called out Nailer. The words seemed to float just above head level, like a fog. "You and your partner are drastically out gunned. There is a fire team with precision weapons levelled on each of you. As you know, we are trained to kill, not wound. I would advise you both to lower your weapons before we get out of our comfort zone."

Kopen began to smile, just slightly at first, but soon it grew, grew into a large, sloppy grin. His shoulders began to heave, and then he was laughing, laughing like he had just heard the funniest joke ever told. But through the laughter, a shadow visibly swept across his forehead. The eyes stayed serious, never straying from Westhead's.

"And the award for the biggest dick goes to JOE-CAG," Kopen finally said, lowering his pistol and holstering it. "Stand down, Neil."

"I'm going to assume you are talking about the appendage and not our personalities," Westhead joked. He couldn't help but be amused. His right hand was extended when he stepped forward. Kopen shook it. "I'll also assume that bumping into you here is not a coincidence."

Despite his defeat, an air of confidence settled over Kopen, even as the three JOE-CAG operators surrounded him. It wasn't so much the lack of humility as it was lack of embarrassment which perplexed Westhead. He soon discovered why.

"No, Chief," he answered. "Not a coincidence. What say I buy you a cup of coffee and fill you in?"

Westhead holstered his own pistol, a new scowl eclipsing his face to contrast the satisfied glint Kopen wore. He sensed what was coming and wasn't happy about it.

"Too early for a scotch? Nailer, Mac, head back in and continue your assignments. Agent Kopen, I have a better idea than coffee. Why don't you come with me to have our chat?"

Westhead walked to his Jeep without confirming the passenger. Only when the engine turned over did Kopen find his legs and jump into the passenger's seat, intrigue defeating pride.

He rolled down the window to address his partner. Westhead recognized him from Arlington National Cemetery. He'd been one of the agents snapping pictures of their group.

"Neil, go with those two up to their safe house." Off Westhead's pending objection: "Allow it, or I shut you down right now. You'll be getting a call from COL Stevens this morning with the president's instructions on how this operation will be handled moving forward. The truth is, your team should already have been pulled. Consider this a professional courtesy."

Westhead gritted his teeth, knowing he was right. The writing had been inked with Hagen's visit the previous night. Now, it seemed Kopen knew something he didn't.

"Go ahead," he told Nailer and McDonald. "Try not to hurt him," he added, equal parts joke and threat.

They hovered over the pudgy FBI agent, enveloping him, frames disproportionately muscular. Shaggy beards and hair made them especially wild-looking against such clean cut and fragile features. Neil's furtive glances made for a poor effort at not reeking of inferiority.

"Have fun," Kopen called out as the Jeep sped from the lot.

The first few miles passed in silence. Westhead delivered his standard aggressive driving performance, perhaps even exaggerating a bit for his audience. For his part, Kopen remarkably managed to not white-knuckle the door handle when they whipped into oncoming traffic to avoid the first red light, tires eliciting an aggressive squeal. Determined to not speak first, even if it meant to ask for a destination, Kopen sat impassively, though seat belt tight.

When they eventually drove under a Naval Air Station Oceana Dam Neck Annex sign, Kopen gave his driver a sideways glance but still said nothing. A uniformed guard checked their identification at a blue-roofed guard hut, and they were on base.

Now carefully driving the speed limit, Westhead wound the car through the subdued order inherent to military installations. He gave a wide berth to a group of sailors running in formation, bright green reflective straps secure across torsos. All stop signs were afforded the strictest interpretation of the law, crosswalks patiently waited in front of as the morning's mostly uniformed pedestrians made their way to drab, yellowed buildings with impeccable but basic landscaping. Finally, he pulled the Jeep into a remote lot ringed by barbed wire and shut off the engine.

"Here we are," he announced, turning to his passenger.

"And where is 'here,' Chief?"

"A place not many people get to see, Seth. It is Seth, isn't it? Do you mind if I call you Seth?"

Agent Kopen's head flicked slightly to get a better look at his surroundings. "Sure," he answered.

They got out, started walking, Kopen still unsure what this place was. Before them, a nondescript building. Behind it, part of a field was visible. The whole compound was fenced and gated.

"Great. I appreciate that, Seth. You can call me Dan, or Chief if you want. Even call me Pig, but that nickname has kind of fallen by the wayside over the years."

"Pig, huh? That because you carried the M60 Echo 4?"

There was a subdued smugness, a sense of honor in Westhead's nod. A pride in the tough jobs.

"I carried the Pig in my Ranger platoon," said Kopen. "Heavy son of a bitch, but nothing makes you look cooler than the twenty-five-pound necklace."

Westhead examined him, gauging something. He seemed to find it. "Indeed, I'm sure you did. Look cool, that is. But I thought we would fire some more advanced weaponry today. Maybe we'll even see some real-life members of SEAL Team 6. If they aren't, you know, out saving the world. This *is* technically their range. And incidentally, where I think that rogue operator is that you're looking for. But hey, that's not my job. Still remember your CQB from Ranger Regiment?"

Kopen's eyebrows rose. "So, which is it? Are you trying to push the heat onto DEVGRU by taking me here? Or is this some trial by fire? Testing my mettle in combat?"

"Who says I have an ulterior motive? Maybe I just want to give you the chance to shoot some cool ass guns."

"That's appreciated, Chief. Unnecessary, but appreciated. Remember, you have your skillset, I have mine. It's been some time since mine included close-quarters battle. But have no fear, I'm still sound in the investigative department. Maybe that's what has you so nervous."

"Nervous? Who's nervous? And don't worry about the degradation of your shooting skills, Seth. I'll make sure you're safe in there." Westhead opened the door, leading into a multistory kill house.

"I wasn't worried," Kopen said as they entered. "But don't be surprised if you're surprised."

"What is that, some ancient Eastern saying?" Westhead screwed his eyes tight, whispering in an unidentifiable accent: "*Only when the wind is at your back can true flatulence be achieved.*" He lurched ahead, chuckling at his own joke.

Kopen muttered to his back, "Funny," before hustling to catch up.

By the time Kopen had followed him into the armory, Westhead already had an automatic weapon in hand. After examining the magazine, the sights, checking the grips, he offered it to the FBI agent.

"This one should do. MP7A. The next-generation SpecOps weapon—why shouldn't our country's premier law enforcement agency get a chance to fire something so cutting edge? Think you can find your way around it?"

As seemed to be his custom, Kopen took his time answering, doing so with few words. He was not a man for hyperbole; let others underestimate you, his father always told him, and their impression of you can only go up.

"I'll manage." He clumsily took the rifle by the stock, holding it away from his body as if poisonous. Then, with a series of smooth jerks and clicks, he expertly disassembled, then reassembled, the weapon.

If Westhead was impressed, he didn't let on. "Would you like Kevlar?" he asked. The tone was a challenge, almost a taunt. Kopen apprised his host with suspicion.

"And why would I need that? Should I be worried about an accidental discharge?"

Westhead offered a wry, if not culpable smirk, still holding out the vest with two limp fingers. "Accidental discharge? No such thing."

Kopen disregarded both the veneer and body armor, accepting eye and ear protection while securing his weapon in the high ready position.

"Good. This way."

Before them, a hallway, narrow, lined with doors. Westhead stopped before the first one, dropped, and began a series of push-ups. Kopen watched him for a moment, head swiveling 180 degrees. After realizing it wasn't a joke, he reluctantly started pushing out his own. Heart rate properly elevated, Westhead popped up and suddenly mule-kicked the first door, dynamically entering the kill house. Kopen, scrambling, followed behind, exercising careful muzzle discipline.

They moved fluidly, one left, one right. When an outline of a bad guy popped up, Westhead engaged, the suppressed weapon sputtering competently in his hands.

"Moving."

"Moving."

An outline of a blond woman. In her arms, a baby. Kopen's finger flinched, but he left the target unmolested. The next cutout wore a head scarf, held an AK. Kopen let loose with a quick burst. "Moving." Scanning for additional targets. "Moving."

"Clear left."

"Clear right."

They safed and cleared their weapons, lifted the ear protection.

"Well I'll be ..." Westhead clucked, walking forward.

Kopen smiled, fingered his target. "I'd say, what, a three-inch diameter?"

Westhead examined it, measuring his thumb over the three tightly spaced holes. "'Bout that," he replied.

Content, they slid to the other end of the room, repeated the process over Westhead's target. Four, if not five inches separated the farthest two holes. Westhead sighed.

"Looks like you got me, agent."

"Nice of you to say so. In case you didn't understand earlier, your team is being pulled from the mosque. The FBI is taking over surveillance. I'm sure you'll be happy to get back to 'ordnance disposal.'" He patted him on the back and exited the room.

Westhead did a good job at hiding his ire, wiping sweat with a smile. The news wasn't anything he wasn't expecting. They retrieved their phones, wallets, keys, and side arms from a locker before stepping into the afternoon. When he checked his email, Westhead's eyes widened, face contorted in anger and shock.

"What is it?" Kopen asks.

"Nothing. Get in. We're out of here, on the double."

Thinking about yesterday's meeting between Bagby and Basting still has my face flushed and heart rate swift. I'm beside myself with anger and hatred.

Similar clandestine meetings had taken place ahead of the Basting Institute's final report to the president before Operation Atlas, and soon after that our ROEs were changed. That time, it had been Imam Shami meeting with Dick Basting. If I had taken them out before they could convince the president that our operating tactics were "affecting hearts and minds," a lot of good men would still be alive. It goes without saying that I can't let it happen again. The whole point of forming JOE-CAG was to protect us from restrictive rules of engagement. Hence why I have to take out the president and his weak advisors. I missed Basting once. I won't a second time.

My hands massage throbbing temples. As expected, the activity gives no relief, and I can only consider tearing my hair out follicle by follicle. I'm just barely able to keep my thoughts in order, the exercise of pacing around the tight office our team is working out of necessary to keep a semblance of sanity. There's a small television. I flick it on. CNN.

The first story tells of the heartbreaking woes of the Kardashian clan, something about a nude pic one of them accidentally put on social media. The colors on the screen start to blur each time my attention goes back to it. I have to look away, quickly, blinking, shaking my head in an attempt to clear the optic palette. It's futile, and soon the screen is dancing all over the room, the greens and reds and whites blending into a psychedelic kaleidoscope that bends my brain until I find myself hunched over, palms tight against my ears, pressing, pressing, with a force unnecessary until finally the pressure is too great and then it's like a valve was opened and I can almost hear the steam whistle announcing that it's over, this episode is over, allowing me to think again, see again, the world unblurred and suddenly dignified. The relief is immediate and doesn't go unappreciated. It occurs to me how complete and total the lack of respect is for a tortured mind.

With the manic incident past, the world is free to rush back at its regularly scheduled pace. My head still feels a little light, the overhead lights a little bright, but I'm able to pull it together. The television again pulls my attention, this time with a report that is of the utmost interest.

"Today in Syria, ISIS leaders celebrated the mass slaughter of hundreds of civilians in Aleppo, mostly women and children. Many, persecuted as Christians, while others were found guilty of other crimes under the Islamic State, such as listening to Western music or smoking cigarettes. The victims were packed into steel cages and lit on fire, burned alive. Ibrahim al-Baghdadi, the founder of the terrorist group, released a statement praising the genocide."

The screen fills with the face of the man I've been hunting for the past six years. The face that fills most of my hours, both waking and sleeping, that has been on the cover of two warning orders and is of course the target of our current mission prep. Any residual fogginess is replaced by a blinding rage, a sharp stab of focus that I am immediately grateful for. Bagby, Basting, the president, and al-Baghdadi, in no particular order. I still haven't decided on Kopen's fate.

"I praise the bravery of the mujahedeen who carried out this beautiful act in the name of Allah the benevolent," the British voiceover says across the confident, evil smirk. "The Zionists and nonbelievers will be expelled from the land, God willing, and the caliphate will reign for a thousand years."

"The brutal ISIS leader is rumored to have been the target of two failed US-led Special Operations missions, both resulting in American casualties, including a former Navy SEAL earlier this month. The first of those operations, in August of 2011, led to the death of thirty US service members, mostly from the secretive SEAL Team 6, when their helicopter was shot down outside of Fallujah, Iraq. That tragedy still represents the greatest loss of life in US Special Operations history."

More grim statistics flash across the screen, more images of prisoners clad in orange preparing to be beheaded, more smoke and fire and death and bodies. They still my pulse, lend a certain focus to my thoughts. It's a singular concentration now, inner turmoil turned outward to direct my rage on my real enemies.

The television flies across the room, a satisfying smash sending pieces to all four corners. I am alone, and the crash is followed by an unnerving silence.

I decide to go for a run.

My pace is fast, despite an already-scorching morning. I belt out Bad Religion loudly as I push the tempo. My headphones are at top volume and I can't hear the world above them.

"Well, now do you feel a little better,
Lift up your head and walk away.
Knowing we're all in this together,
For such a short time anyway."

The miles fly by, and like the sweat covering me in a slick dampness, anger and pain pour out. I'm all too aware that just like the sweat, the anger and pain will always be replenished, no matter the efforts to expel it. That I've come to terms with it doesn't make it any less blood-curdling.

When I get back, there's a secure email in my inbox requiring an immediate brief from JSOC. It's about al-Baghdadi, but has nothing to do with the genocide shown on CNN. I'm informed an F-18 pilot ejected over Syria this morning and is now being held hostage by ISIS. I scramble to find the other guys, make sure everyone has been briefed. This type of mission is our bread and butter, and we expect to be spun up immediately.

Dispositions shudder with rage when the team hears about LCDR Wilson, the downed pilot. Now there's an anger to our preparations, an even colder focus as we go about mission prep. Not a word or action is wasted. Jokes stop, smiles nonexistent. The desire to end alBaghdadi was already at an emotional threshold, but now that there is an American pilot's life at stake, we are biting at the chain, begging to be unleashed.

I, for one, certainly enjoy the underlying threat of violence. It's always a part of me, and seeing my teammates with that same almost frenzied need for carnage allows me to feel comparatively normal. It's not easy being the most bloodthirsty man in such an ultra-violent field. It says something when men who have killed other men all over the world with no remorse or hesitation look at you sideways for your vicious enthusiasm.

Word comes down from JSOC that there will be mission updates when the whole team is together in Arizona. The president has pulled the mosque op and placed the entire team on stand-by for a Priority 1 mission. *Good*, I think, *we're not in the business of protection. We're in the business of killing bad guys*—here, I can't help but hear Brad Pitt's character in *Inglourious Basterds*:" '... *And, cousin, business is a-boomin'!*

LITTLE CREEK

For the return trip from Dam Neck, the base's traffic laws were more suggestive in nature than unflimsy rules. It was another quiet ride, the only conversation when Westhead dialed the safe house number and offered a few grunts to GQ.

"We heard," GQ said softly.

"I'll be back in fifteen. Have everything packed and ready to go. Operations can do a full site scrub after we're gone."

GQ responded in a voice designed not to be overheard. "I take it you're not alone."

"Correct."

"Me neither. Talk in person."

Agent Kopen addressed his driver. "I thought we had just come to an agreement, Chief. What is it, exactly, that you are trying to hide from me?" He didn't get an answer.

Westhead accelerated through a yellow light. They were back at the office building quickly, the return trip taking significantly less time than the outbound.

GQ, Nailer, and McDonald were already outside loading a black windowless panel van. Neil, the other FBI agent, watched them, hands in pockets. There was hardly a pause to their work when Westhead and Kopen screeched to a halt a few spots over.

"Agents, this where we'll have to part. Good luck babysitting the mosque."

Kopen seethed. "Someone is going to tell me what the hell is going on."

The JOEs all paused, looking at him with something like amusement.

"No, we're not, agent. You got what you wanted, what the president wanted. The ICC and Imam Bagby are all yours." Westhead motioned for his guys to get in. He slid the van's door shut. "Enjoy."

The van sped away unceremoniously, leaving the two FBI agents standing alone in the lot, one furious, one confused.

GQ snickered once they were on the road. "What a couple of incompetents. Is the FBI entrance exam given in crayon?"

Westhead headed toward the highway. "Don't be so quick to discount the Kopen guy. There's more to him than he wants you to think."

"Either way, we're done with those dolts. What's the plan? Do they know where the pilot is being held yet?"

"Still unclear. The Activity is continuing to gather information while the president looks at all options for securing his release."

"And for us?"

"Us? We're headed to the airport, gents. The CIA was kind enough to provide us with a jet to Arizona, where we'll join the rest of the team training on the mock-up. That op just got bumped up a priority—intel is trickling in that makes them believe LCDR Wilson is being held at al-Baghdadi's compound. I recommend getting some shut-eye during the flight; no idea when we'll get the chance again."

"Sleep? What's that?" asked GQ, cracking a Red Bull. "Sounds familiar."

No one laughed.

Soon they were in the Downtown Tunnel, racing through the concrete to Naval Station Norfolk. Sleep was the last thing on their minds.

They were too amped, had too much work to do. Westhead popped in his Bluetooth while he drove, able to get further instructions from Stevens in Arizona. GQ spoke with former coworkers in the CIA's Special Operations Group for the latest intel on the pilot's location, while Nailer and McDonald made a checklist of necessary gear.

Once they were waved onto base, they headed toward Chambers Field. The men were too preoccupied to appreciate the naval might they passed as the van travelled up Hampton Boulevard, but if the harbor had pulled their attention, they would have been privy to an impressive row of monstrous gray behemoths making the Chesapeake Bay look distinctly pond-like: Nimitz-class aircraft carriers, battleships, amphibious personnel carriers, even a submarine being towed into dry dock. The bustle of maritime dominance. Overhead, E-3s, cargo planes, F-18s, took off and landed amongst the Nighthawks and Sea Dragons circling Willoughby Bay. But these SpecOps warriors had launched from and staged on, quartered in and been bored silly aboard these ships and aircraft over lengthy careers. If the firepower registered, it was only peripherally.

As they skirted the golf course on Admiral Taussig Boulevard, an SUV pulled up next to them on. A kid, not more than ten, stuck his tongue out. His sister giggled. McDonald stuck his tongue out back at them. The kid pushed his nose up. McDonald did the same. Before Westhead pulled ahead, McDonald had turned his eyelids inside out, and was crossing his eyes at the gaping-mouth youths. He turned in his seat to watch the SUV recede, a contented smile tickling his face.

"What the hell are you grinning at?" GQ asked him. McDonald looked away, watched the airport come into focus.

The van pulled right up onto the airfield, where they found CDR Hagen waiting less than patiently. In a white polo with faded jeans and sneakers, the civilian look came across forced. Engines on the glittering Gulfstream G650 he stood beside were already whirling, making it loud and brisk on the runway. Hagen held the grimness, the weight of this new mission, in his stance, in his flared nostrils, pursed mouth. A low-sitting hat and aviator sunglasses couldn't hide the aggression in his face. Since the Second World War, pilots had held a special place in every soldier's heart; American air superiority was a battlefield equalizer, and the troops didn't just rely on it to get them in and out of combat. Many times, the order for danger close air artillery in an operator's earpiece had given them confident chills, knowing the sky was about to open up and their foes decimated by a precise display of aerial bombardment. There was a special feeling boots on the ground got when they heard the thump of an Apache arriving on station, or the buzz of an A-10 Warthog's Gatling gun chewing through enemy forces. All of these men had cheered from afar as high-flying B-2's dropped their payload ahead of ground assaults, softening up Taliban or al-Qaeda positions and all but guaranteeing successful missions. Now it was their turn for repayment.

Westhead greeted the commander with a respectful nod. It was too loud on the tarmac to speak, and Hagen appeared in a rush. They bounded up the stairs and into the sudden silence of the exquisitely furnished plane. Hagen leaned into the cockpit to address the two pilots checking gauges, his voice muted but authoritative.

"We're taking off in five minutes. I don't care who else is on the manifest, my men will not be kept out of this fight. If whoever we're waiting for isn't here in five, they're getting left."

The taller pilot seemed to be the one in charge, but still unsure how to respond. He lowered his headset to his neck, cleared his throat.

"Sir, we have orders to hold this plane for an additional VIP. We are being instructed not to take off until he has arrived."

"And we still don't know who this 'VIP' is?"

"That is correct, sir."

"Let me be clear. I don't care if it's Bo Derek on her way to do a strip show for the troops, in five"—he peeked at his watch—"four minutes this plane is skyward." He spun away from the cockpit to dissuade further discussion.

GQ contorted himself to let him pass. "Hey, Commander, who the hell is Bo Derek?"

Hagen lowered himself into the beige leather seat closest to the cabin door and stared onto the tarmac, fidgeting. His team leader took the recliner opposite him.

"Any idea who might be riding with us?"

Hagen shook his head without tearing his focus from the port-hole window.

"Must be someone important to give us the big boy," Westhead said, gesturing at the plush accommodations. "They usually stick us with windowless cargo planes. Or worse, commercial."

Hagen placed his sunglasses on top of his hat. "Did you notice the tail number on this jet, Dan?"

He thought about it. "N397P."

"Recognize it?"

"I don't think so."

"I do. It was on a Boeing 737 I flew on from Kabul to Bucharest in 2003. A rendition flight. It also was on a Learjet I watched go in and out of Ankara continually when we were deep undercover in Turkey. And remember on Team 2 when the CIA flew us into Columbia on that Twin Otter? N397P."

"So?"

"So, that means this plane doesn't exist. It's a ghost tag. Most of the Air Branch planes are at least legally registered to shell companies or law firms. The fact that this one isn't means that there will be no record of this flight and who was on it."

"Must *really* be someone important then."

"You didn't think the federal government would spend all this money for us to ride in style, did you?"

"All I ask for is a rifle that doesn't jam and an MRE less than ten years old."

"I'll get you the rifle."

"Deal."

Hagen again looked to his watch. His expression soured. He stood, yanking the cabin door shut with a solid THUMP that immediately muted the plane's interior. His full frame devoured the cockpit door as he leaned back through it.

"Clear us for takeoff and get this plane moving, please." The request was not as polite as its words suggested. Although he did wait for a response, his body language only allowed for a single option. After a nervous trade of glances, Pilot #1 pushed a lever forward, resulting in a stretched surge of the jet's engines. He spoke into his mouthpiece.

"Ground control, N397P requests taxi clearance with information Charlie."

The plane's guarded movement forward was disproportionate to its roaring engines, but together they satisfied Hagen. He exited the cockpit and took the same seat as before, arms crossed, hat pulled low over his face, leaned back in a stubborn recline.

Westhead was happy to sit and observe, the responsibility for flight times above his pay grade. When a hand clasped his shoulder, he looked up to find a smiling Nate standing over him.

"Chief, glad you guys made it when you did. I think the commander was about to leave anyone keeping him from this op."

"Hey, bro. My apologies, the line at security was extra long."

Nate took the seat next to his mentor. "So, I hear a pilot went down over Syria." He was whispering in the hope his pleas wouldn't reach Hagen. "You guys going in to get him? Which would mean that I'm going in to get him, since I'm TAD to your unit for this op, right?"

"It doesn't mean that at all."

Nate leaned forward conspiratorially. "Dan, if there's anything you can do as a team leader to get me on this mission, I'll forever be in your debt."

"First off, you're a newly pinned SEAL with one combat mission to his name. Second, I don't make those decisions. And third, I'm pretty sure you're already forever in my debt." There was no whisper, no insinuation, of what Nate had already done for him in Syria; that wasn't a debt, it was duty. Its mention would have been unneeded, ancillary. More so to spare undue embarrassment or risk degrading the sacrifice made by Darby than a lack of appreciation. Nate himself never considered taking credit for those heroics. That was a sacred chit that could never be traded, but would unquestioningly be repaid should the opportunity arise.

Westhead looked around their unexpected windfall. "There any food on this plane?"

Nate stumbled, but found his voice. "I'm pretty sure I saw some fruit. Banana? I think there was a basket somewhere." Then, to Westhead's back, softer: "What about the pilot? Is it true al-Baghdadi is holding him?"

Westhead didn't turn from the cabinet he was tossing. "We don't know yet. There will be a full briefing when we get to Arizona. It's up to that man "—he referenced a maybe-sleeping Hagen—"and COL Stevens if you are a part of it or not. Now, I know these CIA planes have sandwiches and shit on them. I'd give your left ball for a roast beef and Dr. Pepper."

Westhead's search for a fridge under the mahogany trim and LEDs screeched to a halt, attention diverted to the window. Flickering red and blue flashes bounced off their taxiing plane, which suddenly slowed, the engines decelerating into a high-pitched whine.

"What the—" Hagen called out, jumping from his seat. He pressed his face against one of the portholes. A black Suburban swooped in front of the jet, blocking its path authoritatively with an unnecessary display of lights and siren. When the cabin door opened, a dark-suited agent entered the plane.

"CDR Hagen, as instructed, I have two additional passengers for this flight." The man stepped to the side, allowing the newcomers to board.

"Agent Kopen?" The shock in Westhead's voice gave the FBI agent reason to smile.

"Didn't think you'd see me again so soon, did you, Chief? The director called just after you left. Sounds like the president wanted to have some additional eyes on this op. Guess he thought I'd be better utilized here than reconning the ICC. I think Neil can handle that."

Up to this point, Hagen had stood to the side, glacial eyes surveying the interaction with a cool disapproval. When he stepped forward, his voice was even and commanding.

"The director of the FBI has no input on who is involved in this—in whatever mission this team may or may not be embarking on. I'm not even sure that half the people standing in this plane have the security clearance to be read in on this operation."

The FBI agent seemed suddenly uncomfortable on his feet, but remained in place until a throat cleared from behind him. The distinguished, silver-haired man it belonged to stepped forward.

"You are right, CDR Hagen, the director does not have the authority to create joint task forces between the Federal Bureau of Investigation and JSOC. Or, for that matter, to include a civilian observer. However, the man that he reports to, does. That being, of course, the president of the United States."

While the man had no official authority over anyone present, each man's posture straightened, their words considered with more care. It was Hagen who finally addressed him.

"Mr. Basting, I certainly appreciate your relationship with the president and your position as foreign policy advisor, but I'm afraid there is no way I can allow civilians on this flight."

Dick Basting nodded as if he were expecting that response. In fact, he was about to prove he was.

"I fully, understand that, Commander, I do. But since I no longer have an office, and the Middle East seems safer than downtown DC, the president thought I should travel with your team in my capacity as his advisor." He extended his right arm, revealing a cell phone. "I think this is for you."

Slowly, Hagen reached for the phone. He put it to his ear, listened for a moment, said only, "Yes sir, Mr. President," and handed the phone back to Basting.

"Guess we know why they gave us the big plane," Westhead said, earning a hard look. Hagen continued toward back of the cabin, announcing to his team, "Make room for two more." He then leaned into Westhead, voice lowered: "Make no mention of Atlas Revenge, Palindrome, Bagby, or any intel we get on this pilot. I don't know what he does or doesn't know."

Westhead settled in his seat, glaring in the new arrivals' direction. "This should be an interesting ride. Let's get it over with." Kopen threw him a half smirk and a nod as if he couldn't be more in agreement.

The pilots, understandably apprehensive, suddenly seemed to share their passengers' desire to speedily take to the air. Rushed, they pulled the cockpit door shut while Kopen and Basting strapped themselves in. Soon, the plane was speeding down the runway and they were airborne.

It was almost an hour into the flight before there was any real conversation, and it was Westhead calling down the length of the jet.

"Agent Kopen, you ever get choked out when you were a Ranger?"

The fed opened his eyes thoughtfully, one then the other. His expression remained passive and he seemed almost amused at the question.

"Dan ..." Hagen cautioned.

Kopen stopped him. "It's okay, Commander. Why do you ask, Chief Westhead? Would you like to try?"

"Just curious, I suppose. I know that when I was first assigned to a platoon, all the new guys had to get choked out at least once. You know, kind of like an initiation. I've heard Rangers do that as well."

"Ah, to be one of the boys. Well, I tell you what, Chief, you feel free to try. Although haven't we already been over this? Don't be surprised if you're surprised."

With a plane full of fascinated passengers looking on, Westhead stood, ducking slightly in the narrow berth. His focus remained strictly on the FBI agent as he casually made his way to the front.

"I don't doubt that, sir. But in my experience, eventually, *everyone* goes to sleep." With those words, he flashed suddenly to his side, arms extended, clasping them around Nate in a violent bear hug. The young SEAL fought, but Westhead was able to get position behind him, and, with his knee wedged into his spine, wrap his right forearm around his throat and cover it with his left. Nate struggled. His legs thrashed, knocking over a food tray, scattering those sitting nearby.

He clawed behind him, just getting a hold of Westhead's shoulder, but it was futile. It was with a resigned acceptance and bulging eyes that his face went red, then purple, then white. Westhead eased him to the carpet, slumped peacefully against a chuckling Nailer's seat.

Westhead surveyed their guests as he picked his way back to his seat, repeating, "Eventually, everyone goes to sleep." He opened his backpack, a plastic medicine bottle jingling in his pocket as he made his way to the lavatory. There were still almost four hours left until they landed in Arizona. He could use the sleep.

TOMBSTONE, AZ

"As you know, our mission has changed from capture/kill to rescue and recovery." Stevens opened the mission brief to the full team, plus Basting, Kopen, and Nate. While incensed that the civilians were allowed to sit in, the colonel had received an earful from the president about their treatment on the flight, along with very specific instructions as to their level of access moving forward. A flurry of scowls may have been sent in the civilians' direction, but that was as far as the opposition could go. For operators who did not excel at passive-aggressiveness, maintaining decorum around the gatecrashers would be the hardest part of this mission. For their part, the FBI agent and foreign policy advisor ignored the gestures, smartly maintaining a low-key demeanor.

Stevens stood in the foreground, a translucent blue sky at his back. His men were positioned loosely around him, wiping sweat while rehydrating, taking in each word as a football team would their coach's. The sun's rays seemed to pulsate off the plywood structure to their rear, the smell of sand and sage carrying across the desert on a stiff wind.

"The Activity is working to confirm whether LCDR Wilson is in fact being held at al-Baghdadi's compound, which of course, you are now intimately familiar with." Stevens motioned to the mock-up behind him, a three-level compound constructed from scratch on the edges of Fort Huachuca. The team had been hitting it all day.

A temporary fence had been erected around the mock-up's perimeter, shrouding the new construction, not that anyone else had access to this part of base. JOE-CAG's support team had recreated al-Baghdadi's compound based on satellite and drone footage, as well as photographs and intel reports from assets already on the ground in Syria. The team now knew each nook and cranny of the compound. They knew whether doors opened in or out, if the security wall was fortified, the types of hinges on doors, even which direction the doorknobs turned. They had several plans for infiltrating the heavily guarded building and would be able to adapt depending on situation.

"Flight to Iraq leaves at 0430 tomorrow morning. We have the evening off. It's going to be a long flight. I would expect most of you to be hung over for it. Mr. Basting, Agent Kopen, we will be conducting team-building evolutions this evening in Tucson. You are welcome to join if you'd like."

Basting stood. Although small, he radiated a confident quality. The air of station and intellect he wore had the ability to overpower even the most physical of men. The room fidgeted with unease.

"I think Agent Kopen and I will let you gentlemen enjoy the evening on your own. See you all on the plane tomorrow morning." He reached into his back pocket and came out with a platinum card. "Colonel, if I may, this evening is on me."

An enthused if sarcastic cheer rippled through the tired, overexposed troops. "A bar tab should make up for getting us killed!" Thor's mumble was anything but quiet, although amid the din of their exit it could be reasonably ignored. Westhead walked with Adam. No one so much as threw a sideways glance at the two of them during the short trip back to the barracks.

The team rushed through an abbreviated bathing routine, anticipation for greasy food and intoxicating drink trumping leisurely hygienic indulgences. Hell growled from a toilet stall, "New Guy! Need to see you in my office!" His voice echoed across the cavernous bathroom, designed to accommodate a full battalion's restroom requirements, carrying over hissing steam, running showers, and casual bullshitting. From under a line of industrial showerheads, McDonald's head snapped toward the command. A wry grin purported to hide his apprehension, but saucer-plate eyes fooled no one. His teammates, in various stages of bathing, watched with interest as his bare feet slapped against the tile floor, towel tight around midsection. He stopped outside the stall where the team leader was seated, speaking through the door.

"What's up, Hell?" The voice tight, resigned.

"I heard you smuggled a handle of Fireball into the barracks. As you well know, alcohol isn't allowed in the barracks. What if some tight-ass major walks through here and starts smelling cinnamon whiskey on everyone's breath? I'll tell you what. He's gonna want to know who the drunk fucks are on his base that don't have to abide by the United States Armed Forces grooming standards. And someone —my guess would be your guardian angel, Westhead—might tell him what unit we are with. And then everyone on this base will know who we are and why we are here. Is that what you want?"

McDonald shifted his weight, furled his eyebrows before answering. "I just thought ..."

"What? You just thought what? You just thought that you'd show your resourcefulness by securing alcohol in a dry building? That you'd be a big hero and everyone would take Fireball shots in your honor? That we'd be so impressed you'd no longer be new meat?"

"I just wanted everyone to get fucked up before we left, Hell."

"I just wanted everyone to get fucked up, Hell," he mimicked. The scene was comical, if for no reason other than it was taking place through a toilet door. "You know what? Me too. Call us some cabs or find a POG to drive tonight. You're not DD anymore."

McDonald took a quick step back, relieved, replying simply, "Roger that," before heading back to his locker. As he left, Hell called out once more from his perch: "And bring me a shot, McDonald! I may be in here a while!"

Westhead gave McDonald a fist bump on his way past. The team hurried to finish dressing.

My skin is radiant, tingling with the knowledge that one of my targets is here, with us, delivered to me as if from Providence. There could be a fall, an accidental discharge, poisoning, even a simple disappearance, poof, gone, an empty bed, the man never to be heard from again. It's a big desert out here in Arizona. Even bigger in Syria. The presence of Basting means the last thing I want to do is go out with the guys tonight. To shoot the shit, play pool, drink beer, chase skirts. Act like one of them. Because I'm not, not anymore. That ship has sailed. I admire their singular focus, the linear-minded desire to get from Point A to Point B even if the path leads through a brick wall. That used to be me. My mission is now bigger, more complicated. But the truth is, part of my success is dependent upon appearances. Keeping my teammates' faith. So I do it. I socialize with them. I make jokes, I express my desire to kill terrorists and keep our country free from tyranny. Not untrue, just not with the same targets and methods. Naturally, my reluctance is the exception. The rest of the guys are hopped up like they have one last night of freedom before turning themselves in for a lengthy prison sentence.

Our civility is tested further by the handle of Fireball being passed. It gets chugged while hair is spiked, cologne splashed, the volume increasing as stresses fade into the evening. Some rap shit I'm not familiar with blasts during all this. For a moment, you could almost be fooled into feeling like a carefree civilian getting ready for a night on the town.

"Transpo in five!" someone calls out, and we empty out of the barracks and into the still-warm evening. Waiting in front are two young soldiers from our support staff, on edge but dutiful, having secured two duty vans for the evening.

There's a violent rush to board as hyper-aggressive commandos claw, clutch, grab, pull, and scramble over each other to claim the most prized seats and avoid the middle ones. Shouts of "No bitch!" are largely ignored. There's a prestige that comes with the front passenger seats, making them a particularly costly commodity. More than a few blows have to be traded to earn the privilege of having control of the radio. This is an exercise I can get behind, and happily dive into the fray, earning myself a bloody lip and good-sized knot for my enthusiasm. Well worth it. I'm even able to find a metal station, to the chagrin of some and delight of others. Disturbed's *"The Sound of Silence"* keeps our energy fierce.

Finally, we're settled in, and the drivers, familiar with our brand of camaraderie, tentatively head off Fort Huachuca for the hour drive to Tucson. A few of the guys went to school out west and have spent time in the college town, assuring us that we can't go wrong at Frog & Firkin. Inwardly I groan, incredulous that we plan to take over a college bar. And there is no doubt, when we enter a bar, we take it over.

"You realize a lot of you are pushing forty, right?" I say. "What makes you think sorority chicks aren't going to laugh you out of the bar?" Naturally, that elicits a chorus of jeers and insults questioning not just my masculinity, but also my sexuality. I give it back as good as I get, even returning a few punches, but mean what I said. There's a reason most of these guys are divorced or close to it.

"Go fucking fuck yourself you fucking mo," someone calls out from the back. "Take your fucking fuck all negative vibes and give yourself a good strong assfuck. Some of you fucksticks may have gone to college, but for us fucktards and high school heroes, tonight's our fucking night to fuck some fucking college pussy. We got till 0430 to try, at least. Don't try to take that from us."

The diatribe elicits a deafening chorus of cheers. Pantera goes louder. I watch the frenzy with dispassion, even though I'm its target. Someone tells the black shoe driving our van to pull over at the Circle K, and when he gets back in, he has a thirty-pack.

A half hour later the beer is gone and we pull onto a fresh, palm-tree-lined street. The restaurant, ugly, chipped maroon-and-yellow paint slapped on uncaringly years ago. College kids, some of them mopey, some eager-looking, all oblivious, walk past in Greek letters and backpacks, ignorant, at least to us, as to the ways of the world. The van is quieter now, and I sense an appropriate disdain for the whole scene. Finally, the door slides open, and we tumble out, ready to make our mark on the unsuspecting college town.

TUSCON, AZ

"This is it?" GQ took his seat with the rest of the team at a long wooden table. The tan, blond waitress didn't disappoint, but the rest of the bar did. He turned to her. "Where the hell is everyone?"

Her eyes rolled, shoulders shrugged. "Tuesday. I mean, we have flights of Hefeweizen for six bucks, but it's usually pretty dead on Tuesdays." She pulled an iPhone out of tight, short shorts with the little frays on the end. The boys noticed. "Still early, should pick up around 10:00."

They watched her walk away with their drink orders.

"Is it just me, or did she barely look at us?" Thor asked.

"It's not you," Hagen responded. "Or maybe it is, if you're unsure why the nineteen-year old waitress didn't fall all over herself for a bunch of thirty-plus-year-old cavemen."

"If only you were still thirty-plus, Commander," Hell told him. "That Just For Men 'do says you rounded thirty a while ago and are sliding past your forties. Besides, chicks dig tats and beards."

"You know what women want like Jud knows about scented bath products, Hell. Didn't you get married when you were like fifteen? Just pray you'll still be operating when you're forty-three. I don't care how many smoothies you drink, how many SoulCycle classes you take, you won't be doing what I'm doing in ten years."

"Shit," Hell crowed, "they're going to have to scrape me off the battlefield. What else am I gonna do? Learn how to tie a tie?"

Jud bent forward in his chair, waiting until he had the floor. "I'll say this: The barber who has the best haircut in the room is not the best barber in the room."

Puzzled faces morphed into ones of disbelief, finally dissolving into a round of bemused snorts. No one ventured a guess as to what Jud meant with his latest nugget of wisdom.

The waitress returned, with drinks, assisted by a friend. The table calmed while beers were placed in front of each man.

Then, simultaneously, Thor and Westhead spun toward Nate. He was reclining in his seat coolly, failing in a clear attempt to project innocence.

"Did you just fucking see that?" Thor exclaimed.

"Sure did," replied Westhead. They pulled their chairs closer, examining Nate over the top of fuming noses.

Nailer called down from the other end, "I saw it from here!"

Nate squirmed, looked at his shoes briefly before raising his head and offering a culpable, if not hopeful, grin.

"I have no idea what you're talking about," he said.

"Bullshit! And you're going to sit there with that shit-eating grin on your face too?"

The rest of the conversation at the table had stopped, the focus strictly on the young SEAL.

"What's going on?" Hell asked.

"I'll tell you what's going on," Thor told him. "This FNG—and mind you, not even one of *our* FNGs, but a regular, run of the mill Frogman FNG—is making googlie-eyes with the waitress."

"What?" GQ was pissed. "Doesn't he know FNGs are supposed to be seen and not heard? And sure as hell aren't supposed to step on our tail! They're supposed to get it for us!"

The waitress watched the interaction with a somewhat amused air before really putting Nate in the jackpot. She smiled at him. So he smiled back. The table shook with fists, the air thick with curses. Stevens and Hagen shook their heads, knowing they could no longer help the boy.

"That's your ass, son," Hell spat at him. "You're going to wish you were back in BUD/S building sandcastles, blowing kisses at mermaids."

To his credit, Nate remained stone-faced. He knew he would have to pay the man at a later date, but some things were worth a little pain. He batted his eyelids at the waitress. Flashed what he considered a mysterious half-smile.

"So, what time do you get off?" he asked her. As per the intent, this elicited another, more raucous eruption. He grinned further, awaiting her response.

"My boyfriend, the U of A football player, will be picking me up at 1:30," she replied.

The boys hooted, mixing in some good-natured threats toward college football players. Nate made an exaggerated show of hanging his reddening face.

"That gentleman would like to buy you guys a round," the other waitress informed them, flicking her head at a barstool. It supported a man about their age, thin, with stringy hair and a nervous face. He spun back toward the bar when they looked his way, but quickly rotated back, knowing he was caught.

"Thank you for your service," he mumbled across the room, raising his mug. "82nd Airborne, once upon a time." They returned the gesture, but didn't ask him to join like he had hoped.

"How about shots?" Mutt suggested in the slow, surfer drawl that still managed to sound intelligent when it came from him. "Those of us not in Stevens's van missed out on the road beers. Need to catch up, bro."

Westhead agreed. "That's mighty kind of him, ma'am, please thank him for us. We'll take a round of Jamison, if it's not too much trouble."

"Bushmills for me," Hell told her, scowling at Westhead.

"Me too," Nailer said.

Pos raised his hands in excitement. "And wings!" he yelled. "We need lots of wings."

"Ma'am, can I get a big ol' water, too?" Jud blotted his face and neck with a handful of napkins. "Hotter than a two-dicked dog."

The waitress nodded, snapped her gum at Nate, and disappeared behind the bar.

"I can think of worse things than tying a tie," Westhead said quietly.

The comment was met with blank stares, light laughter, then napkins and straws tossed in his direction.

"Still thinking about that? Fuck. That. Shit," Jud bellowed. "I'd rather dip my testes in honey and teabag a hornet's nest than wear a monkey suit and sit in an office all day. Where's the *adventure* in that?"

"Dan, you'd get fired for sexual harassment on day one!" said GQ.

"Or stealing office supplies," offered Hell.

"More likely drawn and quartered by his coworkers for ratting someone else out for taking home company pens," Nailer said.

"Could you imagine us sitting in an office all day? That'd be like a lion babysitting the zebras." Jud shook his head vigorously. "Just ain't right."

"I'm pretty sure you don't get to blow shit up or shoot people in the real world," Nailer warned. "That leaves me out."

"Seven hours under crisp sheets and three hots sounds mighty nice to me," countered Westhead.

"Shit, I can get that in prison, and fuck the tie!" hollered Thor, clinking his glass with the operators on either side. "The men would be better looking too!"

The waitress returned, setting down the shots and taking more drink orders.

"All right, settle down, you wildebeests," Hagen said, standing, raising his shot glass with the slightest of wobbles. He first aimed it at the man at the bar, indicating his gratitude with soft eyes. "You know I'm not one for long speeches—"

Another flurry of debris fell from the sky as Hagen's men shouted heartfelt epithets toward him. Westhead made eye contact with Adam, adjusting his stare at Stevens. Their OIC was the only one unanimated. He sat stationary, unemotional. He looked like someone who didn't belong at the table.

"Okay, maybe a speech here or there." Hagen lowered his voice and the table quieted. "But I just want to say again that it's an honor to go to work with this team every single day. We took an oath to defend this country, that's true. And we do that, readily. But when we're forward deployed and the bullets are flying, we all know who we're fighting for in those moments. We're fighting to make sure the man to our left and the man to our right goes home. And yeah, that's not always possible"—here he raised his glass and a soft but deep rumble of "Hooyah Darby" rippled across the table—"but we've all pledged to never leave a man behind, and dammit, we never will. You are true professionals, and as we tackle this next obstacle, I know that we will not fail. I know that what we do is worth the sacrifice, worth the pain. Worth missing births and birthdays, worth splintering our families. Because we are brothers. We are our own family. I know each and every one of you has my six, and I wouldn't want to go into battle with anyone else. These are things I know. To the brotherhood."

The resounding "To the brotherhood!" shook the bar. The men were not unfamiliar with the ensuing brand of interest sent in their direction. Some enjoyed it, some did not. It was the mix of curiosity and fear and respect that those who did relished, even if they were loath to admit it.

"To Just For Men!" called out Pos.

"To my future daughter, may she have twice the brains as her daddy and never come across any offspring of Thor!" said McDonald.

"To marshmallow Fluff!" Jud lifted his shot to his mouth.

The boys are already causing a scene, and it isn't yet dark out. Hell, I can't blame them, not really. My effort at being one of the guys is going poorly, I realize, but my head won't stop throbbing and the country music playing in this fucking bar is worming its way into my bones, deep inside my body, and it's fragile down there already, a caustic witch's brew of hatred, disappointment and violence mixing with an admittedly declining grasp on reality that makes me question whether I'm really even here, and I just want to scream and maybe bash someone's head in but I'm not really sure where my rage is directed. Even as I seethe at these men, I love these men, these men are my brothers, and after all, isn't everything I'm doing for them?

"I. Have to. Take a shit," I announce, standing up, it really more of a query than a statement and I don't bother to register whatever looks of concern fall over their faces because I'm moving now, quickly, hovering really, my thoughts coming haltingly and jagged, the order of the words in my mind maybe making sense, maybe not, like when you are not quite asleep but close to it, and you know on some level they are deep and profound thoughts but you realize they will never see the light of day, that they'll vanish with consciousness, and I make it to the bathroom, and I do sit down, for how long I don't know, but when I float back out from the stall the cool water from the sink feels good on my face, and I let it run down my untidy hair, my beard, onto my shirt, and I'm aware enough to blot it with a paper towel, and then I'm back in the bar, the music louder now, or maybe I'm just hearing it more clearly, my senses tingling, and someone suggests another bar, and after a call for shots, I buy a round and we're moving, moving, out the door and into the hot, dry night.

"You guys know that Nelson owns a bar somewhere out here, right?" It was Adam, the last one you would expect to be suggesting bars, but he had been in the same troop with Nelson in DEVGRU and wanted to see his old buddy.

"Nelson?" bellowed Nailer. "From Red Squadron? He's in Tucson? What the hell are we waiting for?"

When they piled back into the vans, the wrestling and horseplay was that much more ferocious, though the ride lasted barely a mile. A couple of ripped shirts and Jud's swollen eye were the main casualties by the time they pulled up to a similar looking building, Trident Grill blazing in fluorescent on the brick facade.

Westhead hung back on the sidewalk while the rest of his teammates examined the college crowd milling around the patio, standing in line. Any previous discomfort, of not fitting in, had vanished with the alcohol.

"Hey, any of you turds have a good protest lined up tonight?" Thor shouted at a group of skinny frat boys coolly smoking cigarettes around two blonds. The group turned slowly, at first unsure it was they who were being addressed. Something like intrigue passed over the girls' faces, while a natural cockiness transitioned into fear when the boys saw the author of the antagonism. Any air of superiority quickly disappeared, youthful self-aggrandizement dropping like a dress after prom. As one, instinctively, they stepped back from this group of imposing, hostile men.

"I wanna protest and get people fired!" Thor taunted.

GQ put a hand on his shoulder, real gentle, soothing-like. "Easy, Thor, brother man. Take it easy, bro. We get in a fight out here, we'll never get in this bar and get a crack at this college pussy. Don't deny me college pussy, bro. I never went to college."

Sweat beaded on Thor's forehead. His eyes, wide. Then, slowly, his demeanor began to change. Calmed. Like he found something, some peace somewhere. He offered the frat boys a big, sloppy grin. Leaning back, chin raised, he howled into the moon, then raised his arm into the air, the universal gesture of bro-ness. Still terrified, three of them hesitantly returned his high five, causing him to whoop loudly with each connection. He then cruised past the bouncer and into the bar, a lion on the hunt.

"Control your men tonight, Chief." The crisp words startled Westhead, and he spun around to find Stevens standing behind him, smoking a cigarette. "If they're still listening to you."

"Roger that, sir." Then: "Didn't know you smoked."

"Rarely. You going in?"

"Actually, I was waiting out here for you. Have a minute?"

Stevens motioned to a bench, and they sat down. Westhead looked skyward, swallowed deep breaths.

"This about Kopen?" Stevens spat. "The investigation? Still worried we have a terrorist on our team?"

"Sir, I never said that."

"Some are interpreting your questions as such. You're losing your men, Chief. And your leadership is in jeopardy. You know that, right?"

"That wasn't my intent."

"Intent be damned. I suggest you stop questioning your teammates and get your head in the game."

"Roger that, sir." They sat in silence for some time, Stevens smoking, Westhead contemplating his words.

"Lots of stars up there."

Westhead watched his commander staring off into the night sky, a childlike smile across his face. "Sir?"

"Up there. Look at it all. Where does it end?"

Westhead cleared his throat. "Sir, that's what I wanted to talk to you about."

"The stars?"

"In a sense. We—you've seemed ... distant lately." He spoke the words cautiously. "I just think—"

Stevens cut him off, but his words lacked emotion. They sounded to Westhead as if they had traveled a great distance. "I don't give a shit what you think."

"I can tell you don't, sir." He adjusted his seat to avoid the smoke. "If you don't think I'm capable of leading my men any longer, I will stand down."

"That what you want?"

Westhead took a moment to answer. "It's not. Not yet. I might as well tell you—I plan to put in my separation papers after we complete this mission. I'm retiring. But I would like the opportunity to see this op through. Al-Baghdadi has taken a lot from me. A lot from us. I would like the opportunity to make that right."

Stevens nodded, but into the night, like he was responding to a separate conversation.

"Sir, you thought highly enough of me to let me know that the men are questioning my leadership. Well, I hope you take my critique as constructively. I'm not the only one who has noticed your—lack of focus."

"That so?"

"Respectfully, it is sir."

"Well, Chief, let me tell you—and whoever else is asking—that you don't know shit about my focus. I have responsibilities that you have no idea about. Duties and obligations to people higher on the food chain than you can fathom. And I don't expect you to understand. That's called chain of command."

"I understand chain of command, Colonel. But when you disappear days before go-time, it's going to raise some eyebrows."

"Are you questioning your officer in charge? Accusing *me* of something?" It was almost a whisper, with no menace in the question. It was as if he really wanted to know.

"Sir, far be it for me to question you, but we all know we play by different rules than the traditional military. No matter rank or status, we have to all be on the same page. You and CDR Hagen taught me that."

"Did we?"

There was a long pause while he lit another cigarette. From inside the bar, a drunken chorus of *"Living on a Prayer"* reached them.

Westhead spun angrily toward him. "Sir, are you going to read us in on whatever you got going on? This whole team depends on you, and right now we don't know that we can." He braced himself, ready for an attack. Maybe that's what he wanted. He didn't get it. The next words were even softer.

"I could say the same for you, Dan."

"Goddammit, Ben! Where were you the other night? I did some reading on the flight over. That ACLU lawyer who worked with Dick Basting's committee got herself killed here in Tucson the other night. The same night the team got in town."

"That's what we're talking about, Chief. You seem to be worried more about casting aspersions on your teammates and sympathizing with the enemy than fighting a war. A war we're already fighting with one hand tied behind our back. That's how you lose the support of your men. And when that happens, strange things happen in battle. I wouldn't want anything to happen to you."

"Don't threaten me! There are rules, Ben. Even with what we do, there are rules. And taking out civilians on American soil is against those rules. No matter what they've done."

"So you *are* accusing me? Some balls, Dan. You just don't know when to stop pointing fingers."

"It would be quite a coincidence that she got killed at the same time you were MIA in the same state as her."

"You're lucky we have a long history together. Am I supposed to feel sorry for her?"

"I don't know. Do you?"

"No."

"That's all you have to say about it?"

"I guess so. It's—it's, interesting. That she got killed."

"Interesting? That sounds like an admission, Blade."

Stevens sighed, ground out his cigarette. "Don't put words in my mouth. You need to get your head unstuck from your ass and do your job. Now, I'm done here. You let me know if I need to downgrade you from CI status."

The colonel stood, head loose on thick shoulders, rotating his neck in a widening arc. His shadow cut an impressive but uneasy figure against the night sky. He looked into the distance.

"Sure are a lot of stars up there. Sometimes you forget that when you're in the city. Guess it takes a desert to remind you that there's more than you can touch."

Nelson is lining up shots for the boys when I enter the bar. I remember him from back in the day. A solid operator. Now he owns this bar.

My head throbs as I watch the guys recon the scene, working in teams, moving and communicating, just like good SpecOps forces do. They operate with military precision, although while they can't see it, from my position of overwatch I am able to tell that one of our hallmarks is not being met—that of stealth.

The guys are too drunk and not quite self-aware enough to notice, but the entire bar is focused on them. From the nineteen-year-old wallflower super-excited her fake ID got her in, to the early-twenties meathead on the six-year plan, they all watch my team operate, their AO not a jungle or desert but this multi-roomed, sticky-floored, sour-smelling bar.

"We're a professional lumberjack team," one of them is telling a wide-eyed girl. "We compete in timber sports. There's an event this weekend in Phoenix. I'm defending my stock saw world record."

"I didn't know that was a real thing!" she says, loud, leaning into his shoulder, maybe so she can be heard over *"Don't Stop Believing,"* maybe not. "That's so cool, it must be so hard."

"I'll tell you this, ma'am, there's nothing like hearing the sound of a good buck saw—we call it the misery whip—chewing through a nineteen-inch white pine in under twelve seconds."

"It's what we live for." It's Nate next to him, chiming in with the straightest of faces. He takes the hand of a second girl, gives her a spin around the dance floor.

Some of the braver males stand close to their feminine counterparts, trying to look at least slightly uninterested while they eavesdrop. Most of them wear faces of suspicion; they're not buying the lumberjack story. But if something tells them there is more to this group of muscular, tattooed men, none are foolish or intoxicated enough to say it.

This goes on for some time, the consumption and volume growing in proportion. As has become my custom, I stand to the side, involved only peripherally in conversations about the election and Zika. An argument breaks out, a near fight. It's only a matter of time. Everything is only a matter of time, I think, just as time begins to bend into that funny, blurry funnel it sometimes finds itself in when the atmospheric conditions are just right. I stand back, observing, aloof and cold, wondering for the life of me what will happen next.

It was Westhead who eventually stepped between the two drunk operators. Nailer and McDonald were growing more incensed with each insult. The bar's bouncers were ineffective, relegated to fringe observers as the rest of the unit encircled their teammates, aware that such a dispute would only be over when the participants decided it was. Westhead caught Nelson's eye, whose expression made it clear their time at the Trident Bar was finished.

"Enough!" he barked, breaking through the red-faced circle egging them on. "I'm not sure you idiots understand how bar fights are supposed to work—you fight other people, not each other!"

"Easy, Chief, they just gotta blow off some steam," Thor said. "Nailer still thinks New Guy should still be treated like a new guy. New Guy disagrees."

Westhead hesitated. He knew this would have to be settled between them. "At least get them outside. They're not doing this in Nelson's bar. Midnight Fights in the desert."

Excitement rippled through the team. Bar night over. Soon they evacuated into the evening and the vans, destination an area where they couldn't do as much damage. Westhead wondered if he would be next.

Five miles outside of town their drivers pulled over, the vans' blinking emergency lights the only visible entities until an orange moon. McDonald and Nailer were the first ones out of their respective vans, having smartly been separated by Hagen for the ride. Nailer began to pace, frenzied and hyper.

"Cherry ass new guys think they run shit now. Your jock rash from The Dump hasn't even healed yet! You want to be a full JOE, I'm going to show you what that means."

He was already shirtless, looking ghostly in the van's headlights, sketches of ink fading into the gloom with no discernable beginning or end. McDonald approached him quickly without appearing hurried. He seemed oblivious to the rest of the team, who, in strict linear displays of tenure, shouted either threats or encouragement.

It was Nailer who threw the first punch, connecting solidly. So did the next, and the one after that. The blows smacked regular and rhythmic, hearty slaps that rang out across the desert air. It quickly became clear that McDonald wasn't interested in defending himself. In fact, he appeared to be enjoying the abuse, his jaw jutted out defiantly, bright teeth glistening in the combined light of moon and headlights, pink blood slicked across a grinning mouth. He shrugged off each strike, refusing to go down. This further pissed Nailer off.

He screamed, "Hit me back you limp wristed motherfucker!" Pieces of spittle flew from his mouth. A few landed on McDonald's face. He flinched for the first time, as if the indignity of bodily fluids touching him was worse than the blows. He wiped his mouth with his sleeve, streaking blood.

They stood facing each other, heaving shoulders the only humanistic features. The rest of the team had fallen into an unbelieving stillness. Everyone waited in the darkness for the next move. It was Nailer's. He turned his back to McDonald and started walking alone down the long, flat road.

TOMBSTONE

When we report to the small airfield at the foot of Laundry Ridge the next morning, it's only hours later. The night's activities are evident across tired and in some cases bruised faces, but that condition will have no effect on our ability to do our job. We're comfortable being uncomfortable.

I'm pleased to find it's a single C-17 sitting alone on the runway. I guess the president's babysitters will have to get used to not flying first class. Our operations team and the plane's loadmaster are hard at work under portable spotlights, filling the gray monster with pallets of the ammo, weapons, and equipment required of war.

"Hope you brought a hammock," one of the guys mumbles at Kopen as we file onto the plane. For some reason the FBI agent is wearing a suit. "Those jump seats can get pretty uncomfortable after fifteen hours in the air."

Next to him, Basting hesitates at the bottom of the loading ramp, dodging a K-loader. He allows the slightest of hesitations while staring into the cargo plane's windowless cavern. Kopen reaches into the canvas bag at his feet, pulling out two netting systems, and begins to string them up between pallets.

"Not my first C-17 to the Middle East," he says, ignoring the team's amused reactions. "I have you covered, Mr. Basting."

I find my own place to set up, and by the time we're airborne, most guys are racked out with Ambien assists. A few, working on college degrees or MBA's, study. Hagen, who has designs on completing The Great American Novel, types alone. The manuscript, which he's never let us read word one of, has been a work in progress for much of his career. Most people would have trouble concentrating in the noisy tube, the weapons and vehicles of war all around them, but we aren't most people. I've seen guys complete timed biology exams on combat outposts while being shelled by the Taliban.

For me, I have my own work to do. As I consider options for fulfilling the ultimate mission, my eyes keep finding Dick Basting, knowing that there is no way he can return from the Middle East alive. I'm still undecided on Agent Kopen. For that matter, Chief Westhead too.

About midway through the flight, Stevens slammed down the secure sat phone. That got the attention of the men, who stopped card games and lowered dog-eared books, waiting for their commander to fill them in. He stared at the two civilian guests and chose his words carefully.

"I've just been informed that The Activity has confirmed LCDR Wilson is being held at one of al-Baghdadi's compounds on the western Syrian border. ISIS is trying to negotiate a prisoner release. Our pilot for four shitheads being held at Guantanamo. Not your average, run of the mill shitheads either. Two were high-level Republican Guard under Saddam, and worked with al-Baghdadi before the invasion developing weapons of mass destruction for the regime. The other two, AQI bomb-makers. You can see where al-Baghdadi is going here."

"Blade, please tell me our commander in chief is not considering doing this deal. If they know where he's being held, send us in," Nailer pleaded. "We've trained for this."

Stevens instinctively glanced in Basting's direction before answering. "We're not in the business of policy-making. I assured the president that JOE-CAG would successfully complete this mission if given it. That's all *I* can do." His face again met Basting's. This time, the look was pointed.

"I tend to agree with you, Colonel, and you, Petty Officer." Basting nodded at Nailer, faced the team. "I will ask the president to consider your group for a direct action raid to rescue LCDR Wilson and eliminate Ibrahim al-Baghdadi. I'm of the opinion that a small, surgical strike is a better option than diplomacy or a prisoner swap."

The words were met with an appreciative, if not surprised, murmur. Basting excused himself, and headed toward the front of the plane to retrieve his sat phone.

FOB MONSOOR

Here we are again. The same dust clouds, the same Ranger captain, the same plywood hooches. My body has no concept of time or even what day it—only that it's dark outside. My body screams for rest, my brain hoping it's time to go to work.

Anxiously, we follow the captain to the SpecOps area, receiving the same energetic speech about the capableness of his Rangers and their respect for what we do that he gave us before Atlas Revenge. Again, it falls on deaf ears.

When we get to our corner of the base I push open my door, but find the room covered in gear. I turn to the Ranger officer.

"Captain?" I ask him. "It would appear as if your men have moved in."

Confused, he steps in front of me and takes a look.

"That doesn't look like my Rangers' gear," he says.

"That's because it's not." I turn to the voice and find Chewbacca, sweaty in shorts and no shirt, towel around his neck. "JSOC moved us over here this morning. Something about a high-level recovery mission?" He looks at the captain, not willing to give additional information. "You guys may be able to find room in the GP, large." He smooths his beard over and over, a decidedly amused look splashed across his face.

Immediately, I look for Basting. He's hovering toward the back of the group, chatting with the SEAL Team 6 commander.

"Mr. Basting," I say, trying to control my temper. "What in the hell is going on here?"

The JOEs stood outside the SpecOps area, exhausted, gear at their feet, wondering what the hell was going on. Dick Basting stepped between the Team 6 squadron and JOE-CAG and raised his hands for attention.

"COL Stevens and CDR Hagen, I just spoke with the president. Despite my best efforts, he is not yet convinced that a direct action assault is the way to go to safely bring LCDR Wilson home. He is still considering the prisoner swap. In the meantime, he is asking both units to stage here and remain on standby should the asset recovery option make sense. If that decision is made, the president has not yet decided if it will be JOE-CAG, SEAL Team 6, or both to go in. He asks that everyone continue to prepare as if you will get the mission, and when the decision has been made, you will be the first to know."

"This is bullshit! You gave us your word!" McDonald stepped forward, livid. His teammates considered pulling him back, but an immediate, almost telekinetic consultation moved them to abandon that instinct. Someone had to say it. The surprise was it was their newest member who had stepped forward, cut lip and swollen nose melding with his anger to create a snarling image.

"You're the reason thirty men died!" he shouted. "Piece-of-shit bureaucrats that have never put a boot on a battlefield making decisions that get us killed!" His audience was rapt, too much in agreement to step in. "Hell, sir, we don't mind giving our lives. I'll be honest with you, every man standing around you right now will gladly do so. Including LCDR Wilson, I'd bet. It's what we signed up for. In fact, most of us are pretty sure that if we do get this mission, we're not coming back. And that's okay with us. But we're tired of men like you making us question just who we're fighting for while making it harder to do our job."

The Team 6 commander finally stepped forward and put a hand on McDonald's shoulder, which tightened under the grip.

"Sir," he spat before walking away.

It's late the next afternoon when I finish a workout. We're all on edge, waiting for the president's final decision. I take a seat alone at a picnic table on the edge of base. Outside the wire, the Iraqi desert stretches out before me. Past that, Syria and LCDR Wilson and al-Baghdadi.

I stare into the haze, across the sand, the berms, the crude HESCO barriers and concertina wire. Every so often a dust devil catches my eye in the distance. One of the guard towers provides some shade as the sun moves. I take another gulp of Ripped Fuel, deciding how to take Basting out without getting caught or risking the mission.

"Guess we're victims of red tape and the politicians again, huh, brother?" Chewie is sitting on another picnic table across the quad with some of his squad mates. They're talking softly, eating chow.

I shrug. "Won't be the last time."

His big face lights up behind the bushy beard. "Too bad we can't just take them out too. Declare martial law. Guarantee we'd end this war within six months. With a victory."

I laugh, genuinely. "I'd be lying if I said the thought hasn't crossed my mind."

"Anyone seen Basting?" The Team 6 commander came out of the TOC, ever-present cup of coffee in hand despite the lateness of the afternoon. Behind him, the Ranger captain.

"The White House is on the line for him," the captain announced, proud of the information entrusted to him.

Everyone perked up upon hearing the news, daring to hope it meant the op was a go. For which team, they didn't know. But they were tired of sitting around. Working out, conducting mission prep, waiting for orders. There had been no additional intelligence on the captured pilot's status in the past twenty-four hours, but both SEAL Team 6 and JOE-CAG had mission plans ready to go should they get the call.

"Haven't seen him. Probably still getting his beauty sleep," one of the SEALs answered. Chewbacca stood, whittling a block of wood that was on its way to resembling a toy car.

"Let the fucker sleep," he said. "He does us no good being awake."

"I'll check on him. He was up late finishing a brief for the president." Kopen came out of the mess tent dressed, like always, impeccably, even in the sandbox. Full suit including jacket, tight half-Windsor knot with a silver tie bar. He somehow even managed to keep his wingtips gleaming, despite the never ending sand and dust.

Adam had secured an old Soviet manual the Russians gave new KGB officers in the 70s and was stretched out in a lawn chair reading from it. He didn't look up when mumbling, "*Ne budi liho, poka ona tiho.*"

Kopen, not understanding the Russian proverb, wrinkled his forehead and started toward the officer's quarters where Dick Basting was staying. Air conditioning and an actual mattress in a private trailer were perks of his position.

All eyes followed Kopen's journey across the gravel courtyard. His path led him directly though the two teams' prep area—SEAL Team 6 on the left, JOE-CAG on the right. Managing to not appear intimidated by either, he stopped in front of Westhead.

"You want me to show you how to shoot that thing, just let me know," he said loudly. Westhead looked up from the rifle he was sighting and grinned at the FBI agent. A smattering of jeers from both sides of the aisle followed.

"I appreciate that, Seth, I do. You ever want me to show you how to pull off proper urban recon, you let *me* know."

Kopen patted him on the back, genuinely, then continued his march, turning the corner toward the officer's quarters. He wasn't gone long. The men heard him before they saw him again.

The shout was not unmanly or frantic; rather, it provoked a sense of control amid disorder. A second call for assistance brought the entirety of both SpecOps groups running to the cluster of trailers, weapons at the ready.

Inside Basting's trailer, they found Kopen performing rescue breathing on the president's foreign policy advisor. He was in bed, still under the covers, cold and rigid.

"What the ..." Stevens started. He shared a look with Hagen, then the Team 6 commander.

We stand around Basting's trailer, unsure of what to do. A corpsman from Team 6 takes over CPR from Agent Kopen, but quickly declares it a lost cause.

"Look here," one of the SEALs says, pointing at a pill bottle on the floor next to the body. He leans over without touching it. "Alprazolam, 1 mg. Empty."

There's a moment where everyone looks from that pill bottle to the body, and back to the bottle. It's clear what happened, at least to the people in this room.

"Guess the prez's man didn't like Iraq," someone commented. "Who could blame him? This place sucks." He laughed morbidly.

The Ranger Captain takes charge, asks us all to leave the trailer. His troops will take the report and make arrangements for the body to be flown stateside.

"Agent Kopen, if you could come with me so we can make our incident report, that would be appreciated, sir. And COL Stevens, maybe you should take that call. As far as I know, the White House is still on the line."

"Chief, what happened?" Nate hustled around the corner, past army medics removing a black body bag. He had his laptop under his arm, headphones in.

"It looks like Dick Basting committed suicide last night. Overdosed on pills."

"Holy shit," was the only response he could muster.

"Holy shit is right. Xanax," said Westhead. He stressed the name with extra emphasis.

"Wow." Nate paused here, the air suddenly very thick. "He leave a note?"

"I didn't see one. NCIS has been notified, but the scene is being secured. I would suggest that if you have any Xanax that's not legally prescribed to you, you get rid of it now. Hell, even if it is prescribed."

"I'm not lying to you, Chief, I haven't touched the stuff in a long time." Then: "What about you?"

"Don't worry about me. I'm off to find Stevens and Hagen. They went to take a call from the White House that was meant for Basting."

"How will this affect the mission?"

"It shouldn't. One dead policy-maker shouldn't have any impact on the rescue of a US Navy pilot. I'd get jocked up, if I were you. I spoke with Stevens—you're going out with us if we get this op."

Nate allowed himself a slight, imperceptible celebration before jogging back to his hooch to prep his gear. Westhead started toward the TOC, but stopped when he heard his name called softly. Agent Kopen, just visible in the shadows, raised a hand in his direction.

"Chief, a word? In private, if you don't mind."

Westhead took a glimpse around, saw they were alone. Kopen held open the door to a tan trailer. Reluctantly, Westhead followed him into the air conditioning.

"Before you even begin, Agent Kopen, I shouldn't be here ... talking to you. I mean, I have no idea why I even walked in here." Westhead began pacing the width of the small room, a single hand running the length of his head from scalp to neck, smoothing stringy hair, pulling absently at his beard. He left his sunglasses on so Agent Kopen couldn't see his eyes, which flitted all over the room.

"I understand that, Chief, and I appreciate you doing so. I came to you because you're the only one on your team I feel I can trust. And believe it or not, I'm trying to help you."

"Don't you see how much of a problem that is?" The question seemed to be shouted though its volume was low. A muffled outcry. "I can't be the one you trust! That's not the way it works! I'm a part of this unit, a team leader. My loyalty is with my men, not some FBI agent trying to hem us up!" He started toward the door, the stink of infidelity suddenly overwhelming.

"We both know there is no way that was a suicide."

Westhead wheeled around. "I know no such thing. Do you have evidence of that?"

"Of course not. And I'm sure there won't be any." Kopen stepped into Westhead's space, his direct gaze fixed on Westhead's eyes. "I just want to know if you know who did it. Truly."

Westhead didn't blink or respond. They stared into each other, a convoluted mix of suspicion and trust, respect and wariness.

"I don't. Truly."

"Before you go." Agent Kopen stepped away from him, from the door. "Before you go. Just hear this. The forensics came back from the house where Imam Shami was tortured and killed."

Westhead stopped, afraid to hear the results. "And?"

"You want to know?"

He could feel his heart beating through his chest. He knew the answer, he just didn't know what his response was going to be.

"I'm still standing here." He removed the glasses.

"Undetermined."

"Undetermined?"

"Correct. For now."

Westhead sneered at Kopen, a real and honest rage sweeping over him. He hit the door with outstretched arms, bright sunlight smacking them both as he brushed past Kopen and exited the trailer.

Agent Kopen called after him. "For now!" Westhead didn't turn around. "Undetermined for now! There *is* DNA from the scene, it just doesn't match anyone in the national databases. But rest assured, we've narrowed it down, we have a genetic profile. It's just a matter of getting a sample from them!" he cried to Westhead's retreating back.

Westhead slowed his departure only after noticing Nailer and Hell perched on a picnic table. They had witnessed the interaction with a concern that visually evolved to disgust. Anger. They stared into him. None of them spoke. Westhead continued toward the TOC, which Stevens and Hagen were exiting. The serious men had serious looks on their face.

"Give me good news," Westhead said to them, trying to shake the conversation with Kopen and the stabbing glares from his teammates. The hair was still standing up on his neck and his voice almost cracked with stress.

Hagen spoke first. "We're a go. Hitting the compound tonight. The Activity has reason to believe LCDR Wilson is there now but could be moved soon. First priority, his rescue. Secondary, capture al-Baghdadi. The president wants him alive."

"Alive? He's not going to throw up his hands and come with us. We should be expecting a suicide vest."

"You must have thought that was a suggestion," Steven said. "It wasn't. Gather the team leaders and go over the plan with your men one last time. Staging area at 2300. Needless to say, this is a no fail mission."

Westhead nodded and went to find Adam and Pos. He already knew where Hell was.

The team gathers at the bonfire, waiting for the still-light sky to blacken. Night seems reluctant to arrive. The sliver of an early moon is already overhead, but in in a pink/purple swirl of space. As I walk over, I see the DEV guys standing by their hooches. They're just visible in the dusk, watching us, the glow of the base's perimeter lights outlining frustrated silhouettes. They're pissed we got the mission. I don't blame them. We would be too.

Our assaulters are kitted up, making those final buddy checks that can mean the difference between life and death: Touching up face paint, checking batteries, shaking packs to ensure noise discipline, shining lights to identify anything shimmering that could give us away. You take care of your gear, your gear takes care of you. Same with your buddy.

Everyone seems good to go.

As I approach the group, I feel more sets of eyes on me than I can handle. Westhead's little rendezvous with Kopen did not go unnoticed or unreported. Not by me, not by the team. The assemblage of exterior distractions continues to leave more than a hint of tension throughout our ranks. On the surface, the whole thing has me ... worried? Angry? Resolute? Inwardly, there's a struggle to resolve the crushing feeling that they suspect me with the distinct feeling that I am projecting, I must be projecting, I have to be; that all the perceived suspicion and furtive glances are nothing more than invented wariness, delusion even. And then, just when I've convinced myself that that is the truth, the bubble is burst, by the person I'm most fearful of.

"How you feeling?" Westhead asks. He had come up next to me without drawing notice.

"I'm ... fine," I tell him, unsure of the question, but leery just the same.

"Ready to do this?"

"Just waiting for H-hour."

"See you got your Lone Star Flag there."

I look down to my hand. My fingers splay the frayed edges of the flag. "Always. You know I don't go operational without it."

"Texas forever."

"You got it, Riggins.

"Just so you know, I don't think for a second Dick Basting took his own life."

I pause before answering, an expert at keeping my face stone. Then: "No?"

His look is one of insulted intelligence, curled lips an insinuation that the question does not deserve an answer. He gives one anyway.

"The guy comes all the way to Iraq to do himself? When he's just survived the bombing of his institute? Give me a break. And an overdose on pills? With no regurgitation? Not a chance."

"Dunno. Sounds like as good a reason as any. Depressed over the loss of his institute. Stuck in a war zone with a squad of A-type personalities hell-bent on making him miserable." I stick a dip in my mouth. Not wintergreen, of course. I spit. "What is it you think happened if it wasn't a suicide?"

Westhead looks off into the distance, answering softly.

"A well-placed shot of potassium chloride would do the trick, wouldn't you say? Maybe in between his toes where the ME won't find it? That is, of course, if a medical examiner even gets to him. Lots of time between now and when he gets back stateside. I'm sure the president's medical staff will give him a once-over, but there's no guarantee they'd catch that two or three days after death. And if they do, oh well. Everyone on this FOB is already under suspicion, aren't they? What are they going to do? And you know what? I don't give a shit. As long as it doesn't affect this mission, my heart doesn't bleed for that liberal crybaby. So I'm not going to question anyone about anything. As long as they got my six, and we complete the mission, I'm good to go."

There is fire in his eyes, a rage to his posture. I can tell he knows, deep down. He doesn't know everything, certainly not the why, but he knows. The question is: Will he do anything about it?

"Good to hear, Chief," I tell him. "I'm sure the rest of the men will appreciate that. Especially after whatever that conversation in the trailer was with Kopen. I think you know how that went over with everyone."

I can tell he's surprised that I mention the meeting. Not necessarily that I know about it, but that I'm actually addressing it. "People talk," I explain, shrugging.

"They do. And right now, my only concern is conducting a successful operation. That's it. But when it's all over, when the pilot is home safely, when we've bagged al-Baghdadi, those questions will be asked. That you can be sure of."

"But not now?"

"Not now."

"Roger that."

The mutual defiance directed at each other lingers. Neither want to concede anything. I don't insult him by denying it; he doesn't make me by asking. We continue in this fashion, light from the fire licking our faces until a few other guys walk up with beef jerky and wisecracks.

"Something doesn't feel right," GQ said from the shadows. Like all of them, he wore a disdasha, the loose fitting robes common to the region, over his normal kit. A spray tan, powder to yellow his teeth, makeup, and hearty beard all made him look especially local in case they had to blend into the city. "Something about this op is giving me the willies."

"Third time is the charm, right?" said Pos.

"Better fucking be," he responded. "Although taking him alive could easily mean the end of our lives. Can't say I like that."

"Could be this mask of suspicion on us," Hell said, readjusting the keffiyeh scarf wrapped around his head. His eyes, tinted darkly with contacts, shot into Westhead. "People more worried about checking in on their brothers than the task at hand."

"Enough, Hell. Me and the Chief had a little chat—he's squared away," called out Stevens. "Aren't ya, Chief?"

Westhead spat, not just to Stevens, "I don't need to answer that. And fuck you very much if you have to ask. But when we got an FBI agent embedded with us and the president worried about our readiness because one of our own might be responsible for these attacks, and oh yeah, HIS FUCKING SECURITY ADVISOR JUST DIED ON OUR WATCH, then we all need to get our shit together. So if it means a team leader asking about guys taking ammo or flex cuffs, or accounting for missing RDX-X, then yeah, spare me your hurt feelings. I'm gonna wonder about you if you're *not* asking those questions. And I'm getting sick of defending that."

"I don't need you wondering about me, Dan." Nailer took a step closer to his team leader. "And here's some news for you. I don't give a rat fuck about terrorist sympathizers getting shot, tortured, blown up or dying in their sleep. If they can't hack the sandbox, then good fucking riddance. I'm happy to say my job is almost exclusively to remove those wishing harm to my country from the gene pool. And to all those who oppose ... well ... Fuck you."

McDonald jumped to his feet. "You sure you didn't have anything to do with it? Those sound like the words of someone happy all those people got killed."

"Just not wasting my sorrow on those who don't deserve it. You wanna feel bad for someone, New Meat, feel bad for Darby. Mourn the men of Operation Atlas, and all the Marines and sailors and soldiers that gave their lives in Iraq and Afghanistan only to have a weak-kneed leader give it all back to the animals. You and Dan can have your pity party on your own time. But I'll tell you this—the next person to question my motives gets a 7.62 through the roof of the mouth."

Stevens stepped between them. He carried his heft quickly, the tan fabric of his robes fluttering almost ethereally.

"Stand the fuck down! Five minutes from the biggest mission of our lives, and you want to do this? This was supposed to be settled in Arizona!" He grabbed hold of McDonald, shaking him. "Does anyone here miss Dick Basting? Does anyone care he's gone? How about the ACLU lawyer? The imam? The intelligence fuck that got Darby killed?" He turned to each of his operators, wide-eyed and serious. "Then why the hell are you spending your energy trying to figure out who killed them?" Deep, stone eyes moved toward the TOC. Kopen stood in the shadows, previously unnoticed. Stevens pointed. "That's his job. Do I need to remind you of yours?"

Kopen eased forward. He was in his own robes, a red-and-white-checked keffiyeh covering his head. He had a HAHO rig and gear at his feet.

"Colonel, that's only part of my job. Right now, my job is to safely recover an American pilot."

Stevens was incredulous. "You think you're coming with us?"

"I know I am, Colonel. The president asked me here to see this mission through, and that's what I'm going to do. I was Airborne and 75th

Ranger Regiment in another life. An assaulter with the FBI's Hostage Rescue Team. I'm just as operational as your men. Ask Westhead there."

"You need a better rabbi that that, Agent Kopen," Stevens said.

Hell laughed. "HRT? Airborne? We aren't busting some hillbilly meth lab, Agent. This is a HAHO jump into a terrorist compound. No static line dope on a rope bullshit."

"I have over a hundred HAHO and HALO jumps under my belt, Gunny."

"Fantastic. Just remember, it's not the fall that kills you, it's the ground."

"You're not worried a friendly might accidentally shoot you in a firefight?" Stevens asked. "We clear rooms a little differently than you did in your battalion, Agent."

"Those threats, Colonel?" The FBI agent stepped forward. If he was intimidated, he didn't show it. "Chief Westhead has seen my close quarters battle abilities. I'm done debating. Unless you want me to place a call to Washington and share some of my concerns about how Dick Basting died, I'm on this op with you."

Hagen and Stevens traded looks. Neither had the time nor inclination to fight this. Their lack of opposition was its own acquiescence.

"You're with Butler." Stevens jabbed a finger at the young SEAL. He stood in the background, quiet and observant. "You two stay out of the way." Then, to the rest of the team, "Load up." Under the jealous watch of the DEVGRU squadron, they started toward the airfield where they wordlessly boarded a waiting C-5.

SOMEWHERE OVER WESTERN ASIA

The men gathered around Adam in the cargo hold, taking knees and lowering heads. A small, worn Bible came from the front of his plate carrier. He pressed it tight against his forehead, not reading from it, but seeming to draw strength from the weathered cover. While not all those gathered regarded themselves as true believers, most saw the advantage in being covered. Just in case.

"More than ever I feel the need of having Thee close to me," Adam began, the words just distinguishable over the whining plane projecting its occupants closer to combat. The prayer was the same he offered before every mission. "At any moment I may find myself in battle. However rigorous the task that awaits me, may I fulfill my duty with courage. If death should overtake me on this field, grant that I die in the state of grace, forgive me all my sins, those I have forgotten and those I recall now: grant me the grace of perfect contrition." Some of the men's lips moved in silence with the words. Most finished with an obligatory "Amen." Adam kissed the medallion of St. Michael, tucked it back under his shirt.

Compulsory spiritual duty completed, the men went off to doze or start the process of pre-breathing. They would inhale 100 percent oxygen to flush the nitrogen from their bloodstreams, a prerequisite for the height from which they would jump. Westhead sat alone, brooding, distanced from the rest of the team. He made a point to stay far from Kopen.

"You mind?" Stevens motioned to the jump seat next to him. After receiving a permissive nod, he lowered himself onto it. "We haven't had a chance to talk about Cheyenne. How's she doing?"

"You know how she's doing."

Stevens made a clucking sound indicating that in fact, he did.

"I do. Without me, she dies."

Westhead's attention snapped toward the colonel, shocked at the harshness of his words.

"'Fuck you say?"

"I know it, you know it. Even more so than I originally thought, actually. I spoke with Doc Soto before we left. I understand she's already started treatment in preparation for the transplant. Once that preparation has begun ..." He stopped there, checking Westhead's reaction, making sure he had his attention. He did. "That's it for her. Her body can no longer produce healthy blood cells. Without mine, she's dead."

Stevens leaned forward before continuing: "It was me. All of it. It was me alone."

Once more, I stare into his face, reading him, making sure he fully understands what I'm telling him.

"It was me. All of it. It was me alone. The Basting Institute, Imam Shami and his mosque, Riley & Porter, the lawyer in Arizona. And yeah, you were right. Dick Basting too. I killed them all. Me alone." My words are not quite lost in the sounds of the jet, and his frozen expression tells me he comprehends them fully. "And I'm not done."

Westhead lunges, pulling his sidearm from a thigh holster. He slams the barrel into my throat, pushing fiercely. I push back. The metal is cold against the soft skin under my chin. My lower teeth grind against the uppers. I taste blood.

"And I'm going to need your help," I continue, hissing through a clenched jaw. "Do it for Cheyenne, do it for the brotherhood, do it for me. But you're going to do it." Face contorted, eyes slits, he cocks the weapon. I put it at fifty-fifty whether he's going to shoot me in the face right here and now. We hold this pose, the seconds thick and sluggish. I almost feel bad for him, but know that this is what needs to be done. Removing choice, free will, from another man, especially a man of this caliber, is not something to be taken lightly. It takes a moment, but his grip loosens. We slump back to our seats and glance toward the front of the plane, interested to see if anyone noticed.

"I am going to kill the president when we return," I state simply. He does not react. "It has to be done. But I can't do it alone. I'll need your help. After that, Cheyenne gets her marrow. Then you can do with me what you may."

Pockets of chatter begin to pop up, slowly at first. Westhead walks to the front of the plane, away from Stevens. Kopen tries to stay inconspicuous. No one engages him. There's more movement around the cabin, guys smacking fists, adjusting the straps on their chute containers. The 30,000-feet call is given. By the time the fifteen-minute signal is passed, everyone is rigged in their HAHO gear: polypropylene knit undergarments, assault packs secured by D rings, oxygen masks on. The rear ramp lowers with an ominous hum, revealing a gaping mouth, an all-encompassing black hole, the infinite ready to consume all who enter. Weapons are strapped underneath armpits as everyone lines up in the wind and cold. The jumpmaster offers each man in line a thumbs-up; each returns it, holding a gloved hand into the frigid dark air for a beat. Westhead stares past the open door, the sky over the desert brighter than its counterpart above. From up here he can see the curvature of the earth, the horizon glowing into space. He makes eye contact with Kopen, who seems good to go. Maybe his chutes will fail, and the agent will no longer be a distraction. Does he actually wish that? Doesn't matter what he wishes when it comes to fate, to the whims of the gods. Does he really believe that?

Two minutes. Thor is first in line. He raises both arms, circling them, popping tense shoulders.

Thirty seconds. Everyone is on their toes now, leaning forward, aware only of the whirl of the jet, the rushing air. The task at hand. A joke directed at Jud, who hates heights, crackles through their headsets. Something about hoping he can bounce. He doesn't even bother flicking Thor off. The jumpmaster straps in with a gunner's belt. He crawls forward on his hands and knees, peering out through the ramp. When he finds his mark, he slaps Thor on the butt. Thor waddles the last few steps into nothingness, arms outstretched, falling chest-first into the black. GQ immediately follows, then Kopen, then Jud, Nate, Pos, Mutt, and so on and so on like freefalling dominos, until all the men are invisible stains slicing through an oblivious nighttime. The air temperature at 33,000 feet is minus forty-five degrees Fahrenheit. They will glide silently for fifteen minutes, covering nearly twenty miles before landing in a precise circle ten meters from each other in the middle of a vast Syrian wasteland.

I'm the last to jump, following Westhead, who of course gives his standard shout of "Geronimo!" while leaping out of the plane. His chute pops while I'm still in freefall. I pull my cord, looking up to ensure it opens correctly; above, a perfect canopy. Behind me, the gray behemoth peels off to the north. We are alone, the sudden serenity a liberating arrival. I float peacefully for a time, enjoying the feeling of weightlessness, falling smoothly except for a quick shudder when steering the canopy into the proper compass heading.

The team lands in a tight pocket. Once on the ground, half set security while the other half get out of their jump gear. There is no communication. It's greener here than I expected. Instead of the familiar desolation of unforgiving desert, ditches filled with human waste and pockmarks from bombs, there are trees, shrubs, even fresh water.

Soon, we're in the local attire, faces, features and hair already darkened to blend in. Most of us speak the language. Jud quickly makes comms with our CIA contacts and informs us the convoy is en route. Minutes later, four blacked out Land Rovers come into focus on the horizon, leaving plumes of dust in their wake. It is the only movement on the landscape, occasionally disappearing behind clusters of trees or changes in topography. Past the trucks, the few lights of Homs twinkle anonymously in the distance. We wait in the land's besieging black and quiet. It's not a long wait. It feels like one. I try to make eye contact with Westhead, but he looks away. I'm not worried about him. He knows mission failure is not an option. I find Kopen, but instead of a pointed glare, I offer a half-smile. I don't want to raise his alert level.

The Land Rovers arrive without ceremony. We load up quickly and head toward the town of Al-Rastan, an ancient city built on the edge of the Roman empire. It's seen near constant battle for thousands of years and was one of the first localities to rise up against the Syrian government in their current war. Now, arguably the most wanted terrorist in the world and his American captive are supposed to be somewhere in its midst.

My driver's name is Khaled. He talks too much. He wants to know my name, wants to know where I'm from, what America is like. Blade, I tell him. I tell him I'm from Canada and don't know what America is like, but that I imagine it's better than here. He agrees, taking no insult.

"Okay, I get, you no talk, you no talk, okay," he says, his arms raised off the wheel in deference. His teeth are rotten, his breath reeks of tobacco. I shoulder my rifle, lower my NVGs and scan the skyline. Except for the three other Land Rovers, it's motionless, nearly void of light. Khaled tells me that Al-Rastan is a half hour away, but we will have to take the long way to avoid government checkpoints and rebel roadblocks. Fine, I say, but keep your hands on the wheel. The last thing we need is to break an axle in the middle of the desert. I check the GPS again and we're on track.

AL-RASTAN, SYRIA

Westhead's driver speeds through the ancient city, crumbled and broken from a new war, or at least a new version of the old one. Different war, same result. Sharply, they turn down an alley. Two men sit at its entrance on folding chairs, AK's across their laps. They look expectant of the convoy, but that doesn't stop JOE-CAG snipers in each Land Rover from painting them with laser designators as the team passes. Everyone monitors their area of responsibility from the roofs to the rear. By the time they pull into a gated compound in what probably passes for decent shape in this town, their pocket of earth is just beginning to glow.

"You stay here until nighttime," Khaled says haltingly once everyone is inside the house. He seems to be the ranking Syrian asset. Khaled is tall, lean, with small, confident eyes on an overly animated face. A hawkish nose, with a patch of hair darkening the wide forehead. One gets the impression he's younger than he appears. Hard years, living here. Even in ill-fitting, dirty clothing, filthy fingernails, he carries himself nobly. You would venture that if he were from a Western country he would be a pharmacist, an entrepreneur. Successful and happy. But he's not. He was born here.

"You sleep, relax. We come back with food, water." He starts toward the door, but Stevens steps in his path, blocking the exit.

"No can do, Tonto," he says. "No one leaves until we do." He shoots Abe, their CIA contact, a look. "You take their cell phones?" Abe's eyes divert to his feet. He shakes his head.

"Everyone, cell phones out," Stevens barks in Arabic. The JOEs move swiftly through the room, taking the cell phones from their incredulous hosts. Mutt holds a mesh bag, where they drop them, batteries and bodies separated.

"Get comfortable boys. You don't leave until we do." GQ throws Khaled a three-cheese tortellini MRE and a bag of skittles. "See, we're not all bad. Just don't eat the lime Skittles. You'll get us all killed. And watch out for Pos. You turn your head for one minute, he'll eat your whole meal. Could lose a finger you try to stop him." Pos nods in agreement. Khaled wears the confused look of someone who doesn't get the joke.

Stevens barks, "Dan, you know the drill. Get everything set up."

Westhead begins spreading shooters throughout the house. The rest of the team finishes unloading. The safe house is large, three stories, and once upon a time was undoubtedly a lovely home to a fine family. Tall ceilings, whitewashed walls, dirty shadows where paintings, maybe a watercolor, a landscape of a date farm or a family portrait, once hung. Maybe the house belonged to a doctor or government official. Now, anything of value has been removed. Graffiti in Arabic, some smashed walls and a plethora of bullet holes complete the décor.

The men move to fifty-fifty security—half sleeping, half on watch. They will switch off this way throughout the entirety of the hot day, bull-shitting, eating MREs, drinking as much water as possible in between naps and watch until it gets dark again. No mention is made of the building isolation of Westhead. Like this they will wait until they can move out and conduct their operation under the protection of night, the noises and smells of another burnt out city wallowing through and around them.

Agent Kopen finds me during a period of downtime. I'm sitting alone on the second floor, eating almonds, observing my men load mags, check gear, munch MREs. Those on security are at their posts: on the roof, in the windows, on comms with circling air assets, alert and ever-vigilant for signs our cutout has been compromised. Those not on duty play cards, chatting quietly, very few sleeping like they should be. Pos annoys us with knock knock jokes, Thor regales whoever will listen with tales of feminine conquests. The standard bullshit, even as we all keep watchful eyes on the locals. They wait to be released with scowls across their faces, still pissed at being held against their will. Tough shit.

"Colonel, have a minute?" The FBI agent looks just slightly ridiculous fully kitted and in native garb. I motion to the dusty floor next to me, and he squats, close. "Impressed with my jumping abilities?" he asks. "It had been a while, but I gotta say, I enjoyed that."

I smile. "You made it, so there's that."

"I'd being lying if I didn't say I was a little worried, since it was your men who packed my chute. I get the feeling I'm not the most popular guy on this op." His smirk is disarmingly severe. "At least if something had gone wrong, I had the rest of my life to figure it out. Then again, no one's ever complained about their chute not opening."

"Not true. One of my boys would have docked to you before pulling their own. We're not going to let you die on our watch, Agent Kopen. It would make us look bad." I don't mention that if he is killed by any number of other, more innocuous threats in this warzone, JOE-CAG's reputation will come through unscathed.

He shrugs, acquiescing. "I suppose that it wouldn't look great for you if *both* of the president's observers came home in body bags. But I don't plan on dying. Not yet, at least. I do plan on arresting those responsible for the attacks back home, though. And guess what? The lab work came back from the crime scene where the imam was found."

"And?"

"And Westhead didn't tell you?"

"How would he know? You find a mole in my unit, Agent?"

"Mole? Nah ... Just a friendly face."

I focus on pushing my anxiety down. If I had left DNA, the whole mission was blown. But if that were the case, why aren't the cuffs already on? Or more realistically, why wasn't I laid out at the morgue after an FBI SWAT team showed up at my house? Unless Kopen had just discovered the results and doesn't have the manpower to take me out here. No matter what the forensic evidence says, this investigation is getting too close. Maybe I *should* have turned Agent Kopen into a lawn dart. Not that it's too late. With the lead investigator out of the way, there's no doubt mission success will come easier, that conclusion as unavoidable as rain in the spring.

"So are you going to tell me, or keep making me guess? Or should I wait for Chief Westhead to loop me in?"

"Actually, he's doesn't know either. We're not at liberty to reveal the results just yet. But it's safe to say, we're getting closer. I don't expect there to be another attack."

"Good to hear," is all I say. I finish the bag of nuts, place the wrapper in a burn bag. We'll destroy all evidence that we were ever here before leaving. "That all?"

"Yes, sir," he says.

"Keep your head on a swivel out there," I can't help but tell him.

It's a cluttered scene, twenty or so unwashed men strategically placed throughout the home based on comfort and tactics. The JOEs are alert, even when not on watch. The Syrian assets' earlier frustration and boredom seems to have been replaced by mounting fear. When someone asks Khaled about it, he says his men are concerned that when the ISIS commanders discover their city has been infiltrated by Americans, their absence will be noticed, they and their families tortured and killed. When the ominous call for evening prayers envelops the air, all adjust themselves accordingly. It won't be long now.

Westhead is on the roof, pulling watch alone, when the incantations fill the sky. The few people remaining in the city scurry to cover, for fear they'll be discovered not offering the Maghrib prayer and be punished heavily.

"What was that with you and Stevens on the flight over?" McDonald had come up to scan the neighboring rooftops with Westhead. The air around them is stagnant under a still night. Both men hope for a breeze that the evening never promises.

"You saw that, huh?"

"I did."

"Call it a difference in military tactical philosophy."

"Looked like a pretty stark difference."

"It was."

McDonald lowers his binos and his voice. He studies his team leader carefully. "Is Stevens the one responsible for the attacks on American soil?"

Westhead doesn't flinch, but he doesn't answer either.

"Chief, I think the men deserve to know if the commander of this unit is a terrorist."

"Our mission is a go, and that's all you should be concerned with," Westhead eventually responds. He squints into the setting sun, something on the other end of the roof piquing his interest. Then, gruffly, "aren't you supposed to be resting right now?"

"Roger that," McDonald replies. As he exits, his attention carries Westhead's gaze. They both stiffen at the sight.

From the far corner of the roof Stevens sits in the shadows, fixated, coldly sharpening a knife. The faintest of echoes from his scraping comes into focus. He wears an expressionless face, blank maybe from the shadows, maybe not. The two leaders lock eyes in the dusk. Communication passes. Westhead decides he is more upset at not placing the sound than he is at the image of his boss, black-eyed and surreptitious. He turns away, back to the scope, scanning the skyline with no acknowledgement or distress. Stevens follows McDonald back inside.

It's been a long day, but night is now finally upon us. If we don't move out soon we'll have to contend with sunrise. I hang up the sat phone, hand it back to Jud. The president has finally pushed us into H-Hour, and not a moment too soon. I gather everyone on the first floor of the safe house.

"We're a go," I tell them. "Load up, rolling in five." The activity throughout the room is immediate and purposeful. I make eye contact with Westhead. Nate stands next to him—I've noticed the two stick close together. I've made a decision.

"Agent Kopen, New Guy and Dan, you're hanging back at the safe house as overwatch. Keep an eye on the natives and monitor our frequencies. You'll be our eyes and ears with the TOC. We're going to depend on you to get us out of here—make sure that our exfil and extract go as smooth as possible."

There's a clatter as the rest of the men hop to, rifles slung and hot. Westhead grabs my arm, teeth showing.

"What the fuck, Blade? You forget what I'm holding over you? I know your secret. I would think you'd want to keep me happy."

I stare at the fingers clenched around my bicep until he lets go. Only then do I respond.

"And you must have forgotten what I have over you. So shut your mouth and do your job. Believe it or not, this isn't personal. Mission success, that's all I'm concerned with at this point. Despite what you may think, I need someone here I can trust. And I can't think of anyone I can rely on more than you right now."

"At least leave Nate here with me. I can use his gun."

"So can I. He goes with us." I'm not oblivious to the insurance policy Nate represents and walk away without giving Westhead an opportunity to argue further. It's difficult to tell whether Kopen is angry or relieved to be hanging back.

We load back into the Land Rovers while the squad remaining in the safe house barricades the windows and doors behind us. The house stays blacked out. As we pull into the alley, they take up positions on the roof to provide perimeter security. It won't be a long drive to al-Baghdadi's compound across town. If all goes right, Westhead's squad will spin up our extract shortly after mission completion, the full team, prisoner, and rescued pilot whisked to safety by the expertise and skill of the United States Army's 160th pilots.

In the meantime, I study what I can of the desolate neighborhood through tinted windows. I tell Khaled to step on it. He mutters something in Arabic as we accelerate into the night.

The town seems deserted, the night what passes for tranquil here. They settle in on the rooftop, each focusing on their fields of fire: The neighboring windows and rooftops, the empty, cratered roads. Green and black through night vision. An irrigation ditch lined with rocky, reddish clay leading to an open sewage field. Crumbled houses, hidden alleyways, burned out cars. Kopen whispers into the night.

"Hard to believe this is the same world as ours."

"It's not," McDonald replies softly.

"Same planet, different world," Westhead says, almost an afterthought.

Kopen can't help but chuckle. "Amazing how the prospect of immediate and violent death in a foreign land will make you wax philosophical." A half smile into the black.

Westhead continues a composed observation of the scorched city. There are few lights and less movement. At least half the buildings are collapsed and blackened; where thousands of palms grew in the past, only stubborn, singular trees rise now, almost as if they had been placed by a giant's random touch. What allowed those trees to survive? He sighs, his exhale the only stir in the crusty setting.

"Stinks here. What would you call that potpourri?"

"Death," McDonald answers simply.

"Camel shit mixed with hopelessness?" offers Kopen.

Westhead is able to snicker. "I was going to say progress, but ... what the ... that is not the stink of Syria—who ... ?!"

Kopen readjusts his position behind his rifle, stifling a combination giggle/groan. Westhead's arm goes to his face.

"That was you? My God! That's something, when you can overpower the stench of a war-torn country. You better check your draw's."

"MREs," Kopen laughs like it's a joke between fraternity brothers. "It's been a while since I've enjoyed the processed cuisine of the United States government."

Westhead lifts a hand into the night air, suddenly serious. "Hold it," he says. On his right wrist is a small screen, footage from their dedicated drone playing across it. "Looks like they're on the target street. The Apache just painted the house."

Khaled is getting more nervous the deeper we drive into the city. He knows the streets well, and thus far has been adept at avoiding roadblocks and checkpoints. A scout team of well-paid locals, unaware of who they were clearing streets for, had travelled the exact route unmolested just fifteen minutes earlier. In my ear, a combat controller from the TOC lets me know the route is still clean.

"Route Alpha is clear, Khaled," I pass along. "Continue to the end of this street and make the last right."

"I know the route, Mr. Blade," he tells me, his anxiety noticeably rising with each decimated building we pass. The roads and structures are in even worse shape in this neighborhood, and intelligence lets us know they will be nearly impassable on al-Baghdadi's block. I imagine what the town looked like in the past, when Khaled was growing up. Palm clusters and date tree–lined streets. New, whitewashed buildings with markets and fruit stands out front. Busy sidewalks, old women yelling at children from the balconies above. Soccer fields and schools. Now, only the mosques are close to damage free, and even they sport bullet holes. There are still some civilians left in al-Rastan, but they live in fear and under ISIS laws and curfew, the amenities of their old lives gone with their jobs and freedom.

"There," Jud says from the backseat. The men in our vehicle lean toward his finger, see the fluorescent green beam coming down from the heavens. I know that's the only help we'll get from an Apache on this op.

"Titan One, we see your paint," I say into my throat mic. Then, to Khaled, who is not wearing night vision: "One block over, last house on the left." The Syrian mumbles something unintelligible, and guides the Land Rover around a scorched sedan. It's unnervingly tranquil, the dilapidated street giving the impression of being uninhabited. In the side view mirror, I watch our other SUVs follow. My earpiece comes alive with Nailer's voice.

"Blade, I got tangos on the roofs on either side of the target house," he reports.

"Roger that," I tell him and get back on with the Apache pilots, knowing the answer before I ask. "Titan One, we have tangos on the rooftops. Can you engage? Over."

It's a minute before I hear back. "Negative on that. Too much collateral damage." Bullshit, I think, anyone still in this city is an enemy combatant or at least sympathizes with them. Before I can finish the thought, I feel myself fly forward, slamming into the dashboard with authority. I recover quickly, a little stunned, my weapon at the ready.

"Roadblock," I hear Khaled mutter, immediately followed by the familiar sound of AK-47 fire pinging off the up-armored Rovers. An RPG explodes at the rear of our vehicle. It begins.

"Ambush!" I call out evenly. "Dismount and assault on foot through the kill zone!" Since we're so close to our target, there's no point in pushing the convoy through. We'll take defensive positions then assault toward the compound. I pop my door and take a firing position behind it. Behind me, I can feel Khaled moving frantically, the SUV starting to rock. I wheel back to him, H&K pointed at his face.

"Do not move this fucking vehicle!" I order over the automatic fire raining down. My finger slides over the trigger guard. I give him one second to put the car back in park before I take his forehead off. He sees that, reads it in my face, knows that his only chance of survival is to stay where he is. He throws the gearshift forward, and ducks under the steering wheel. "Coward," I breathe, turning back to the houses in question, engaging two more targets.

"This is Ground 2. Troops in contact," Westhead says sternly into his radio. "Request air support. Over."

The response is immediate. "Negative on the air support, Ground 2." Westhead curses and slams the radio down.

"Dammit. This is the shit we're talking about. You can thank Basting and his cronies in Washington for deciding these hajis' lives are more important than our men's." He doesn't look at anyone when he speaks, but it's clear who it's directed at. Kopen is unsure how to respond. He knows he's not the problem, but as part of the Washington bureaucratic machine bears some responsibility.

"So what do we do?"

"Nothing we can do. We wait. And we make sure those birds are ready for extract the second our guys say it's time to go."

"What about a QRF?"

Westhead consults his wrist, watches the beginning of the firefight from the monitor. "That's Stevens's call. Team 6 is on standby at

Monsoor, but they're at least an hour out. Unless it gets really bad, I'd say we're on our own. But this is what we train for, Agent. Believe it or not, that's the way we like it."

"I believe it," Kopen answers. They all go back to their fields of fire, Westhead checking in with the TOC every few minutes.

It's a glancing blow, but holy shit does it sting, even through the accompanying surge in adrenaline. Incoming from the rooftops thickens, and with no air support, we're sitting ducks in the Land Rovers, fortified or not. I check my arm—it's a graze, barely drawing blood. But a gunshot nonetheless. More than anything it pisses me off. I quickly wrap it with gauze and pressure dressing, continue directing the men.

"Out of the kill zone!" I call, ordering them to form up on our primary entry point. Half leave the cover of the trucks, making a dash for the front of al Baghdadi's compound, shrapnel kicking up all around us during the trip. The other half stand upright, sending covering fire into the surrounding homes until we skid to safety against the front wall. Then we reverse the maneuver until the entire team is stacked against the outer compound wall.

The whole thing looks just like the mock-up. The clay house is larger than the other homes on the block and in much better shape. For now. The same security wall we practiced breaching rings it, angry barbed wire running the length. At least they got that right. No matter, we don't plan on climbing over. Or, for that matter, using the gate. We expect that to be IED'd.

"Breacher up!" I shout, automatically knocking twice on my helmet. Bump bump. Thor rushes forward through the attack and on a knee deftly sets a shaped charge against the wall. He checks to make sure we're behind cover before cooking it off. A quick FIZZ then loud BOOM that I can feel in my chest, brain properly rattled. When the dust settles a nice four-foot circular hole invites us into the courtyard. We stack and enter dynamically. Thor puts down one of two ISIS fighters who greet us; I take out the other with a double tap to the face.

Our assault train moves forward into the courtyard. The home's front door is tantalizing close.

I call for Hell and Nailer. They rush forward. Across the street an apartment building, half decimated and burned out, overlooks our target. I point into it.

"Gents, I need overwatch in that building. Can you get in there to set up an OP?"

Neither hesitates or even bothers with a response. The answer is understood. The rest of us prepare to cover their movements. "Popping smoke!" Thor hollers before tossing a smoke grenade onto the street. There's a lull as a dense white fog begins to drift ethereally across the destruction. Hell and Nailer turn, poised, waiting for my signal. I give it, shout to the rest of the men through the wafting fog: "Cover fire!"

To a man, we step back from the relative safety of that wall, again aiming into the surrounding buildings. The rising smoke makes for an eerie setting. Somehow, it seems to have stifled all noise, slowed down the pace of action. There are a few muffled shouts, the sound of suppressed rounds spitting down the line, but they come lethargically, as if covered with a blanket. Nate is shoulder to shoulder with me, his belt-fed SAW thumping and grating with violent authority. Plaster and rock shower down upon us as we send hundreds of shots into the accompanying structures. Tracer rounds slice through the sky, a spectacular laser show. Pos and Mutt's 40 mike-mikes explode into the tops of the homes straddling the target compound where we've been taking sniper fire. "Cease fire!"

When I lower my rifle, Hell and Nailer are across the street, scrambling over piles of rebar and concrete through residual smoke. The ground ahead of and behind them lights up with return fire, but they reach the building safely. Once they're inside we crouch back behind the wall.

I radio Hell after a moment. "Status?" It's a minute before I get a response. His breathing is heavy.

"Fucking stairs are blown out. Give us a minute, we're going to have to boulder our way up the rubble."

"Secure the doors and set claymores around your perimeter before you go up."

"No shit, Blade. We've actually done this before." The line goes dead. I turn back to my men.

"Hold tight," I tell everyone. As I do, a WOOSH goes off over my head, followed by a screech and splintering of the security wall. I'm thrown into the air, landing on my back. When I come to, I can't move my arms or legs. Something heavy is holding me down.

"Get the fuck off!" I yell, squirming. It's Jud. He's lying on top of me, covered in concrete and other debris. His face, previously darkened, now looks ghoulish, freshly painted a dusty beige. Surprised I'm conscious, or even alive, he rolls off.

"Damn, Blade, I thought you were cooked," he coughs, shaking his head to clear the cobwebs. Dust rains off his broad shoulders like snow. He looks genuinely happy I'm alive. "That was pretty much a direct hit."

"Takes more than an RPG to kill me." I've forgotten that I'm also shot. There's another WOOSH, then another, and we dive toward the front façade of the home. Behind us, our Land Rovers are engulfed in flames. There is no sign of Khaled or the other drivers.

"Guess we're going to need to find another ride home," I say to no one while scanning for targets.

"They're in the shit now." Westhead is fixated on the drone feed. "Looks like they're about to breach. Incoming RPG and small arms everywhere."

"You sound jealous," Kopen says tightly.

McDonald rises from his sniper position urgently, crouching on the roof. "Come on Chief, we're doing them no good here! We have to get in that fight!"

"Get back to your sector, McDonald! Our orders are to stay here and organize extract. It's mission failure if we don't get that pilot out of here safely."

McDonald sulks back to his corner. Kopen watches the interaction, fascinated.

"You guys really are like little kids," he tells them.

"SpecOps is 13th grade, you know that," says Westhead. "You were a part of it." Then, to everyone: "They're inside." He changes the settings on his screen, and instead of black and white, it glows in shades of reds, oranges and yellows. Friendlies show up as blinking sparkles of light. He keys his mic.

"Blade, I got two heat sigs on the first floor, four on the second and six on the third. The roofs are quiet. Looks like a pretty straightforward breach."

"Roger that," Stevens says. Westhead can hear the explosions, close, in the background.

"You want me to start that QRF?"

"Negative," Stevens breathes before the connection cuts out.

Westhead turns to McDonald. "Get that HLZ cleared. We could be leaving in a hurry."

I knew I could count on Westhead. Aside from the fact that he would never do anything to jeopardize the mission, I'm banking on him wanting Cheyenne to live more than he wants me to die. My whole mission plan depends on that premise. So far he's on point. I look over at the young SEAL he's so fond of.

"Moving," I say, my left hand squeezing Butler's shoulder. He spins to his left and immediately engages the bad guy spraying fire at us from around a corner.

"Moving." We're stacked in two lines and winding gracefully throughout the house, clearing rooms. It's a masterful choreographed display, a result of extensive CQB training, muscle memory, and hundreds of real-world ops that make it look seamless and instinctive; to us, it is. The other train, led by Thor, peels to the right and lines up at the base of the stairs. I flash four fingers at him. He nods, gives a "crash out" call and tosses a flash bang up the stairs. No one flinches when the house shudders with the ensuing percussion. That element swiftly but tacitly enters the smoke and unknown, each footstep and muzzle

movement meaningful and precise. I hear an immediate reply of au-
tomatic fire, followed by the even THWAK of our suppressed rifles.
No one yells out and then there is the stark shock of sudden silence.
My group finishes clearing the first floor and makes our way upstairs.

Thor is standing apart from the men. His eyes are wide, his chest
heaving. It's hard to picture him like this, even as he stands in front of
me. The makeup, the local clothing, the dyed hair. He looks like a Syrian
peasant, but he's not; he's an elite United States commando, and he's
standing over the body of a woman, a girl even, her chest wet and red
and she looks cartoonish, her eyes still open, despite all odds maybe
even with a flicker of life left in them, and then Thor drops, pushing on
her chest, opening her airway, and we all know it's hopeless, and that
we're not yet out of the fight anyway, but even when GQ and Jud grab
him, he fights to get back to her, he yells about needing to save her, and
it's not until I smack him purposefully across the face that the blank
look leaves and he clutches his rifle with a new anger and determination and then Westhead is in my ear and he passes along the news that
unfriendlies are pouring into the building on the floor below. We step
over the AK-47 at the girl's feet and prepare to be overrun.

"We gotta get over there!" McDonald is shouting, and Westhead
has to hiss at him to shut the fuck up or the hajis are gonna be all over
the safe house and then they won't be able to help anyone. The truth
is, Westhead is glad he has to calm the junior JOE, has to order him to
stand down. It's as good an outlet for his frustration as any. He wants
to be at the target compound with the rest of his team just as badly, it's
a testament to his sense of duty that he doesn't race over.

"So what are we going to do?" Kopen asks again.

Westhead's face is cold, his patience, waning. "We're going to make
sure that HLZ is secure. Then we're going to find an alternate exit for
them, and then we're going to kill the shit out of al-Baghdadi, all his
men, and rescue the pilot. That is what we are going to do." He reaches to his chin and tries Stevens again. No response.

Fucking Dan. Can't he tell I'm a little busy? I hear the crackle of him trying to raise me, but I'm in the middle of a major fucking fire-fight and can't come to the phone right now. Asshole. He just better remember that he needs me alive.

Additional ISIS fighters are pouring into the courtyard, leading with grenades, spraying and praying during their mad dash. They're well armed. Not as well as us. We are dropping most; some make it inside and fan out, away from our fields of fire. We've formed a fortified perimeter on the second floor, Nate behind the SAW at the top of the landing, the high ground perfect for him to rain brass on any mujs rushing up the stairs. His focus is complete behind the bi-podded machine gun, strings of full metal jackets strung across his shoulder. He looks like Rambo. I make a mental note to tell him that after we're back in the world—every young operator wants to hear that they look like Rambo. The weapon bucks rhythmically in his hands, calmly and effectively mowing down screaming, bearded fighters as quickly as they can run up the stairs to their death. I try not to focus on their features, but can't help noticing how young most seem, as young as Nate; clad in black, callously step-ping over and across their fallen comrades on blood soaked stairs. I can't help but be amused at all the white sneakers, or worse, the socks with sandals combo. Not the most battle-effective attire.

Ammo is not yet a problem, but we can all see it becoming one if the influx of suicidal holy warriors doesn't slow. My biggest concern is LCDR Wilson, who I still believe is one floor above, mostly likely with al-Bagh-dadi ready to make his last stand. But this ISIS cell is doing everything they can to make sure we don't make it up there. We can wait no longer.

"Squad 1, take third floor!" I yell. We lay down another blanket of cover fire as they move, led by Thor. My gun rises, spits twice, and an-other black-pajama-wearing haji falls. The chaos of battle is now full and non-negotiable, but I take solace knowing that our experience, technology, and training make it less so for us than the enemy. The flow of terrorists coming up from the first floor begins to slow, although I can hear scattered intones below calling out orders in Arabic for what I can only assume is a counter-attack. The voices filter upward frightfully: Arabic spoken off screen is always particularly haunting, causes me to grip my weapon just a little tighter, shoot a little faster. Despite their losses, despite the absurd pointlessness of their task, the fighters call to each other confidently, unwavering cadences of "*Allahu Akbar*" bolstering each other like a parent's encouragement. They are not unaware, I suppose, merely uncaring that they are about to die. The drugs they take—strong amphetamines—help, as does the message they've been force fed since childhood emphasizing the rewards to be received in the afterlife for killing nonbelievers. *Kafir.*

I use the lull to get SITREPs. Hell and Nailer are dug in on the roof across the street, taking out targets of opportunity trying to IED our building. Thor's squad reports sporadic fighting on the third floor, but no sign yet of al-Baghdadi or our pilot.

"Nate and Pos, stay on two. Don't let anything make it up those stairs still breathing. Everyone else, third deck with me. Thor, coming up."

"Come up!" is the enthusiastic response. There's a burst of clicks and snaps as we reload, then make our way up the stairs. It's again quiet, another ebb in the flow of war.

Thor briefs me as I scan the open, vacant floor. Four dead enemy fighters and a ton of brass lie on the chipped linoleum. "We've cleared the floor, save the back left room," he says. "It's fortified, and I didn't want to blow it in case the pilot is being held back there. The overpressure would kill anyone in the room."

I nod, move to the side of the door. It's steel. Thick. Out of place in the otherwise unsophisticated compound. I run my index finger—my trigger finger, the glove cut off below the middle knuckle—over the hinges. No sound comes from behind it. Ideally, I'd like to wait out whoever is back there, but according to Westhead's updated report of additional ISIS fighters heading to our location and the lateness of the night, we don't have that luxury.

"Dan, what do you have for heat sigs?" I whisper into the radio.

"Two people in the room in front of you," he squawks back. "Roof is clear, first and second floors are clear for the time being. But the surrounding neighborhood looks like ants converging on a hot dog. Ten minutes before the house is overrun."

"Shit." I put down the radio. "GQ, can you get me video from inside that room?"

He examines the iron door, checks the clearance at the bottom, then steps forward, pulling a tube from his chest rack.

"Check," he tells me, approaching the door cautiously. The steel is thick, and while your standard AK round wouldn't penetrate it, there's always the possibility that whoever is in there could open the door and toss out a grenade or spray a volley of fire. GQ crouches to the side and slides the tube under the crack at the bottom. He takes out a small monitor, and I huddle next to him. Thor stands beside us, weapon shouldered should the door open.

The feed is clear, full color. The room is small, square, nearly empty. The first thing I see is our pilot, tied to a chair. My heartrate accelerates. He is here. Not another dry hole. Next, I bury my excitement, continue my triage. It appears his restraints are the only thing keeping him upright. He's still wearing a tattered flight suit, his face purple and covered with dried blood. I can't tell if he is conscious, but his head does roll to the side several times, involuntarily it would seem, but indicating he's alive nonetheless. GQ slides the camera toward the only other person in the room. My heart stops. The image on the screen is unmistakable. Al-Baghdadi. Finally, after everything, here he is. Our Great Ghost, the individual responsible for so much pain and suffering, just a few inches of steel separating us. He's dressed in all black, with white sneakers, a black keffiyeh covering just the top of his head. His features are fully visible, and I see true evil in them. The beard covers only the lower part of his face, below his mouth. The sudden realization that he is dead, no matter what, settles upon my shoulders pleasantly.

He's staring at the door, intense but unworried. He doesn't seem to notice the tiny piece of tube jutting under the crack. In his left hand, an AK is held loosely. But it's what is in the other hand that takes my breath. I have GQ zoom in on the right. It is, in fact a detonator. He's waiting for us. There's a bulk under his loose-fitting shirt, and I can only come to the conclusion that he is wearing a suicide vest. He's perfectly content to die, as long as he takes all of us with him.

"Dan, what's the ETA on the enemy reactionary force?" I'm whispering again into the radio.

The response is fast and clear. "They're two blocks away. I'd say five to eight minutes on the first wave. What's the SITREP there?"

There's no time to answer, so I don't. "Spin up that extract, now!"

The bad news comes almost immediately. "That's a negative on the extract, Blade. JSOC says the LZ is too hot. We'll have to rendezvous at Bravo."

Shit, I think. The secondary LZ is two klicks outside of town. We're going to be pressed to make it out of here before daylight. I don't bother getting upset at the news. No mission ever goes as planned. We have more immediate problems, both behind this steel door and coming in the front one. One problem at a time. I instruct Westhead to leave the safe house and get his squad to our compound. He's more appreciative for the order than I am for the additional guns. A half-thought forms: Kopen, not trained to the level of my men, running through a war zone. That issue could easily solve itself. I push it aside, refocusing on the door before us.

A solution comes to me. "Who's got gas?" I ask. GQ steps forward, already removing a thin, oblong canister from his webbing. The fogger sprays a mist of 3-methylfentanyl, the same chemical I used to knock out the imam in Virginia Beach. I squat before the door. GQ extends the camera feed. On it, Al-Baghdadi doesn't flinch as I aim the nozzle under the door.

"The first group of hostiles is approaching the house." Westhead's voice comes through my earpiece again. "I count five MAMs. Small arms."

Hell joins the conversation from his overwatch position across the street. "I have eyes on two." Then, after a short break: "Two tangos down. We don't have eyes on the other three." On the screen, al-Baghdadi attempts a crooked step that could belong to a drunk. No one's attention leaves that right hand. We step back, farther from the door, eyes still locked on the monitor.

"Nate, pucker up," I say, going to the inner-squad channel, breath quickening when I watch al-Baghdadi stumble on the other side of the door. The hand holding the detonator falls to his side, limp. No dead man's switch. "You should have company shortly. Three hostiles coming in the front door."

"We'll get 'em," he reports from the floor below. "Do what you gotta do up there and let's blow this pop stand."

When I click off, I find the men watchful, waiting for my order. Looking back at GQ's screen, we see al-Baghdadi fully react to the chemical. He's sniffing the air, face crinkled in confusion. A jolt of awareness hits him and he suddenly seems more alert, clawing frantically for the detonator hanging at his sleeve. If he finds it and presses the button, that could be it. He, the pilot, and probably us will be blown to hell. An urgent swipe causes him to drop the rifle. He falls to his knees, wobbling, but his chin remains up, defiant, the wrathful face announcing he's not yet ready to concede.

"Broco torch!" I call out, but Mutt is already next to me, the exothermic cutting torch out and ready. Once he sparks it, red and orange flames dance in the otherwise dark room. It cuts through the fortified door like butter. Thor leads the thermal breach and then we are inside the room, screaming at al-Baghdadi to get on the ground, racing to liberate the pilot. The pungent smell of the airborne sedative is strong. We hold our breath, but still I can taste it, feel it working my nostrils, singeing my eyes.

LCDR Wilson is completely out, Al-Baghdadi just this side of consciousness. He's upright on both knees, crazed eyes wide and angry, probing us, his brain wondering where he went wrong while simultaneously scrambling to find a reasonable solution. He finds one, and with a last gasp of effort, grasps at the detonator.

"Bomb!" I call out, diving at the terrorist just as he grips the button. Time seems to freeze. There's a clamor of confusion when my body collides with his. Laying over him to absorb the blast, I tighten and tense, waiting for the explosion, anticipating death. When it doesn't come, I wonder if I'm already dead, or if the breath-taking pain is something else. I have al-Baghdadi pinned, but I'm not sure how long I can hold the position. My vision is retreating, black drapes sliding in from my peripheral. I realize that there is no overwhelming smell of fire, and that makes me think that maybe his suicide vest did not clack off. But why is everything so foggy? As I slide into unconsciousness, what limited vision is left makes out Thor in a similar position on top of the pilot, using his body to shield him from the explosion. Then,

"We're moving out—now!" Westhead yells to McDonald and Kopen. They hit the stairs and soon are running through the graying streets, which are just beginning to stir with a sleepy lethargy. A new day has arrived. Westhead's blood freezes when the call to morning prayers echoes through the gloom. He can't help but wonder if it's not a plea for additional holy warriors to join the fight against the crusaders. On the screen strapped to his wrist he counts more than a dozen bad guys sprinting toward the same destination as he and his men.

"Take a right here!" McDonald has a handheld GPS device and is guiding them through smoked out, derelict streets. From one of the few remaining balconies an elderly woman stares down at them as if three large white men with automatic rifles sprinting through her neighborhood is status quo. They continue through the town, the ominous calls in Arabic louder and more intense now. There is no doubt what they are saying.

When they're a block away from al-Baghdadi's compound, they encounter the first enemy fighters a block over. Clusters of intense men, running through the haze, hunched over, most carrying AK-47's, a few with RPGs or belt-fed machine guns. Westhead glimpses the first group down a parallel street; he's able to hit the deck just as their rounds crack close. The three Americans immediately take firing positions and begin to engage, putting down several of the jihadists. Others scatter back into the rat holes of the city. Two sprint across the street, scurrying into a burned-out storefront.

"We need to get an angle on that building," Westhead says. Both McDonald and Kopen nod, chests heaving. They entertain a quick mag check and visually confirm each other's readiness. Everyone's good to go. The three men are shoulder to shoulder, tight against the trunk of an SUV, the only cover available. Until they can neutralize the threat in that storefront, they're pinned down. As Westhead starts to call out an order, a burst of machine gun fire rocks the truck. Sparks fly off the hood and windshield, sending them lower to the ground, heads now level with the truck's bumper. The men can do nothing but clench their helmets and grit their teeth, hoping one of the rounds doesn't have their name on it.

"Anyone hit?" Westhead calls down the line after the barrage subsides. Each take inventory, confirming they are still whole.

"This truck doesn't give us the best cover," McDonald points out.

"No shit," responds Westhead. "Our best bet is to pop smoke then leapfrog out of here. You two go first, I'll keep their heads down. Meet at the far corner."

"How are you going to do that without exposing yourself?" Kopen asks.

Westhead's sneer is answer enough, a deterrent to further debate. He takes a deep breath, reaches for a smoke grenade from a pouch on his vest. Before he can pull the pin, a longer, more sustained shower of fire propels them lower. A rocket explodes close, sending clumps of concrete raining down. The blast rocks the SUV, crashing it back to earth smoking. Another rocket hit and the only thing between them and their dug-in enemy will be demolished. Westhead makes his move, standing high to toss the grenade. A pause, and when the fog sets in, he motions to Kopen and McDonald. All three step from behind the truck, Westhead sending rapid bursts of fire into the storefront while his teammates sprint across the street. As the smoke lessens, the two fighters raise themselves, machine guns pointed at Westhead. He's out in the open, completely exposed, only a ruined city street between him and two terrorists with automatic weapons. Time moves in a sluggish crawl. They are close enough, and the wafting smoke has thinned enough, that Westhead can make out the features of his enemy. The men look similar: animated, drug-fueled eyes, electrified that this American is out in the open, that they have him dead to rights, as if Allah himself had delivered him into their crosshairs. Westhead makes eye contact with both, recognizing that they have already assumed the kill. Both the holy warriors allow a slight, if not surprised smirk, raising their weapons to put down the infidel, faces bright, their trigger fingers flexed. Then:

A CRACK rings out above Westhead. One of the fighters slumps, his machine gun discharging into the air. Another CRACK. The other falls. Westhead spins, weapon raised, searching for the sniper. Nailer's voice comes through his ear.

"You're welcome, Chief."

Westhead exhales, unclenches his butthole, and offers an appreciative thumbs-up into the morning air. He scans the rooftops for his teammate, who makes himself temporarily visible against the lightening sky. It's two middle fingers into a sweeping gesture at his crotch. Nice.

Across the street, McDonald's confused face angles upward. He freezes when he sees Nailer's silhouette on the roof, sniper rifle aimed in their direction.

"What's wrong, New Guy?" Nailer hisses into his ear. "You look like you just crapped your britches. Maybe show a little appreciation? And look alive. You have three hajis about to turn the corner at your six."

McDonald wheels toward the threat just as the aforementioned ISIS fighters turn the corner. He puts all three down, and after an appreciative tip to the head for their overwatch, the squad continues toward the target compound. Kopen brings up the rear, huffing just a little more than his brethren. Westhead gives him an encouraging smack on the back when they reach the front wall of the compound.

Adam greets them in the courtyard with a grease-smudged smile. "Welcome to Shangri- La, boys," he says, yanking open the security gate with a groan. The three newcomers slide in, taking in the bullet-and-bomb-riddled compound. The enemy bodies, the crumbled security wall, the courtyard covered with brass.

"Looks lovely," Westhead tells him with fondness. Walking by, he grasps Whitey's shoulder, the gesture brief but meaningful.

0640 hours

When I fully come to, it takes a minute to remember where I am. I try to lift my head. It feels like it weighs a thousand pounds. I have trouble opening my eyes, focusing.

"I think he's coming out of it. Colonel, can you hear me?"

I recognize the voice, but can't place it. It sounds young. Even and calm. It takes a minute to connect shards of thought, discount them as dream.

"Did. He detonate?" I'm finally able to get the words out, or at least I think I do. They seem distant, broken. For a second I'm not sure if they were audible, if I actually did speak.

"No, sir. He dropped the detonator after you tackled him. Another second, and he would have."

I try my eyes again. It's Butler, the young SEAL. Through the slit, I recognize admiration in the kid's face. Awe. Then, as if anticipating my next question: "Al-Baghdadi is alive, bagged and gagged. LCDR Wilson, conscious and ambulatory. Seems like a tough son of a bitch. He's good to go."

I nod, more to clear my head than communicate affirmation. "Good.

What, uh, what exactly happened?"

"The gas must have knocked you out."

I groan, embarrassed. If we make it out of here alive, I'll never hear the end of this. I'll probably be known as Gas or Sleeping Beauty from now on. Not that it will matter shortly after that. Without warning, my stomach heaves and I vomit. Wiping my mouth, I ask, "So what the hell are we waiting for? Where's our extract? Where's Dan? Kopen make it?"

"I'm here, sir. We all made it." Westhead sounds close, and when I extend my arm he takes it, helping me sit up. "The sun is up, Colonel. JSOC won't send in the cavalry until tonight. We're going to be here for a while."

I curse inwardly, but am unwilling to vocally express my concern about a second day in the village. "Why isn't Butler on the second-floor landing? We have security in place?" I'm able to get to my feet, grabbing Westhead's arm again.

"Yes, sir. We've fortified the compound. We've got guys on the roof and are communicating with the TOC and air assets. Pos and Mutt are dug in at the stairs. Nailer and Hell are still providing overwatch from their hide across the street."

I look up at him. Any misgivings, any hatred he may be harboring is not evident, at least not at the moment. It's as if our conversation on the plane hadn't happened. *Good*, I think, but am not naïve enough to hope it won't reappear after this day is over. If we make it out alive, which seems like a long shot. But for now, it's business as usual, and we have a mission to complete. I take water from Kopen, try to read him. I don't get much. Does he know? The liquid feels good on my face, the back of my neck. I suppress another gag, chug the rest, glance at my watch. 0650. I must have been out for a while.

"Only twelve hours or so until it's dark enough for an extract," I say. "How are we on ammo and water?"

"Okay for now—we've divvied up the mags and grenades. The pace of their attacks has certainly slowed, but they know we're in here. Mostly indirect fire at this point. Mortars."

"Regrouping. Make sure everyone stays on their toes." I get to my feet, collect my weapon. "Sounds like it's going to be a long day."

"The longest, sir."

0800 hours

We don't have to wait long for the next wave of attacks. A baking sun is still making its way overhead when the air fills with the crackle of automatic weapons splintering the front of the compound. Hell and Nailer quickly find the source on a neighboring roof and send a volley of sniper fire to eliminate the threat. Just as the shooting stops, a beat-up sedan turns the corner and stops at the entrance to the street, idling. Nothing moves. The silence, unnerving. Then, the car begins to roll. It picks up speed methodically and deliberately, the aged engine struggling under the driver's urging in his last seconds on earth.

Westhead radios an update from their roof. "Guys, looks like a VBIED at the end of the street. A thousand meters and gaining." He clicks off. The car shudders while increasing velocity, headed straight for the front wall of their compound.

"We don't have the fire power to do much from down here," Adam reports from the courtyard. The words come flat and unurgent, even if the slightest of strains can be detected in his voice. "But I don't have to tell you what's going to happen to me and Pos if that thing makes it through."

"Seven hundred and fifty meters."

"Jud, get that .50 cal up and take out the engine block!" I order evenly over the team net.

"I'm trying!" Jud's voice is higher than usual. "I don't have an angle!" The car accelerates, now quickly closing the gap from street to house.

From my vantage point through a second-story window, I watch our snipers' rounds ping off the car. The insurgents have jerry-rigged metal plates to cover the windows, and the fire has no effect. Nailer and Hell immediately change tactics, taking out the tires. This slows the car and sends it skidding, but the driver quickly adjusts, and soon it's again rolling toward our position, slower now, but still with a stubborn resolve.

"Less than 500 meters."

From inside, we're helpless. There's no point wasting our ammo. I think about calling for an evac. We watch the car continue a deliberate, steady approach.

"Shoot at the trunk, see if you can make it detonate prematurely! The trunk has to be filled with explosives," Adam calls from the courtyard, a little more frantic. "This guy is getting close!"

There's a commotion to my rear, and then Mutt is shoving me to the side, peering out my window.

"I got this," he says as casually as making a drive-through order. I duck just in time to not get smacked in the face by his Carl-Gustaf rocket launcher. He hauls the weighty tube onto his right shoulder, carefully taking aim through the laser range finder, an 84-millimeter anti-tank round already loaded. For a split second, my attention drifts to the identical rocket launcher I have stashed back in a Virginia Beach storage locker, but quickly redistribute it where it belongs. The car rattles as it accelerates, rear wheels low, straining under the additional weight. It's just outside the security wall now. I can imagine the excited "*Allahu Akbar*" on the suicide bomber's lips, and not for the first time I wonder when it will hit him that there aren't seventytwo virgins waiting for him on the other end of that explosion. Hopefully not simultaneously with our confirmation.

Mutt's call of "Rocket!" rings out just before the room seems to lose air. An immediate and consecutive THUMP and WHOOSH knock me to my butt, hands automatically covering my ears. Firing that weapon is like getting hit in the head with a baseball bat. Standing next to it isn't much more pleasant. When I pull myself up and back to the window, I'm able to watch a squirrely vapor trail winding through the street, followed immediately by a direct hit into the driver's side of the car.

The street explodes in a mammoth fireball, what's left of the car shooting straight into the air. The compound shudders, seemingly alive with the strain of the blast. But it holds, just another blow it has no choice but to endure. Part of the mud wall caves in, covering the front of the house with smoke and rubble, but after a quick count, I confirm no casualties.

"Threat neutralized," Westhead reports from our rooftop. His call is cool and composed, without the slightest trace of satisfaction. No one bothers to follow it up with a "for now."

"No big deal," hisses Adam from the courtyard, groaning. "Me and Pos just lost our eyebrows. And our hearing."

Pos's voice comes through the radio next, giddy and excited. "What's that you say?" He coughs before clicking off.

Mutt lowers the weapon assertively. "Better than your legs."

Then, silence. We all know it's just the beginning of this long day.

1019 hours

"Yo, let me get that Meatball Marinara." GQ's face is serious, watching Kopen struggle with an MRE packet. The FBI agent looks just slightly out of place, a little older, a little more clean-cut, a little more rotund than the other operators. He pauses, contemplates the meal in his hand.

"This?"

"Yeah, that. I got a cheese omelet here. They're delicious, you just need to add hot sauce," he explains, moving forward, brown packet extended, assuming the swap. Kopen, unsure, surveys the room. He finds expressions of intrigue, the audience riveted by the pending decision.

"I was born at night, but not last night, GQ. Meatball Marinara is my favorite."

"Bullshit. What do you know about your favorite?"

"You think this is the first Meal Refusing to Exit I've ripped into sitting Indian-style on a dusty floor, rifle as a tray? Meatball Marinara with crunched up Combos in the sauce is the shit. You should try it." The FBI agent holds up a bag of cheese Combos, and, removing a glove, starts to crush them into the pasta. "But you enjoy those powdered eggs." The room is impressed.

"Damn, GQ, that fed pretty much just told you to eat your shitty breakfast and fuck off while doing it." Thor laughs, tosses Kopen a package of candy. "Here you go, Fed, you can have my Charms."

Kopen swats them across the room with a sneer, eliciting a vigorous round of laughter.

"You know what you can do with those," he says, sticking a spoon into his Meatball Marinara with Combos.

1059 hours

"How you feeling, Thor?" I ask. Worrying about my men lets the mind dawdle away from my injuries. I'm already fidgety, and it's still morning. My stomach is sour from the gas, my head is ringing, and the patched bullet wound stings. Not that I would mention any of that out loud. Each minute crawls by, every second filled with anticipation. Waiting for the next attack, curiosity as to what it will be and how it will come. Nightfall can't get here soon enough.

Thor grins at me. He's out of the local clothing, having ripped the sleeves off his loose shirt, one of them now repurposed as a headband, the other armbands. He seems to have recovered from killing the young woman; his expression, his mannerisms all say he's put it past him. Her and the rest of the EKIAs have been piled into an empty room, DNA samples taken and distributed for transport between at least two men. Al-Baghdadi is still flex cuffed and sedated, a hood covering his head, positioned in a corner on the first floor where we can keep an eye on him.

"Feeling dangerous, sir," Thor sings in between the clicking sound springing off the magazine he's loading. "What do you need?"

"Go relieve Westhead on the roof."

"Roger that. Who's got sun screen?" Thor asks the room, leaving his post at a rear-facing window to stand and stretch. Mutt laughs, calls him a "pasty chicken-boy."

"I don't even know what that means," he says, smearing lotion across his face, ears, and neck. "But don't cry to me when your dysplastic nevi turn into melanoma, surfer-boy."

"Unless it sets in before sunset, I don't think I'll have to worry much about skin cancer," Mutt replies with a morbid enthusiasm.

"I don't know about you, but I plan on seeing the good ol' U.S. of A. again," Pos yells from where a kitchen once stood. There's something in his open expression, the declarative announcement, that makes you think he's not just playing a part, not just living up to his moniker. I wish I could be as confident. He still sports pieces of plaster and cement on his shoulders, in his hair, from the suicide car bomber. His round face, after a squirt from his Camelbak, is now starkly clean against the residue from the blast. "I didn't come this far to only come this far. They ain't killed me yet, and I don't plan to let them start now!"

"You're yelling again," Adam calmly tells him from across the room. No response. Adam spits sunflower seeds while scanning the neighborhood, a growing pile of shells at his feet. Suddenly, he rocks into a squat at the edge of his window. "They ain't killed you yet, that's true, but they're about to try. I got two clowns trying to sneak around the back here. They're not armed, but one has a cell phone."

"Scouts," I say and jump on the radio. "Dan, you see these two as-shats in the back alley?"

His reply comes from the roof. "Affirmative. Peekers. No weapons, but they're definitely reporting our position. What are our ROEs?"

I make a quick decision. "Fuck our ROEs. Take them both out." *Better to be judged by twelve than carried by six.* There's no response, and I don't hear anything from the roof, but don't need to. Adam's reaction says it all. It's a thumbs-up, and I radio back to the TOC to report the action.

1124 hours

"Commander, how are you feeling? Hungry?" Hagen crouches next to the pilot. Although battered, he's gaining coherence. A slight shake of the head, then dilated eyes scrutinize the second floor of the house. He's already refused morphine twice. The effects of the gas are wearing off, and although he still seems to be a little confused as to who the white men dressed in local garb are who saved him, he's becoming more alert.

"We're with the United States military, and you're safe," Hagen tells him before he can ask again. He puts a fist on the pilot's chest. "We're waiting until nightfall to extract, and then you'll be on your way back to the States to see your family." He reaches under his armor, pulling out a ragged circle of cloth. It's his NYFD patch, the one given to him by the fireman's mother. "A little memento for you. It's gotten me through some tough times."

LCDR Wilson's chin quivers just slightly. He has to narrow his eyes. "Thank you, sir," he croaks, clutching the patch with a new strength. Hagen, embarrassed, turns to their prisoner, giving him water, which he refuses, letting it dribble down his chin.

1341 hours

"I don't know, man, what are they waiting for? This isn't good, man, I really got a bad feeling. We should just patrol out of here now, vamos, disappear, poof. Gone." GQ's face twitches involuntarily, but it tends to do that.

"Shut up, we're not going anywhere during daylight." Pos's response comes from under a camo boonie hat. He's stretched out on the floor with the hat covering his face. It rises and falls with each sentence. "Let 'em come, bro. We'll keep knockin' 'em down. You need to get some sleep. Dream about a porterhouse, a cabernet, and a big-tittied blond to feed it to you. You'll feel better, dude."

GQ continues his pacing, pulling back the cardboard covering a window and peeking out at each pass. "I don't need need a big-tittied blond. I need an evac. Who the hell can sleep at a time like this?"

"No one, you don't shut up," Hell tells him.

"I don't know, man; I can feel it in my bones. I just don't like it. Too quiet out there."

"GQ, please sit still, you're giving me vertigo," Hagen tells him.

"Come here, let's see that new ink."

GQ pauses, half-smiles, takes a knee next to Hagen. After a deep breath, he raises his sleeve. Sinewy muscles, a spackle of scars and deep bruise adorn the extremity.

"Finally finished that cover-up," he says, pointing at his shoulder. Constant ragging from the other guys had convinced GQ to rid himself of the high school-era tattoos obtained in a more immature phase. It had taken years of expense and pain during every bit of downtime, but the combination of laser removal and cover up work had finally erased the old flaming baseball, tribal band, and angry skull, leaving his left arm, chest, and back full of art more appropriate to job and personality.

"My brothers' initials with birth and death dates," he explains, elbow jutted, pointing. "This one is Zeus's labrys. Then there's Twin Tiki's featuring the Eye of Horus—it's a talisman to ward off evil. I got Thor's hammer—" off Thor's look: "Not yours, Smurfette. Thor's hammer up here, with a Viking valknut, and a Spartan shield. The shark teeth are entwined with octopus tentacles and plants to symbolize mastery of the sea and the circle of life." He dropped the sleeve and pulled up his shirt to expose a wide, decorated chest. "You've seen the Knights Templar shield, of course—"

"Of course," Hagen replies.

"But the rampant lion is new, and so are the names of the thirty men lost in Operation Atlas across my rib cage." He twists to reveal his side covered in tiny lettering. "When you gonna get yours, Commander?"

Hagen, a wry smirk across his face, nods slightly. "Never know. Maybe if we make it out of here I'll get my own lucky charm. And I'll expect you guys to keep up your end of the bargain if I do."

1500 hours

"Colonel, we're showing at least a dozen MAMs grouping two blocks south of your location. Over."

We're getting regular updates from the TOC, where they can observe drone and satellite feeds we don't have access to on the ground.

I motion to GQ, and he comes over with our monitor. A dirt-encrusted finger swipes across the screen until he finds the insurgents. From overhead, they look like scurrying amoebas. GQ zooms in, and I get a better look at what we're about to be facing. They're splitting into two groups in an attempt to flank us.

"We have eyes on," I report back.

"We about to have company, Blade?" Nate asks me.

"The neighborhood welcome wagon. Everyone to their firing stations. We have two groups approaching, one from the south, one from the east. Remember, every round counts."

"All right, all right," Pos crows in his best *Dazed and Confused* imitation. Mutt responds with the requisite, "they stay the same age" as everyone moves quickly and confidently to their sectors.

I collect my MP7A and stick four magazines in my chest rig, brushing past Westhead and Whitey on the first floor. They've fortified the front door and are dug in on either side. They—at least Adam does—offer a grin and thumbs-up as I pass, faces dirty and tired but gung-ho. I climb out the first floor window into the courtyard. It's hot, the late afternoon sun high and angry. Thor and Mutt have taken positions behind murder holes they've punched in the security wall and both are on the scope.

"Anything moving?" I ask, avoiding the openings in the wall. Neither turn toward me when answering.

"Negative. Quiet so far," Thor says from behind his weapon. Then: "Didn't mean to jinx it. I got a tango at the corner. Poking his head out."

"Wait until they bunch up," I say. Ammo is most definitely a concern. I grab my binos and crouch in the dirt next to him. Through the eight-inch circle, I have good line of sight to the corner he's referring to, 250 yards away. Sure enough, a figure in dark tracksuit, AK poised, pops his head around a crumpled building. He watches the compound for a second, then motions back behind him. He eases forward into the street, and then,

THWAAAK. I hear the spit from across the street, see the fighter drop, dead before he hits the ground. Nailer's voice comes though my earpiece. "Tango down." Before I can appreciate the work of our overwatch, the dead guy's buddies make a break for it. I count an even dozen, and they're rushing the house with little regard to tactics or techniques. It's a shooting gallery, and between Nailer and Hell on the roof across the street, us out front, and Kopen and McDonald on our roof, the action is quick and deadly.

"Cease fire!" I order. I count nine new bodies in the street, meaning at least four made it through. One of the casualties, an RPG-7 rocket launcher at his feet, stirs slightly. He tries to make it to a knee. I let him. I know how valuable that weapon is to these fighters. A moment later, I'm rewarded. Unseen, a frantic voice calls to the wounded terrorist. The cry echoes through the neighborhood. The wounded turns to it, pleading for help. He's answered sharply and lies back down. Then, from behind a collapsed building on the corner, a man sprints toward him. He ignores his wounded comrade, grabbing the rocket launcher instead. My rounds are only two of the many sent into him, spinning him 360 degrees like a top, until he crumples into a bloody mess on top of his buddy. The rocket launcher lies next to him, a juicy enticement.

1650 hours

"W-A-R, WAR!" Mutt slams a king down, to the chagrin of Pos and his jack. "Game over. Another twenty to the Navy SEAL Foundation."

If there's anyone on the team who can take a loss graciously even while suffering innately from it, it's Pos.

"I can think of worse things to spend eighty bucks on," he says through tight lips. "But there's no way you beat me four times in a row without cheating. I'm not mad, I just wanna know how."

"I could tell ya ..." the bro operator slurs, a twinkle in his eye. One handed, he shuffles the deck with dexterous expertise.

"That's why I stopped playing poker against him years ago," Hell says. "I've never seen Mutt lose at cards. Go fish, gin rummy, doesn't matter."

"Deal 'em," Pos says. "This time you're"—he pauses at a shrill whistle, which is followed by an explosion on the side of the house. Another off-target mortar—"going down."

The rest of the room laughs. "You know what the definition of insanity is, right, Pos?" asks Jud.

"All I know is that before the sun sets and our ride arrives, Mutt will have a date with some tiny-ass yoga pants."

"Excuse me?" It's Hagen's turn to get involved. Mutt clears up any confusion.

"That's the bet. Every time *I* win, Pos has to donate twenty bucks to the Navy SEAL Foundation. On the rare chance that *he* wins, I have to wear yoga pants for twenty-four hours. He picks the size."

"Mutt, I hope you keep pulling those aces from your sleeve," Hagen says. "Not sure I want to see your boys in yoga pants."

1713 hours

"Don't talk to me until you've read the Hottell memo." Nailer's voice comes through the team channel from across the street, rousting me from the closest I've been to sleep the entire day. "That's all I'm saying. Don't take my word for it. The government has confirmed at least eleven crash landings. They've documented them."

"Dammit, Nailer, shut up about the damn aliens," I spit back over the net.

"Blade? Don't tell me you think we're alone in the universe. Not you, there's no way you believe that. You're too strange. And you read—comics, yeah, but you read."

Pos takes over the counter-argument. "I'm just saying, if they're really here, why don't we know about it? And don't tell me the government is keeping it a secret. They can't keep anything a secret."

"Ever heard of the 'Zoo Hypothesis'? It basically says that they are here but have chosen not to communicate with us. That our civilization isn't advanced enough to be worth their while."

"I guess I can see their point."

"Exactly. The size of the universe is beyond our comprehension. It's ridiculous to think our tiny, *tiny* piece of that universe, this grain of sand we call Earth, is the only place that can sustain life. NASA has basically admitted there is life on other planets. And the FBI found three crashed UFOs in 1950 alone. That memo is public record! You just gotta open your eyes."

"And Hilary is an alien, right?" Pos asked.

"I'm not going to say she isn't ..." Nailer goes quiet for a minute before getting back on the radio. "I got movement in the building to your south. Hold tight, this motherfucker thinks he's being slick. 'Bout to smoke check somebody ..."

1808 hours

Most of us are on so much Ripped Fuel that at this point, sleep is no longer even attempted. Besides—I glance for the hundredth time at my watch—sunset is at 1949, and we all expect the main assault to come before that. The enemy is familiar with our tactics and know that once the light is gone, we will be too.

I look around at the men on the second floor, tired, wired, ready for a rack and hot meal. They're watching and waiting. Nate is dug in behind his machine gun at the top of the stairs. He's barely spoken all day and only infrequently left that post. I can tell he would take it as a personal affront if any enemy fighters made it up those stairs. Adam is reading from his miniature Bible, rifle across his knees. Mutt and Pos are back to their card game, Mutt's fashion sensibilities still intact. GQ and Jud are at the two forward-facing windows, scanning the streets and neighboring buildings. Thus far, they've only managed to capture Hell taking a leak in a Gatorade bottle across the street. When they mention it, I'm reminded that our supplies, including water, are dwindling.

I head up to the roof to check in with Westhead and Agent Kopen. I have to admit, he's been an asset, this shoe, cool under fire. When I tell him so, he asks when I'm going to respond to the subpoena. My answer is "never" and then I check in again with the TOC.

It's been several hours since there's been an organized attack. Intermittent mortar rounds continue to fall, but with little effect. Our satellites and drones don't show any enemy fighters gathering. In fact, the town is completely still. That gives me almost no solace—I assume they are organizing elsewhere for the big showdown. Sunset is still an hour away, and not for another hour after that will it be dark enough for the cavalry to come get us. Plenty of time for a good gunfight, I'm sure.

I don't have to wait long. The Air Force controller back in Baghdad, his young, intense voice familiar now, rouses me from my trance.

"Colonel, we have movement a klick to your east. Check that, east, north, and south. Bulldozers. Three of them. At least two dozen MAMs grouping." My butt cheeks clench, knowing that we don't have the firepower to knock down bulldozers.

"TOC, again, I'm making an official request for air support." This time he at least checks with the higher-ups. The answer comes back too quickly.

"Negative, Colonel. ROEs will not allow for air support over inhabited cities. Sorry, man, you're on your own until dark. Out."

I fling the sat phone to the ground, pissed but not surprised.

1837 hours

The minarets suddenly come alive again, the tinny voice calling in Arabic for the true believers to come out and do their duty, to send the crusaders to hell. Through our exhaustion, our injuries, our ringing ears and empty stomachs, against the never-slowing numbers of enemy perfectly happy to donate their lives to their cause, there is a stubbornness, a defiance, a willful decision to win the fight, to complete the mission, to go home alive. No matter what it takes. I see it in every man's face, their determination to fight for those next to them. For LCDR Wilson and the good name of our unit. Their demeanor says: We will not be denied victory.

I'm sure the enemy feels the same way.

Usually, I go into firefights with no doubt about success, fully confident I'm coming out the other end alive and victorious. But this will not be your average firefight. This time, I put it at fifty-fifty.

My thoughts wander to childhood. An image of my stepfather entwines itself in my mind. My mother, standing behind him, face nervous over his shoulder. Then the curtains swish shut, and they're gone. I turn to face what comes. The Millen brothers, two years older and bigger than that. I strike preemptively, fists tiny but sharp, a satisfying crunch when one lands solidly against the nose of the one with freckles. Blood spurts out, but I only see it for a second before a lightning bolt connects with my head, and then stars, lights, oh-so-many stars, dancing and bobbing all around me, but my arms keep swinging through the stars, through the darkness, and when I catch my breath the one without freckles is pulling at the one with freckles, trying to get him to his feet and off my yard, and they're both covering their heads and then I realize the shouts, the vulgar words are coming from my mouth, but I can't stop them until finally the tears come and the world becomes real again. I don't know why I'm crying. If I'm happy or angry or maybe hurt, but the tears come, and I stand on the edge of my yard, victorious. I hear the front door unlock behind me. I didn't get a beating that night.

1851 hours

The final attack starts innocuously enough with another shower of mortar fire. The rockets land closer than in the previous shellings, with several exploding against the roof. Our snipers are forced to take cover, the house further crumbled. No one is seriously injured, but it's then that I know for certain how bad this is going to be, that the enemy has been resupplying all day while we waited in the compound, thumb firmly in ass. Not that we had a choice.

When the mortaring slows, GQ shows me the bulldozers on the

screen. Still a few miles away. Three of them. Driven by suicide bomb-
ers, weighed down with explosives. That's when my heart sinks. I know
I am not alone with that sentiment.

I wonder aloud, "How the hell are we going to stop those bulldozers?" I realize not the most leader-like comment, but when you've had a
day like this, hey, who can fault a little stream-of-consciousness honesty?

No one has an answer.

The cold angry machines have started rumbling toward our position
from their chosen directions. Scores of black-clad fighters with white-let-
tered headbands take cover behind each, high-stepping and chanting serious, rhythmical prayers. These are not your run-of-the-mill brainwashed
kids looking to prove themselves. These are the battle-hardened warriors, the professional fighters who have traveled from Iraq and Jordan
and Turkey and Australia and the U.K. to kill Americans and die hon-
orably for their god. I recognize the ISIS flags, both hanging from the
bulldozers and being carried by optimistic goose-steppers. It's quite a
production, I have to admit. A well-equipped and vicious production at
that. I get an updated ammo report and discover we have one Carl-Gustaf rocket, twenty-three frag grenades, ten claymores and two pounds of
RDX-X left, in addition to the few mags each shooter still carries. Without bothering to do the math, I try to ignore the fact that we don't have
enough firepower left to repel this attack. That fact is lost on no one.

There seems to be a quiet resignation amongst the team. Not a lot
of chatter, just firm chins and narrowed expressions. The room grows
murkier by the minute, and I look into each man's shadowed face,
gloomy pockets and crevices visible by the various fires highlighting our
surroundings. Eyes are electric and especially white, jumping around the
room, thoughts transitioning from what we're leaving at home to what
we're about to face. No one on this team would ever consider giving
up, but no one is fooling themselves about the daunting task at hand.

"What I wouldn't give for a Red Cross girl and a sponge bath,"
Mutt casually tells the room.

"A Collalbrigo sparkling rosé and some Siberian sturgeon caviar," offers GQ.

"Shit," says Jud. "I'd lick the fuzz off your taint for a bacon ched-dar cheeseburger."

"I'd just take a few Hellfires from a Predator," Hagen says.

He gets agreement, a "Fucking Chair Force," but no one's heart is in it.

"I have an idea," Kopen says suddenly. He jumps to his feet, face contorted in thought. Our attention, piqued. "But we have to hurry. Round up the frag grenades and RDX. I need twenty feet of time fuse and all the claymores."

Westhead turns to him, expression wide and excited from a simi-lar bolt of inspiration. "I'm with you, Agent. I'll get the blasting caps, tape, and a fuse igniter. McDonald, grab all the remaining RDX-X! Meet you out front in two."

They bolt down the stairs before anyone has a chance to ask them just what in the hell they're talking about.

1901 hours

A peek onto the street sends a tingle through my gut. The town re-mains still as the cover of evening descends casually upon it, but it's not a peaceful stillness. Still like the pause at the top of a roller coaster. The neighborhood is starting to tint in an ominous shadow, the tops of build-ings painted a darker hue. The scene suggests a ghost town, one of the mock-ups the army builds for us on Bragg or Benning, the kill houses we train on in Mississippi and Niland, the deserts of the Mojave. Empty save for the wreckage and bullet holes.

Focus is intent, grips and muscles tight as we wait.

Kopen and Westhead's plan is quite a gamble. If they're wrong, we're out of grenades and almost all our explosives. Then again, if it doesn't work, it won't much matter.

Across from me is Nate, dug in and motivated. You can tell he's trying to look tough, to appear unafraid, which doesn't mean he isn't, just means he's conscious of impressions. I'm amused by it, at least as amused as one can be in a scenario such as this.

The creaks and groans of the bulldozers reach us well before they are visible. The monsters move slowly, if only because they can. Neither side is rushed, which makes for a paradoxical calm. The waiting not to be misinterpreted for patience. Enemy mortars and small arms fire lead their way, rocking the house, sending plaster and drywall showering down on us. We hunker down, saving our ammo. Watching drone footage, I'm shocked at the number of fighters in the procession. An unorganized formation tracks the churning, orange machines creeping to our position. We have time until they reach the compound, but our preparations are already complete. So we wait.

The work out front had been done quickly. Westhead and Kopen raced from street corner to street corner, eerily unmolested as they went about their work. After setting up the claymores, dozens of small holes were dug and filled with explosives and grenades, then time fuse run back into the compound. Now we wait shoulder to shoulder, the sweat beading on each of our brows not just from the heat.

"Not yet," Westhead mutters to Kopen over comms from the rooftop. The FBI agent had volunteered to remain on the first floor, M-60 fuse igniter in hand, anxiously waiting for the bulldozers to come within range. The rest of us suck mud on the roof, preferring to crumble with the building rather than be buried under it.

"Come on, Dan, don't let them get on top of us, or this won't work. All that will be left of our little group will be dust."

"I'm aware of that, Agent, but if you pop the fuse too soon, there's going to be a big bang and that's it. I did the math, I'll tell you when to cook it off."

The rest of us remain immobile, watching, waiting, hoping like hell Westhead and Kopen know what they're doing. It's an unnatural state, not having ownership or control, but like everything we do, we do it because it needs to be done. I do it with the rest of them.

1903 hours

After a long two minutes, with the growl of the heavy machinery growing each second, Westhead clicks the timer on his watch, keys the radio. He murmurs, "Pull on my mark," with the intonation and drama the order deserves. Then: "3 ... 2 ... 1 ... Execute!"

Three floors below, I can picture Kopen pushing in the time fuse, rotating it 90 degrees and pulling it out. Seconds later he calls out, "I got smoke," before he's scrambling back to what's left of the stairwell, racing upstairs. If the test burn was accurate, the time fuse is now burning at 32 seconds per foot, meaning that the first of 22 grenades, each sitting on an ounce of RDX-X, will start exploding in less than six minutes. The American versions of IEDs should detonate just as the explosive-laden bulldozers arrive at our doorstep, followed shortly by the claymores. If the timing is off, if our charges clack off early or late or the bulldozers change their pace, well ...

1904 hours

It's mere seconds after Kopen's yell of "Coming up!" that his frantic figure dives onto the roof, breathless. Our amusement at his entrance can't be helped, but is brief. Westhead stares into his watch, counting down the time until the first of our IEDs is set to blow. We're lying in a line, close enough to touch the man to our left and right, just peeking over the edge of the roof. Below, from three directions, we can watch the bulldozers creaking toward us. The battle cries of the ISIS fighters accompanying them grow louder with each step.

1909 hours

"Thirty seconds," Westhead announces, not that he has to. Each of us are counting down on our own watches. When the time comes and goes with no activity, eyes widen and stomachs drop. Then, as we're sharing looks of alarm, BOOOOM! The first smallish blast from the street pulls everyone's attention in that direction. It's followed immediately by a string of louder, more intense explosions. They continue in quick succession, dozens of them, until everyone is of the mind that the shaking of the earth will never stop. One after another, the eruptions come, filling the air with choking black smoke, and we're awash in shrapnel and heat and I imagine this is what it will be like when the world ends. Maybe it is. All we can do is hunker down, helmets on, mouths open, and ride the concussive waves until the world is ringing with such venom that it's hard to tell when the blasts stop. When we're convinced they have, we peek over the edge of the roof. It's disconcertingly hushed through billowing smoke.

Westhead's excited shout fights through the chaos. "It worked!" he yells, and as the fog clears, it's a decimated moonscape that greets us. The street, unrecognizable. More craters than flat land. Our building, like the ones surrounding it, seems to be missing its front half. The first bulldozer comes into focus. What's left of it. The blackened shell is smoking, barely recognizable, flames leaping high. The other two husks, flaming as well. After a relatively calm moment, one jumps into the air with a sudden BOOM, a massive fireball whose flames reach as high as our third floor. I can feel the heat on my eyebrows as we jump back, awestruck at the flying machinery. The secondary explosion is triple the size of the one which stopped it. The dozer eventually lands twenty meters from where it launched, crashing into the rubble of Nailer and Hell's compound. Their reaction over comms does not disappoint.

1911 hours

"That's one problem solved." I'm out of breath, although not necessarily from physical exertion. Westhead and Kopen, those two new BFF's, bask briefly in their success, but the outpouring of ISIS fighters through the haze gets us back on point. "But we got about a hundred more trying to overrun our position! Claymores!"

From Hell and Nailer's OP across the street and our positions on the roof, calculated fire rains down upon the jihadists with what ammunition we have left. They seem to be everywhere, scattered throughout the fiery block trying to infiltrate our compound. Jud calmly informs us he's got it, and initiates the detcord rigged to the claymores circling the house. There's a hiss when the cord cooks off, burning at four miles a second. A high-speed flaming snake shoots down the side of the house, and ten nearly instantaneously choreographed explosions burst from downstairs, sending 700 steel ball bearings 135 degrees from each device, with a kill range the length of a football field.

"Front Toward Enemy," Thor murmurs with appreciation, and there's a quick huddle around GQ's monitor for a battle damage assessment. Dozens of insurgents are immobile, sprawled across the streets, bleeding against the security wall, dying where they lie. There's no time to count casualties, but the claymores did their job. We rush to take defensive positions throughout the house, happy to be back in the fight. My new Air Force friend tells me that the HLZ still needs to cool before they will attempt to bring in the Chinooks for extract. Naturally.

1933 hours

The battle is frenetic, enemy targets everywhere. With the front of the building completely gone, I'm able to slide down a slab of concrete from the second floor to street level. Westhead and Nate are in shooter's stances directly in front of me, back to back behind a remaining chunk of the security wall. They send fire evenly and coolly into the dusk, with much more returning.

"What do you got?" I ask, taking cover beside them. The concrete at our head fragments so we crouch lower. I spit rock.

"A pocket of insurgents is in the first floor of the building at three o'clock," Nate tells me while sending a tracer burst into it. "We've seen at least twenty go in and none come out. That's where we expect the next wave to come from."

"How are you on ammo?"

Westhead grimaces. "Almost black. I'm down to one mag, plus my sidearm."

I reach to my chest and hand him one of my remaining two. "Don't miss," I tell him. Then: "Where's Kopen?"

"Last I saw he was dug in on the roof. Why?"

I don't answer. His glance lingers on me.

"When's the cavalry arriving?" Nate wonders aloud. "Not sure how much longer we're going to be able to hold them."

"I thought Chief was going to call an Uber."

"Nah, I cancelled it. Three-times surge rate? I'm not paying that shit."

"Then I guess we're on our own." My gaze rises to the murky fields lowering too slowly above. "Our extract is loitering a few klicks from HLZ Bravo, waiting for nightfall and a lull in the fire. Once it's darker we can try to leapfrog there, but it's going to take ammo."

"It's going to take ammo to make it to nightfall," Westhead points out.

"And therein lies the conundrum. One of them, whattacallit, 'catch 22's.'"

"I don't know if you're using that term correctly, Colonel."

"Chicken or egg?"

"Nope."

"Oh well. It'll come to me. Keep knocking them down; I'll keep working on extract."

"We need CAS if we're going to cool the LZ, Blade, you know that," Westhead says.

"I do. Doesn't mean it's going to happen. You know the new ROEs—no air support anymore over inhabited villages. We either repel this attack or die trying."

"How about a supply drop then? I don't mind running out of bullets, but some shit paper would be nice."

"I'll see what I can do." Before I can leave, Westhead calls me back.

"Blade!"

"Yeah?"

He addresses Nate, tells him to go inside. When he's gone:

"You owe me. You owe Cheyenne. If anyone gets out of here alive, it needs to be you. Don't leave her mother widowed and childless. That woman, her family, have given enough."

I nod. "I'm going to do what I can to get us all out of here, Dan."

1949 hours

The team is down to our last mags. Mutt and Thor have procured AK-47's from dead mujs. We're doing our best to collect additional-al weapons, but for every terrorist we put down, two seem to take his place. The streets and courtyard are littered with corpses. Somehow, aside from my forgotten flesh wound, we're for the most part intact. For now. I gather everyone on the first floor. A collection of dirty, battered men stands before me. They are tired, they are ragged, but they are no-where near breaking. For these men, no breaking point exists. Death is the only condition that can take them out of the fight. Looking back at me, I see eyes sparkling behind the filth, shoulders tired but upright. Worn but defiant postures. Still in the fight. Always, still in the fight.

"All right, men, this is it, our last stand. Our Alamo. Let's hope it ends better for us. Rockets are gone, grenades are gone, claymores are gone, ammo's almost gone. ADM Bradley can't risk pulling us out when the AO is still hot. Air support is not an option, and a supply drop is an hour out. There's still probably close to fifty terrorists running around out there who would like nothing more than to hold your head up on Al Jazeera." I pause here, take inventory. "I don't know about you, but I'm feeling pretty good."

Their response is resigned amusement, if only for lack of suitable alternatives. No one here is afraid of dying; the only fear is acting like you are.

"So you're saying there's a chance, Colonel," says Pos. "We got knives, fists, the butt of my rifle. Hell, I'll chew one of these fuckers' ears off if I have to."

"I hear terrorist tastes great this time of year." Westhead picks up the briefing, earning a round of tired smiles. Any chance for laughter is greedily accepted in times like these. "Just ... save two bullets. One for al-Baghdadi ..." He looks over at the pile of shit still tied up in the corner. He may or may not be conscious, a black hood covering his head. "The second ... well, I'll let each of you decide what to do with your second round Me? I know where mine is going, should it come to that. I'm not trying to be a YouTube star. That's all. Fan out, and get as many of these bastards as you can."

As we move out, I can hear excited, rapid Arabic outside, circling the house. Lingering calls of "*Allahu Akbar*" surround us, whispered across the wind like smoke. The incantations coming from everywhere and nowhere all at once, supernatural musings carrying across the battlefield. I meet the pilot's wide eyes and hand him my pistol. For the first time, I truly wonder if I'll ever have a chance to complete my mission. I make out Westhead across the room. The chief wears the most intense sneer I've ever seen on a human face. He's ready to kill. So am I.

Next to him stands Kopen, ashen-faced and intense. He's chewing on his lower lip, over and over, and it's bleeding, and he licks at the blood every so often, seems surprised at its presence. Like his body is above displaying its distress. As if it's immune to all this. I know better. He meets my stare, attempts an optimistic face. If he thinks I've forgotten about him, he's wrong.

2033 hours

Westhead feels outside himself, as if viewing the battle from up high, a place of security, a perspective of omnipotence. All around, his teammates fight in slow motion, moving, shooting, and communicating like their lives depend on it, which of course, they do. Flames dance against any sections of wall remaining of the house. The smell of smoke and all the stenches that come with war, familiar as they are, register just peripherally.

The second floor has collapsed onto the first, forming the stage for the fiercest fighting yet. The only stairwell has been decimated, funneling combatants from both sides into the living room, kitchen. ISIS fighters pour into the compound, not all at once but in a steady, even trickle that makes it seem like a never-ending, albeit slow-moving, parade. It's close quarters battle in the truest sense of the phrase. Gut-check-desperation, grab-your-sack-pick-up-your-balls time. When Mutt's sidearm clacks loudly at point-blank range, a shrieking holy warrior not ten feet in front of him, GQ wheels toward the threat. A violent stroke from the butt of his AK-47 drops the insurgent just as his weapon cackles, sending a fracture of bullets into the floor at their feet. Mutt raises his eyebrows at his brother appreciatively before leaping on the enemy fighter, fixed blade raised high. When he stands again, his arm is stained red and the terrorist at his feet is gurgling through a bright crimson line running the width of his throat that bubbles with each lessening gasp. Mutt snatches the AK from the dying fighter's hands. Two more insurgents rush in through what's left of the front of the home. Westhead cuts them down with his own repurposed AK. He scans the scape for Stevens, but can't find him. Kopen either. There's a call for the team to consolidate at the rear of the house. There he finds the rest of the men, their weapons now mostly varieties recovered from the enemy: Dusty AK-47's, a PKM, two RPK light machine guns, and some RPG-7's. Pos came across a shoulder-fired FIM-92 Stinger but no rounds for it. Nate's SAW rests on his shoulder, the two remaining belts of ammo draped across his chest in an X.

The only men missing are Stevens and Kopen. Westhead attempts to raise them on the radio. Everyone else is catching their breath in some form, taking personal and team inventory, anxious to discover if anyone is badly hit.

2041 hours

Red splatters across my field of vision, blurring everything. My lips purse, lightly spitting warm liquid. I clench down, swinging the stock of my rifle again, and in doing so there's the satisfying sensation of soft tissue crunching under me. The sounds of hand-to-hand battle are all around, the screams of men dying and killing, and it's the other senses that are highlighted now, allowing the smells to come purposeful and strong, each one playing off another, separate but conjoined, and there are so many men in such close proximity in the dark room that it's almost like this isn't happening, but it's the realization that the sun has set, our ally has returned, that makes suppressing this wave of terrorists so vital. I raise up, enraged, seeking my next target. The room has calmed. Mutt and GQ stand over a dead enemy fighter, crazed but calm. They don't notice me as they fall back. I move in the other direction, but pause when I hear Westhead calling for me over the team net. On the other side of the kitchen, Kopen doesn't see my movement.

2049 hours

Stevens's voice comes through the team net, strained and urgent. "Coming out onto the rear courtyard!"

A minute later, the commander is staggering toward the rest of the team, an unconscious al-Baghdadi slung across his back. LCDR Wilson lurches through the dusk behind him, dragging his left leg but alertly sweeping the pistol in front of his body. A surge of heat quivers through Westhead when he sees Agent Kopen bringing up the rear. Despite everything, the mission is on track.

"Blade!" Westhead exclaims, running at him to help. Kopen falls in, and together they relieve Stevens of his charge.

"Everyone present and accounted for?" Stevens breathes.

"Affirmative, we're up." Westhead reports. "Hell and Nailer are still in the OP across the street, but the rest are here. Everyone is at least ambulatory."

"Good," he says. His face is especially sinister in its streaked paint and grime from the now three-day-old op. Oddly angled light from so many fires plays with his features. Westhead stares into him, disbelieving that this is the man responsible for so many deaths yet at the same time holds the life of one little girl in his care, in the blood leaking out onto his blouse, his face. He has to grit his teeth to deal with the unfairness, but then notices Nate along their edges, chest heaving and an expression that says he is ready to eradicate the enemy, and he remembers his mission and his focus returns to getting everyone out alive.

"Blade, we gotta get the hell out of here, now." There seems to be a lull in the action, but the drone pilots let them know that they have movers coming from at least two directions. "We don't have the ordnance to hold out any longer. It's dark enough. Time to bug out."

Stevens's response is quick. "Break into fire teams and consolidate ammo. We'll leapfrog to the tertiary LZ. Jud, get comms with the TOC and make sure that bird is waiting. We'll be coming in hot. Moving in two minutes."

When they regroup into fire teams of four, it's Westhead, Nate, McDonald, and Kopen who are together. Along with the other elements, they crouch in the new and welcome night, silent, listening for any sign of the enemy, waiting for the right time to move. The smell of destruction, of cordite, of death encases them just as substantially as the eerie billowing smoke. Through NVGs, the compound and surrounding buildings glow in a green hue. A whisper comes through the team net.

"Ones and twos, get ready to move," Stevens orders. "You take the prisoner. I'll rendezvous with Hell and Nailer. Meet you guys at the HLZ."

Westhead rotates to his six, contemplating Stevens's figure behind him. He stands alone, AK at the ready. Something about the form gives Westhead pause, increases his pucker factor. Instinctively, he glances toward Kopen, who seems to be thinking the same thing. Westhead raises a finger to his men, and starts back to Stevens through the haze. To his shock, Stevens raises his weapon fluidly, stock against shoulder in a firing position. Westhead freezes, his whole body tingling. Is this it, is this where it ends? Then, as suddenly as he had raised it, Stevens lowers the gun and hisses.

"What the fuck are you doing, Dan? I almost took your head off.

You don't move without calling it!"

Westhead, his heart beating again, lifts his NVGs to the top of his helmet. He knows the colonel is right. "Sorry, Blade. But I don't think it's a good idea for you to stay back." He glances down at al-Baghdadi, hooded and flex cuffed at Stevens's feet. "We need to move as a unit."

"Don't let your personal need for my safety outweigh our TTP's, Chief. This is our mission right now, and we're doing it the right way. This is the call."

Torn, Westhead knows it is the best plan for mission success, while still leery of Stevens bringing up the rear. Either way, it doesn't matter; the decision has been made. Al-Baghdadi can't stifle a grunt when he goes roughly over Westhead's shoulder.

"Roger that, sir," he says. Kopen's anxious face greets him when he rejoins the fire team, al-Baghdadi now in their charge. Westhead gives the agent a slight shake of the head. Kopen knows what he means: *Keep your head on a swivel.* Seconds later Stevens gives the call for the ones and twos to move forward. Westhead and his men rush through the open field, staying as low as possible while the threes and fours send whatever firepower they have left into the surrounding buildings. They finally skid to a stop in an irrigation ditch, thick sludge to their waists.

"Are you fucking kidding me?" McDonald spits. "Can this op get any worse?"

"Don't say that." Kopen can't help but laugh. "It can always get worse."

"Agent, I'm up to my balls in goat shit, how can this get any worse?"

"If you think this is goat shit, then it's already worse."

McDonald groans, and then it's their turn to lay down covering fire. Minutes later the third and fourth fire teams scoot past, Jud tapping Nate on the back with a hoarse call of, "last man" as he passes. Like this they continue for a couple of uneventful klicks, the pursuing fire more distant and sporadic with each rotation, until a single CH-47 Chinook shines in the distance, a suddenly bright moon reflecting off its wide body.

Westhead smiles, for the first time allowing himself a consideration that maybe, just maybe, they have a chance to get out of here alive. Then he remembers that Stevens, Hell, and Nailer have not yet arrived, that he has no way of knowing if they are even alive. When he tries to get Stevens on the radio, he's met with silence.

Kopen places a hand on Westhead. "I wouldn't worry about him; the Colonel is like the undead. The Terminator or some shit."

"No one is above taking a round in the face, Agent Kopen, not you, me, or COL Stevens." He raises his FLIR binos, scanning the landscape for the telltale sparkle of an American IR strobe. For a minute, there's nothing but green and black. Then, a rapid flicker of light. Followed by nothing. Then a flash, and soon there's no mistaking the strobes, three of them, invisible to the naked eye but blinking brilliantly through night vision, moving swiftly in their direction. Behind them, the sky suddenly opens again with streaks of light, tracer fire trailing their teammates as they hustle to link up with the rest of the team.

2123 hours

"Miss us?" Stevens asks. He's crouching beside Westhead and their prisoner, breathless. Nailer and Hell offer their own vulgar greetings. Kopen clenches his weapon tighter, eying them alertly.

"Like the clap," Westhead replies. "Can we get the hell out of here now?"

Stevens flicks his head up at the sky, and when Westhead looks that way, the Chinook is beginning its glorious decent. Finally. It seems to him like a gift from heaven. The approach regal, heroic. The muted thump of whirling blades sends his heartbeat faster. When he feels the rotor wash on his face, he lowers his head and purses his lips to block the moondust. The chopper pauses, hovering just overhead. Suddenly, a single spark dings off the rear rotor. The chopper rises a few feet, then suspends in place as if making a decision. The thump of an enemy machine gun makes it for them. A shower of flashes erupts against the side of the chopper, sending it accelerating upward and the JOE-CAG team grabbing cover wherever they can find it. Dejected, they watch their ride float off into the distance.

"Son of a bitch!" GQ yells across the jarring quiet. "Why is there no Apache support? We're no longer in the village! And it's night!"

Stevens holds up a hand, covering his ear with the other. Weary men wait for instruction, turning back toward the sound of approaching fire. It's to their rear, the burning village they just exfil'd from setting a gloomy backdrop. They set a security perimeter with expectations that the pursuing enemy will soon be back in range.

"TOC says the bird is loitering two klicks west, out of the range of RPGs and small arms. It's low on fuel, so if we're catching a ride, we need to move quickly. Needless to say, we have to deal with these persistent-ass mujs first." To solidify his point, an incoming mortar whistles, its explosion harmlessly kicking up rock and dirt. The night is re-energized with a shower of muzzle blasts, a thick wall of projectiles. It sends them to the ground, instructions given for a counterattack. And then Westhead hears the call that chills his blood, every time.

"I'm hit! Son of a bitch, I'm hit!" It's GQ shouting down the line, his voice only rising in volume to be heard over the competing sounds of gunfire, mortars, RPGs.

Westhead crabwalks toward him, coming to a stop over a pale face. GQ's eyes are saucers as he grits his teeth through the pain. He clutches Westhead's arm with one hand, the other holding pressure dressing against his neck. Even through the dark, a circle of red can be seen extending outward, dampening his fingers.

"Fuck, man, sorry. Took one in the neck, I think."

"Let me see," says Westhead. He peels the dressing back. The sucking wound is black freshly shredded flesh. Westhead can hear his heart in his ears. Everything is moving slowly, in gelatin waves. He places GQ's hand back over the wound and rummages through his teammate's blowout kit, already ripped open on the ground next to him. He works to control his own breathing, to steady his hands. They find a hemostatic clotting bandage. He tears it open with his teeth, shoves it into GQ's wound the best he can.

"That should slow the bleeding," he tells him. He searches GQ's face. It's growing paler. His breaths come heavy, but infrequent. Eyes flutter, then droop. "How you feeling, buddy? You good? Want morphine?"

GQ's face lifts, a temporary bolt of energy flowing through it. He shakes his head. "I'm good," he breathes, blood-soaked fingers going from his neck to the soil around him, sifting through sand and gravel until they clasp his rifle. "I'm good!" he yells louder, rising to a sitting position, weapon shouldered.

Westhead gives him an atta-boy before racing back to his position, when another call of someone hit comes through the radio. He's unsure if they're talking about GQ or someone new, but the pace of battle has picked up and he knows they have to win the fight before they can apply buddy-aid or land the chopper. Over his shoulder, Westhead sees Stevens directing the men.

"Blade, we gotta get everyone to the LZ or that bird is going to leave us again!" he calls to him. "You go. Take the others. I'll stay and cover you guys."

2149 hours

I hesitate, considering Westhead's plan. If he stays to cover our movements, there's a good chance he won't make it back. And I need Westhead's help to take out the president. But we have a wounded, high-value prisoner. The rescued pilot. This mission hangs precariously. The team is watching, awaiting my decision. GQ lays flat, still shooting, but growing weaker by the minute. It's the right call. When another report of a man down goes out, I give Westhead a nod and pass down the word.

Soon, Chief is heading back the other way, most of our remaining ammo and Nate's machine gun with him. The rest of the team races forward through the gloom, al-Baghdadi on my back once more, Hell and

Nailer assisting a weakening GQ. A form brushes by me going in the other direction. I lower my NVG and recognize the gait. Agent Kopen.

2152 hours

"Chief, I'm with you." Kopen's voice sounds hollow, but the statement does not leave room for argument. He takes a murky knee next to Westhead, grabbing one of their few remaining banana clips. He clacks it into his AK-47 and turns toward the approaching enemy. Westhead gives an appreciative nod and turns his body in the same direction. Behind them, the rest of the team is moving out, leaving them alone with only the moonlight and advancing enemy force.

"Who else is hit?" Westhead asks, making out Jud and Mutt's bodies carrying a form he can't quite place.

Kopen turns, watching the rest of the team exfil. "McDonald. It didn't look good."

Westhead cringes, but has no time to worry about his newest teammate. The incoming fire is growing thicker, and while they dig in the best they can, the flat ground is not an ideal fighting position. The insurgents are as yet unaware that it's only two Americans left to defend this empty field, and they send an alarming volley of artillery in their direction. Westhead and Kopen answer it the best they can, moving and firing from different positions to give the impression of a larger force.

"Blade, status?" Westhead croaks into his throat mic when they are each on their last mags. His mouth is so dry he can barely get the words out. His battered and broken body screams. He can't help but feel pretty sorry for himself, pretty alone, but knows that if they can't stop this attack, the chopper will never be able to land, and Stevens, the pilot, Nate, the rest of the men, will end up dying here on this cold, foreign battlefield. And that is unacceptable to him, even if it means he does.

Arabic carries closer across the battlefield. Its haunting notes get closer; ISIS fighters are sprinting in their direction, trying to interdict the departing chopper. The SAW vibrates in Westhead's hands, sending the last of a 200-round belt downrange. Some insurgents go down; more get through, and then they are on top of his position, their footsteps crunching in the sand, shouts and shots wafting through the atmosphere. *So this is it,* he thinks to himself, *this is where I die.* A dark-robed fighter towers over him and as Westhead pulls his knife the screech of a mortar splits his ears and he can't help but cover his head as the air is sucked out of the earth and then everything goes blank.

2219 hours

I'm initially alarmed when I open my eyes and still see nothing. I can't breathe. It takes a moment to remember where I am. Then I taste the grit, feel the gravel embedded in my skin. The enemy mortars must have landed right on top of us. I'm half buried. My arms and legs tingle, and it takes a minute until I can rise to a knee. My helmet is sideways on my head, but my NVGs are still working. When I lower them, I see Westhead not fifteen feet in front of me, face down, unmoving. There's no sign of Agent Kopen. A light wind is the only movement, its gentle touch somehow getting through the five-alarm fire going off in my brain.

"Dan, you alive?" I'm able to squawk through a mouthful of sand. I can't hear my own voice. Urgently, I scrape dust and dirt off Westhead's body. There's no reaction. I hunch over, check for a pulse. His body seems cold and heavy when I try to open his airway. Suddenly, he emits an involuntary groan, then a deep, wild gasp as his lungs search frantically for air. I lift his head, causing him to squirm in pain as he pants, sucking oxygen.

"I hate to tell you, bro, but you gotta get up," I say. "This is no place for a nap."

He squirms, groans once more, face scrunched in agony. His head is awash in blood. When he sees me crouched over him, there's first confusion, then alarm in his face. He scrambles backward.

"Easy, Chief, if I wanted you dead you'd already be. You forget I need ya? Now let's get the hell out of here."

"Wh—What—What are you doing here? Where's the pilot? Al-Baghdadi? Nate?"

"Gone—all in one piece. Extracted on the first bird. Mission success. I came back for your ass," I tell him, casual.

"Kopen?" Here his features go hard, accusatory.

I decide to wait before answering. The truth is, I don't know if he is still alive. I grunt, motion next to us. Kopen is contorted in the dirt. As if knowing he is the topic of conversation, he twitches, fighting hard to turn himself over.

"Looks like the bastard is fine. You thinking about proposing?"

Westhead struggles to a crouch, tight smile masking the pain. He clasps Kopen's arm and together they rise. "Don't ask, don't tell," he croaks.

"Your secret is safe with me." Then: "A second chopper is inbound for us. We just gotta make that LZ."

There is no other movement or sign of the enemy as we patrol out of the field. Maybe they forgot about us. Maybe they gave up.

2301 hours

The three of us reach the designated HLZ with no further enemy contact, generating contented, if not wary, glances. After everything we've been through, are we really going to make it out of here this easily?

I go to the frequency for the incoming Blackhawk. The pilot lets us know he will be on station within minutes. Westhead cracks an IR stick and we take a knee in the moonlight, awaiting our ride.

Westhead pulls me to the side while we wait. "So what now?" he hisses.

He looks smaller. Angry. Injured but not broken. "Nothing has changed," I answer.

"You know you won't get away with this. I won't let you." He glances over at the FBI agent, bouncing on the soles of his feet, staring anxiously into the night. "Kopen won't let you."

"Let me worry about Kopen. As for you? I think you've made it clear what your position is. I think you'll continue to protect my life as if it were your own. In fact, I'm counting on it."

Before he can respond, the air once again comes alive with explosions. The enemy has found us. We take cover, pissed and unbelieving. All sets of eyes go skyward, relieved to find our salvation incoming, but dreading that it won't be able to land. The Blackhawk is overhead, but banks before lowering further. It's directly in the line of fire, chinks of automatic rounds echoing off the tail. The pilot is immediately in my ear, tells me they're dropping a SPIE rig for us. Westhead catches the rope, and begins helping Kopen connect his harness to a D ring. He works quickly. Both of their backs are to me. Now is my chance. I raise my weapon with one arm through the rotor wash. Westhead blocks Kopen as he unscrews another carabiner. I hold, waiting for an open shot. The rope spins, and they trade positions, Kopen suddenly sketched evenly against the mottled background. It's just as I squeeze the trigger that I can feel bullets tearing into me like a sledgehammer. I fall, fighting against whatever is happening, trying to stay conscious, but it's futile and everything is upside down and I wonder if anyone will ever pay for this.

2315 hours

Everything is so bright. Clean, crisp. Not bright like an abundance of light, bright like all filters have been removed. This is what the world must really look like, an impartial, true-in-the-truest-sense of reality, or more likely, the absence of all distortion. Something tells me not to head toward that light, and I bolt alert, struggling for breath, numb but alive.

A gentle wind grows in force, and then I'm hit with a harsh, thumping sound that dizzies me further. Suddenly, everything speeds back up maniacally. Maybe everything isn't as clean as it just appeared, because the pain is real and jagged and there's no denying it, so I gasp, gasp fully and deeply, and then I can see the world again, my eyes jerking open, mouth urgently working to fill my lungs. Body parts seem unattached, unrelated.

"Relax, Blade, we're getting you out of here!" It's Westhead's voice in my ear, much closer than I would expect, coming long and narrow as if through a tube. I feel his breath on my face. It makes every attempt to soothe, even in the midst of chaos. After another deep breath and several determined blinks, I'm able to take in my surroundings and achieve a semblance of recognition.

Above me, the Blackhawk's rotors blur, their wash pounding down on us. I can see Kopen, already dangling in the air. A rope crosses my shoulder. Westhead fastens it to my harness. It occurs to me that we're attached, face to face, connected by several carabiners. He holds me upright in a clumsy bear hug. My head feels heavy, lolling from side to side like a baby's. We're being supported by the rope and that seems to be the main thing keeping me upright. I can feel the crack of sonic booms all around us, can feel the air from the bullets whizzing by rather than hear their report. A grenade lands somewhere close, then another. Westhead extends a thumbs-up to the helo directly above us. Before I pass out again I try to clear my vision, but a heavy curtain is lowering. I fight it, squint into the rotor wash. When the helo starts a sturdy lift, Westhead begins to run, dragging me, and then we're pulled into the air with a shudder and we're dangling, rising swiftly under the stars and moon and wind. I feel Westhead grunt, then wheeze and slam against me twice but the pain is too much before it all fades to black.

BETHESDA

Eight bullet holes. Nine, if you counted the one that grazed my arm in the initial contact. My body armor stopped most, but still. Normally, I'd be pretty proud of that statistic, but the deaths of GQ and McDonald during the operation have dulled my glee. What losing two more of my men did do was sharpen my anger, steady my resolve. Lying in my hospital bed at Walter Reed I couldn't help but smile when Phil was wheeled into my room.

"Don't be too pleased with yourself," he breathed in that rattling haunt of a voice. "Those are paper cuts compared to my wounds."

I sat up as best I could. "You are the king of battle scars, my man. My Purple Hearts are pink compared to yours."

He whispered, "And don't you forget it," especially softly, maybe from his injuries, maybe not to be overheard. His wounds may have been old, but they were still more painful and debilitating than my fresh ones and always would be. Softer now: "This mean your personal war is over?"

I scowled. "Not even close. Soon as I'm out of here, I complete the mission. Failure is not an option."

He nodded knowingly. His goggles misted. He exhaled jaggedly.

"Had a feeling you'd say that. Guess what, soldier? You'll be leaving here in handcuffs, you don't agree to my conditions. There was a nice FBI agent who came to visit when you were still unconscious. Older guy. Was on crutches, but said he was going to be fine. Some sort of accident, I don't know. He was short on details. But he did seem particularly interested in finding out who's taking out everyone associated with Operation Atlas. Really wanted to talk with you before you got released. Something about trace DNA at one of the crime scenes, that they've found their man. We chatted for a while after finding out we were in Ramadi together."

"That so? He sure is good at making friends." Then: "Can't believe my oldest buddy is willing to sell me out. When everything that I'm doing is for him."

"Guess I'm just disloyal like that. Does that mean you're going to do it?"

I nodded. I didn't have a choice.

"Hear you're getting discharged tomorrow," said Westhead.

"You heard right." Stevens was upright in bed. He'd regained his color, some of his weight, but still had a way to go. "When did you get out?"

"A few weeks ago. Wasn't much to it."

"Two rounds."

"In the shoulder. I'm fine."

"Glad to hear. Heard Kopen pulled through too."

"One in the back. Just missed his spine."

"Lucky man."

Stevens looked to the window. Outside, it had cooled. The tree branch scraping the glass danced with color. A squirrel ran past. Westhead didn't notice either.

"Was sorry to hear about GQ and New Guy."

Westhead dug his nails into the back of his hand until angry concave indentations ran across his knuckles. "Don't give me that shit. Don't act like you care about those men. You're a discredit to their memory, to their sacrifice."

Stevens struggled to raise himself higher. He looked truly surprised. "You can't believe that. Everything that I'm doing, that I have done, is in the name of the men who gave all. It's for them, and those who come after them. *That's* why I have to complete this mission. Don't you see that?"

"The only reason I haven't already put you down is because of Cheyenne." Westhead paced the length of the room. "Kopen has you, just so you know. That's what I came here to tell you. The DNA sample you left at the marrow drive? He subpoenaed it. They'll have it next week and when they do, they'll match the attacks to you, and you're done. So whatever we have to do, it needs to get done before that. Let me hear you say you're donating that marrow, or I'll end this right here." Westhead came closer, loomed over the bed.

Stevens's dark eyes bored into his team leader. "As soon as this last op is completed, the marrow is hers. If something happens to me before that, she dies."

"Then you better get your ass out of that hospital bed, Colonel. Because she's no longer producing healthy cells. We're running out of time. And so are you."

"Hand me my pants."

WASHINGTON, DC

Westhead had already parked the stolen ambulance three blocks east of my location on Constitution Ave. I was alone in my truck, smack between the Washington Monument and White House, a perfect portrait of the South Lawn stretched charmingly ahead. I sat in the driver's seat, simultaneously checking Twitter and the sky as I waited. The day was frigid but picturesque, a fluorescent sky glowing deep and full. I sat and I waited, tourists and commuters streaming by. Pink ears and scarfs, foggy breath and quick feet. Selfies in front of the White House Christmas tree, sipping coffee from the Starbucks on 14th and H. A few hearty visitors were bundled on the top of the red open-roofed buses crisscrossing these streets, unaware that the first presidential assassin since Lee Harvey Oswald was within touching distance. That when they got back to Topeka and Florida and Italy and Silver Spring, they would forever be a part of American history and have the tale to accompany it. My hand continually reached back to graze the plastic case in the bed of the truck. Six more Advil in a losing attempt at sating my violently throbbing head and shoulder.

The first thing I had done after discharging myself from the hospital—after two temporary releases for the funerals in Arlington—was to outfit the truck with a camper shell with a retractable roof. When Marine One hovers over the South Lawn sometime in the next ten minutes, I'll be able to pop out of the top and fire the Carl-Gustaf rocket launcher virtually unseen. Once the president's helicopter is aflame, Westhead will pick me up in the ensuing mayhem, the ambulance sirens and lights allowing for a quick and unnoticed extract.

"Shouldn't be long now," I told him through a Bluetooth headset. "Looks like our buddy just finished his round and should be headed back home soon."

Westhead's reply was stiff. "Roger that." The chief was what you would call an unwilling ally in this mission, but as assumed, he'd rather go down in history as an accomplice to one of the most famous murders in history than let that girl die.

I checked my phone again, a tweet from *People* magazine letting me know that the president's helicopter escort had left Joint Base Andrews, where he had played, by most counts, his 311th round of golf since taking office. It wouldn't be long until anywhere from three to five VH-3D Sea Kings or VH-60N White Hawks appeared suddenly on the horizon, scattered over the National Mall in multiple formation shifts to throw off anyone tracking the one carrying the president, and landed on the White House's South Lawn to deposit their charge safe and sound. The fleet of Marine One choppers were outfitted with state-of-the-art defensive mechanisms like infrared decoys and dual spectral flares to throw off heat-seeking missiles, but none of those countermeasures affected my plan—I won't be firing any rockets until the single helicopter has set down on the emerald carpet covering my target's backyard, not giving the Marine pilot at the controls any time or space for evasive maneuvers. Since the Carl-Gustaf is recoilless and quickly reloadable, I will be able to get all three 84-millimeter anti-tank rockets off in under thirty seconds. With my experience and accuracy on this particular weapon, there will be nothing left of the president or Marine One seconds after the helicopter touches down.

"Five minutes," I reported while crawling into the back and opening the case. The green tube-like weapon went comfortably to my shoulder. I had previously loaded the first round; two more were within arm's reach.

When I opened the hatch and stuck my head out, sunlight and cold air streamed through the top, numbing the tip of my nose even while warming my forehead. I began to slow my breathing and heart rate, focused on the smell of clean air, the chirping of birds, the rhythms of traffic. In front of me, a postcard, a staunch illustration of the mighty USA—the fountain of the South Lawn framed impressively by 1600 Pennsylvania Avenue, its continual stream of water shooting into the air in a symbol of wealth and power. Uniformed and undercover Secret Service agents milled throughout the crowd, on high alert, covered eyes scanning the crowds and traffic. I lowered my head, patient, and then heard the sound I'd been waiting for.

Westhead heard the approaching choppers at the same time Stevens alerted him over the phone. He spun from his perch in the back of the ambulance, legs dangling out the open doors, to watch the three Marine helicopters circle and intersect over the Mall. One shot directly over the Washington Monument. The other two split it. There was no way of knowing yet which one had the Marine One call sign. For their purposes, it didn't matter.

It was the one flying directly over the monument that didn't peel off. Westhead studied its movements coldly. The green-and-white aircraft crossed Constitution Avenue just before him, low, soaring onto the South Lawn before slowing and rotating. Thousands of tourists stopped in place, cell phones out, gazes elevated. They watched it hover just off the ground, the nose turning ninety degrees before gently lowering itself to the grass. No one noticed the ambulance a thousand yards away, rear doors opening wider. The athletic man pulling a cover off a bi-podded sniper rifle, taking a prone position in the shadows of the ambulance's interior. They never heard the shot, an emphatic spit from the suppressed TRG M10. And they barely flinched when the ambulance shot into traffic, a dark tinted Tahoe following close, both vehicles' lights whirling and sirens blaring.

When the helo began its final descent, that's when I took aim with the Carl-Gustaf. A mere seconds from achieving my ultimate goal. I would have thought I'd have been more excited. That completing this final mission would give me resolution. A sense of all-encompassing achievement. It didn't. At least not yet. Once the rocket connected with its target, I expected the hollowness to fill. Marine One hovered before me, just above the grass, fountain spray blowing sideways. Before touching down, the chopper rotated majestically, nose pointed at the West Wing, pausing in air as if saluting or maybe waiting for something to happen. It remained stationary for a second, big and immobile and clear through the rocket launcher's scope, and then, as the wheels were about to find earth, I lowered my finger to the trigger and ...

"Direct hit," Doc Soto said to Westhead once he had collapsed the sniper system and scrambled into the passenger seat of the ambulance. Soto, narrowed eyes focused on the rearview, flicked the lights and siren and whipped into traffic, guiding them toward a parked pickup truck with a tall camper over its bed.

"Better of been," Westhead growled. "Aim small, miss small."

The ride was short, only three city blocks, but seemed to be taking forever with traffic, even with the assistance of the emergency vehicles' signals.

Then they were pulled over, the ambulance blocking the eastbound lanes of Constitution. The accompanying official-looking Tahoe assisted, blocking westbound traffic. There wasn't much of a commotion around the pickup truck, not yet, just a few rubberneckers beginning to turn their attention from the White House, where the president offered a lazy salute to two Marines and a short wave to the throngs before hustling through the cold into the White House. Soto and Westhead, in white EMT uniforms, jumped out of the ambulance, stretcher between them. They quickly breached the pickup, finding exactly what they were expecting: COL Stevens's still-warm body, blood leaking from a tiny hole in his chest.

They hustled him into the ambulance, Westhead now behind the wheel. Soto jumped into Stevens's pickup and they screamed into traffic, heading west toward the GW Parkway with a madman's urgency. The Tahoe followed close behind, lights and sirens equal to its predecessor, sandwiching the pickup. The pickup made a right on 23rd, where Soto would park it in a George Washington University garage and head to Bethesda in another vehicle. The ambulance and SUV continued on, hitting the 66 onramp at close to triple digits. Unsuspecting commuters, the Kennedy Center, the Georgetown waterfront, all flew by their peripheral, the caravan making haste for Walter Reed Medical Center and a bone marrow procedure that had never before been attempted.

BETHESDA

Even when the boy was young, during the time when his life had been flipped upside down, there had been an air of maturity about him. His carriage, his curious eyes, the confident angle of his chin, had all alluded to a wisdom beyond the dozen or so years bony shoulders and mussed hair suggested. In any event, he most certainly had inherited the responsibilities of a grown man as soon as it had happened. He hadn't a choice.

Over the next few years he grew. There were ups and a lot of downs. Eventually, he became the rock his family needed. For his mother, his sister. For his grandparents, those tough patriarchs who took them in after it happened. He had a lot to learn, but he learned it. And he excelled.

There was no way to sugarcoat the events that had brought what was left of his family here, today. He's handling it now, as he had then, more or less just as his father would have wanted and expected. And that is what led him to where we are today, to this position as protector and warrior.

But if those characteristics and experiences had pooled to construct Nate into that man, conversely they must bear response for his inability to stand idle in the face of adversity. No more so than when well-meaning attempts at assistance are less than helpful. It was to his credit that Nate became a man of action; it was to his mother and loved ones' annoyance that he was such while they waited for news of Cheyenne's procedure.

"Nathan, for the twelfth time, will you PLEASE sit down?" His mother was exasperated. Exasperated, exhausted, confused. Next to her in the waiting room sat her parents, nobly silverish in a way declaring they still had a lot of living left to do. They waited dispassionately, content to be seen and not heard under the tense setting.

Gayle was still unsure as to the series of events which had led them here, to a rushed marrow transplant for her daughter with a donor she did not know. Westhead, having already instructed his protégé once not to leave his seat, shot the young SEAL a pointed scowl, leaving no ambiguity as to intent or consequence. Nate plunked into the nearest hard plastic chair, exhaling loudly.

"They should have been done an hour ago," he complained. "What the heck is going on back there?"

No one answered the rhetorical question, deciding instead to focus on the boxy television bolted to the wall, the peeling yellow paint, the scuffed floor tiles. Westhead and Doc Soto intended to limit those in the know, which explained the closed-off portion of Walter Reed and the late hour. Even Nate had no idea that it was actually the deceased COL Stevens's marrow being delivered to his sister. He had been issued the same official story as everyone else: That COL Stevens had died in a training accident and a second donor had been identified. Doc Soto, Chief Westhead, and Agent Kopen had decided they three were the only ones who would know the truth.

It was Doc Soto who finally broke the tension, hurrying through the waiting room door.

"First round is done, folks. She's resting, but in good shape."

The celebration was optimistic if muted. Kopen put a hand on

Westhead's shoulder. Gayle looked ecstatic but still confused. Her eyes were hollow, hair tied off in a stringy ponytail. She pulled West-head aside.

"Dan, I'm still not sure what's going on. The back door, the sectioned off part of the hospital. The sudden late-night procedure. Who was the donor? I thought the man in your unit who was a match, COL Stevens, died in a training accident."

"He did. Turns out there was another match. He wishes, uh, to remain anonymous."

"Is he important? High ranking or something? I would imagine he would have to be to get this treatment." She waved her arms at the empty hospital wing.

Westhead smiled. "He was."

LAUREL, ONE YEAR LATER

"Pass the soy sauce, please, Uncle Dan." Cheyenne reached over Westhead, taking the bottle from his hand. "And the shrimp tempura."

"Slow down, honey, you're going to make yourself sick."

She made a face, the kind teenage girls have been torturing parents and boys with since the beginning of time. "I've *been* sick, Ma. Eating too much sushi isn't going to make me sick."

"It's gonna make me sick watching you, little piggy," Nate teased, tilting toward his little sister. He took in her stubby hair, the pink cheeks, the bright eyes.

"What about you? You have rice in your beard!" she exclaimed while leaning into him. "You think *that* is pleasant to look at?"

They were eye to eye, still as much thirteen and seven as twenty-one and fifteen. The fondness was real; it was deep. Shaped over adversity and tragedy, multiplied by blood. Nate didn't take his eyes from his sister's while addressing Westhead at the other end of the table.

"Chief, last California roll. You want it?"

Westhead released Jan's hand and patted his growing belly with greedy satisfaction. "Best part of being retired, Little Warrior. I can eat as much as I want. Pass that puppy over here." Jan smiled at the hostess, flattered to be in on the joke, and handed her boyfriend the roll.

Gayle let loose a giggle as Westhead popped it into his mouth. They all watched with anticipation. His eyes immediately began to water. No one said a word through unrestrained laughter.

THE END